Film Society

For my mother and my daughter

FILM SOCIETY

a novel

Gilaine E. Mitchell

A Simon & Pierre Book

THE DUNDURN GROUP
TORONTO › OXFORD

Editor: Marc Côté
Copy Editor: Don McLeod
Proofreader: Barry Jowett
Design: Jennifer Scott
Printer: Webcom

Canadian Cataloguing in Publication Data

Mitchell, Gilaine
Film society

ISBN 0-88924-296-8
I. Title

PS8576.I8693F54 2000   C813'.6   C00-930053-8   PR9199.3.M497F54 2000

1   2   3   4   5   04   03   02   01   00

THE CANADA COUNCIL | LE CONSEIL DES A
FOR THE ARTS | DU CANADA
SINCE 1957 | DEPUIS 1957

Canadä

We acknowledge the support of the Canada Council for the Arts, Ontario Arts Council, and the Book Publishing Industry Development Program (BPIDP) for our publishing program.

Care has been taken to trace the ownership of copyright material used in this book. The author and the publisher welcome any information enabling them to rectify any references or credit in subsequent editions.

J. Kirk Howard, President

Printed and bound in Canada.

Printed on recycled paper.

Dundurn Press	Dundurn Press	Dundurn Press
8 Market Street	73 Lime Walk	2250 Military Road
Suite 200	Headington, Oxford,	Tonawanda, New York
Toronto, Ontario, Canada	England	U.S.A. 14150
M5E 1M6	OX3 7AD	

Acknowledgements

Many thanks to my husband, Gerry Fraiberg, my family, and the friends who encouraged me during the years it took to write *Film Society*; Lindy Powell for her unfailing support as my dearest friend, and for always reminding me that it is important to honour your voice; Marc Côté for believing in the book and giving me the freedom to make it what it needed to be; Kirk Howard for publishing it; the Ontario Arts Council for assistance at a crucial time; and to Margaret Laurence, who helped even from beyond.

Film Society

Fade In:

EXTERIOR — TREE-LINED STREET — NIGHT

Chapter One

This tree-lined street with Victorian homes and large front porches could be any street in any small Ontario town. It just happens to be in the Village of Stirling, where a group of women meet once a month in the red brick house at the end of Anne Street to watch movies.

It started one winter night, upstairs in my bathroom. Jenny was sitting on the edge of my tub, which badly needed caulking, while I was busy smearing deep red all over my mouth. She was telling me caulking isn't so hard, the trick is to make sure you tape it in, and don't stop once you start spreading the white goop.

"If you stop, you'll fuck it up. You'll get blobs," she said from behind me.

I removed half of my lipstick with a soft bite on a single square of toilet paper then flushed it down the toilet. Jenny inspected my tub, pushed a small piece of loose caulking back into place and advised me on what type of caulking I should buy.

"Don't be cheap," she said. "It's never a good idea to skimp on good caulking. You'll just end up with that black mould again before you know it." Then she sat on the toilet to pee, told me I should tighten the wooden seat before someone falls off and breaks their neck, and asked me how much toilet paper I buy in a week. I sat on the edge of my tub, closed the curtain behind me to block out the mould and the maintenance and my impatience with perfection.

I've never had much luck with bathrooms.

I've anticipated many happy endings in bathrooms. I've made love in bathrooms. Changed my mind in bathrooms. Can't forget some bathrooms. Like the one at the Legion with the bad paint job, where I saw my aunts reapply their makeup and discard their disappointment, where I followed suit and made my way back out to the dance floor to waltz with a man I no longer loved.

I've washed away the semen of men I barely knew in bathrooms I saw only once, where cold, grey water lay in puddles on Formica counter tops and football-shaped soaps hung on thick ropes over the shower head — honestly, I didn't know they were there until it was too late — either that, or there was nothing anywhere but a few sheets of toilet paper dangling from a broken holder and a black towel hung in a hurry over the curtain rod, tiny hairs all over the floor.

One bathroom saw me through infidelity and the birth of my children, where I soaked my swollen, cut, and stitched vagina in the same tub I soaked my leaping heart, hiding the aftermath of lusty afternoons with Johnny Marks behind plastic curtains, burying my post-natal state of panic in porcelain and hot water, a cluster of candles burning in the corner by the faucet.

I watched shadow flames flicker larger than life all around me as I soaked my pride the day my husband told me he was leaving, he'd found somebody else. I already knew anyway. I recognized that euphoric look, the sudden lift in his spirits, which didn't come from being with me, but until he said it, I could ignore it. I could tell myself he wouldn't do it, couldn't do it, couldn't leave, like I couldn't, wouldn't, didn't. But he did.

I got over it in the bathroom.

In the bathroom, you mourn and you celebrate and you start over. Film Society began during a pee break in the middle of *My Left Foot*, with Jenny on the toilet, myself on the edge of the tub and then in the mirror, pinching cheeks that seemed pale and puffy, which I blamed on too much drink and not enough air — the hazards of winter hibernation.

"You should fix that leaky faucet," Jenny said from the other side of the room. "How much do you pay for water every month? Would it be okay if I brought along a friend the next time we watch a movie?"

That winter, two of us grew into four of us, which grew into seven of us altogether. Seven women, a television, and one bathroom.

We gather every month around the table in my living room and fill up on guacamole and Grace's stuffed pumpernickel and Alex's homemade salsa, then wash everything down with generous amounts of wine and beer and ice water as we hastily catch up on each other's lives. There's always some urgency to this, to get it in before we start a film. We squeeze and condense and talk quickly — anything to bring our stories up-to-date, to say *this is where I am now.* And every once in a while, our own lives make us forget about the ones waiting for us in the cassette on top of my television and it's nearly midnight before we sit down to watch.

Somewhere along the line, I became keeper of the Film Society stories, most of them told to me in further detail in first person, in a quiet corner of my cluttered kitchen, or in the privacy of my small and somewhat dysfunctional bathroom. The faucet in the sink is still leaking. The toilet seat is missing a bolt now and hangs off to one side.

My film friends don't expect my bathroom to be any other way, but they do expect me to keep their story lines straight, to guess at what will happen next, to remember what went wrong before. They expect me to be truthful, but on their side.

It was Del who suggested our lives might be better if we had rushes or dailies to look at — the uncut film printed for viewing by filmmakers the day after it's shot; the object is to check for errors before the set is taken down. Everyone agreed even that's too late to change what has taken place. We're not living celluloid lives where life comes at us in carefully crafted scenes and builds to a contrived climax and fitting resolution. There is no paradigm at work here, no guaranteed formula to follow or tell us how our story's going to turn out. A moment simply comes, then leaves you with the rest of your life to live with it.

Sadie

THE STORYTELLER'S JACKET

Chapter Two

The night Ben and I got stuck while making love was a night like all the others I'd seen at Oak Lake.

That's how I'd begin.

With something familiar.

With the same dark sky that greeted me every time Ben called and I drove out in the middle of the night to see him — on the wheels of one long-ago moment — under a sky full of stars, sprinkling specks of light on a lake rumoured to be bottomless. That's what made me clamp down on him with a force I never thought possible. The bottomlessness of the lake.

The temporary loss of footing.

Even after it happened and Ben lay sleeping beside me, I was sure there was a point to this bizarre occurrence. I just wasn't sure what it was yet, since it only developed in the last several hours of my life, placed in the lap of my artistic sensibilities, a metaphor I couldn't imagine would do me any good.

If I were a writer, I might reach for a pen and record the details while they're still fresh — the black water; the green and white fireflies glowing around the shoreline; Ben's unbelievable release of control. How he nearly drowned me in his eagerness to take me with him.

If I could paint, I'd splash the canvas with underwater lovers and a horizon of black binoculars. Big, eyeless binoculars with glassy stares that threatened to make intimacy a spectacle. Something ugly. Something laughable. Something punishable.

I thought I saw someone watching us from a cottage down the lake. A stick figure against the dim porch lights. Maybe that's what kept me from going with Ben to a place, he kept panting, was the best he's ever been.

If I could write it all down, I'd have an accurate, detailed account of what happened. But I'm not a writer or a painter. I'm a storyteller of the verbal kind, with a wandering mind. I can't stay on course and land in the middle of the end of the story. I have to go off here and there and make stops along the way. I have to take a walk on an island I think no one else has ever discovered and describe what I see before I make my way back to the point of the whole blurry mess.

I've had my share of impatient lovers, and an ex-husband who was forever asking, "is there a point to this story, Sadie?" So I've learned to pace myself and periodically inject, "and there is a point to this story," into my ever-changing, always-evolving, becoming-something-else monologues.

And just how will I tell people what happened?

Will I start at the beginning, which some would say was earlier in the evening when I met Ben at Oak Lake, in the dark, so no one could see me. I drove my car down John Meyers Road and parked it on the side, just before it forks to the left for Sid Oaks Lane, then walked the rest of the way in — the same way I'd been doing it for over a year. Of course, that's not really the beginning. They'll want to know

why I met Ben in the dark, why I didn't want anyone to see
me at this winterized ramshackle cottage he calls home.

Why does a forty-nine-year-old woman sneak around
in the dark to meet her younger lover? A respectable
woman who runs an adult literacy centre, has two teenage
children, a mortgage in a small town, and a shitty car that
empties her pocket every other week with its needs-this-
needs-that attitude, and a nagging feeling she should have
bought some registered retirement savings plans twenty
years ago.

That's the beginning of another story.

Or the beginning of this one.

I have so many. I collect them, and at this very moment
I'm wearing most of them on my back. Literally.

"It's a case of vaginismus," Mary-Beth said on the phone,
"an involuntary contraction of those muscles. It'll go away if
you just relax."

I was standing in the small kitchen of Ben's cottage,
where the phone is. Ben by this time was an involuntary
appendage and shuffled along the floor with me, the two of
us wrapped in a blanket that smelled of cigarettes we had
grabbed from the couch after we manoeuvred our way up
from the lake. I was cold and had put my jacket on. Ben was
wearing his black Levi's shirt, faded and marked with the
remains of too much clumpy laundry soap, which he doesn't
see or doesn't bother wiping off.

"Usually fear or pain makes you clamp down like that,"
Mary-Beth continued. "If you can relax those muscles, you'll
release him."

"Why can't he release himself? Won't he lose it soon?" I
was panicking. Ben kept sighing and shaking his head and
didn't know what to do with his arms, which were tired of
holding me and bored with hanging idly by his sides. Mary-
Beth was calm, and I could picture her sitting up in bed under
her crisp sheets in some freshly laundered summer nightgown,
which she had hung on the line to dry that morning.

"You've probably cut off the blood supply," she said
quietly. "That'll keep him erect."

"Jesus Christ, Mary-Beth, what if we're stuck like this forever!" I could already hear the cries of humiliation from the mouths of my children, the gossip and whispered enjoyment that would spread throughout town.

She's the one who got stuck.

"You just have to relax," Mary-Beth kept saying. "Do some deep breathing. Lie down and talk calmly. I could come out with some Valium. Where exactly are you?"

I didn't tell her. I said I'd call back if I needed to. The last thing I wanted was Mary-Beth showing up, knowing Ben's name before I even introduce them, asking him about this bad back, telling him he should quit smoking to get rid of that cough he's had for a while now.

I only called her out of desperation.

I'm not friends with her.

We meet every now and then on the street, or we go for a drink. It's always Mary-Beth's idea. How can I say no? She gives me yearly Pap smears and listens to my complaints about my sore neck and recommends Kegel exercises to keep my bladder and all those other things up where they should be.

She knows how much I weigh.

Besides, I tell myself, she hasn't been in town that long, and doesn't appear to have many friends. Any friends. She only moved to Stirling from Ottawa two years ago, after Dr. Reynolds retired, and lives alone in the apartment above her office, a pale blue home on the edge of the Mill Pond with white shutters and a parking lot with five spaces reserved for patients.

"How about a drink?" Mary-Beth will say when we run into each other. We'll go to Jim's, the sports bar on the corner, where a ball game or hockey game will flicker above us and the smell of pizza and stale beer fill the air — where Mary-Beth pretends to be like me and I find myself acting like Mary-Beth, leaving things out, rearranging, talking in a language not entirely my own.

After a drink or two, we'll go our separate ways. I always have a reason to get on with the evening. Groceries. Making dinner for my kids. Or film night with my friends.

I'll watch Mary-Beth walk back down Mill Street in her comfortable shoes and navy suit and cropped, chin-length hair, and I'll get an urge to rush home and burn anything in my closet that isn't multi-coloured or beaded or bright, or scented with Patchouli Oil, which never bores me and fills my pores with nights I'll never forget.

I'll go home and put on my Storyteller's Jacket while I scramble eggs for dinner and wait for Ben to call, which could be anytime between 5 p.m. and midnight. I'll stand over the stove in my jacket made of silk ties and plaid shirts and a snip or two off a pair of faded blue jeans — the fabrics of love — crazy-quilted with cross stitches and blanket stitches and two-lane stitches that remind me of love on the road in the back of a Volkswagen camper.

Purple velvet and red silk and paisley greens and gold. Years ago, I took a navy jacket and began covering it with pieces of my lovers' clothes. I wear it now, as I lay otherwise naked under a blanket in Ben's cottage, with a piece of his black Levi's shirt in my jacket pocket. I snipped it earlier, a small piece from the bottom right side, near the seam, so he wouldn't notice it missing for a while.

Ben shut his eyes a few moments ago.

He didn't want to talk.

Sleep will take care of this, Sadie. Sleep, he said.

Quit talking.

Quit thinking.

Just go to sleep.

I was in between men when Ben showed up. A knock at the door. There he was. Canvassing for money for a family whose home at Oak Lake burned to the ground earlier that spring, just after the warm air began melting the ice on the water. I was making dinner, the television was blaring from another room, my children were whining about their grumbling stomachs and why can't I stop being so cheap and buy some extra channels so there's something worth watching.

I went to the door with a black-handled flipper waving in the air, yelling for the kids to turn it down, watch the burgers, and set the table — which I wouldn't have done if I knew who was standing on the other side, listening to another frantic, bitchy, burned-out woman. At least, that's the way I imagined he saw things, or how I see myself when I let the reel roll back in my mind. A frantic woman I hardly recognize who takes me by surprise, knocks me out of breath with her hurried, scattered state.

I could have just given him some money. I had close to thirty bucks in my wallet. I could have let it go at that, but I didn't. I didn't see a wedding ring.

No, he didn't know what caused the fire. Yes, he knew the family. They live across the lake. Or they used to. He's just trying to help. Everyone needs help from time to time.

I could arrange a big yard sale at the literacy centre to raise money, I said. I've done this kind of thing before. I'll call him with a date and the details. What about a yard sale *and* barbecue?

An exchange of phone numbers and the door closed and I watched him walk down the street to the next house with his good looks and good intentions and all of my thoughts in the palm of his hand.

It often happens this way for me.

I'll go for long periods of time without seeing anyone then all of a sudden someone shows up like a gift on God's wind and consumes my every waking moment. The sleeping ones, too. A complete takeover of my daydreams and night dreams, and the precious few moments when I'm actually alert and aware that another world exists outside the new one that's just been created and tossed into the universe, waiting for its history to begin. How will this turn out?

Even in my brief moments of awareness, he's there — when I'm teaching someone how to read a newspaper, or defending my right to wear the clothes I do to my embarrassed and hopelessly conservative seventeen-year-old daughter. I can hear the sound of the telephone ringing before his next call. What he might say. What I might bring up. How we'll get from here to there. It always happens this way for me and I kick myself for still obsessing about boys at 49.

I make myself wash the car and shop for hot dogs and talk to people on the street. I tell myself I'm doing all these things and functioning and at worst appearing only slightly distracted. See. I'm not paralyzed by my obsessive thoughts. See. I'm in control of them, letting them in fully one moment, when I lie down for a nap after work before making dinner, shrinking them to a smaller screen against the bigger picture in other moments — multi-tasking with whatever demands my attention at the time.

I toast buns, fry Spanish onions, and try to talk everyone into buying a date square for another $1.50. It's for a good cause. He shows up and carries larger items to people's trucks and car trunks and tells me I've really done a wonderful job and aren't we lucky it didn't rain. He was sure it was going to rain the way the wind picked up last night and covered the stars with a sheet of cloud and pushed the waves up over the dock. Have you spent much time up at the lake, he asks.

Several summers, I tell him, with my kids, at the little beach where the canteen is. I keep forgetting there really is a lake up there. It's strange, I say, the way it sits at the top of the Oak Hills, a tiny lake smaller than most of the farms that surround it, just five minutes from town, in a bedroom community of expensive suburban homes with fenced-in pools and central air, and long and winding heated driveways that melt the winter snow. Even some of the old cottages on the lake are being replaced by three-storey Cape Cod-style homes with cathedral ceilings and state-of-the-art kitchens.

It's hard to think of it as a lake, I tell him.

Lakes are supposed to take you hours to drive to, with miles of wilderness around them and nothing but endless water ahead of you when you stand at the shoreline — not something you pass on a regular basis along the highway, and hardly ever notice, and never think of when you long to

be lying on a hot dock with a gin and tonic and a good book
and no worries beside you.

I hadn't thought about Oak Lake in years.

We packed up the barbecues and let the other volunteers
divvy up the unwanted yard sale items and took some of the
leftover food up to his cottage. It was late in the afternoon,
on a Saturday, the only time I would see the cottage in the
daylight. Darkness would usher me in for the next year.

You see, he has this girlfriend. Everyone likes her. All
the neighbours, his friends, everyone. She's a nice girl. She
wants to move in with him. He doesn't want to hurt her. He
doesn't want to live with her, either, so he puts her off. The
cottage needs fixing up. His ex-wife is suing him for more
child support.

He loves his kids.

He does what he can.

He's in between things.

He just wants to fish all summer and make decisions
with a rod in his hand and a smoke in his mouth.

He's being honest, he says, at least with me. Can I handle
it? He doesn't have the energy to deal with anything else.

We made love against my better judgement, which I've
learned to set aside with frequency and consistency over the
years, and toasted his thirty-ninth birthday, which was the day
before, and picked a place for me to park my car the next time
I came up to the lake — after dark, so the neighbours don't
notice, so no one will say anything to a certain someone, so his
life doesn't get more complicated than it already is. We picked
the fork in the road, not far from the cottage, and sort of
chuckled over the irony of our choice. The heavy scent of
calcium chloride that kept the dust down followed us out to
the highway, then disappeared into the midnight air as Ben
drove me back into town.

I keep thinking about standing at my kitchen sink in my
Storyteller's Jacket, scrambling eggs for dinner, waiting for
the phone to ring, for Ben to call. How the anticipation ran

up my sleeve, skipping like a stone over a quilted history of similar moments, putting its arm around my shoulders and rubbing my back with nostalgic affection, time passing.

I scrambled back and forth myself, between the counter and the stove, adding salt and cayenne pepper, and throwing utensils into a sink full of eggshells and dirty bowls while Van Morrison sang about old loves. I grabbed a salad out of the fridge and vowed to take down all the posters advertising concerts I couldn't afford to go to, which hung like dangling carrots under borrowed inspiration. The scribbled lines and curves of my own handwriting formed the words of some other, wiser souls on sheets of recycled paper from the literacy centre. I retained nothing and carried on, forgetting what it was I felt I needed to remember.

The phone rang and I talked quickly, breathlessly, to a friend about the downside of love on the sly, trying to fit all the details into one long, uninterrupted sentence before my daughter or my son walked into the kitchen looking for dinner or something to drink, throwing a look of disapproval my way.

Ben can't go to concerts with me, or to dinner parties, or meet my friends, or my ex, who drops by every other week to pick up the kids and keeps asking me when I'm going to get a real life as he bitches about his new wife and their rambunctious three-year-old son and drinks my beer.

Hal tells me I've picked another loser who hasn't got a job and doesn't take me out. He closes the door and leaves behind empty bottles in a beer puddle on my pine table and the lingering image of the purple and black striped shirt he wore to my sister's wedding at Wasaga Beach twenty-five years ago, where he sat by the water's edge flirting with a cute blonde, lighting her cigarettes and fetching her drinks. I watched him as I followed my sister and her new husband around, passing out wedding cake wrapped in doilies and silver ribbon to guests who would forget to take it home or would discover it at the bottom of their purses two weeks later, rock hard and turning colour.

You can't know for sure how you feel about a man until you end up stuck to him — with him — with him in you. You think you like him, maybe even love him. You create scenarios as days pass and he doesn't call. His mother died and he went away. His girlfriend keeps showing up and he wants to call you but can't get a moment's peace from her. He got a job and left town.

You tell yourself he didn't mean much. He was just another lover, someone to pass the time with. You were going to break it off anyway.

The phone rings. It wasn't so long ago that you saw each other, was it? No, you're not mad. Of course, you understand.

Then you hop in your car at eleven at night and your daughter calls you a whore and your understanding son says he'll look after things, and you drive out into the darkness, rationalizing your right to your own life, praying, bargaining for *him*, or *her*, or *it* to keep your kids safe until you get home.

You go.

Just to get there.

Just to get there one more time.

Some of your friends say you're too available. You deserve more. Make him choose. You or her. Secrecy or out in the open, public declarations of affection that make everything alright.

How can you drive out there in the dark in the middle of the night? It's not safe. He shouldn't make you do that.

You're a disappointment to women everywhere. Weak and boy-crazy. A horny middle-aged disappointment who can't tell what it feels like when you get in your car and put on Patsy Cline's "Walking After Midnight" and smell the lavender as you back out of your driveway, and breathe Patchouli Oil, and the fresh smoke of the cigarette you've just lit, and the ripe smell of the hay that's been cut in the fields you pass as you climb the hills and reach the bonfires and the black water of the lake, and remember a thousand times in your life when you couldn't smell anything but disappointment with yourself.

How can I not go, I say.

Sometime over the last year, I started telling Ben about Mary-Beth, and Mary-Beth about Ben, and this is what really bothered me about Mary-Beth coming up to the cottage to fix our problem. They know too much about each other.

Ben knows all about the man Mary-Beth dated who had the latest, greatest fishing boat with all the gadgets and gismos to help him spot a fish five hundred feet away; how the kids on the dock where he parked the super fish-finder caught more fish with sticks and string than he ever did; how Mary-Beth said he was never any good at finding the right spot on anything, which surprised me that Mary-Beth would even bring that up.

"The only things he ever found out there were mosquitoes and a good place to pee," Mary-Beth had said, and I repeated it for Ben hoping he would shed some light on what answers he might be finding out there on the lake with his rod and his smokes. He was on his second summer of soul searching and as far as I could see he hadn't caught a single decision.

Once, after we had made love and Ben fell asleep, I went outside on the porch, which threatened to give way at any moment and send me down a grassy slope into the cold night waters. I stood there and watched the blackness roll in towards me and wondered what Ben thought about when he was out there alone, fishing in the weathered aluminum boat that came with the cottage. It bobbed up and down and back and forth against the dock — *yes, no, yes, no* — as indecisively as the man who climbed into it and went fishing for answers.

The precarious life of a fisherman.

I never told Ben about Mary-Beth's theories on why he can't make a decision, or what she thinks about the way his girlfriend has begun following him around and showing up without notice, which is really beginning to irritate him. I've never said a word about my "aftermath cycles," which Mary-Beth named and asks about whenever she sees me on the street and I'm looking anxious.

Days one through five after I've seen Ben, I'm fine and can live with or without him. Days six through ten, I teeter between calm confidence that I'll see him again soon and a state of questioning despair when I'm sure he's chosen the other one, or someone entirely new, and won't even call to tell me. By day eleven, I'm ready to break it off and get rid of the headache that's been sitting above my eyebrows for the past four days.

"What day are we on?" Mary-Beth always asks, then we'll go for a coffee or a drink, or just stand on the street, the two of us backed up against the hardware store, analyzing the meaning of the ring-less phone.

"Everyone thinks I should dump him."

"Why," Mary-Beth says, "you like him. Love doesn't just have to happen in the daylight or between 6 p.m. and midnight, for all the world to see. To hell with convention. What's it got to do with love?"

"You're right," I say, "why get messed up with that."

"He's been honest with you, from the start," she says with a serious tone to her voice.

"You're right, he has."

"So, he's not as honest with the other one. What does that tell you about their relationship?"

"You're right again," I say. "I'm really glad I ran into you."

And I am glad until Mary-Beth tries to turn the helpful advice into a commitment for dinner at her place the next night. I didn't mind our impromptu meetings on the street, every now and then, but Mary-Beth wanted some kind of payoff — friendship — for listening to the aches and pains of my heart that she solicited in the first place.

I decline her invitation, saying I have to watch my son play basketball or something like that. I can't remember now. I regret ever telling her anything about Ben. Mary-Beth assumes she's now part of our relationship and can bring it up in conversations on the street corner, the way most people talk about the weather.

"Are you awake?"

Nothing.

"Ben?"

Nothing.

I can feel him slipping away, a weakening of the walls that hold him in place.

Not yet.

Not yet.

He sleeps. His body rises and falls, and he breathes as though he might stop and be gone forever. In the dim light, with only a thin line of pale yellow coming in from the kitchen, he could be anyone, or everyone — if I let what I already know about him drift out the window onto the night's breeze, and I clear the slate for nothing but the shape of his silhouetted shoulder as he lies on his side facing me with closed eyes, like the others who've clothed me with their passing love.

He breathes.

He stops.

He breathes.

And I remember standing in line at a post office, years ago, with a brown package in my hands, waiting my turn.

And the striped T-shirts Johnny Marks used to wear.

And the way he used to sit on the front porch of his sister's house with his back against the pillar, with one leg over the edge, resting on the ground.

I still think of him every time I cut asparagus and go to yard sales and cover tomato plants with tin cans to protect them from frost.

I stand at my kitchen sink today, waiting for the phone to ring, and I'm there again — back in the gardens of vivid recollection, listening to music on a transistor radio, the smell of anticipated love sitting in the damp morning soil, which I turn over and run my fingers through and carry around for hours under my nails until I wash my hands.

I'm in the barn, stripping wash stands and flat-to-the-walls and dry sinks. I feel the heartburn from breathing the chemical stripper as I peel back the layers of paint, removing my gloves, using my bare hands to get every bit. Waves of prickly heat run over my body thinking about him, the possibilities, the unknown, as I get down to the original finish and realize I've hardly noticed the time.

Then Hal's voice mumbles something about it all being a waste of time, this stripping. People — the ones with real money — want everything "as found." If it's still got bird shit on it, it's worth more, he'd say. The rougher, the better. And a little bird shit is as good as gold.

Most of the people who used to drop by our barn on a Saturday or Sunday still wanted what we called "honey money pine" finish by Min-Wax, so I continued to strip and peel away the layers — and wonder about the furniture that was once a backdrop for family photos, or a reminder of a bad fight where fists were slammed and legs kicked, or the place where love rolled around under the sheets and children were conceived.

In winter, we would work upstairs, in the empty bedrooms where we planned to put our kids some day. When we had kids. I'd help lug cupboards and weigh scales and bedroom sets up the narrow staircase as Hal cursed the sharp turn at the top and yelled for me to move back a little, to the right, to the left, to the extra space that wasn't there. Then we'd work for months inside one of the bedrooms, opening the frozen windows when we could, to breathe. To let the cold, grey air into our lungs.

In the workaday haze that was my life, I didn't see Johnny Marks coming.

I saw Hal and our barely-make-a-living antique business, and the vegetable gardens behind our house, and the empty rooms we planned to fill upstairs.

I didn't see Johnny Marks coming, even though he'd been part of my life ever since I was old enough to yearn for the kind of love that didn't demand silence and the occasional quick look the other way — didn't ask for tradeoffs and trade-ins of tidbits, and parts, and whole chunks of your being, and the oddest appreciation for what you got in return, no matter how much less it was worth to you.

Pawn shop love.

Johnny came to housesit at his sister's while she went travelling for a year in Europe with her husband and her two daughters. He moved into their farmhouse, on the seventh concession, two roads over from our place. He looked after their beef cattle, and repainted the house, and carved the faces of old men and old women on the cedar fences in the fields behind the house, and along the road — a series of bumps and grooves you wouldn't see unless you knew they were there, secretly sitting in the man-made boundaries of dead wood.

He showed up one day, when Hal was someplace else. He brought a chair. It used to belong to his grandmother, he said. He remembered sitting on it when he was a kid, watching his grandmother make his favourite fudge. Maple walnut.

He found the chair in his sister's barn, with peeling white paint, and red paint under that, and flecks of pale green paint under that. He wanted it restored. How much would it cost? He'd pay any price. He couldn't stand seeing it painted in three different colours and covered in dust and chicken shit anymore.

"Some people would pay a fortune for a chair like that," I told him, "especially with the chicken shit on it."

"Some people have chicken shit for brains," he said.

"My husband always prices the jobs," I told him, wondering in my own mind how that came about in the first place when Hal always asked me how long I thought it would take to complete the task, and what the cost of the materials would add up to.

"Well, whatever it is, I'll pay it."

Johnny stood in a three dimensional picture, framed by the thick beams that outlined the huge doorway to the top of the barn, with a horizon of summer-green behind him.

"What difference does it make what it costs," he said, his face shadowed by the strong afternoon light behind him. "If you're going to do something, are you going to change your mind because it costs a hundred bucks instead of fifty?"

"To some people, the price you pay makes all the difference," I said. I was conscious of the way the light pushed past him and spilled over my face, a spotlight on every micro-expression he might catch if he was paying any attention at all. I tried not to give anything away.

"Then their minds weren't really made up, were they," he said, a question and an answer at the same time, and I wasn't sure if we were still talking about his grandmother's chair, which stood only a few feet away with his past, and maple walnut fudge, and my future lying in the crevices of the spindles I'd be stripping tomorrow.

He hung around for a while, wandering through the maze of refinished furniture and works-in-progress, asking me about this piece and that, and did I make a living doing this? He carried his cigarettes under the sleeve of his striped T-shirt and ran his fingers through his hair, which was thick and messy and made him look like he just woke up.

"You should soak your hands in aloe," he said, a thought that came out of nowhere.

"Do they look that awful?" I held them up for inspection. I was used to the dryness and hardly noticed how much the chemicals were changing the texture and colour of my own skin.

"My sister has half a dozen plants lining the kitchen window serving no useful purpose in life. I'll bring you a couple when I come back for the chair."

He shook my hand before he left, the softness of his skin bathing my own chapped hand in tenderness that wasn't part of a quick business handshake, and I couldn't remember the last time Hal had held my hands. Or I held my own. They were for work. A separate entity. I had forgotten they were there, at the end of my arms, with all the pleasures of touch at their mercy.

I told Johnny to come back next Tuesday. I would have the chair finished by then. I walked with him through the barnyard, over to the driveway where his car was parked. The ground was dry. It hadn't rained in weeks. I was listening to the sound of our feet moving in unison over the cracked dirt path, and the chatter of the barn swallows that lined the telephone wire stretching in from the road. Something from inside of me leapt into the air as the swallows picked up and flew away above our heads in a single, sudden move of force and unanimous decision.

After Johnny left, I remembered Hal was going to Toronto the following Tuesday to deliver a few pieces to one of our regular customers. He wouldn't be home when Johnny came back for the chair.

I never planned to have an affair with Johnny. There wasn't time for that — for planning. Sorting, sifting, thinking things through. He appeared that day in the doorway of the barn with his grandmother's triple-painted chair. He came back the following Tuesday to pick it up, stripped and waxed and restored to its original finish. By Friday morning, we were walking through the fields behind his sister's house, looking at the faces he carved in the fences — the old men and old women who knew what we would know one day. That's what he said.

By Friday afternoon, I gave myself up to him and let him have me right there in a field, and all the way back to the house, and in the kitchen, on the floor, near the chair. It was meant to be, he said. He knew it was going to happen, since the first moment he saw me. He said I knew it, too. And I guess I did. I didn't plan it, but I knew it, and I couldn't pretend I didn't.

In the fields that day, I only knew not having him was more unbearable to me than any act of disloyalty I was committing. Grabbing my chance was everything. Planting myself on the ground, letting him, and his perception, and certainty, push me into the soil where I had a chance to grow all over again, and do it differently.

I went home hoping Hal wouldn't smell our lovemaking and cooked him asparagus country pie for dinner. I complained about the heat and headed for the bath, and my heart skipped a few beats when some blades of grass floated to the top. I sat soaking, lingering, putting off washing Johnny away. I could still feel him between my legs when I got out of the tub and dried myself off and dabbed Patchouli behind my ears.

That summer, I retreated to the front porch of my mother's house — the third house on the left past the Harold Cheese Factory — where the McCann women regularly gathered for cheese curd and tea and Aunt Viv's homemade cherry wine. Of course, their last names changed when they got married, but they always thought of themselves as the McCann women. There was something reassuring about it.

Hal thought I was there more often that I was. When I wasn't with Johnny I did go, to sit with the women who had always been in my life, to see if I'd spot something of myself in their eyes, to see if they noticed any change in me.

My father would retreat to the drive shed whenever the McCann women arrived. He'd go off and fix some old boat motor he'd found at the dump, for the fibreglass boat he brought home years before, which still sits to this day, dry-docked in the tall barnyard grass, with a bird's nest under the hull.

My mother never learned how to swim and didn't like the water and refused to go out in it with him. It sits — a symbolic reminder of the one thing she wouldn't do for him — in the same place where those rusty relics he called farm implements used to sit. Just throw a little Massey-Ferguson red on them, Charlotte, and they'll be as good as new, he'd say. And she would. She'd stand out there in the hot summer sun, swatting horse flies, painting bright red the spokes and the prongs on the hay cutters and the rakes and whatever other ugly contraptions he'd drag home, boasting about his keen eye to spot a piece of rusted machinery that could still be useful.

I was the only McCann woman of my generation who was still in the area. My younger sisters and female cousins were scattered throughout the province and rarely made it home anymore. My brothers were here and there and made the odd appearance with a girlfriend or new wife who was interested in sniffing out the past.

I was the one who sat on the porch with them — with my mother, and Gran, with Aunt Viv and Aunt Ruth — and I was accepted as their equal, expected to understand their

private jokes and recall the lost lyrics of songs they danced
to when they were young. Don't you remember that one,
Sadie? Surprise. Surprise. They were always surprised to
remember I was half their age, less than a third of Gran's life.
I never said a word to any of them about my affair with
Johnny, but it hung like a question mark in my own mind at
the tail end of every subject we covered.

I told Ben part of that story already. I remember because he
asked me if my father would be willing to sell the boat for
fifty bucks and I couldn't imagine him selling it at all, and I
really couldn't imagine Ben driving up there, to the place
where I grew up, talking to my father, and hauling that boat
away, leaving his footprints on sacred earth. My earth, which
he barely knows about and stomps on frequently when he
doesn't call or makes me wait four weeks to see him again.

It all slips away. My tight grip on where I came from. He
walks all over it and clouds my vision with the dust he kicks
up in his silence.

I never told him this.

He'd only interrupt me, or stop my words with his
beautiful mouth, or say I've got it all wrong and rationalize my
rationalizations until I forgot what it was I was trying to get
my head around to begin with.

I only told him about the boat. He asked me if fifty
bucks would pay for it. I told him I couldn't bear going up
there, seeing it tied to the dock, sitting in the lake, bobbing
up and down in stormy waves, being caressed by gentler
waters under a sliver of the moon. Being where it should
have been all along.

That's as far as we got.

His phone rang and Ben ran inside to answer it, leaving
me on the dock to wonder why he couldn't just let it ring
until it stopped. When he came back, he had a dismissive
look on his face, as if it might persuade me it was only his
friend, Bill, drunk and distressed over the sudden flight of his
wife — the one with the beady eyes and the beak-like

mouth, the one he said never stopped complaining about how bored she was living in the country, how she missed the sound of six-lane traffic and screaming sirens and pollution warnings on the radio.

I might have believed it if it didn't take him another half hour to move closer to me, to separate the words he'd heard over the phone from what I was saying, to return to the position we were in before he leapt to answer the call. My legs over his legs. His arm around my shoulder. His feet hanging over the dock. His free hand catching fireflies and drinking beer and smoking cigarettes. Running his fingers through his hair.

He was asking me about the pale blue silk patch on my right arm. I was telling him it came from a scarf that belonged to a man named Glen, a sculptor who spent half the year in Italy working with the finest marble, how it reminds me of my Aunt Viv, who once planned a trip there. I was telling him all of this when his free hand began unbuttoning my blouse and he suggested we take a swim. Was Glen a good lover, he wanted to know. Did he do anything special? Yes, I said, as a matter of fact, he did do something very special. He rubbed my feet like he was sculpting clay. He'd rub them for hours with his strong hands, and he listened to my stories. He liked my stories.

Ben said he liked my stories, too, and would like to hear more about Aunt Viv and her trip. I said she never went away. She only planned to. He said I could tell him all about it. Later.

I didn't think about it at the time, when he was stripping me and kissing me and telling me how much he wanted to fuck me, but I thought about it before.

About telling him why Aunt Viv never went to Italy. The way Aunt Ruth used to paint her house, over and over again. The kitchen, the bathroom, the stairway, the kitchen, the bathroom, the stairway.

About the shirts my mother mended and made do with, and the flea markets she used to wander through, looking for a small item that would give her a lift. A candle too pretty to burn. Some old rhinestone buttons. Something luxurious and frivolous for under five dollars.

The way Gran used to complain about everything. The money Ruth wasted on paint. The food at the nursing home. The mystery person who kept stealing everyone's hand lotion. How Gran sat, rigid and frayed, like the broken threads of woven osier in the seat of the rocker. That was her chair, near the purple clematis, the shadiest spot on the porch.

They were there in the beginning, that first summer when Johnny Marks showed up with his grandmother's chair. They were still there the following summer, after I mailed that brown package and left the post office without any blood in my veins.

They remain as bookends.

They sit on a shelf I pass regularly and sometimes stop in front of, letting my fingers touch the volumes that stand between them, holding the details I've managed to keep in good shape. Crisp and clean, without dog-eared or ripped pages, like new every time I see them. Separate from everything else.

Under the roof my father patched a dozen times — behind tiger lilies and irises and three generations of peony bushes — on a wooden floor with peeling grey porch paint and splotches of cherry wine stains, I learned how to build the shelf that love sits on. I learned how to make it sturdy and unadorned so it looks like it belongs. Plain and simple, another piece of furniture holding some untitled books, which become obscured by the pockets of air that puff out of Ben's mouth and make their way into a bag of endearing things about him, which I carry with me when he's not around. Of all the things to cling to. Apnea. And the streaks of laundry soap on his shirts.

I'll think about them when I'm trying to knock him down a peg or two. He snores. He walks around looking like yesterday's laundry. He doesn't work. He can't even catch a good fish.

He stumbles through.

He stumbles.

And makes me wish I could, too.

Stumble and fall, and not bother getting up right away to brush myself off, but lie instead, on the ground I land on, and stay a while. Fallen and still. With half a chance to remember what it is I couldn't do as I stood in the kitchen of my mother's house, waiting for a kettle to boil, while Gran demanded to know what happened to her mother's ring.

"I hope one of you didn't go and pawn it or something," she said.

I could hear her, and the rest of them, through the screened door in the kitchen, where I stood, eavesdropping, until an image not unlike my own caught my eye.

There was a picture of my mother lying on the table, a photograph leaning against a candle. Taken long ago, on the porch. A picture of her wearing a straw hat, leaning on a pillar, staring out over the peony bushes. Behind it, there was a picture of my mother painting a rusted rake in the barnyard. Behind that, another picture of my mother squatting, her back to the hushed lens, painting the same rake, and Aunt Viv standing beside her with a paint brush in one hand and a bandanna on her head, her mouth moving, caught in mid-sentence as she spoke to the camera. Protesting, no doubt, against being in such an unflattering setting, sweating, in clothes she'd only wear to paint in a barnyard.

"That ring's worth a fortune," Gran went on. "It's a whole carat. The detail on that carriage, they don't make them like that anymore. Of course, my father had taste. Taste *and* money, which is more than I can say for your father."

"Dad tried, mother," I could hear Aunt Ruth say.

"He forged cheques!" Gran snapped back.

"The worst time," Aunt Viv joined in, "was when the police came to get him just as my date showed up, that Robert what's-his-name. You know the one, Charlotte. He drove the red convertible."

"Robert Davidson," my mother answered without hesitation, plucking the detail from her mind as she plucked thread with a favourite needle, up and down, through the thinning fabric of one of my father's shirts. "He lived in town, on Emily Street," she continued. "His father was a butcher."

"My God, dear, your memory never ceases to amaze me," Aunt Viv said with her own mix of drama and sarcasm. "Thank you for carrying around the details of my life I can't be bothered remembering."

"You can't be bothered remembering, Missy, and I'll never forget." Gran began rocking back and forth, faster, enough to make the chair inch closer to Aunt Ruth. "I'll never forget that time your father went all the way to Florida to keep from going to jail again. He came back three hours before Charlotte's wedding, with no money and no suit to wear. Remember that dear? He had to borrow that awful powder blue suit from Norman."

"It wasn't awful, mother," Aunt Ruth said. "My husband paid a fortune for that suit."

"It was the ugliest suit that ever came out of a store!" Gran yelled, her anger at everything and nothing squeezing into the first opportunity she'd had all day.

"It was an expensive linen suit, mother." Aunt Ruth's voice was controlled, with exasperation only a few more words away.

"Ugly as hell, and wrinkled too," Gran pecked again.

"It wasn't wrinkled, mother!" Aunt Ruth yelled. I could see her shaking her head, sighing, turning to face the flowers that had gone limp in the beds below her. She was a tired as they were of the unrelenting heat and the burning words from the yellow goddess who sat across from her. Gran wore the same yellow smock dress most of that summer.

Just as Aunt Ruth yelled, my mother dropped her sewing box, and straight pins and spools of thread scattered all over the porch floor, and Gran switched to the old sewing machine she gave my mother, and why didn't she ever use it, and how many times is she going to mend the same shirts, and isn't that husband of hers ever going to make a decent living so she can go to the store and buy some new clothes.

The rest of the McCann women stayed low to the floor, picking up the mess of pins one at a time, while Gran ranted on to no one in particular about the heat, and the weak tea, and the intolerably long distance between the porch and my mother's only bathroom at the top of the stairs.

I slipped into the pantry off the side of the kitchen when I heard Gran coming. I stood behind the door and pretended to be looking for more sugar. In case. I heard her climb the stairs with a steady pace at the start, then slow, staggering steps. I could hear the aging anger go out of her when she got close to the top — it wheezed its way out, and was replaced by confusion and indecision about which direction to head off in.

I read the labels on soup cans while I heard her feet shuffle one way, then the other. A door closed and she moaned slightly as she sat down on the toilet. I stayed in the pantry until she flushed and went back to the porch — and the pump in the cellar below me kicked in, drawing water from the well in the field behind the house, with a motor that was growing louder and slower, deadening the sound of her return and the question of what happened to her mother's ring.

The pale blue silk patch over here never found out. He went back to Italy and fell in love with a model with nicer feet than mine.

The plaid flannel on my elbows didn't even want to know I had a grandmother, or a mother, or children of my own, and frequently called at the last minute on a school night to get together, and planned weekends with beer and pot and sex at *my* house because he was married and we couldn't go to his house.

Earlier, Ben asked me about this funny green material on my hip. It wasn't like any shirt he'd ever worn, he said. It feels like polyester, but thicker, he said. I was going to tell him, but then I had to put my mouth on his and take my jacket off, and everything else, and slide into the lake with him because he made me think of Bobby and his nice strong body, and why I clipped a few pieces from one of his ball caps.

I was going to tell Ben how every time I went into

Bobby's closet or dresser drawers looking for a patch of cloth, he walked back into room and made love to me again, and again, and I couldn't think of clothes at all when I thought of Bobby, only his tireless, muscular body. But as I lay under him one night, drained by love's rough touches and his inexhaustible probing and acrobatic curiosities, I couldn't help but notice the swollen fabric on his collection of ball caps, which hung on hooks in perfectly straight rows on the back of his closet door, and when Bobby got up to shower before another round of spinning and hanging and tangled limbs, I snipped away at his Scout's hat with the Swiss army knife he kept on his night table.

It sounds like a fable, not a real life, and I don't sound at all like the same person when I tell that story and the one about my grandmother's ring. I can hear the difference in my own voice.

I hear it.

The way my voice loses its smile and becomes guarded, and unsure, as I stand under the covered bridge on Mill Street and watch the flow of Rawdon Creek and tell Mary-Beth once again how Ben romanced me in the wee hours of the morning, faking surprise at myself for letting it all happen. The midnight rambler, we call him. His name is rarely spoken anymore, not even by me and my handy little bad girl voice. Shame, shame on me, trailing the verbal journal entries I make every time I see Mary-Beth.

Except that one time when she cornered me outside the Sears Catalogue Store and invited me up to her apartment for a drink and I couldn't think fast enough about what else I had to do.

When she did most of the talking and I walked around her living room scraping fragments, excavating amongst her brown Lazy-boy leather furniture, and the dying fig tree in the corner, and the pictures on her bookcase, which sat near a heap of seemingly uninteresting rocks and pebbles, until I looked closely and turned them over and found the embedded vertebrae of something tiny and unknown.

Mary-Beth dropped names like gastropods and

cephalopods and trilobites, and did I know they were pre-Cambrian, five hundred million years old? She collects them from the beach at Presqu'ile. She drives out on weekends and scours the shoreline, looking for historic backbone.

She's never had any of her own, she said.

"I'm not likely to leave any marks on this earth." That's what her clinical doctor's voice said.

"Nothing that'll last beyond tomorrow."

When she said it, she was standing in front of the bookcase and she spoke with resignation, which I hate and find presumptuous, since none of us know what will happen tomorrow to change our view. She could meet someone, she could do something. I don't know what. Something.

I looked at those pictures on her bookcase and figured I did a good job of picking out her mother and her father and her brother, the one in the white frame with his blond, well-groomed wife and their two impeccable children. It was the man in the gold frame I couldn't place — the one who was standing beside a small plane, leaning on its wing with a cigarette in one hand. I wanted to know who he was but I didn't want to know the story. There had to be a story behind that picture, and why she chose brown leather, and why she doesn't move that dying fig into more light, and how she ended up here, without anyone in her life but a bunch a patients who only need her twice a year when they get a runny nose or find a lump.

We sat on her couch and drank scotch and soda and she asked me what I was going to do about the midnight rambler. Was I getting past the conventional crap that says I have to have him all to myself, like the rest of the normal world? That he has to call me three days before he wants to see me, not eleven at night, and promise me exclusivity on his penis and his heart.

Had I gotten past all that, she wanted to know. Could I close my ears to the rest of it, to what I'm supposed to do?

Sure, sure I have, I said, as I chugged my drink and couldn't figure out why I said I'd have soda, which I've never liked and which sits in my stomach, burning, bubbling, until it works its way back up and settles in my chest — carbonated rain against my bones. Like that man in the picture, the one in the small gold frame on the bookcase, fizzing and spitting at me from behind a piece of glass. Staring at me. Shaking his head in between drags on his cigarette, and throwing looks of disappointment my way.

I left Mary-Beth's apartment and walked home, after that.

Then I drove out to Johnny Marks's sister's farm.

I stopped a short distance before the house, pulled over, and parked in front of the faces he carved in the fence along the road. They were still there, a lighter shade of grey.

Of course.

Think of all the suns that have risen since then, casting fading rays of hope on the bumps and grooves he left behind. The boundaries we didn't cross still stand and get splashed by passing cars after a heavy rain has filled the potholes on the road, their wooden eyes never blinking in response.

Dead wood.

That doesn't flinch.

Or ever move.

Like I did, from the kitchen to the pantry, when Gran went upstairs to the bathroom and came back down and returned to the rocker on the porch and demanded to know what had happened to her mother's ring.

She had a right to know.

She had given it to my mother, her eldest daughter, years before, and never spoke of it again, until this time. She wanted to see it.

Suddenly.

Suddenly, it was the most important thing in the world, the only thing her failing mind could focus on. The ring. The ring. That fucking, fucking ring.

I didn't tell Johnny Marks about the ring.

I told him Hal begged me not to leave.

With his eyes.

His silent, silent eyes.

I told Johnny I owed Hal another chance.

That I had an obligation.

I'd made a promise.

To be there.

I wrote it all down and mailed it in a brown package along with that shirt I embroidered for him. That jean shirt with the pearl buttons. I sewed tall blades of grass and grey split-rail fences and simple outlines of old faces. Half-faces, with one eye, part of a nose, half a mouth, carefully placing them on the front and back of the shirt just below the collar. I added a red barn and a chair and some birds on a wire just before they leapt into the future.

I folded it properly, the way my mother taught me, and tucked the note I scribbled one morning when Hal was out into the pocket, with a little hanging out over the top so Johnny wouldn't miss it.

And I wondered if it would send him flying up the driveway to get me.

To save me from myself. Or convince him I wasn't capable of leaving, of trusting what we had.

I kept waiting for Johnny to tell me to leave, even though he said he'd never say it, wouldn't tell me what to do, wouldn't tell me — that I should hear it in the way we made love that year, but all I heard was silence when I got out of bed at his sister's house to go to the bathroom.

I couldn't hear my feet on the floor when I got up, after we spent the afternoon loving and talking and sleeping for minutes here and there until it woke us up for more, before I had to go.

I couldn't hear my feet, or feel them on the carpet at the end of the bed. On the plank boards in the hallway, painted deep red, bleeding love at my feet.

I took that jean shirt out on the porch after I made another pot of tea and sat beside my mother to finish what I'd started.

"That looks like a man's shirt," Gran said.

"It is," I answered.

"You mean to tell me, Hal's going to walk around with whatever it is you've got on there?"

"It's a lovely shirt," Aunt Viv said.

"It's a silly shirt," Gran snapped back. "What man would

wear a bunch of birds, and, and — what is that? Is that a fence? My God, what man is going to wear a fence embroidered on his chest?"

"Mother," Aunt Ruth piped in, "just because you can't imagine something doesn't mean it's bad."

"I never heard of such a silly thing. Birds and fences on a man's shirt. A tablecloth or a pillow, yes. But a man's shirt?"

A car went by, breaking the conversation with the sound of shifting gravel. I looked up and saw the haze left behind by speed and dust, then continued sewing the beaks on birds, swatting flies that tickled me with their nothing legs as they ran across my arms.

I felt a sense of urgency. With finishing the shirt. With getting home. With getting to the next moment. It sat in my gut, pounding, as though my heart had sunk to my navel and was banging from the inside like a growing child, restless, uncertain, torn between the dark safety of the womb and the enticing warmth of light on the other side.

His sister was coming home, Johnny said, and it was time for him to go soon, back to Toronto, maybe, or north to Sault St. Marie. He might go there, he said, and spend some time at a cabin in the woods, outside of town, he wasn't sure. He stared at me from the pillar on his sister's porch, which he leaned against, with one leg stretched in front of him, the other dangling over the side, his eyes on me, on what I wasn't saying.

I never told him how Aunt Viv took his shirt out of my hands and showed me how to make tulip stitches, which she placed with precision along the split-rail fences, with green stems and red petals. How Gran grew impatient over the failure of my mother to produce the ring. How Aunt Ruth kept trying to change the subject, pulling out paint swatches from her purse, asking us what we thought of lavender for the hallway.

Any one of them could have pawned it, Gran said. Every one of her daughters had a motive, she pointed out, then went down the list. Aunt Viv wanted to go to Italy. Aunt Ruth had put too many paint and wallpaper and new linen

purchases on her credit cards. My mother had to replace the
roof on the house, which had started leaking and was losing
shingles every time the wind picked up.

Aunt Viv opened a bottle of cherry wine. My mother
got some glasses. Aunt Ruth poured and took a glass out to
my father who was still puttering in the drive shed. I stayed
quiet in my corner, tying off the threads with three or four
knots, obsessed about the pictures of our story staying in
their proper place on Johnny's chest plate and shoulders.

I guess I knew then I was going nowhere. I was stuck.
With myself.

With Hal, worried and upset we weren't making enough
money. Needing me to put my arms around him and tell him
everything would be alright, looking at me with eyes that
knew I'd been someplace else for the last several months,
and not with him, not really. He knew I was slipping, he had
to know, and he reached out to me and told me we didn't
have enough money to pay the mortgage and the insurance
and couldn't I, wouldn't I even consider —

I took it in. So he'd quit looking at me, quit involving me.

In the kitchen that warm summer day, while I waited for
the kettle to boil, and Gran came down the stairs from the
bathroom, I wanted to tell her — in those few seconds it
took for her to cross the kitchen — I wanted to tell her my
mother gave the ring to me and I'm the one who pawned it,
traded it for a couple of mortgage payments and some car
insurance, and that I was leaving, going off with my lover,
and isn't it the right thing to do, Gran? Wouldn't you have
done the same, if you could have? Don't you wish you did?
Don't you wish?

And I almost did.

I stood outside the Legion in Stirling on a Saturday night,
the week before Johnny left, while everyone else was inside
celebrating Aunt Ruth's twenty-fifth wedding anniversary. I
stood there while it rained, waiting for my feet to take me to
my car.

I was coming.

I even opened the door and sat inside and turned the

key and the wiper blades kept saying *yes, yes, yes, yes.* Then I saw Hal, standing outside under the white light. He didn't move. He just stood there in the rain. Waiting. Pleading, with his silent, silent eyes.

I told Ben about the Legion scene once before, when we were talking about defining moments, when he was in a talkative mood, pensive and worried about what he was going to do next, concerned that he couldn't hear that voice that always tells him what to do. It seemed it had have left him for good.

We were sitting on the dock and I told him I knew I shouldn't have stayed with Hal, that night in the parking lot of the Legion, I knew it. I told him I should have gone off with Johnny.

When I asked Ben if he was listening, he said yes, but he continued looking out over the lake with other things on his mind, so I stopped, and didn't bother telling him how I never saw Johnny again, that I mailed the note and the shirt the next day, that I stood in the post office feeling faint, afraid I was going to vomit on the marble floor, or crawl into the corner and wince.

I didn't tell him what happened in the bathroom at the Legion that night, that I ran into Aunt Viv and Aunt Ruth just before I thought I was leaving for good — that Aunt Ruth was crying because her husband told her his anniversary gift was paying off the debts she'd piled up on the credit cards, which Ben wouldn't understand anyway, because he didn't know anything about Aunt Ruth's obsession with redecorating or how Uncle Norman had spent their entire marriage telling her, her home is her life and it should be enough to make her happy.

How could I ever explain the frazzled excitement she experienced when she pulled out swatches of paint and wallpaper and laid them across the red metal table on my mother's porch? Or tell him about Aunt Viv's sarcasm, which vented anger at her husband's unwillingness to die. He was dying for years. No one should live that long like that, with oxygen tanks and soiled beds, and a leash around her neck, keeping her from going anywhere.

I didn't tell Ben I saw Aunt Viv and Aunt Ruth embracing, wiping each other's tears, fighting to get past the rush of truth, which had caught them both unaware in the freshly painted bathroom of the Legion. I said Uncle Norman was a son-of-a-bitch and they scolded me for talking that way. He was a good provider, they said. He just didn't understand women. I apologized and watched as they washed their faces, and Aunt Viv pulled out her lipstick and green eye shadow and rose-red blush, and they made themselves up all over again before they walked back out to dance to Frank Sinatra and Dean Martin.

I stayed in the bathroom for a while and smoked a cigarette and couldn't help but notice all the spots the painters had missed with the beige paint. Flecks of old white paint were still showing in the corners and in the indentations between the cinder blocks on the wall. It was a sloppy job, I decided, and they should never have been paid.

Of course I left the bathroom certain I wouldn't have to look at its poorly painted walls ever again, never imagining I'd be back in less than hour, reapplying mascara that had run down my face on the dance floor and onto Hal's white shirt. Never imagining that I'd end up here, all these years later, divorced and lying next to Ben, losing him as he slips away and leaves me empty and barren, down there, where I've filled myself with dozens of lovers and still find myself — never mind. I've collected a few good stories along the way. We only covered the pale blue silk patch on my left breast, the plaid flannel on my elbows, and the swollen green polyester near my hip, on the right side.

I'll probably never tell Ben I was thinking about Johnny earlier tonight, when we were making love in the lake, when he cried out *this is the best, this is the best*, and he gave himself up to me, completely, and I had him, all of him, everything in him, in my hands and between my legs and we went further and further out, deeper into the blackness until I couldn't feel my feet touching the bottom.

I was thinking about Johnny, then. About the article I read last year in a Toronto paper, how he's been commissioned to carve hundreds of faces in logs for the city parks. There was a picture of him, inset, in the top corner of a larger picture of three logs he'd already carved, with the faces of old men I could have sworn I'd seen before staring out at me.

He looked the same. Older, but the same. And I wondered what ever happened to that shirt — if his wife, an artist from northern Ontario, the article said — if she found the shirt one day while she was cleaning out closets, if she threw it into a pile for the Salvation Army, if someone else in the world was walking around with our story on his back. Some unknowing soul clothed in split-rail fences and tulip stitches and birds on a wire just before they leapt into their future.

The night Ben and I got stuck while making love was a night like all the others I'd seen at Oak Lake.

That's how I'll begin.

With something familiar.

With the same dark sky that greeted me every time Ben called in the middle of the night and I drove out to see him — on the wheels of one long-ago moment — under a sky full of stars, sprinkling tiny specks of light on a lake rumoured to be bottomless.

And then I'll tell the story.

How I drove home the next morning with a piece of his black Levi's shirt in my pocket, thinking about my Aunt Ruth and my Aunt Viv, who still hasn't booked her trip to Italy even though her husband died three years ago, afraid to leave the house alone. About my mother, who asked me the other day if I thought the way she fixed her hair made her look older than she is. I suggested she go to a hairdresser for a new style, but she shrugged and said my father always trimmed it and she managed fine.

We were all sitting with Gran, in the dining room at the nursing home, on her ninety-sixth birthday. There was a

cake with candles and the staff was about to sing for her.
Gran was in between my mother and myself, looking at a
bird on a feeder outside the window, not knowing or caring
what all the fuss was about.

Not remembering I told her that day on the porch that I
was the one who had her mother's ring, while my mother
looked the other way to hide what she knew was the truth.

Not remembering the ring at all.

I rubbed Gran's back and thought of Mary-Beth's rocks,
the embedded vertebrae of the tiny and unknown, and how
Gran's skin had become thin and barely covered the bumps
and grooves of her own disintegrating spine.

And how I left Ben's cottage just as the sun was coming up,
left him sleeping, shrivelled and retracted from inescapable
decision. Safe. How the heavy scent of calcium chloride
followed me on the cottage road and out to the highway, then
disappeared in the early morning air as I drove back into town.

Chapter Three

"He's probably afraid to have sex with you now," Alex says.

"Really," Sally laughs. "Shit. Talk about going to extremes to get a man to *stick* around."

"God. I know dogs get stuck," Storm adds, "but people … I've never heard about that before."

A week has passed since the blessed event took place with my beloved. Ben still hasn't called and pride has kept me from calling him. The way I see it, it happened to me as much as it happened to him. And yet, I lie awake every night wondering if he is laughing about it, as I sort of hope he is, or if he really does fear me — me, the penis-clamping woman I'm afraid he thinks I am now.

"How the hell did you get out of the lake and into the cottage?" Jenny wants to know.

"What did Mary-Beth call it?" Grace asks. "Can you spell that?" "Did it hurt?" She isn't holding a pen or paper, but she is making her notes just the same. She can't help herself. She's a writer. I oblige and tell her how to spell vaginismus, and that, yes, for a while, it did hurt, and then it went away, or I just got used to it, I'm not sure which.

It is the July meeting of Film Society and Storm has brought *Babette's Feast*.

We've seen it before.

We're in a nostalgic phase now.

We've gone through the sex phase and the art film phase and the Canadian-films-only phase. Not long ago, we decided that after several years of movie-watching, it was time to revisit a few films, like old friends, even if their initial impact wouldn't be experienced in the same way again, even if it changed dramatically. It was a risk we were willing to take, and it didn't always work out, and was sometimes disappointing. Like it was with *The Big Chill*, which we saw last month, which made us nod in awe and recognition the first time we watched it, years ago, which we had trouble sitting all the way through this last time.

"Oh, for Christ's sake," Sally said before the film ended, "what woman is going to let her husband knock up her girlfriend? Tell me. Just because she screwed around on him, we're supposed to think she'd make this big sacrifice, and they all live fucking happily ever after. Him, because he gets it. Her, because she lets him. And the girlfriend, because she's pregnant — maybe. Talk about contrived."

And then there were other films like *The Company of Strangers*, which seemed more real to us than it did the first time around. Real. And closer to home, now that we could imagine ourselves as old women, facing our own mortality. It didn't seem so far off anymore. We watched those old women stranded on their bus trip in complete silence. Nobody moved for two hours. Nobody was talking, even when the closing credits rolled.

Tonight, it's *Babette's Feast*, and Jenny has already cried out, "I hate subtitles," and Sally has followed her lead and proclaimed, "If I wanted to read dialogue, I'd pick up a book," as I knew she would.

Jenny doesn't usually care what we watch, as long as there's lots of wine to drink.

Sally complains but is always the first to lose herself in the flickering images.

Grace likes to point out the great lines, the honest dialogue, and the subtleties she thinks the rest of us have missed.

We put up with her.

It's only Sally who loses her patience with Grace's constant commentary, who tells her to shut the hell up and watch the movie. Their distant and roundabout family connection gives her permission. They are cousins by way of someone's mother's husband's cousin's daughter — enough of a family connection to impose opinion and lay a dismissive hand on the normally acceptable boundaries of friendship, making them feel they ought to know each other better, like each other more, that there is something to their relationship other than proximity, other than the fact they share the same circle of friends.

Grace talks. Sally yells. Storm sometimes closes her eyes and listens to a film.

Lately, everything makes Alex weep.

Delaney, when she's here, makes us rewind scenes, to see how they were shot. She is the only one missing tonight. She is buried beneath the old photographs of a few dead women, trying to piece together their stories. Normally, she is the clerk at the Sears Catalogue Store on Mill Street. Now, she's suddenly a documentary filmmaker and she says she can't come out.

"Have you told Del yet?" Storm asks.

"I wonder if anyone saw you like that," Sally says. "Christ, can you imagine some old geezer up there getting up to take a piss in the middle of the night and he just happens to look out the window and sees the two of you stuck like dogs?"

"You don't stick like dogs," I say.

"How the hell *did* you get out of the lake?" Jenny still wants to know.

I tell them I found it funny, to be stuck like that.

Can you picture it, I say. There I am, wearing nothing but my Storyteller's Jacket, lying in bed with my lover stuck inside of me.

I say they wouldn't believe what it took to get out of that lake and up that slope to the cottage, tangled limbs and the weight of another body fighting the necessary synchronized movement. It was nothing less than an acrobatic achievement, I say. A walk on a tightrope with your dignity falling farther and farther below you, its promise of return as unlikely as you forgetting the exposure, the undignified exposure, revealing you as the awkward, fleshy being you are, at the mercy of your own involuntary reaction. God, help us all.

I say it, and then I let it lie, let the silent space around it finish the story, and watch. Watch as Grace makes her mental notes. Watch as Sally sits in her chair in the corner of my living room and feels the empty crevice between her legs as it tightens and twinges with another reality. Watch as Alex looks down at her feet and thanks God, over and over again, that it happened to me and not to her. Watch as it calls her to attention and back to my words about involuntary contractions, how Mary-Beth said it was rare, but it happens — the clamping, the force, the inevitable prolonged erection.

The sensation of being stuck for good.

This silences them and we start the film, and let the familiar quiet settle in, settle us down, and transport us once again to Babette's kitchen, to cinematic lovemaking with culinary art, to what we remember when we first saw it, to what we've forgotten or see differently now. Only Alex shifts in her seat and sighs repeatedly and throws inquisitive glances my way, worry and sympathy all over her face.

At the end of the night, after everyone else leaves, while she is standing in my doorway, it's Alex who says, "at least you didn't have to explain it to anyone else. It's not such a predicament, Sadie. You're free to be stuck with whomever you choose."

Then she disappears into a mid-summer's night, leaving behind the words free, stuck, and choose, and I cannot separate them from the images of a woman making an exquisite feast she herself will not sit down to eat.

Alex
MARRIAGE BY NUMBERS

Chapter Four

In twenty-four years of marriage, Anthony Roy never produced a single painting of his wife. It was something that had been on Alex's mind for some time, although she never brought it up. She let it go by, like everything else, and chose instead to drag it around with her in a suitcase full of self-imposed illusions that never quite worked.

She took it along in her aging blue truck as she drove to the Stirling farmers' market. It sat next to her the entire morning while she sold her zucchini and tomatoes, and made small talk with women who didn't seem to recognize her nagging disappointment.

It wasn't until later in the afternoon that Alex realized how heavy and burdensome the whole thing had become. She saw herself from the rooftop of the Stedman's department store across the street and allowed one more illusion — of being in the good care of Anthony's strong, tanned arms, his palette and his brush giving her their undivided attention. The painting would be *Lady at Market, Oil on Canvas. There she'd be, sitting on the tailgate of her truck, in a pair of jeans that were starting to feel tight and a faded navy T-shirt. Both had dry dirt marks from carrying armloads of tomatoes out of the field at 5 a.m. Her long, greying, black hair would be pulled back out of her sun-reddened face. She'd be surrounded by other trucks and cheap beach umbrellas, and tables full of heat-beat vegetables. The humidity would hang in the air. She'd rub the dull ache above her eyes and sip on a bottle of warm water. She'd be anxious, almost hysterical in her thoughts, hating herself for her lack of calm. She'd try to strike a pose of ambivalence.*

On the drive in to the market, clover fields and red barns and the clear sky lent their lines and colour to Alex's vision of Anthony painting some woman's breasts. Streaks of alizarin crimson and cerulean blue half-circles erased the politeness and distance of pure white canvas, while Anthony's layered paint strokes teased swollen nipples until they stood erect to catch the light from the northern window. Alex could picture them winking in delight at the man who caressed them tirelessly in cadmium yellow and Acra red.

This happened every time Anthony painted a nude. Alex imagined her husband having sex with his subject the minute she wasn't around. It didn't matter that he repeatedly told her they weren't women to him, but lines and curves, and light, and energy. Not to mention these paintings were the only source of his meagre income — supported by women who wanted to surprise their husbands or treat themselves to a nude portrait by the renowned artist, Anthony Roy. It kept him well stocked in oils and canvas, and with very little left to contribute to their modest living.

None of that mattered to Alex anymore.

She could no longer believe that when these masses of curves and light crossed their legs, and positioned themselves this way and that way, Anthony didn't see their vaginas, neatly shaven and moist from the summer heat, and stinging with excitement over being seen by a man they hardly knew. How could he say he only saw a black triangular shape and cobalt violet curls? And what about the sexual energy, with a heartbeat of its own, pounding and begging him to embrace it and devour it for the eternity of the moment?

Those were the thoughts that ran through her mind on a Saturday afternoon at the farmers' market, when the light changed and cast shadows all around her from its harsh, unforgiving place above. It was defeating when Alex realized, once again, she was seeing herself through her own eyes. Anthony's continued to elude her.

At some point, Alex started talking to herself — out loud. She did this in her truck when she drove the back roads home from the market and as she sat in the spare room, cutting clothes that used to fit her into square rags for Anthony. He was always saying a painter could never have too many rags.

It had become an annoying habit — this talking to herself. But she no longer trusted the mute voice in her own head to sort things out. To pay heed to what went through her mind.

A few weeks earlier — when she was at the market — dazed from a lack of sleep the night before, and weakened by another day of unrelenting heat, Alex mumbled something about thick arms and unreachable happiness. She was thinking of Picasso's *Seated Nude*, and how the woman's arms were rounded, like parentheses, "bracketing what she could not reach but longed to hold."

She caught herself quickly, but Alex knew Vincent had heard her, the man who sold sunflowers out of the truck parked beside hers. He never said anything, but she was sure he looked at her differently from that moment on — as if he was waiting for the unbalanced woman selling zucchini beside him to mumble more spontaneous, incomplete thoughts.

In the spare room, Alex cut a pair of beige pants that were destined to be smeared with a burnt sienna and Viridian green hillside, and she thought about the *swish-swish-swish* sound she heard the other day. It was the sound of friction between her legs. The top of her thighs had rubbed together when she walked down the gravel driveway to check the mail. She had never heard it before and tried walking with her legs farther apart. But it didn't do any good. She decided she would have to walk bow-legged to separate her newly joined thighs and that seemed extreme and ridiculously vain.

What other betrayals of the body did she have to look forward to, she wondered? Would her sagging breasts eventually reach the crease that formed when she sat, like some kind of stupid grin across her belly? Would she end up with large pockets of cellulite behind her rubbing thighs? Would they look like lumpy beanbags?

No wonder Anthony never cared to throw such horrors of the flesh at his virgin canvas. Even the greatest impressionist must paint with at least some hint of the living creature before him, no matter how unpleasant the reality.

The first time Vincent invited Alex for a drink after the market, she declined. She was afraid he was only curious about the state of her unstable mind. If she was capable of talking out loud to no one in particular, what other strange behaviour might he be entertained with? She'd heard he was a psychotherapist in Toronto before he divorced and moved to the old Ryan farm on the fifth concession. Apparently, he was on some kind of sabbatical from life and didn't want to do anything but grow sunflowers and fix up the dilapidated farmhouse he had bought a couple of years ago.

The next time Vincent invited her for a drink, Alex accepted. She told herself he was probably just lonely, in need of a little conversation after spending all of his time tending his towering sunflowers, and filling cracks in plaster walls with spackling compound. A person could go mad living the quiet life, especially after being used to the traffic and buzz of the city. Even a woman who talked to herself was better company than no company at all.

After they packed up their unsold goods at the end of a long day, Alex followed Vincent along the back roads to his farmhouse. The sun was already burrowing into the horizon, skipping stones of deep yellow light across the tops of passing trees and turning the metal rooftops on barns into slanted sheets of rippled gold.

She knew Anthony would be admiring the same sunset from the studio window, standing in its path so he could feel the light on his weathered face. She knew he'd eventually close his eyes to watch the private light show of the sun's after-image. She assumed he wouldn't be thinking about her. She hadn't been gone long enough for that yet.

The last time Alex drove down the same road, Vincent had just moved into the greying, white stucco house. The fields that lined the narrow laneway were full of thistles and in need of cutting. She was surprised to see how they had changed, to see them full of sunflowers as tall as any man, with faces glowing as the sun settled down to sleep and gave them one last kiss of light.

She couldn't help but think of van Gogh, and the number of times his much-loved sunflowers came up in conversations with Anthony. Van Gogh, Chagall, Matisse, Monet, and Gauguin. They weren't dead at all, she thought. They lived on. On a dirt road in Ontario — the eighth concession of Rawdon Township — in the rags, canvases, and hundreds of tubes of paint in a converted chicken coop.

Anthony always spoke of them as family, as distant relatives whose genius had somehow been passed down to him, deserving of his constant verbal recognition of their technique, passion, and madness.

He never mentioned the wife of Henri Matisse, who supported their family with a millinery before he was able to make a living selling his paintings. Every fall when she found herself back at school teaching the young and the uninterested about the colour wheel — and when she dropped into the tub exhausted from weeding and picking and selling vegetables for extra money in the summer — Alex thought about Madame Matisse.

Anthony never mentioned Chagall's wife, Bella, either — never talked about the way Chagall celebrated every wedding anniversary with a painting of himself and his wife. Anthony didn't see what that had to do with anything.

He did give Alex a painting once — early on in their marriage. She never understood it, but dutifully placed it in a prominent place in the house, in the living room, where she could spend the rest of her life trying to figure it out. Most of the space on the canvas was untouched. In the middle, there were a series of shapes and outlines of half-drawn figures, painted in primary colours, in lines that never joined and sometimes trailed off faintly until barely visible. It was untitled.

Alex wondered what Anthony would make of that picture now. Would he see *her*, or only the colour of her white summer shirt, softened by the onset of darkness? Would he even notice she was some place she'd never been before?

Lady on the Porch, Oil on Canvas. Seated on a red chair, shadows of a dozen sunflowers standing in line along the porch of a freshly painted white stucco house. The woman would be waiting for a man named Vincent, handsome in his dishevelled, introspective way, to bring her a glass of red wine. She would sit with her hands on the sides of the chair, anticipating the burning pleasure of the wine passing her parched lips, making its way down her throat into her chest and her aching back. She'd be looking off to the right — out over the field of a thousand faces, wondering why she was there, and if she would ever want to leave.

"My daughter thinks I'm an aging hippie and my husband's an irresponsible loser." Alex and Vincent sat inside, at the kitchen table, after clusters of annoying bugs had chased them off the porch. She told him about Felicity, the daughter she had during a brief relationship before she met Anthony.

"The day of her wedding, she tells me I'm a disappointment because I didn't register her for Royal Doulton china at the gift store in town."

"Do people still do that?"

"Apparently. And I blew it. That, and I didn't bother getting my hair done."

"Are you supposed to?" Vincent sat sideways, along the table's edge, his legs stretched out, crossed and relaxed. He ran his index finger slowly along the top of his wineglass.

"Her fiancé's mother did." Alex took a few gulps of wine

and a little ran down the corner of her mouth. She wiped it with the back of her hand. She was certain that Vincent noticed the drooling and now thought of her as some hick who can't even manage to keep the wine in her mouth.

"Do you think you're a disappointment?" he asked.

"Is this therapy?"

"I thought it was a conversation."

"Sorry."

"For what?"

"For being accusatory."

"You're so formal." He made it sound like a request, an invitation to stop the verbal dance of the defensive and the guarded. Her shoulders dropped to level comfort. There was nothing to lose. Her pride had been replaced by vanity, and vanity was something she was more than willing to part with.

"I talk to myself. Out loud. Occasionally."

"I know, I've heard you."

"Is that a sign?"

"Of what?"

"That I'm losing it."

"I doubt it."

"I sometimes think I am."

"So."

"What do you mean — so?"

"So what if you're losing it? What difference does it make?"

None. None at all she wanted to say, and mean it. Sure, she could be eloquent, even dazzling with words, captivating onlookers at a gallery opening with talk about enticing nuance and engaging manner, throwing in something about the unending delight and the fullness of form of the impasto style. So what if she ended up walking the streets in town blurting out incoherent excerpts from her internal prose, about unreachable happiness and sagging breasts, and the sound her rubbing thighs make.

"I guess it wouldn't make any difference," she finally said, "because you no longer care when you lose it, do you?"

"The only thing you're in danger of losing, Alex, is your idea about what life was supposed to be."

During their conversation, Alex thought she saw him gazing into her eyes for long periods of time. She couldn't be sure, though, because she kept looking away — at the antiques around the room he'd refinished himself, at the aluminum kettle sitting on the stove with a small dent in one side. She could picture Vincent making himself coffee in the morning. She wanted to be there — in the morning — to walk up behind him and put her arms around his still-flat waistline.

When she went to the bathroom upstairs, Alex caught a glimpse of his bedroom and the rumpled mess of sheets on his bed. She wanted to climb in and stay forever. She returned to the kitchen feeling as though some sort of intimacy had passed between them.

He didn't kiss her when she left, didn't suggest she come again. He thanked her for an interesting evening and walked her to her truck. It seemed like the wrong ending for the kind of intense conversation they'd had — the wrong piece of footage edited onto the final moment of a film about a completely different night. Alex drove home replaying their conversation over and over again in her mind.

It wasn't until she pulled into her driveway that she remembered she hadn't bothered calling Anthony to let him know where she was. The light from the studio was still on and she hesitated before she walked towards it. She decided she'd tell him someone from the market invited her over at the last minute, that she didn't call because she didn't want to interrupt him. He wouldn't pry, or be suspicious. She was sure of that. She'd never given him reason to be before. Besides, nothing happened.

The morning after the evening she spent with Vincent, Alex was picking tomatoes from the field beside the house. Her knees were soaked from the wet earth. It had rained in the middle of the night — a heavy rain that woke her up and sent her downstairs, where she sat in a chair in front of the painting Anthony gave her years before. She had stayed there until it was time to go out to garden, holding a glass of cognac in tired hands she admitted needed more touching, more stroking — less time holding things together, patting someone's back, and framing someone else's soul.

"Visual innocence," she said on her way out the door, a pair of garden gloves and a few baskets under her arm. She could no longer look at a field and simply see a field. She saw a carpet of green, which seemed to stretch into forever, and herself, standing at the other end, tiny and insignificant, holding an empty basket. "Nothing is as it once appeared."

Almost two weeks passed by before Vincent asked Alex over for a drink again. She accepted and told him she'd like to take a walk through his fields of sunflowers. It sounded like the romantic idea of some young virgin who thought love and sex had more to do with setting than anything else — she wished she hadn't said anything.

Vincent seemed to like the idea, so she stopped second-guessing herself. They packed up a little early that day and ignored the questioning looks from the other farmers who saw them leave at the same time.

As she followed Vincent out to his house, she knew then that she would make love to him. She also knew she'd feel guilty about it later. But she told herself, she'd learn to live with it. She had learned to live with so many other things.

At least there would be pleasure before pain, she rationalized, and she hadn't felt pleasure for a long time. She was used to rationalizing — accepting Anthony's art as more important than her own desire to return to the canvas, dismissing his lack of affection towards Felicity as a lack of genetic connection. The list went on, but even Alex had grown bored with it, tired of the impossible task of keeping peace at any price.

Would it have made any difference if she hadn't bothered rushing in to clean up the mess all those years? Would more blood have been spilled? Would more unspoken truths have been heard by knowing souls? Pity the woman, she thought, who thinks she's made a real difference in the lives of those who don't even notice her slipping away.

Just that morning, after the sun came up and Alex came in from the field with arms full of tomatoes for the market, Anthony had offered to wash her hair with the rainwater they collect in a barrel behind the house. She couldn't remember the last time he offered to do this. It had once been a weekly ritual — a prelude to lovemaking and quiet mornings spent talking about all they wanted to do with their lives, together. It eventually waned to a monthly, then yearly event, trailing off to non-existence like the mysterious figures in the painting he had given her, now hanging in the living room.

Alex sat by the barrel with a towel around her neck, her head tilted backwards, resting on the back of her chair. She jerked slightly when the first drop of cold water ran down the side of her face.

"Sorry," was all Anthony said. Alex said nothing. She sat there listening to geese fly overhead. Most likely, they were headed for the pond in the woods at the back of the property. She opened her eyes to see them but they were already out of view.

Anthony ran his fingers through her hair after each ladle full of rainwater, carefully separating the knots along the way. Alex heard the odd car go by on the gravel road and the distant sound of a chainsaw cutting through wood. It brought the smell of wet leaves and earth to mind. It would soon be fall when Anthony and Alex would head to the woods themselves, to cut trees for the old wood-stove in the studio. If they were lucky, nature would provide enough fallen trees to avoid cutting any that were still standing.

Alex was going to ask him how much wood he thought they would need to heat the studio all winter. She also thought of mentioning the thank-you note Felicity sent the other day, for the painting they gave her as a wedding gift. She was even considering talking about the weather, just so they'd have something to say to each other. Instead, she only said "thanks" when Anthony finished towel-drying her hair.

The damp, cool earth in Vincent's sunflower field welcomed Alex's body and spread before her the possibilities of endless lovemaking. A thousand faces would witness her release, she thought. She had already managed to shut out all concerns of what's right and what's wrong — what's good and what's bad. There was no room for the remains of dying love in a field full of golden sunflowers.

She lay there waiting in the pencil-thin red light of the fading sun as Vincent undressed, his head lowered in her direction, silhouetting his face and hiding his thoughts. There was no way to tell if what he saw was disappointing to him. She decided she didn't care, and it helped to know Vincent wasn't the sort to voice it anyway. So far, everything he had ever said to her was spoken without criticism. There was no reason to ever hold back or change things in mid-sentence at the first sign of judgement coming her way.

Alex wanted Vincent to take his time unbuttoning his shirt. She wasn't in any hurry. She wanted to lie before him — exposed — and to have the chance to get the perspective absolutely right.

Lady in a Field, Oil on Canvas. Lying naked in a field of sunflowers, one arm resting at her side, the other on her stomach, just above her navel. One leg stretched flat against the ground — the other bent at the knee. Nothing to be embarrassed about. Her hips might have grown slightly wider over the years, but they were strong and bore her a daughter who was feisty and opinionated and determined.

Her thighs were thicker than they once were, but they were part of sturdy legs she could rely on for hours of weeding, and to hold her up during tiring days in the classroom, where she made a living and, sometimes, a difference in a kid's life.

She would be lying there, waiting to make love to a man she barely knew — waiting to make love to herself. She'd be thinking of the field beside the one she was in, and the one beside that, and how their lovemaking could go on forever, and how comfortable she would suddenly feel lying naked before him.

Fall came with cooler-than-normal weather, changing the

leaves earlier, making them more brilliant than Alex could remember. The tall maple near the mouth of the pond — usually a deep yellow — surprised her with its new dark orange leaves. She trailed behind Anthony, carrying a thermos of hot chocolate and looked for other transformations in the season of change.

She was no longer conscious of the *swish-swish-swish* of her rubbing thighs, or the hours that passed by with hardly a word from her husband. She walked with pleasure through the woods, passing familiar rocks, taking in the smell of the spruce and pine.

Part of her was wishing Vincent could be there. Part of her was happy to be with Anthony, whom she had followed down the same path for what seemed like a lifetime. He still wore the same thick blue and red plaid shirt, and carried the same rusty chainsaw. He still walked with his back straight as a board, his legs barely bending as he moved.

She thought if she could push memory aside, she would see Anthony only as he was that day. A man in the woods. A man walking tall, carrying death in his hands to the hundreds of trees that surrounded him and bathed him in their glory. It wasn't evil she saw but vulnerability, and his failing eyes, which no longer saw the beauty of what stood before him.

Then memory intruded, and the fleeting freshness of what she saw was lost in the cool air blowing in her face, reminding her of the purpose of the day, and the stale truths about the man who was walking before her. It wasn't easy to close the private gallery behind her eyes — to leave behind the long-running show of scenes of their life together.

Alex couldn't look at Anthony without thinking of their time living in Toronto, when they first met after university. She still remembered every inch of the house they rented in the Beaches, and the corner smoke shop where she used to buy licorice pipes for Anthony and Felicity on her way home from teacher's college.

She couldn't erase the day they moved out of the city to the old farmhouse they slowly furnished in antiques collected together at auctions and early morning yard sales.

Anthony could hardly contain his excitement. He jumped up and down, and sang and danced, as he unloaded the U-Haul and carried their possessions across the threshold of the house he could call his own. He had come home to the country, just a few miles from where he grew up.

Everything about the place was endearing to him, even the downstairs windows that had been painted shut, the bodies of dead flies decomposing in the sun between panes of glass. He was going to transform himself into a handyman and fix them in no time, he said. He called a contractor after a week of unsuccessful bouts with several bent paint scrapers. It was the first of many defeats imposed on him by the old house, but nothing it did could ever kill his love for it. The well never ran dry. That was the important thing. He made it a mantra for their life in the country, and their marriage.

The real estate agent who sold them the farm told them it was an artesian well, and that it once supplied five other farms. While their neighbours regularly had their water trucked in during dry, hot summers, Anthony stood proudly on the porch watching the water trucks pass by, then went inside and washed his hands with the taps wide open.

For several years, they worked at restoring the farmhouse to its original beauty — stripping and sanding the hardwood floors, repairing and reinstalling the tin ceilings that had been stored in the attic. They converted the chicken coop into Anthony's studio. Alex put in flower gardens and eventually a huge vegetable garden in the field beside the house.

There was always work to do, plans to draw up, materials to shop for — the before and after pictures recorded every moment. There were very few pictures of a family having fun. Even Felicity helped with the work, pounding nails into the heavy cedar boards Alex and Anthony held to the outside walls of the studio.

At one time, Alex thought about having another child. Her marriage didn't seem complete, and she wanted Felicity to have a sibling. Anthony never talked about it much, and didn't respond when she brought it up. She assumed he didn't want the responsibility or the intrusion on his life, so she never pushed it. She felt she had already imposed Felicity on him and he had accepted the imposition without complaint.

As they walked on, past the pond and down the path towards a heavily wooded area, Alex tried to recall the day Anthony actually said he didn't want a child. Nothing came, and she felt a chill in the middle of her back, and heaviness in the pit of her stomach. She watched Anthony's reflection, rippled by the breeze running along the pond's dark water.

The truth was Anthony never did say he didn't want a child. He never said she should give up painting, or go to teacher's college to support him, either. Or that she should sell vegetables at the market every summer. He never said Felicity was an imposition. They never talked about any of those things. Alex always made the decisions based on what was never said.

"I don't think I've ever been able to talk to you."

She said it out loud, like a statement in the middle of a conversation that up until that point had been conducted in the silence of her own mind. It intruded on the scene, creating a cloud of tension over the spot where they stood, where lightening had placed a large spruce at their feet, sparing them the depressing task of having to choose which tree would die for their firewood.

"Where is this coming from?" Anthony was squinting in the sun, straining to see, and to grasp the meaning of what had just been said. The chainsaw hung by his side.

"I'm not sure," was all Alex could manage.

"Well, why did you say it?"

"I don't know. Let's just forget it." Alex put the thermos down and pulled her leather gloves out of her pocket.

"Let's just cut the tree — please." She fussed over the fit in the fingers of her gloves so she didn't have to look up and see her husband's face.

Finally, Anthony started the chainsaw.

"That's the thing about an affair," Alex said when her fear of being heard was drowned by the deafening sound of the rusty chainsaw, and Anthony was busy pushing it into a thick limb. "It awakens the dead."

Alex held onto the fallen tree as tight as she could while Anthony methodically cut it up. Yes, she thought, it awakens the dead, and the self-conscious, long-denied greediness of an aging libido, and the youthful courage to expose oneself without a care about repercussions or rejection. That — and it brings about the unfortunate surfacing of truths about yourself you managed to shove into the dark corners of your mind. Those convenient man-made cubbyholes you forget exist until your house is shaken up, aroused by the pounding of your own heart and a renewed interest in what the next day might bring.

"So this is what it's like."

She wasn't surprised or disappointed, only certain that Anthony didn't suffer the same way after his trysts with naked women in the converted chicken coop. That's what bothered her the most. The guilt and self-blame about what had gone wrong with their marriage had landed squarely in her lap.

On a cloudy Saturday several weeks later, Vincent and Alex got into his truck and drove south with no particular destination in mind. They ended up in Prince Edward County, where tri-coloured gourds and apples of every kind imaginable were on display at tiny roadside stands, with names like Windwillow Farms. They drove past well-run orchards and quaint towns with more antique shops than houses — through valleys and hamlets where people rode mountain bikes in large groups and ate in sophisticated country cafes, then spent the day perusing the area's artisan shops.

Vincent and Alex passed by it all, opting for the ambiance of the desolate ruins of Lakeshore Lodge on the rocky shores of Lake Ontario. They ate the tomato and red onion sandwiches Vincent had packed for them in the shell of one of the lodge's cottages — where steady lake winds blew through glassless windows and banged the loose whitewashed boards on the wall against each other.

It wasn't the first time Alex had been here.

Two years before, she had been standing outside one of the studio windows watching Anthony paint a nude. The young woman looked no more than 25, with brunette hair cut just about her shoulders, streaked with red highlights. Her breasts were on the small side, but her nipples were huge and dark brown. Anthony had matched the colour perfectly on the canvas.

The young woman looked off into the distance, towards the door. Her breathing was shallow, as instructed by Anthony, her life briefly suspended as she sat naked on a white sheet Alex knew she would find later. It would be waiting for her on top of the washing machine in the house. Anthony always used the same sheet.

As she stood watching, nothing happened that could be considered upsetting, except for the way Anthony looked at the woman. He was so intense, so captivated. His eyes smiled at her, amused and smitten. He occasionally made one-word observations. Beautiful. Perfection. Lovely.

Alex soon walked away and got into her truck. She drove aimlessly for hours, talking to herself above the steady drone of the radio, which she turned on in case someone spotted her babbling out loud. They would just think she was singing along — a middle-aged woman who no longer cared about making a fool of herself, belting out off-key songs about love gone wrong.

She eventually ended up at Lakeshore Lodge, after hiking through the huge sand hills of Sandbanks Provincial Park. She stood on the foundation of what was once the main lodge. Parts of it were blackened from the fire that had flattened it a few years before. Then she sat inside the smallest of the remaining cottages, on a tree stump, and emptied the sand from her shoes. There were cigarette butts near her feet and an empty bottle of gin in one corner.

The view from the glassless window looked out over the endless waves on the lake, with a couple of tall cedars to the left, on the crest of a ledge that dropped off sharply. Below the ledge, there were. huge flat rocks, soaked from the slapping water. Alex imagined the view had not changed much over the years and that others, who sat in the cottage decades before, had also been calmed by the surroundings and the sound of the seagulls sitting on the rocks nearby.

Something about the place conjured up images of a young woman sitting on a bed in the same room, looking out the window in the late afternoon, tired from playing shuffleboard earlier in the day. Alex had seen the remains of a shuffleboard court in front of the foundation of the main lodge — a flat grave for buried pleasures in the lives of those lucky enough to afford a stay at this old luxury resort.

She had also found the cement wading pool with peeling bright green paint, half-hidden in the tall grass. The pebble-speckled marble floor of the old dance hall, still scuffed from the shuffling feet of those who would have danced to Glenn Miller across the floor and over the embedded Lakeshore Lodge emblem, with the sun and the waves on its crest.

At the time, Alex felt she had been there before — sitting on the edge of the bed in the later afternoon, tired out from a hot day in the sun, anticipating the dance that night and the solitude of the flat rocks in the moonlight. Feeling alone and at home, in the place with the calming view, with water reaching out beyond all that she carried inside her.

Two years later, she was sitting in the same place with her lover, seeking shelter from the wind in a cottage that had seen better days and more love and discontent than the weak and tired walls could reveal to inexperienced eyes. A simple cottage that remains forever in good condition in the memories of those who stayed there — remembered, because of their sudden displays of affection, or the nightmarish release of feelings of emptiness and unhappiness. People either left there more in love than ever before or with the realization that love had died.

Now it was Alex and Vincent who had come to sort things out among the falling walls. Alex knew that they too would become part of its history, and when the cottage finally collapsed and was dragged away, bit by bit, they would still live on there with all the others — that their love, however short it might last, would continue to blow in on the winds. For nothing could ever take away the lake and the flat rocks below. They would always be there even when the last trace of the lodge was gone. She would always be able to come back and remember what it had been like.

After a while, after very little was said about anything, they headed over to the Outlet Beach on the eastern side of the park. A wooden snow fence had already been erected along the top of the beach, to protect the fragile dunes from the oncoming winter winds and frazil ice. Alex and Vincent walked along the water where dark green algae had washed up for the gulls to feed on.

They passed a young family trying to capture the joys of summer with one last chance to build sandcastles. The rest of the beach was empty, hard and wet from an early morning rain.

From a distance, nothing else could be seen. But Alex was walking with her head down, making a mental list of the debris before her — plastic white spoons and baggies, and straws. Bottle caps and cigar tips, and bits of coloured plastic from broken shovels. And a scattering of dull white feathers, where a pack of seagulls stood waiting for a rippled chip to be thrown by a playful child, who was later scolded by annoyed parents who couldn't stand walking on sand splattered by the gulls' mushy grey shit.

"Did you ever come here with Anthony?"

Alex spotted a Tootsie Roll wrapper and remembered Felicity sitting on a towel at the age of seven, eating candy and burying her feet in the sand.

"We used to come once in a while, when Felicity was young. Anthony always hated it. Said he didn't see the fun in roasting like a pig in the hot sun."

In the two months they had been seeing each other, Alex made a point of not talking about Anthony too much. Partly out of guilt. Partly out of her own need to live for a brief time without him at the back of her neck — something she could only achieve when she was with Vincent, making love in his rumpled bed. The cold nights had forced them inside, reluctantly abandoning the golden fields.

"We can't expect someone to like everything we do." Vincent's detached tone was similar to the tone he had used the week before, when he suggested that Anthony might not be having affairs with the women he paints, that perhaps the turn-on was in not touching them, that he used the sexual energy merely to paint. At the time, Alex didn't respond. But what he had said had been nagging her ever since.

"What are you saying, Vincent, that I expect too much? That I'm too demanding because I wanted my husband to come to the beach with his family?"

"No. I'm not saying that. I'm simply saying that other people — even our partners — don't always like the same things we do. It's just a fact of life."

Alex stopped walking.

"I don't understand why you feel the need to take his side all the time. What is it? Guilt? Or you just can't help yourself. You have to psychoanalyse everyone who crosses your path?"

"I'm not taking his side, Alex."

Vincent moved towards her and reached out with one of his hands.

"I don't need this from you," she said, stepping back. She walked away from him, briskly, for several hundred feet, before she looked back. When she finally turned around, she saw him sauntering along the beach, looking out over the lake. He wasn't in any rush to catch up with her.

As she watched him, the sun peaked out from behind a cloud. It was harsh in its sudden mid-afternoon entrance, the first it had come out all day. It had been trying earlier, when they were still sitting in the shell of the cottage at Lakeshore Lodge, where the mood of the day had taken an odd, uncomfortable turn and they seemed out of place with the rest of the history of the place.

Alex turned away from the sight of Vincent walking along the beach in the sunlight, closing her eyes for a fraction of a second, allowing Vincent's after-image to appear — the outline of his body in bright yellow lines with trailing dots of light all around. She continued walking down the

beach, slowing her pace a little, letting what had passed
between them make its way out of her. And then it came —

*Lady in Oil on Canvas: Her after-image was painted in half-drawn
multiples of herself, in reds, yellows, and blues, in the middle of the white
canvas. On the right, she was dance-like in her motions, her arms
sweeping towards the sky. In another image on the left, she was sitting,
her legs bent, and her head lowered; resting on her knees. In the middle,
slightly above the other images, she was walking away with her arms at
her side, into the wilderness of the stark white forever.*

She was all of them and they'd been staring back at her
from the wall in the living room, where she lives with the
man who painted his wife, a wife who failed to recognize
the basics any artist knows. Who forgot about primary
colours and after-images, and how the eye makes up for
what is missing.

On the beach, the sun disappeared from sight again,
behind a cloud that promised to move on before their eyes got
used to its flat, soft light. Alex looked back at her footprints in
the sand. Her feet had always been too large for her liking.
Anthony used to say that was because she carried the world on
her shoulders and she needed the support. Alex only saw the
impressions they made in the sand and thought about how
they'd be gone the next day.

"Washed away."

She stopped long enough for Vincent to catch up and
they walked the rest of the way in silence, while the waves
rolled up along the shoreline in a continuous, cautioning roar
— never dipping or quieting, never telling her what to do.

Chapter Five

In August we watch *'night, Mother* with Sissy Spacek and Anne Bancroft. Delaney brings it. She tells us she couldn't think of what else to get. Besides, she says, she needs to keep her head in the stories of mothers and daughters, for the sake of her documentary, which she has set aside for a few hours.

"I need the break," she says. And I almost believe her until I catch sight of the note on the videocassette cover and see "porch scene" and "couch scene" scribbled at the top in her neat and tidy writing. She has already made a list of scenes she wants us to replay.

I expect complaints to come from every corner of the room when she announces the movie she has brought with her — most of us were depressed for a week the first time we saw it. But no one says a word. We are all in some kind of end-of-summer funk. The nights are getting cooler and darkness falls earlier. I still haven't heard from Ben and have weakened and started calling, but he's never there. I am thankful and disappointed all at the same time.

"How's the documentary coming along?" Storm asks.

"I agonize over it," Delaney answers. "Did you know Sally agreed to be in it?"

"Reluctantly," Sally adds.

"What's it called again?" Alex asks.

"When Women Lose Their Mothers," Del says.

"It's the first in a series," Sally jokes. "The next one will be, When Women Lose Their Fathers, and I'll be in that one, too."

A few of us smile awkwardly. Delaney heads for the bathroom. Sally rolls a joint.

In my kitchen, Alex makes an arrangement with miniature sunflowers. She reminds me that it has been a year since she first started seeing Vincent. "It goes by quickly," she says, "when you only get together a few times a month." There isn't any particular tenderness in her voice, or excitement, or a hint of anything remarkable about her love affair. In one breath, she mentions Vincent. In the next, she talks about Anthony. Except for the names, I cannot hear any difference between the two.

Have I heard from Ben, she asks me. Did he leave town or something? Have I sewn the patch from his shirt on my jacket yet? She eyes me up and down looking for it, picking up on the coincidental patterns on my back — likening them to fields I've sewn with perennial regret. From a distance, she tells me, the fields are as clear as day, when I'm standing at the other end of the living room, or down the hall near the dining room. Anyone can see them, she says, if they forget they're looking at a piece of clothing, at the random assembly of fabric and thread — if they can ignore all suggestion of whim or misguided direction.

Alex walks out of the kitchen, leaving me to wipe up the water drops and the clipped stems off the counter and to clear the dust she has just stirred in my head. She leaves me alone to deal with Grace, who comes rushing in to tell me in private that her novel has been rejected by another publisher and she's about to give up and can I say something, anything, to make her feel better, to keep her going. Can I?

I walk back out to the living room with a beer in my hand — thankful that Storm is the quiet type and Jenny is at The Cottage and not here to watch the movie and hear all the talk about mothers and daughters, which puts her on edge and the rest of us on guard. Then I remember that for Jenny, a trip to The Cottage is like being stuck in the same movie, over and over again, and could just as easily star Sissy Spacek and Anne Bancroft, only it needs a cottage and a lake. And if you could take Sissy Spacek and Anne Bancroft and put them *On Golden Pond*, and take a little of the Elizabeth Taylor *Who's Afraid of Virginia Woolf* character and make her part of the Anne Bancroft mother character, you'd pretty much have the movie of Jenny's life. Only it wouldn't end in less than two hours. It wouldn't end at all.

I settle into my chair with Del's note and my aging remote and I'm ready to rewind the porch scene and the couch scene and all the others she has written down with as little disruption as possible.

She was still looking for a few more visual ideas for her own work. That's what she told me earlier in the week, when she asked me to describe, quickly, without thinking, five images that came to mind when I thought of my mother. She wrote them down while the two of us were driving the back roads, looking for the perfect shot of perfect clouds in a perfect sky: An empty porch. An open sewing box. Wavy fields. Burning candles. And cheese curd.

"Cheese curd?" she repeated.

"Cheese curd," I shrugged.

She made me drive while she sat in the back of my car and spent most of the ride leaning out the window with a video camera in her hands. She needed the perspective of someone looking out the window of a moving car, looking up at clouds. They had to be the right clouds, she said. They had to line up in a certain way and cross a certain type of sky.

"That's kind of a tall order," I suggested, "considering the formation of the clouds and the sky is completely out of our control."

"It'll happen," she said, "just keep driving. Don't you have any faith, Sadie?"

"I do," I said, and I did, but I lost it after two hours of zipping up one road and down another. Each one looked like the last, like all the roads that criss-cross the township, the landscape is surprisingly consistent. By car they appear as one long, liquid blur. The same watered-down images whir by, seen but not noticed. Only a house painted in an unlikely colour, or a particularly beautiful farm, or the shifting stones of a century-old cemetery provide visual breaks. Landmarks. And the odd hill, which is steep and distinct, instantly recognizable, and felt in the pit of your stomach as the road drops away beneath you.

"It's the most important part of the documentary," she pleaded when I suggested we go home, that the clouds weren't listening. "Please," she said. So I stayed out there and eventually passed a road, fleeting and familiar, while Del sighed and clung to the camera and rode with her head leaning out the window, restless and agitated, and increasingly desperate.

I could hear it in the way she breathed. As if it were a chore just to be there.

You can't ride so close to the rails, to the nitty-gritty task of compilation — the putting-together of life stories, summation and conclusions, capsulated and abbreviated, told — then walk back into your own life as Del was trying to do and live it as it comes at you, moment by slow-moving moment. Not without thinking of where it might lead, or won't lead. Not without the taste of the earth, as it once moved from underneath your feet, appearing suddenly on the tip of your tongue, a mineral taste, distinctive and lasting, it takes days to go away. You can still feel it between your teeth. Your body shivers whenever you think about it, about where you once were.

The same can be said of a certain kind of love.

You can't go there — not there — and come back unchanged.

I returned to my husband — that night at the Legion, that night when I didn't go off with Johnny Marks, I returned and I stayed. Partly because I felt I should, partly because Johnny never came to take me away. It was months before I finally stopped looking for him, half-expecting, half-hoping he'd come speeding up our driveway to get me.

I returned to Hal and to my garden and to cooking asparagus country pie. I filled two rooms upstairs, one with a son and then one with a daughter. Hal left before they ever started school — left me agitated and restless, with the taste of missed opportunity swimming around in my well-behaved mouth. I let him go without much fuss — told him I only wished he'd done it a few years earlier when I still had a chance with Johnny.

"That's just it," he said as she stood in our kitchen. "Now, I get to be someone's Johnny."

It ended without drama or raised voices. He just left one morning while the kids were out with my mother — with as much as he could carry at one time in his long, anxious arms. I watched him go. Peering out from behind the curtain on the front door, I watched him drive away, then I went for a walk.

I didn't go very far. I walked along Sarles Road, not far from the road I lived on — a road no one lives on. A short stretch of side road with nothing but fields of hay, clover and straw, and fence lines held in place by high piles of fieldstone, some large and flat, perfect for garden paths. I'd taken my share over the years.

I kept thinking I should cry — not for the loss of a great love, for that would have been a lie. For what then? The loss a family? For my children's father? Hal had promised to see them every other weekend and one night through the week.

No — if I had wept, which I didn't, but if I had, it would surely have been for myself. For failing to trust what I knew years before, for failing to trust that Hal would have survived without me, for failing to see it wasn't love for him that made me return, or pity, or duty, or anything like it. Pity and duty would have kept me from loving Johnny Marks.

It was on Sarles Road that I met the plaid patch, which sits on my left shoulder, next to my collar. My first patch. My first choice, the first time I realized I had any, that the world wouldn't end when I made it.

His name was Zeke.

Yes, he had a last name, but I've thrown last names away in favour of the fabrics by which I've known them. Zeke Plaid and Glen Silk and Bobby "Ball Cap" Polyester. Shortcuts to the memorable moments in the life of Sadie McCann. Belittling details I admit trivialize and hide my fonder memories of these men with last names and snipped shirts and lives that go on without me, Sadie what-was-her-name?

Still, the shortcuts work and save me time. I think of Zeke Plaid and I instantly feel the overworked muscles underneath the flannel squares and the thick lines that only partially covered his heaving, hairless chest when he stopped shoveling gravel and asked me if I lived nearby.

"Around the bend, third house on the left."

"The old Chalmers' house."

"You know it?"

"I've worked on these roads for fifteen years."

"A lifetime for someone your age," I said. He barely looked older than thirty and wasn't sure if I was teasing him — I being the older one — the older woman who had to throw age up into the air, to see if it made any difference, if it made him run.

He didn't bat an eye.

"In this job, you eventually meet up with everyone — or you hear about them." It was his turn and he took it. Or you hear about them. Putting me in my place.

Zeke was an employee with the township. His dark blue pickup was parked nearby with the township emblem painted on the side of both doors. He was repairing Sarles Road that spring. It was only a matter of weeks between Hal's leaving and my meeting Zeke. Hal left the first week in April. Zeke was working on Sarles Road in the middle of

May. The heavy rains had washed part of it away, had thinned it out in places that threatened to split it in two.

I was on one of my walks, which I took whenever Hal had the kids, or my mother or my aunts came by to give me a break. It had become routine — counted on — this time to myself when I quickened my pace and lengthened my stride and walked from one end of the road to the other and back again, slowing down on the last few hundred feet, dragging out the minutes it would take to get home — back to the busy life that awaited me. Motherhood. A return to college. Stripping furniture at night and on weekends for a store in town to help pay the bills.

I walked down Sarles Road whenever I could, rain or shine. I practically ran out of the house to greet its knolls and potholes known to me as well as the scars and moles on a lover could ever be. Its trees and bushes and roadside boulders, and the one-wall remains of an old tree-house were as much a part of my walks as street signs and skyscrapers and store windows would be to any urban dweller — minus all human contact.

I never ran into anyone on Sarles Road. Not until the day I met up with Zeke.

He was bent over, a shovel in his hand, stopped in mid-motion, looking up at me from underneath his Rawdon Township hat. Raindrops were landing on his chin and around his mouth, resting on the clean-shaven strip of flesh between his nose and his upper lip, until they rolled down the creases that formed when he smiled and waited for me to say something. The creases, I figured, came from working outside, from sitting behind the windowed sun, driving the back roads of the township since he was practically a boy, before he became the man I met.

He stood up and leaned on his shovel. He was taller than I would have guessed.

"The rain's getting pretty heavy. I can give you a lift."

"I'll be fine," I said.

"It's no trouble for me. I get paid no matter when I'm doing out here."

I liked the fact he wasn't giving up but I wondered if it had anything to do with me, personally. Maybe he was this nice to everyone he met up with.

"I'll be fine," I repeated. "I do this all the time. And I have my umbrella." I wasn't even halfway through my sacred walk. I wasn't about to abandon it on the chance there might be more to his politeness than a genetic predisposition to gentlemanly behaviour — something he might have inherited from his father, and his father before him.

I continued on down the road, feeling his eyes on my backside. I walked with a great deal of concentration. I suddenly felt tipsy and clumsy, as if I'd had too many drinks and might lose my balance and trip over my own feet. Or walk, absent-mindedly, off to one side of the road — on an angle that would reveal my self-conscious, school-girlish concern over what he thought of my ass.

With all the grace of an insecure, ganglylegged teenager, I eventually walked out of his sight. I went to the end of the road, until my feet were soaked and my jeans were drenched, soaking wet and heavy, yet I felt light and serene in my puddly path — in the prolonged gaze Zeke had given me. In the chance he'd still be there when I turned around and headed back. In the very fact I could ask myself, What do I want to happen next?

It had already been decided, on his first offer for a lift.

No — before that.

Before I ever set eyes on him. When I walked out my front door that morning, or some other morning. When I stepped outside and began putting distance between what had been and what was to come, and what I chose not to live without.

It was only a question of would he still be there, or not? And how fast could I make it happen? I didn't want to make it complicated. I barely wanted to talk. I only wanted to walk up to him and start.

It wasn't like Johnny Marks who came upon my life with some kind of fateful impact written all over his face. I wasn't going to fall hard, and be forever changed by my experience.

My head was still present, still walking with me, still demanding equal time with my libido, maybe more.

It wasn't like Hal, either, where everything was tied up in married love, measured in quantity and endurance not quality, or interest — just how often, as long as it was often enough, normal enough for married couples.

It had more to do with a guy who laid me down in the grass by the roadside — another road, another time — a guy who told me I was getting too excited, that I didn't have to move so much. Who said my urge to pee was part of it, part of losing my virginity, that he'd forgotten what a drag it was having a chick for the first time. Did I know I would bleed later? Did I know it gets better each time? But it didn't. Not with him. Not while I continued to lay under his body, motionless, holding back urges I finally knew had nothing to do with peeing.

I realized how fast I was walking and slowed my pace, left it up to the gods who had orchestrated the whole thing in the first place — the rain, the road, the man with the shovel with the moist mouth. Planted in my path. Temptation waiting in the knoll before the turn where the rest of my life was waiting less than half a mile away.

That night I'd be cooking spaghetti with tomato sauce, fighting with my kids to eat more, they never seemed to eat enough. I'd be playing the god of rain myself, holding the shower head above them in the bath while they pretended to be sailors at sea during a sudden storm. I'd be reading one more story, just one more story, about moons and bunnies and cats that wore funny hats. And then I'd be in the spare room, off the living room, sanding a washstand, sanding until two in the morning, at least until two in the morning, to get it done.

I quickened my pace. I decided — yes — only the gods could make it rain. But only I could move my legs fast enough to get there. To get to him before he left. Before he drove off. Before all his work, his freshly laid sand and gravel, washed away in a rain that threatened to never stop.

He was cleaning up, throwing his shovel in the box of the truck, when I appeared from somewhere farther back, the knolls in the road and the graduating hill making me arrive in bits and pieces — my head, my torso, my soaking wet legs. I was aware of his waiting for me. He walked to the other side of the truck and grabbed the handle of the passenger door.

"I'll give you a ride," he called out over the sheets of rain that fell harder, harder and louder, throwing us together inside his pick-up, dripping from head to toe, exhilarated by the force of the storm around us, knowing we couldn't do a damn thing about it. We were made to sit still, together.

"There's no point trying to drive in this." He was eager to accept it. His resignation was obvious and pin-pricked, with thin rays of excitement and anticipation seeping through his what-can-we-do-about-it tone of voice. He placed his keys in an open slot below the radio, above the ashtray, a funny kind of dead space that seemed overlooked at the auto factory, forgotten and unfinished.

"That's fine," I said, watchful of the eagerness in my voice, shaving the smile and the pitch, dulling it, following up with a nonchalant, "I'm not expected anywhere. Not for a while, anyway." I looked at the clock on his dashboard. Hal wouldn't be dropping the kids off for another two hours.

We sat in the thunderous shower, exchanging names and observations about the weather, watching the further destruction of the road before us, eventually moving on to more compelling information, dropping not-so-subtle clues about each other's marital status. He was still — although there was a hint he may not be for much longer. He guessed I knew all about that, the way things turn just before the end. He was okay with it, he said. In fact, he'd be glad when it was all over. Did I have any advice?

The windows in the truck had become foggy from our talking, from our breathing — from the rain that was still pelting down on us, making it impossible to open a window even a fraction without soaking the interior of the truck.

"I'm not good at advice," I said, before I got the idea to draw a happy face on the window beside me — with filled-in eyes, not open eyes, remembering my daughter's insistence that open happy face eyes are scary eyes. Crazy eyes. The solid ones are friendly, good eyes.

"Be happy. That's your advice?" The creases around his mouth were still moist, rain-soaked, like the rest of us. I could feel a huge wet spot forming behind my shirt, on the back of the seat. I would leave dark patches, traces of my body, when I got out of the truck. They might last overnight, if the windows were kept shut, if the drying air couldn't make it inside and evaporate what remained of me.

"Be happy," I began, "and —" I stopped in mid-sentence and looked away, looked down at his work boots, which were scuffed and scratched and covered in mud — the mud of my road. My road, because it's where I walked, where I moved my feet and my legs and my arms, where I used my body to get me from here to there — to transport me from one state of mind to another. To get me from one end of the road to the other and back again. Back home where I hauled furniture in and out of my narrow doorway, renewed and restored. Home, where I manoeuvred my limbs around the kitchen, cooking, cleaning, cutting, chopping, fixing, mixing and so on, and so on. Where I hunched over on all fours and carried my kids around the living room, pretending I'm the horsey, you're the cowboy or cowgirl — using my body for function, for horseplay, for what needs doing next.

"Be happy, and what?" Zeke asked.

I drew a heart, larger than I intended, next to the smiling face, which was already beginning to disappear under a second coat of fog.

"Love?" he said.

"Yes," I said.

"Find it?" he asked.

"Make it," I said, with a forwardness that was a little weak, only semi-bold, a starting point. Yes, make lots of it, I thought to myself, and kept to myself — kept it between my body and me — a secret. Something not entirely or deliberately decided, but arrived at, on a stormy afternoon with a man named Zeke, who wore a plaid shirt — who would wear it often and leave it lying on my bedroom floor, time and time again. Not knowing that, one day, I would snip a small patch from underneath the collar while he slept off another lunch hour of hungry sex, before he went back to work, before he went home to the wife he was never going to leave, after all.

A gathering was all I could think of — a collage of some sort. Like the crazy-quilted pillows my Aunt Viv used to make out of discarded silk ties and little-girl velvet dresses, and the odd bit of tatting she'd find in antique stores.

Gather a collection, I said to myself.

Wear it, or something.

Zeke left me used up, my energy spent, my body reveling in the accomplishment of pursued pleasure. For the possibility of repeating it. Repeating it elsewhere when the time came, when my time with Zeke was up. I wasn't saddened by the thought. It seemed — necessary.

After our physical gorging, it always took some time before I could get my body up off the bed, before I could return it to its other uses. To function. To purpose. To the sometimes mindless and constant movement through the rest of the day.

He wanted to talk, too. About his wife, who was always on the verge of leaving him. About his sheet metal sculptures, which he cut and welded and poured most of his non-linear thoughts into. About how he spent his workdays driving along township roads, thinking about the nature of love, the properties of tin, and why the cuts he gets feel like punishment — retribution for delving into the mysteries of man and metal.

Zeke liked what wasn't easily explained, the fact that his wife had one foot in the door and one foot out.

"I can't figure her out," he said. "She packs boxes. She makes lists. What's hers, what's mine. And then she still crawls into our bed every night, puts her back to me, and in the morning I find her arm around me, sleeping the same way she's been sleeping for our entire marriage."

He liked being on the brink of discovery, of impending knowledge. What makes metal metal — the truth about its properties somewhere in the nearby distance, but still unknown. He was happiest when he thought he had me, before he unraveled our mysterious attraction, before he figured out our time was up, that these two bodies could not occupy the same place at the same time forever.

The reasons for carrying on a little longer — loneliness and horniness — would only drag things out, and add a few more scenes, better left on the cutting-room floor. Comfort and dependency were always hovering above our cloudy heads.

It was on Sarles Road that the clouds aligned as Delaney had envisioned them. A stroke of luck. We had to stop.

"See Sadie. Faith."

She had me drive as slowly as I could up and down the road, three or four times, until she was satisfied she had the shots she needed. Who was I to argue that by will alone, she had managed to get the clouds and the sky to cooperate? Who was I to question the significance of the porch scene and the couch scene in 'night, Mother which she was eagerly awaiting tonight?

"See Sadie. Faith." There had been as much surprise in her voice as anything else.

Did she really believe it?

Did she only want to?

Still, the gods had bestowed a man with a plaid shirt and an active libido upon me when I needed it most, placed him in my path by merely opening the skies and letting the rain fall as I've never seen it rain since. At least that's my version of it — the one I'm going with on this August night, as I sit with a room full of women who believe as much as I do that there is life of some sort in the spools of a videocassette. Even when our minds tell us, no — no. It's only make-believe — good camera direction, set design and realistic dialogue written by a screenwriter working in seclusion, mouthing the words all of us speak at one point or another.

"We believe it because we want to," Sally once said. "But it's all in our fucking heads. Everything is."

Maybe, I think.

And tonight, I believe I'm every bit like that Susan Sarandon character in *Bull Durham*. I send my men, like Zeke Plaid and Bobby "Ball Cap" Polyester, back out into the game, with perfected technique and renewed enthusiasm.

I am contributing.

And that fills me up.

Sally
THE LIST

Chapter Six

Sally has always believed that there should be a special book devoted to the subject of proper etiquette for florists. *How to Prune Annoying Customers from Your Life, Without Pissing Them Off* was her personal favourite for the title. She even had the book cover planned, with a crazed florist holding pruning shears, ready to snap the heads off a bunch of miniature, miserable people who stood, planted in terracotta flower pots. She also envisioned an entire section on this subject included on the Master Gardener's exam and, as Lily Grosvenor stood on the other side of the counter in Sally's store, the first question popped into her mind.

A woman you know, who is unhappily married with three kids, walks into your store and wants to send flowers to a single man, who probably has kids in every town between Toronto and Thunder Bay. She takes up most of your morning trying to decide whether the Bird of

Paradise is too exotic to include in a bouquet of tiger lilies and red dogwood. The woman has never expressed any interest in a flower before — suddenly she wants to know where it comes from, how it got its name, how long it lives, and so on.

Do you...

(a) Advise her to pick something less exotic because she obviously isn't ready for such a leap. Having an affair with Tom Dick (real name) is a piece of cake in comparison.

(b) Suggest she forget the whole order. Why should she send flowers to some guy just because he laid her?

(c) Say, "Who gives a shit? Get out of my store. You're really getting on my nerves, lady."

Lily left Sally's store still uncertain that the Bird of Paradise was a good decision and spent the rest of the day playing the same scenes over in her mind. First — the flowers came to the door, Tom opened them, loved them, put them on the oak table in his kitchen — just one of many places he had her the other day. Next time, the scene changed — the flowers came to the door, Tom opened them, laughed at them, threw them in the garbage.

It was all a waste of time. The following day, Tom called Lily to thank her for the weird flowers and to see when she could drop by for another tryst with her "personal bird of paradise." Lily hung up feeling that all the time she spent at Sally's Flowers had been worth it.

Sally Harrison has been Stirling's only florist for almost fifteen years. She was just 21 when she bought the store from the Weavers when they retired. It was shortly after Sally's parents were killed in a car accident. She took her inheritance, bought the flower shop, and moved into the apartment above.

On a particular Friday night, not so long ago, Sally was puttering, killing time until she could call Josh Mann, an orchid grower who lives on the Island of Kauai, who also happens to be her phone lover. She was perched on a stool in the back room of the store, with a package of cigarettes and a beer, and the radio playing an Eagles tune she's always liked — foreplay for long-distance love.

It was there, in the back room of her store, among clipped stems and rolls of decorative plastic wrap and thin glass vases, where Sally worked on baby's arrival bouquets and funeral arrangements and flowers for every occasion in between. She often worked at night, after her employees went home. She liked being alone.

Sally lit a cigarette and started leafing through the yellowing pages of a National Geographic book on Hawaii. She always called Josh late in the day — his day — which was six hours behind her day. He always had more time to talk then. That's what they did. Talked. That's how they made love. Talked and listened, and talked and listened. A small-town florist and an orchid grower with a quarter of the world's circumference between them.

Sally sometimes thought — if her customers weren't such pains in the ass, she'd feel more empathy towards them. She was capable of it, when she let herself. But, mostly, she just found them so fucking annoying, the way they spent so much of her time on the smallest fucking details. It was hardly the work of a Master Gardener. More like Master of Ceremonies for every life-altering event in a town filled with people who seemed to think flowers could fix everything. Guarantee forgiveness. Sustain a relationship hanging by a thread. Comfort the dying. It's what they expected from her.

Don't stop loving me. Forgive me for that black eye. Oh, excuse me for not coming to see you while you lay dying in the hospital — I can't bear to see you, so here are some bright and cheery daisies. At least you know I'm thinking of you.

That was the language of flowers, as Sally heard it. That's why the dead had always been her preferred customer — their obituaries, her palette. She often worked long into the night, in the seclusion of her back room, painstakingly adding hues and textures until she completed a portrait of the person who would receive one last bouquet. They were deserving of her time — the dead. She had all the patience in the world for them. Unlike the living, they had learned not to get so hung up on the stupid, fucking details that didn't matter. Not to her, anyway.

Whenever Sally called Josh, she never told him what she had for breakfast, or how the dentist said she should have her wisdom teeth removed, or that her delivery van needed a new front-end shock.

She knew he was in his early forties. He knew she was in her mid-thirties. She knew he had spent most of his life living in Iowa where he had been a graphic artist until he moved to Kauai seven years ago, to grow orchids. He knew she had always lived in Stirling and that she had a brother in Vancouver, which was halfway between them.

Sally never told Josh that she won't eat butter unless it melts on hot vegetables, or that she wears overalls all the time because they don't grab her at the waist or in the rise. She can't stand anything tight around her body.

She did tell Josh about the way the funeral director talked her into buying expensive caskets, lined with mauve-coloured silk, so she could rest easy knowing her parents were buried in the very best.

"I've had dreams ever since about my mother's red hair and that fucking mauve silk."

"Don't beat yourself up over it," Josh told her.

"My mother hated mauve." Sally said.

"You're too hard on yourself, Sal."

"But she hated that colour and I went and fucking buried her in it."

Josh told Sally about his younger sister, Pam, who died of cancer. Just before she slipped away, she held Josh's hand and asked him to tell her a story, the way he always did when they were kids.

"Sometimes, I can still feel her hand reaching out for me," he once told Sally, "like a brush of cool air that comes out of nowhere." After that his voice had trailed off, and Sally waited for him to pick the conversation up again. They had always been comfortable with the wordless moments between them, and never rushed to speak just to fill the dead air.

As Sally sat, leafing through the book in front of her, she decided she would tell Josh about Lily Grosvenor, and about her dream he had played a role in earlier in the week. How she had been in a shopping mall with him, riding an escalator down to another floor. How they were waiting to reach the bottom, to step off and go into a clothing store for men to buy Josh some black socks, but the escalator kept going deeper into the ground. How they passed through several layers of the earth, cluttered with caskets and old bones and artifacts from another lifetime. That's how the dream had ended — with the two of them stranded among the remains of the dead, in the quiet stillness of the dark below the blinding, hurried, noisy lives of the living.

Sally's parents died on a grey, snowy day in December. After they were officially pronounced dead at the hospital, Sally went home and walked through every room in the house — taking in all the details. Touching things they had polished, things they had sat on, things people had given them — things they had never liked, but kept on display anyway, for the sake of others. The round and square multi-coloured crocheted pillows on the sofa in the den, which her mother would straighten every time someone got up. The beverage coasters with huge ships in the middle of rough journeys on the high seas, which her mother always kept stacked, all facing the same way, with the ships' masts pointed upwards. The bottles of Johnnie Walker sitting on the kitchen table, which her father always delivered Christmas Eve morning — one to his mechanic, one to his dentist, and one to his barber. The brass watering can on the floor in the sunroom, which her mother used to water the impatiens she planted every spring under the maple tree in the front yard. Red and white and purple. Red and white and purple. In that order — exactly six inches apart.

In the foggy aftermath of death, Sally could only think of the thousands of times her mother must have straightened those fucking pillows in the den. For what, she thought. So they'd be perfectly neat when she went out to do some last-minute Christmas shopping with her husband and never came back.

With Josh, Sally knew there was never any chance of drowning in the details. There wasn't enough time in a half-hour conversation for that. In the two years since Sally first called him to order orchids for a customer, they never once talked about groceries or car repairs or Christmas gifts or empty toilet rolls.

Sally and Josh had better things to talk about. Things that really mattered. And after each conversation, Sally could go to bed and fantasize about the man on the other end of the line, without worrying about what he would want for breakfast the morning after the night before, like she would if he was really lying next to her. She would have to worry about what he'd brush his teeth with, and would he expect her to have sugar for his coffee, and would she wake up before him so she could comb her hair, which always sticks out in six different directions in the morning. What a sight, she thought, to greet you first thing.

She would have to worry about all those details if Josh were with her — if Josh were a real lover. It was the ongoing argument — in her mind — for keeping things the way they had always been.

A girl who barely looks old enough to get married is in your store trying to choose flowers for a wedding bouquet. She is with her mother, who looks old enough to be her grandmother. The bride, who wants purple and pink flowers, argues loudly with the mother, who insists red and white would be more traditional and would go better with the mother's new dress, which is red. After all, they'll be standing together for the photos and everyone knows red and purple don't go.

Do you...

(a) Side with the bride? "It's her day, so pick another dress and let the girl have her fucking purple and pink flowers."

(b) Side with the mother? "Look, honey, you're footing the bill. If she thinks you're going to buy another dress just to match her fucking purple

and pink flowers, she's got another thing coming."

   (c) *Excuse yourself. Retreat to the back room and have a smoke. Then go back out and suggest an all-white bouquet. (Be sure to have a few samples of white roses, white lilies, and white tulips in your hand to get your point across. Send the fucking flowers home with them if you have to.)*

   Clara Whitehead retreated to her bedroom when she and her soon-to-be-married daughter got home, to see if there was another dress she could wear. Beige and cream were the only colours she had been wearing for years. She bought the red dress because she thought it might make her look younger, maybe even make her stand out a little.

   She stood in front of the large mirror on top of her dresser and stared at the wrinkles and the crow's feet on her face — the same ones she saw reflected in the eyes of everyone that looked at her and wondered, Whatever happened to the silky skin Clara Whitehead used to have? She thought the red dress might give them something else to look at. Couldn't she at least have that?

   Clara called Sally later that day and told her she thought the white flowers would be perfect, and she was sure she could convince her daughter to agree. Clara wasn't a bad person, just a little controlling. When you raise nine children, it's a matter of survival. Sally knew this about Clara. You can't live in the same small town all your life and not know it.

Cars drove by. A few people wandered up the street. Dogs barked off in the distance. Sally heard the sounds outside the store window but they were weakened by the majestic Waimea Canyon, and the heavy silence that Sally imagined hangs above the deep lava slopes of ochre, rust, and brown.

   Kauai. "Garden Island." Sally flipped through the National Geographic book on Hawaii from 1970, and then a travel book published in 1987. June Chapman at the library said they didn't have anything newer. Even still, the musty smell from the books couldn't take away the fresh ocean air Sally felt rolling in with the indigo and turquoise waves along Kauai's rugged Na Pali Coast.

She found Waimea on the map, the small town where Josh lives. He once told her it means "reddish waters," because of the red volcanic mud that washes down from the top of Waialeale and into the sea.

She read about Waimea's historic buildings — the Waimea Foreign Church, constructed in 1853 of coral and sandstone, and the remains of Fort Elizabeth, built by the Russians in 1817, which cover the bluff above Waimea River and Bay. Both were a far cry from the historic Stirling Hotel, which had been home to the Sears Catalogue Store for as long as Sally could remember.

As she turned the pages, Sally could feel the fingertips of those who had scanned the pages before her. The eager lovers who planned a honeymoon, and the bored schoolchildren who were forced to write about a place they had never been to, who had to stand up and tell the rest of the class what it was like, the way Sally once did about Australia. She had picked Australia because her parents were watching National Geographic on television and they said they'd like to go there. And Europe. And Africa. And Egypt. Great adventures they shared on an overstuffed, fading paisley print sofa, while the tan-coloured hard-cased luggage with dark leather trim stayed neatly tucked away in the hall closet upstairs. Except when it was hauled out for an annual dusting, to get the once-over before it was put away for another year.

Palm trees and mountains and emerald fields of taro. Waialeale, the volcano that rises over five thousand feet at its highest peak — Kawaikini. The tallest structure in Stirling is the water tower, painted pale green, on the east side of town, beside the Pentecostal Church.

Sally never bothered looking for books on the Hawaiian Islands before — not because she wasn't curious. She just didn't want to know about the landscape Josh saw every day and how hot it was when he wakes up. She didn't want to know what his life was like on a daily basis. Who he ran into on the street. How often he argued with his wife. Or made love to her. Or ate in silence with her.

Sally knew Josh was married. He mentioned it once and then they both forgot it had anything to do with them. In their half-hour conversations, all that mattered was the moment, and for a short time, the physical distance between two people was unreal and unimportant.

Sally started a list. If she was ever going to go to Kauai, she knew she had better make a list of reasons why she shouldn't toss all physical distance between them into the reddish waters of Waimea. It would be easy to fall into an affair of the body after making love to each other's souls over the phone.

Then what?

She made a list and decided she would take it with her if she ever went, so she could quickly look it over in the bathroom of some restaurant when she was feeling weak and ready to say fuck it. Especially after those potent fruity drinks and a heady day of heat and ocean air, and Josh's voice two inches behind her while they were standing at the lookout over Waimea Canyon, over those ochre, rust, and brown lava slopes. That would be enough to make the earth move for Sally.

Samantha Whitehead's (Clara's daughter) wedding picture had appeared in the *Stirling News Argus* around the same time Lily Grosvenor had become the talk of the town for running off to Winnipeg with Tom Dick.

The day before Lily left, she had come to Sally's store to buy a bunch of lilies. Star Gazer, Stella D'Oro, Sammy Russel, every kind of lily Sally had in stock.

"It's for the children," she had said. "So they won't forget me." She had started crying, then sobbing heavily. Sally took her into the back room.

"If it wasn't for Tom, I'd probably be dead by now."

Sally sat at the work table where she once made bouquets to celebrate the births of Lily's three babies, and listened to a mother sever herself from her children, in a desperate move to cling to a man who made her want to go on living.

"I was going to take my car and ram it into that telephone pole at the end of our road. People would just think I had misjudged the turn."

She had it all figured out, she had said, and then Tom came into her life. She knew then — that day — that everyone was going to call her crazy and uncaring for running off. But she couldn't stay any longer, and the price she would pay for leaving would be the faces of her babies forever carved into her heart, which would never stop bleeding for them. That's what she told Sally.

"I'm not even sure, in the end, it'll be worth it. Is anything?"

She left the store resigned, freed by defeat and power-lessness, with a dozen lilies wrapped in cellophane and a tiny card asking for forgiveness she wouldn't be around to see, even if given to her some day.

Ever since Sally started walking past her family home again, she had been thinking about how much it would bother her mother to see the way the place had been let go. She'd hate the patchy grass under the maple where she used to plant her impatiens. Sally hated it, too. Hated the way the new people never bothered to fix the crooked shutter on the front window.

Sally used to sit there as a child and look out at the world. That was the world to her then — the view from a house on a quiet street off the main drag of a small town. Stirling, Ontario, Canada. She had never been any place different.

Sally knew she could go to Kauai and take a boat tour along the Na Pali Coast and look up at the towering cliffs and that she might feel put in her place — relieved to know there was something bigger than her out there, and maybe it could tell her what it was she needed to know.

Maybe the Na Pali Coast could tell her. Or the emerald fields of taro, or the indigo and turquoise waters of the sea, or the ochre, rust, and brown lava slopes of Waimea Canyon.

There must be a price for living amidst such beauty, she thought.

They should straighten the fucking shutter and cut the fucking grass and weed the goddamn gardens and throw a coat of paint on the old garage. Her father always painted the huge white boards while her mother worked away at the fidgety black trim. When they were finished, they always sat at the picnic table in the backyard and admired their work. Her father would rub her mother's sore shoulders and she'd kiss one of his hands and thank him.

Sally had forgotten all about those details. The way her father used to draw hot baths for her mother when she wasn't feeling well, adding lavender beads to the water, and closing the bathroom door to keep the room warm. She had forgotten how her mother used to slip out to the cemetery with fresh flowers the day before her father went to visit his parents' graves, to make it cheerier for him.

She could go to Kauai, Sally thought, as she sat at her work table fingering the dog-eared edge of a page in the travel book. The day's clipped stems and fallen flower petals were still lying in front of her. She knew she could go, but she was afraid she might end up wanting to stay — wanting to know more about Josh. What he liked to do. Where he liked to go.

Did he like to lie in bed for hours on a Sunday morning? Did he like to take walks at midnight when the moon lit up the streets, just because he decided to at that very moment? Did he like things unplanned? Unusual. Messy. Could he stand not having everything in its place? Could she?

At 11 p.m., her time, Sally called Josh. She told him about Lily and Clara, and the dream she had had about him the other night, in the mall, on the escalator. As she talked, she played with the list beside the phone, folding it up, unravelling it, and occasionally glanced at Waimea Canyon.

The books were due back at the library the next day. June Chapman would return them to a shelf in the section marked 851 to 935, where they would sit with their musty pages and fresh fingerprints.

That night, on the phone, Sally never said a word about the books to Josh. Their conversation was familiar and easy, yet Sally knew everything had changed.

Chapter Seven

"I think Sally should go to Kauai," Delaney says. "Or she'll spend her whole life wondering if she should have."

Grace shakes her head and swallows a corn chip. "The guy's married."

"He's probably unhappy," Alex suggests.

"Who the hell isn't?" Jenny says.

"It's not even real," Grace says.

"And *your* fantasy man is?" Sally snaps back.

"I wouldn't hop a plane to Hawaii to find out."

"I never said I was going."

I watch the two of them and I know I'm not the only one who is given to obsessing more than I should about a love that may or may not exist. That by my enthusiasm alone, I can make something out of very little, out of nothing at all — embracing the kind of relationship that depends on the senses to tell us they are so, for everything else points to delusion and we are afraid to ask, Are you real?

Like Grace's Dr. T., whose subtle flirtations she took as signs of genuine affection. Imagined or not, they left her going over and over the same ground — the way he held her hand between his when he told her, her baby was breech, that she might need a Caesarean. The fact he used two hands, that he wrapped both of his around hers, convinced Grace he was attracted to her. She wasn't just another pregnant woman with a substantial stomach in for another fetal heartbeat check. The way he blushed when he gave her her first internal examination, as if medical science had nothing do with his exploratory hand. How he dropped by her hospital room after the birth of her second child to ask her how her bum was.

"How's your bum?" she repeated for us. "Do you think he's that informal with everyone? C'mon. It can't just be my imagination. How's your bum?"

She sits now, convincing Sally — convincing herself — the mind cannot be trusted.

"Shirley Valentine would go," I say.

"Jesus Christ," Sally rolls her eyes, "now I'm fucking Shirley Valentine."

"I rented it tonight," I say.

"On purpose?" Sally asks.

"No. Tom Conti makes me horny. That's all."

"Who doesn't?" Jenny says sarcastically, slurring, drinking. Is that number three or number four? She gets up to get another one before her glass is even empty.

"It might not be coincidental that Sadie just happened to choose *Shirley Valentine* on this particular night," Alex says. "Maybe it's a sign."

"Oh, for God's sake," Jenny cuts in, "you look for signs in the strangest bloody places."

She is bitchy and out of sorts and looking for a fight. I will tell everyone it's P.C.V. when she leaves the room. Post-Cottage-Visit. It happens every September, after she's been to The Cottage in August, and usually lasts for a month or two, until the leaves change colour and start to fall and all traces of summer are gone.

"You're the one who once told me you looked for answers in the swaying branches of a tree," Alex says to her.

"What's all the fucking fuss about anyway?" Sally asks. "I'm not going anywhere."

"I was a kid then," Jenny says sharply to Alex. "I know better now."

Storm doesn't say a word. She is quieter than usual and when I ask, she says it's just the time of year — the onset of fall. I can hear the season's melancholy dripping off the end of the word as she says it. It swirls and sways and falls to the floor, slowly, gracefully, without a sound, it lands and embeds itself in my mind.

Fall.

"If you're looking for a sign," Grace says, "look for the one that says TAKEN and save yourself the trip. You'll only be disappointed, anyway."

"Christ," Sally says. "I never said I was going." She leaves the room and retreats to the bathroom where I know she'll roll herself a joint and smoke it in peace, and rearrange my dried flowers, which sit haphazardly in a basket near the toilet.

"You know, Grace," Delaney says, "she doesn't have much else."

"That's my point," Grace answers. "I wouldn't want her to lose everything."

"It isn't up to us," Storm finally says.

Grace sighs and shakes her head and lets it go.

She hardly ever mentions Dr. T. anymore, aware of the dullness of her own conversation — the repetition of it, the unanswerable question of did he or didn't he care? She has retained him for whatever usefulness he offers — a diversion, something to put her to sleep at night, the lead in a private film she has the option of running at her own discretion, making the necessary script changes as she goes along, as life changes.

In the last few years, Grace has transformed much of that energy onto me, in her role as my confidant, vicariously weathering my stormy relationships, pondering their realities out loud for my benefit, as well as her own, for the sake of her writing — and her marriage. She hangs onto it the way a drowning person hangs onto a capsized boat, relying solely on the mind to get her through, to resuscitate her, bring her back from a state of marital unconsciousness.

She soaks up my life to keep her own from becoming parched — parched and dehydrated and delirious over long stretches of difficulty and disconnectedness, before the pendulum swings back the other way and she finds herself content once again.

It is Sally who once said, "Oh, for Christ's sake, Grace. Get a hold of yourself. It's all in your head." She left the room after she said it. She went into the kitchen for a glass of water, left Grace rolling her eyes in scolded embarrassment over Dr. T.'s seemingly insignificant gestures, left the rest of us wondering if there wasn't more to Sally's outburst, something other than familial concern. Was she really talking about herself and Josh? Had she thrown her caustic comments out just to see what would come back? To see if any of us would rise up to meet her challenge — to convince her that love can reside in the head and still be real. That her own imaginary lover is rooted in reality, even if he is made real only by the sound of his voice and by the reasons she needs to believe he exists.

Are you real?

Shall I love you?

It could have been the moon that did it.

It could have been the annual check-up I had with Mary-Beth last week. "So," she said while she listened to the sound of my heart, "you and the midnight rambler still clamping onto one another?"

Or maybe, it was just because it was mid-September — Fall — and nothing was happening.

Something made me get into my car the other night to go see Ben.

On the way to the lake, I put him through the ropes, mumbling out loud above my beloved Patsy Cline, How insensitive of you not to call! It's not everyday you end up stuck to someone — didn't it mean anything to you? You're lazy and insensitive and you have absolutely no sense of humour. Didn't you find the whole thing funny? What's your problem, anyway?

I had him dead — drowned one night while fishing. Finally getting the big one on the other end of the line and falling into the water and hitting his head on the side of that stupid boat of his, and drowning.

I had him dead — or chained to his bed. Handcuffed by his girlfriend, who would have found him the day after the night we were stuck with a huge smile on his face, which told her everything she needed to know.

He was chained and he couldn't get to a phone.

He was malnourished and sad, a broken man.

She wasn't feeding him or making love to him or talking his head off about the silly patches on a strange jacket.

He was broken-hearted and waiting for me to come to the rescue, to release him as I have before.

He was dead.

Or he was chained.

Or he was just a son-of-a-bitch.

Either way, I was going to tell him exactly what I thought of him.

I was.

It was the moon that did it.

That night as I stood at my front door looking up, debating, should I go, shouldn't I go, the moon was exactly as it was the first night we were ever together. A half moon, which Ben had said was half full because it was waiting for someone like me to come along and give it reason to be whole again. I never knew if that was one of his rare poetic moments, or just a line he came up with to get me into bed. When he said it, there was a grin on his face. I assumed it was a grin. Now I'm not so sure.

It was the moon that made me speed along the highway, and turn down the road to Ben's cottage, that kept me going despite my resolve never to go again. He was there. I know he was there. And so was she. She drives a red car. It was there.

A red car. And red and white gingham curtains on the front door window, which used to be bare, which I always said needed something, a bamboo blind, or something, for the sake of privacy.

It was the moon.

Up there.

Half full. Which followed me back down the road — back out onto the highway with a lump in my throat, wondering why it was like that on the night I finally decided to go.

Are you real?

Shall I love you?

When Sally comes back downstairs we start the film, and sit, transfixed, looking for signs in the flickering images before us — from a woman who talks to the wall. A middle-aged housewife who is unhappy with the way her life has turned out, who runs away to Greece and finds herself.

Grace
IN SEARCH OF PARSLEY

Chapter Eight

The steep hill on Boundary Road wasn't enough to bring Grace back. The view and the sudden decline hardly phased her. She had made the same trip a million times before. At least it seemed like a million. She no longer felt the need to pay attention to every turn and every crossing, as she once did — as if her alertness alone could avert misfortune. She drifted off willingly, her mind going in a hundred different directions. A hundred. A million. Everything was exaggerated on their drives — exaggerated, or dismissed altogether, depending.

Grace kept waiting for the car to crash and kill her, and scatter her pages along the roadside. The wind would pick them up and dance with her words, and lay them down in the dirt and the gravel and the dust-covered grass. Her young daughters slept in the back seat. Grace and her husband rode without speaking. She looked up at the clouds and thought about all the places in this world she'd probably never see, and how she had an affair with her gynecologist the night before.

It was only a dream. She woke up a few times then made herself continue her tryst with Dr. T. as she tossed around trying to get back to sleep. If it had taken place entirely in dream-state she wouldn't have felt guilty, but she did plot the affair out in her mind, awake and aware. Still, it wasn't real. Although, as they continued driving, Grace did have that aching longing that comes when your lover is someplace else and all you have is the memory of your lovemaking.

She kept thinking — if the car did crash and she died, and her pages were scattered along the roadside, they would find their way into the hands of someone who needs to read them. A woman named Hannah, perhaps, would be travelling the very same road the day after the accident. She'd get a flat tire, and as she was changing it, she'd notice a few pages in the ditch, which the police and the clean-up crew never bothered with because it didn't seem important at the time. Hannah would read the first page of Grace's story and feel compelled to follow the paper trail into the freshly cut hay field where the rest of the manuscript would lay waiting. *In Search of Parsley*, by Grace Walker.

That night, Hannah would remember a story she heard earlier that morning on the radio — about a car crash that killed a local woman, and how the woman's two children and husband, a former newspaper journalist, were unharmed in the accident. She'd see Grace's name on the manuscript and realize she was the one who was killed. She'd feel obligated to return the manuscript to the bereaved husband, but morbid curiosity or a sense of fate, or, most likely, desperation about her own life would make Hannah read it first.

It was those few words she read out there on the side of the road. The ones that made her forget about the flat tire, and her hungry kids, and her unemployed husband, who was wrestling with his usefulness and underachievement. It was those few words that made her spend close to an hour walking through a field picking up one piece of paper after another, sorting and shuffling, making sure every single page was found and in order.

Of all the ingredients in the homemade spaghetti sauce she was making for dinner, the one that would be least noticed if it was missing, was parsley. She didn't have any. It might have been the zombie-like routine of cooking the same sauce the same way for years, or just plain fear of what might happen if she didn't follow the recipe exactly. Whatever it was, she set out in search of parsley, knocking on the doors of the other tenants in the building who might have the missing ingredient. What she found was herself.

Hannah would head home thinking about this, the last twenty years of her life stirring and bubbling within, like a thunderstorm taking forever to rumble in from the west with all of her yesterdays riding on its merciless wind. Who knew what debris would be left behind? All because of a few words she found in a field, on a day she didn't expect anything extraordinary to happen.

Hannah would have to wait until her children and her husband were all asleep before she pulled out Grace's manuscript. She would be anxious to know how a person finds herself. She thought about it all through dinner, after hearing everyone groan about how late she was getting home and how awful the fish and chips were. Rubbery. Like they were cooked yesterday and re-heated in a microwave. Why couldn't she get pizza, they asked? All Hannah could think about was spaghetti sauce and parsley. She longed to know how a person finds herself.

The day before, Hannah was sitting in the garden with her sketchpad when she saw a monarch butterfly out of the corner of her eye, prancing about the purple coneflowers and the black-eyed Susans. She had a brief vision of it flying over and landing on her leg, and her hand swatting it away before she could even process the fact it was a butterfly, not some irritating nuisance of a bug. It was the reflex that bothered her. Her shortsightedness and the impatience with what was coming at her. What else had she misjudged lately?

Instead of making dinner the next night, or ordering more food that would bring more complaints, Hannah thought she'd rather take a walk in her garden with a glass of good Scotch and sit and watch the butterflies and smoke cigarettes. When it got dark, she'd watch the fireflies and the clouds pass under the moon, and listen to Bob Dylan, and call a young man she once made love to on a wet dock — on a lake up north, while the loons sang and the wolves howled. In the morning, she'd rise at ten and go to the beach, and stop at a hole-in-the-wall that served good wine and hummus for lunch. She'd meet an interesting man who didn't know her and would believe her if she told him she was off to New York to negotiate a huge contract with Calvin Klein, who saw something in her and loved the clothes she designed.

The thing about parsley, Hannah kept thinking, is that even though it doesn't affect the taste of the spaghetti sauce all that much, you get used to seeing those dark green flecks floating around in that red sea.

The quest to find parsley had led the woman in the manuscript to a number of apartments where she met up with all sorts of people who were also searching for something. Love. Approval. Fulfillment. But no one had any fresh parsley.

One man offered the woman a bottle of dried parsley flakes, but she declined, certain someone in the building would have fresh parsley. Fresh parsley made all the difference in the world, she told him.

That really confused Hannah. If parsley was so unimportant in the first place, why was it so important to find fresh parsley?

Hannah put the manuscript down and sipped on a Scotch in the middle of the day, while her children were at school and her husband was out at a meeting with a transition counsellor, who felt Hannah's husband should become self-employed and start his own management consulting business. This scared the hell out of her — the prospect of not having a regular paycheck.

The grandfather clock in the corner ticked away and seemed exceptionally loud to Hannah, warning her to do something with her life. *Now. Now. Now.*

She opened the small red address book on the table beside her drink and found his phone number. Ever since she remembered that night at the lake, she had been unable to get him out of her mind. She just wanted to talk to him. Although, if he suggested meeting in Toronto, she would go, just to have lunch or something. Although, if he suggested she get a hotel and stay the night, she would.

She wouldn't have ever done it before. But now, she'd be gone before anyone got home. She'd leave a note and go without letting anything stop her, including guilt, which lies beneath her skin, waiting for an excuse to ooze out of her pores and make her wet and sticky and repulsed by her own disgusting smell.

Hannah got a busy signal that sang in unison with the ticking clock, buying her more unwanted time to question herself. What was she going to say anyway? She would have to tell him she never did make it. That she spent most of her time sewing clothes for her three children and a few self-indulgent, wealthy women in town who liked to think of her as their personal designer.

Hannah tried again. It was still busy. She returned to the manuscript, to pass the time, and to search the words on the dirt-smudged paper for reassurance that what she was about to do was the right thing.

It must have been meant to be, she thought. How else would she end up on the side of the road at precisely the spot where the manuscript's first page was lying in the ditch? How else would she manage to find every single page in the hay field? Why hadn't it all blown away? Why hadn't it rained and smeared the words to the point where she wouldn't be able to read them? There had to be a reason.

The last time Hannah saw him was on the morning he was leaving for a job in Toronto. They were both 22. He never came back to Stirling. He married someone else and had two sons.

Twice a year, for years, Hannah looked for him in the city crowds, when she visited Toronto. In the summer at the Exhibition, she stood outside the haunted house with arms overflowing with stuffed monkeys and half-eaten cotton candy, waiting for her children to come out, and for his hand to touch her sunburned shoulder. "You were the last person I expected to see," she had planned to say with as much surprise in her voice as she could put into it.

At Christmas time, she took the kids on the Voyageur bus to Toronto to shop and to see the windows at Eaton's. The enchantment of the busy elves and the flying reindeer was lost in the reflection as Hannah kept a careful eye on her blowing hair and plastic smile. She wanted to look her best — the picture of happiness and beauty.

"Imagine running into you here, after all these years," she would say, when he walked out of the store carrying blue bags filled with pastel angora sweaters and expensive perfumes for his wife.

Hannah was told he never forgot her. She was told he asked about her all the time. She was told he realized he probably made a huge mistake. Then his sister moved to Nova Scotia and she didn't hear anything more about him — not a word. Until she saw the article in *The Globe and Mail*'s business section. She put it away in her sewing box, after calling Information for his company's phone number. She wrote it down in her red address book — under his old number, which was scratched out in a fit of anger a long time ago — in green ink. Dark green ink. Parsley green, Hannah thought.

She would try his number once more. First, she had another Scotch. The manuscript was lying in front of her like death to her soul if she didn't make that call. *In Search of Parsley*. She had to give it up soon, before her kids and her husband came home. When she tried again, it wasn't busy. His secretary asked who was calling, then put her on hold. What was she going to say? Would he even accept her call?

The questioning stopped when she was greeted by the voice whose whispered love was once echoed by a loon looking for his mate in the darkness. At least she had shaped it this way, still refusing to let in another sound — that of her own voice crying out when he broke skin, it was just as haunted and abandoned and needy.

On the phone, he said he'd heard about her clothes. A client's sister regularly commissioned her for new designs. He even saw one — the marigold-coloured linen sundress — at his client's summerhouse last year. She was surprised. A piece of her had been in his presence and she hadn't known it. Hadn't felt it. Hadn't had the pleasure of seeing his eyes take in the beauty of the lines and the curves and the completeness of her vision.

I still love you, he said.

Had she asked? Had something in her silence begged to know?

He said it in the same nostalgic tone he used when he talked about how much he loved living in the country and working on farms, and going to small-town fairs. A pleasant memory that no longer tugged at him to replay it, rekindle it, change his life for it.

Grace let her mind glimpse a disappointed woman who sat staring at a telephone, and then she let it drift back to her gynecologist, Dr. T., while the scenery became out of focus and her eyes settled on the passing ditch. Grace's husband, Steven, drove on, and spent most of his time looking in the rear-view mirror at the silver Volvo wagon riding their bumper. Grace didn't have to look at Steven to know this. She saw the car in her side mirror, where *objects in mirror are closer than they appear* only added to her discomfort.

Usually, Grace told Steven to be careful — not to blip the brakes like he often did in his venting anger. "The kids are in the back," she usually reminded him. "We don't know what kind of asshole we're dealing with." And then Steven usually swore under his breath and pounded on the four-way flash button with his finger and gestured for the asshole to back off.

This time, Grace didn't say anything. It was only another opportunity for argument between them and she was busy thinking about Dr. T. Over a year had passed since Grace last saw her obstetrician-gynecologist, after her second daughter had been born, although he never completely left her mind. His tender touch and quiet reassurance during the births of her children were only ever a concentrated thought or two away. The fact that he was as attractive as he was didn't help — more like the kind of guy she used to pine for in university than the elderly family doctor she used to spread her legs for all through her twenties. The one who seemed just as eager to get the whole thing over and done with as she was.

With Dr. T. it was different. She used to linger in the examination room afterwards and take her time getting dressed, in case he remembered he forgot something and returned, giving them a few unguarded moments together without the chatty nurse by his side.

Grace was no longer consumed by the embarrassment of being seen. She was no longer concerned with the discomfort of the probing and the poking. She had to think about shaving her legs and taking a bath at the last possible minute, to smell good, to make the point of entry as pleasant for Dr. T. as she could.

She knew if she wanted to, she could see him again. All she had to do was call his office and book an appointment for a Pap test, or go in and discuss her decision to end her baby-making days — the one she was putting off, foolishly perhaps, holding out on the chance there was meant to be one more life. She could almost feel it in her arms and at her breast.

She could call his office when she got home, she thought. Then that little voice inside said, "Oh, c'mon, have some grace, Grace." It was something she always heard, or said out loud to others when she was telling a story, when she reached the part where she was about to do something distasteful or selfish. "And then I said to myself, c'mon, have some grace, Grace."

She had been cursed by a name that forever eluded her and left her with imaginary trysts with a caring doctor who was only doing his job. How else should a doctor behave while half his arm is shoved up inside of you, feeling around for your baby's head? Curt? Disinterested? Sarcastic?

After the Volvo finally passed them, Steven relaxed. He exchanged one-finger insults with the driver and mouthed vanities through panes of glass knowing he'd never end up on the same road again. The Volvo's plate said Indiana.

"Fucking American prick," Steven grumbled.

Grace didn't mind that he dealt with his frustration that way. She knew he didn't hate Americans, or anyone, for that matter. Steven hated the driver because he probably had a good job and no worries about feeding his family and keeping a roof over their heads.

She didn't mind that he swore under his breath or that he shoved his middle finger into the air. What she did mind was his insistence on showing the other driver who was right and who was wrong — and which one was driving like an idiot. And even though she told herself this no longer bothered her, and she wasn't going to react, her pulse had quickened and her feet were pushed so hard against the floor of the car her calf muscles were beginning to hurt.

"If you want to be a cop, join the force."

"What do you expect me to do? The asshole's practically in the back seat."

"That's the point. How do you know he's going to stop when all of a sudden you start braking? How do you know he'll respond fast enough?"

"Just relax, Grace. Just relax."

She replayed one of many similar conversations in her head and wondered if he was doing the same. She was sure he was still thinking about the guy with the shiny new Volvo and how much they cost and how he probably has a good job with bonuses and profit-sharing, and that he's still an asshole for driving the way he does. She could tell this by the way Steven was sitting — slightly hunched over, shoulders drooped, a non-expression on his face. But he was the winner of the battle of the moment.

Sure, Steven was probably thinking to himself, sure, he got the guy to pass, to get off his back. But the Volvo had disappeared from sight and left him in his dust, probably racing off to close an important deal while Steven had nothing better to do but drive his wife to the post office — his wife who gets so uptight, squirming in her seat the way she does.

They continued down the road in their private worlds, making silent, inaccurate assumptions about what the other was thinking — filling the air between them with their non-verbal finger-pointing — suppressing any impulse to strike out for the sake of a greater good.

Motion made this possible. The very sense of moving forward while sitting still demanded it. Buckled up and restricted, and travelling at a speed that could crumple and dismantle in a fraction of second, they were forced to make the rest of the journey together amicably — it dangled as the only option from the rear-view mirror, swayed back and forth, back and forth. To ignore it would have invited argument, guarantee a riotous ride the rest of the way. To embrace it would give them as good a chance as any of arriving safely — without waking the two sleeping beauties in the back.

Amanda had drifted off first, not far below the hill on Boundary Road. Then Maura slipped away shortly after, reluctantly giving up the long succession of familiar scenes. At four, she had already begun recalling — naming the towns they regularly passed through, pointing out the house where Maura once saw several pairs of red underwear hanging on a clothes line.

"There's the red underwear house, Mommy," she said every time they drove by.

It was the intrusion on memory Grace was thinking of. To wake Maura out of her deep car-sleep because of an argument would only add a sense of uneasiness to motion — something vaguely unsettling that would accompany her always on journeys of her own. She wouldn't necessarily understand why she equates the two — tension and motion. They would travel alongside old memories of a particular landscape, and a certain kind of cluttered country store where she used to stop for strawberry ice cream, on days when even the motion of a moving car couldn't put her to sleep.

For the sake of Maura and Amanda's future car trips, Grace kept her thoughts about Steven and the Volvo to herself.

It was her idea to live in the country. Steven still got annoyed about the amount of time it took to drive to stores. Everyday, everyday, they had to drive somewhere to get something. This time is was to the post office, to mail Grace's manuscript. She suggested they take the long way — their usual drive — which lasted about an hour and a half by the time they got home again. It would let the kids sleep, and get Steven out of the house. A scenic tour down country roads that needed grading after a torrential downpour — through tiny villages nestled in the rolling hills of Hastings County, and along the Trent-Severn Waterway, where tanned vacationers sailed through on boats as big as houses, waving to envious onlookers having picnics out of their cars.

She would have preferred to make the trip into town alone this time. She would have mailed her manuscript, then walked the streets of Stirling looking at everyone's gardens, smoking cigarette after cigarette, bought at the Becker's store. She'd get a small pack because she quit smoking years ago and she wouldn't want to take them home — she hates throwing money away. Since Steven lost his job, and she had already quit hers at the library, it would seem too selfish to buy a large pack.

She wasn't very graceful that day when Steven came home and announced he'd been terminated. Downsized. Let go. She drank a lot and swore and put the girls to bed early so she could drink some more and not worry about them seeing her drunk.

Steven stared at the wall downstairs in the living room and sipped on what must have been his tenth beer that night, while Grace soaked in the tub with her sixth or seventh glass of wine and wondered how much time she had to write before she would have to abandon her work to find a job again.

She knew she couldn't go back to the library. She had already been replaced and the replacement was working out just fine. June Chapman had taken great pleasure in telling her so. It wasn't that June's voice sounded cheerful over the phone. It just didn't sound the least bit empathetic.

Fifteen years ago, Grace would have been sitting at Steven's feet, talking incessantly, nurturing him, picking up his fallen ego and heavy sighs, and replacing them with lies about how it's all for the best. She would have been completely focused on him. She would have stripped naked and performed any number of fantasies just to take his mind off everything. She would have done that, then.

Where does all the grace and goodness go?

They passed a car accident as they crossed the bridge over the Trent River. Grace knew Steven still fought the impulse to stop and ask the police what happened. For seventeen years he had covered accidents and fires and local politics. Now he drove by, like everyone else. The privileges of a press pass no longer sat in the front window of the car, defining him at a moment's glance. At 42, he suddenly found himself without instant identity, tossed into the jobless statistics they always ran in the paper he once worked for.

Months earlier, Grace started saying things like, "At least you don't have to go out to car accidents in the middle of the night anymore." And Steven started saying things like, "At least I don't have to look at dead bodies anymore." But as they passed the car accident on the bridge over the Trent River, they let it go by and said nothing about it, and simply followed the rest of the traffic as it was waved around the orange markers.

Steven had been getting up late every day and going to bed early. He made phone calls and checked the paper for jobs. He went for walks without Grace and hovered over her when she tried to sort out the bills. He tried to pretend things were normal. She heard him crying in the shower.

As they continued down the road, she stared out at the scenery, which was cut and pasted with fragments of the previous night's heat and flame. A naked back. Soft hands cupping her face. Deep breathing from the heavy body on top of hers. She followed Dr. T.'s lead and breathed in rhythm, giving up her own naturally shorter pace.

The night before, Grace and Dr. T. made love on several occasions in his office. She met him on his days off and they embraced on the dark brown leather couch she used to see on her way to one of the examining rooms. They talked about how much they missed each other in between the times they managed to get together. A month or two would pass before they met up again, making them greedier, more willing to show up late wherever they were supposed to be just so they could grab a few more moments of pleasure with each other.

About halfway through the night, after the second time she woke up and went in to check on the girls, Dr. T. told Grace his wife had left him. She was tired of having no life while he spent most of his time delivering new life. Grace remembered her face from a picture on the wall in his office — him, his wife, his three children, the blue swirling background. She didn't know what to say. Dr. T. told her he was completely happy with their situation — that as a lover, Grace fit into his life well. She didn't expect much from him — a few intense hours a couple of times a month. Was it okay with her to carry on as usual? Sure, she said, hurt like hell that he hadn't suggested she leave Steven for him — relieved that he hadn't suggested she leave her husband for him.

She got up to pee halfway through the night. Steven went downstairs to sit in the dark. When she got back into bed, Dr. T. called and said he needed to see Grace right away. She made up some excuse and ran over to his condo, their new meeting place since his separation. When she arrived, she barely had time to step inside the door and he had his arms wrapped around her, kissing her tenderly, slowly, staring deeply into her eyes. Something was different about him.

There was a pattern to it — regular intervals of puffing sounds. She knew what it was as soon as she heard it.

"What are you doing?"

"I can't sleep."

Grace sat up and saw Steven on the floor at the foot of the bed, pushing himself up and down, exceeding even his own expectations — adrenaline pushing him on. Faster. More. Until he stopped and stood up, exhaling as though he'd just completed a race — a race he'd won — his chest muscles flexed to show he still had it. Then he slowed down and everything sank back into place. Part of the definition in his chest fell away. Part of it stayed, surprising even Grace.

"Why don't you read something?" Grace was anxious to get back to her dream. "That always works for me."

"I don't feel like reading."

Steven lay down beside her on top of the covers and started deep breathing — to annoy her, she thought, to make sure she couldn't ignore his presence. It had become a pattern with him lately and usually precluded a statement about their predicament, which usually turned into an argument. In. Out. In. Out. He was being insistent.

Grace rolled over anyway, to show him she wasn't going to be baited. When he saw that it wasn't working, Steven began coughing and kept it up until she had no choice.

"You're keeping me up." She tried to say it as nicely as she could, considering her impatience with his tactics.

"What? I'm not allowed to cough?"

She refrained.

"Next time, I'll hold it in. I suppose getting up to take a piss is a no-no, too."

"Oh, please — give it a break, Steven. I'm not in the mood for a fight."

"Then don't start one."

She really wanted to get back to Dr. T.'s condo and the strange look on his face, but Steven's verbal prodding rolled her over. She raised her upper body, bracing her weight on one arm for what had been coming at her with more regularity than she cared to think about.

"I am simply trying to sleep," she said looking down at him, seeing only one side of his face — the side closest to the dim light on the clock radio.

"I'm glad one of us can," he snapped, as if she didn't share the burden of their troubles, as if it lay entirely on his shoulders, above his pulsating, pumped-up biceps.

In the last several weeks, Steven had been lifting four-litre jugs of water and old phone books — the big fat Toronto ones he used to need for work — showing her his progress along the way. "Feel these," he kept saying to her every other day, as if change was occurring rapidly, as if his resourcefulness and perseverance were paying off, as if he was doing something tangible and she was not.

Grace was finishing her manuscript. She almost showed him a few pages to prove him wrong, to lay the words in front of him — paper and ink — proof she had made real progress and was nearing the end. But she never knew how that was going to turn out — showing him excerpts from her work.

Before Steven lost his job, there was restrained editing, pointing out spelling mistakes and typing errors, the odd misuse of a word. Since he lost his job he kept changing her prose, telling her her sentences were either too short and clipped, or too long and loopy, and grammatically incorrect — something worrisome considering she had quit her job to write the book.

As far as Steven was concerned, that's when everything started — everything being their decline into joblessness and frugal living.

The summer Grace decided to leave the library, they were staying at a resort on Stoney Lake, not far from the village of Lakefield. They were both still working and decided to splurge, to take the girls away for a real vacation. They used their credit card and forgot about it, booked the seven-day, all-inclusive package. Deluxe suite overlooking the lake, full-course meals, swimming pool, water-skiing, horseback riding, Yuk Yuks comedy troupe, free babysitting. They could even take a boat over to the golf course, if they golfed, which they didn't.

At two-and-a-half years and fourteen months, Maura and Amanda still took their afternoon naps every day in the room. Grace and Steven sat outside the screen door, on the patio, overlooking the lake and the pool, drinking some of the white wine and beer they had brought along and kept in the small refrigerator beside one of the beds. It didn't work very well and everything was only slightly chilled. But they enjoyed it anyway — the chance to be alone, to talk, to have a few drinks in the sunshine — the lake breeze keeping them comfortable, the splashing and the hoots and hollers from the water-volleyball game rising up from the pool to remind them they were indeed on vacation, away from it all.

Steven grabbed her thigh one afternoon and hinted at the possibility of some frisky sex since the girls were sleeping. Where? In the bathroom? In the Jacuzzi tub? Grace had taken a bath the first night with too much bubble bath. The jets in the tub practically buried her in white, orange-scented foam. They laughed and joked about Steven's new nickname for her — "Sudsy" — and they stayed out there on the patio. Neither one of them got up to start something. That's when Grace mentioned it — the little trip she wanted to take into Lakefield to see the house where Margaret Laurence had lived. "Little trip" made it sound less inconvenient, less time consuming.

"Wasn't there a lot of fuss over some book she wrote?"

Steven wasn't the literary type. He read newspapers and computer magazines; Maclean's, Time, and Saturday Night.

"The Diviners," Grace told him. "It was a long time ago."

Grace had all of Laurence's books. She bought them from a bookstore in Belleville. Some books were too important not to have to herself, without the fingerprints and the smells of an entire town on the pages. She liked her books, her private collection at home, because they still smelled like books, and weren't fingered to death with stains — coffee, herbal tea, sherry. Grace would know, with some borrowers, exactly what kind of stains the books would come back with. Her boss, June, never seemed too concerned.

"That's what makes them library books," she'd say. "The stains, and the greasy prints. Life gets all over them."

Grace often wondered why June ever became a librarian. Her lack of attachment to books — any book — seemed odd, wrong even. Whenever someone returned a book with a ripped cover or a torn page, all June ever said was, "Not to worry, not to worry. These things can be taped up."

These things.

Before she went to Lakefield, Grace had only seen the house on Regent Street in black and white photographs, in a memoir, and a biography. It was no wonder they drove right by it the first time. They had made the fifteen-minute drive down the highway from the resort and came into Lakefield along the main drag — Queen Street, which looked as if it might stretch on for quite a while. The storefronts were strung together on either side in two long, uninterrupted lines. But then the street suddenly veered off to the left, and before they knew it, they had reached the end. The road came to an abrupt stop at the Trent-Severn Waterway, with the Lakefield Chamber of Commerce just off to the right. They had missed the house completely.

"You can see it from Queen Street," a woman at the Chamber said. "It's pretty much right there at the corner of Regent and Queen."

Grace had Steven stay in the car with the girls while she ran inside to get directions.

"Just turn around and go back downtown until you see a church on your right hand side, then make a sharp turn. It's right there. You can't miss it." She handed Grace a pocket-size pamphlet on historic downtown Lakefield and a flyer advertising Lakefield's Literary Festival — a weekend event that was starting the day Grace would be leaving the resort to head home. *In Remembrance of the Legacy of Margaret Laurence, Catherine Parr Traill, Susanna Moodie, and Isabella Valancy Crawford*, it read.

"Too bad I'll miss it," Grace said to Steven when she got back into the car. Staying a few more days at the resort was out of the question. They couldn't afford it.

"Maybe next year," he said. He was always agreeable when things were far off and likely to be forgotten.

Grace went down the festival itinerary, reading it out loud
to Steven. A tour of Lakefield's literary heritage. Readings.
Discussions. Dramatic presentations. An open house at the
Margaret Laurence Home. Dinner at Lakefield College.

"Isn't that where — "

"Prince Andrew went to school. Yes." Steven finished her
sentence with a slightly elevated tone, as if now there was
actually something worthwhile to see in Lakefield. "We'll
drive by on our way back," he said.

Grace had picked Wednesday to come into town, partly
because it broke up the week at the resort, partly because
the weather forecast was calling for a cooler, cloudier day. It
turned out to be anything but, and Maura kept complaining
about how hot it was.

"The next car is going to have air," Steven said, and
always said in the summertime. The rest of the year he prided
himself on what good shape his thirteen-year-old car was in
and talked about how much he would miss the old thing,
maybe he'll just keep driving it until it won't go anymore.

Hot and sunny is how the day turned out. By the time
they pulled up in front of the house on Regent Street, Steven
and Maura were already talking about getting back to the
resort to swim in the pool. "Of all the days to do this, Grace,"
Steven sighed.

Amanda was crying for more apple juice. "Firsty.
Manna firsty."

"I won't be long," Grace promised as she handed Amanda
a bottle, then shut the car door, left them to deal without her.
All she wanted was five minutes, just five uncluttered minutes.
Who'd think it would be such a production.

She stepped away from the curb onto the front lawn and
stood in front of the historical plaque that sat atop a steel pole.
She was uncomfortable with standing on the grass but blamed
it on poor planning on someone's part — the historical society,
maybe. Even if a person could read the plaque from the
sidewalk, who would stand there? It seemed too far away.
Then she was struck by the thought that perhaps everyone else
did stand on the sidewalk and wasn't as rude as she was. She

retreated to the concrete and stood at the very edge, her toes almost touching the grass. It was as close as she could get without actually crossing the well-trimmed line.

It was lunchtime. A taupe-coloured car was in the driveway. People were probably sick of the intrusion, she thought. She could hear them complaining, "Christ, another one standing out there gawking at the upstairs windows. This one's really hanging around. What's she waiting for? Read the plaque, take the picture, and leave, will you?"

"Grace, it's really uncomfortable in here," Steven called out to her.

She motioned him with her finger — just a minute, just one minute. She could see Maura banging her head against the back of her car seat, an annoying habit she had only recently developed, rocking back and forth in the car, and on the couch at home. Amanda, thankfully, was still busy sucking on her bottle.

Grace turned back to the house, which seemed out of context, not lying flat before her in black and white, cropped and settled nicely on the page — a two-storey brick home — old, with a porch across the front. Now she could see the brick was a sandy-beige colour and the pillars were white, like most of the trim. White and deep red, or brown, it was hard to tell which. No — brown, she decided. Definitely, a reddish-brown. And there was too much going on around it. A plane was soaring above, unseen and shrieking across the sky. A dog was barking from somewhere nearby — barking and barking. A curtain was being drawn in one of the upstairs windows.

"Grace! C'mon, it's too hot," Steven yelled.

"Mommy!" Maura screamed. "Too hot, too hot."

Grace recognized the plastic white summer chair on the porch. In a picture in one of the books she'd read, there had been a few chairs, and a table, pushed into one corner by the front door.

"Grace!"

She heard the lack of tolerance in the last call and followed it over to the car, to the front passenger window, which of course, was rolled down, all the way down.

"Take them for an ice cream, will you?" she asked, leaning in.

Little beads of sweat had formed on Steven's forehead. She could see herself reflected in his sunglasses — her two faces were large and distorted and they almost covered Margaret Laurence's two homes. She could see both sets of thin lips mouthing the words at exactly the same time. "Take them for an ice cream, will you?"

"C'mon, Grace. It's a house," Steven said sharply. "How long do you need?"

"Please. There was an ice cream store further up the street. I saw it on the way in. Please."

She was begging. She knew it. She didn't care. It worked. Steven let out another impatient sigh. He shook his head and looked away from her, like she knew he would, like he had to do to make sure she knew none of this pleased him. He was making a sacrifice.

It could have been that he knew she wouldn't give up easily. Or he remembered how she took the girls back to the room the other night so he could stay at the resort's bar and play pool for a while — something he never did. She didn't know he even knew how. Whatever it was, Steven started up the car and told her to enjoy herself. He'd stretch it out. He'd clean them up. He wouldn't order anything with nuts for Amanda.

She watched herself pull back out of view in his black lenses, before she stood up. Then she saw herself again — this time in the dark-red paint on the car — in the panel of space between the front door window and the back door window. A stretched and skinny image of herself, arms at side, hair hastily pulled up off her sweating neck, wearing cutoffs and a mauve *Stoney Lake* T-shirt — standing in front of a house that disappeared from sight at the same time she did when Steven drove off for ice cream.

It couldn't bother them too much, Grace thought. Whoever bought the house, they must have expected it, that people would hang around out front staring into their windows. The literary festival itinerary said the festival office was located there. They had to be literary types. What was she thinking before? Of course they wouldn't be annoyed.

To look less obsessed, Grace walked away from the house down Regent Street, past other houses that became important to her simply because they were on the same street, part of it all. She passed an elderly man who looked dazed and confused, who was wearing faded blue overalls and a white short-sleeved polyester shirt that looked as old as he did, and a straw hat that was chewed away on one side. He was inspecting his flowers, a rather sparse mixture of zinnias and geraniums scattered across the front of his house. He nodded, put up a hand, and looked as if he might ask her who she was, what day it was, what town he was in.

Grace couldn't help but think, he must have known her — that Margaret might have walked by the same house frequently, admiring the man's green thumb, the constant effort and the pride he took in making the place look nice. For although his garden was sparse, each flower was perfection, tall and healthy, and seemed to be growing faster than the rest on the street.

She might have known him, and his zinnias and his geraniums, when he didn't have a thin veil of film over his eyes, when his body was less of a disappointment to him, when he used to watch her coming down the street, silhouetted against an amber screen of evening light — when he could tell it was her just by the way she walked.

After she went a little further down Regent Grace turned around. She almost crossed the street to avoid the old man's suspicious stares on the way back — suspicious or pitying, she couldn't tell which. How many women had he seen over the years, wandering up and down the short block, aimlessly, hopelessly, with too much riding on the house near the end?

She tried to block him out, and the traffic that was making its way down nearby Queen Street. She could hear the cars cutting the air with their passing presence. She could hear the tires as they dipped and rolled over the sewer grates from somewhere behind her, rounding a corner too close to the edge, hitting the same spot, one after the other.

Clunk. Clunk. Clunk. With a bouncing metal sound following each clunk.

Grace had only read Laurence's books. She'd never touched her hand or laid eyes on her, not in person. She had never heard her voice — not the one that ever lifted off the page, spoken out loud in notes. All the *Jesus Christs*, and *Oh, my Gods*, and *those fucking stupid bastards* she might have said. Everything might have sounded different then — or maybe not.

There was a wave — a mourning of some distant sort Grace didn't feel she had a right to, considering. It isn't her tomb, it's her house, she kept telling herself.

A pigeon was sitting on the roof when she came back down the street, cooing and cocking its head left to right, right to left, looking down at her, then looking away — looking over at the bell in the tower on the church across the street. She kept thinking, it should be a dove — a dove, not a pigeon.

As much as she was drawn to the house, it was the church that kept catching Grace's eye. She stood in front of the plaque on Margaret Laurence's lawn, but this time she was facing the church, trying to figure out which way the sun rose and which way it set, and how it would look at twilight. How it must have looked to Margaret in the middle of the day — stark and striking against a clear blue sky — in contrast to the rest of the world, 135 years after it was erected. And on a dreary day, it might not have seemed out of place at all, summoning Margaret's thoughts in the dull and introspective rains — greeting her reflective moods with little distraction, giving her something permanent to look at. She would have seen it from inside, through several different windows, and every time she stepped out to move about in this village — this last, this final place.

Steven took two pictures of Grace when he came back to pick her up: Grace standing directly in front of the historical plaque, facing Steven; Grace standing beside the plaque, pretending to read it, the house in the background. She picked them up after they were developed at the drugstore in Stirling, the week after they returned from their vacation. She pinned them to the cork board in the small room off the kitchen where she writes, hung them in the middle of a mess of small scraps of paper — notes to herself. Bits of dialogue and inspiration, and rules to write by.

"Looks like just another brick house to me," June said, flipping quickly until she got to a picture of Steven on water-skis. "Nice ass," she added.

"I should have had you point to the historical plaque," Steven joked when he saw the pictures, "like those stupid tourist pictures everyone takes, pointing to the attraction. Look! Here it is!" Chuckle, chuckle.

Grace still wondered about the missing pigeon — the one that kept flying back and forth between the rooftop on Margaret Laurence's house and the bell tower on the church across the street. Leaving white streaks of shit baking in the sun, cooing its head off, preventing her from having the kind of moment she had gone there to have. It had been there just before Steven made her pose. It was there a few seconds later, flying overhead, dropping a load near her feet. Grace backed up to avoid it and then some unfortunate woman came by and stepped in it. But she didn't know it. She was too busy looking at Grace and looking at the house and back at Grace and back at the house, a comradely smile spreading across her eager face. She was tall and slender, a youthful looking woman for someone in her late thirties or early forties, with a knapsack on her back. She was holding the same pamphlet and literary poster Grace was holding in her hand. She would have seen Grace posing for the picture just seconds before.

"Wow," she said, looking at Margaret Laurence's house, then back at Grace, then back at the house.

Steven got inside the car. Grace took her time opening her own car door, delaying her departure — curious about the woman who held one hand across her forehead, above her eyes, squinting against the sun to read the plaque. Tourist, she thought.

Steven started the car and Grace got inside. As she was

buckling the seat belt, the woman turned to Grace and said, "I interviewed her once, a long time ago."

Grace returned the comradely smile and mumbled something inconsequential like, "enjoy yourself," while Steven pulled away slowly from the curb. The woman shook her head in awe over being in front of Margaret Laurence's house and gave Grace a thumbs-up. Grace waved goodbye.

"What did she say?" Steven asked quietly. They were still fairly close, close enough for the woman to hear if Steven said it loud enough.

"She said she interviewed her once."

Steven turned his head to take a fast look at the woman he hadn't paid a second of attention to the moment before. "Probably for the CBC," he said. "She looks like CBC radio."

They were stopped at the corner of Regent and Queen waiting for a break in the traffic. Grace took the opportunity to grab one last look at the house and noticed the woman was already walking away from it, crossing Regent Street behind them, heading for Queen herself. Grace could see her in the side mirror, then over her shoulder — the one nearest Steven. She watched her through the back window.

The woman walked with a bit of a hop, with a perpetual smile on her face and a song on her lips. It was as if she could hear music, Grace thought, as if she was wearing headphones and a compact disc player on her belt, and was about to start mouthing the words any minute. Pigeon shit on her shoe.

When they were in motion, Grace turned her head in the opposite direction, back to her open window, to make sure the last image would be the house.

June said she understood why Grace wanted to see the house that belonged to one of Canada's most famous writers. She didn't care herself, though. Laurence's books were too real, she said. She preferred John Grisham. What did she need to read about an unhappy housewife for? Or an old woman who's dying, or a frustrated old virgin? She wouldn't have left the resort and the pool and the free water-skiing to visit it. She had seen the house in a book. What was there to look at?

She said she would go to Elvis's house if she ever made it to Memphis. Or the White House if she ever went to Washington. She told Grace she was actually inside the huge Claremont house, up there in the Oak Hills, where it's true, the half-mile driveway is heated and the garage has a floor that moves and turns your car around with the push of a button.

"You can drive in at night and in the morning you can flip the switch and turn your car around to drive out. Imagine — I wouldn't have thought there was so much money in the creamery business," she said. "You and I, we'll never have that kind of money, will we, Grace?"

That's what bugged Grace the most about June — the way she always lumped them together in the same category, as if they lead parallel lives. We'll never have that kind of money. We'll never take a trip like that. We'll never win the lottery. Our kids this. Our husbands that.

June and Grace had worked together for more than eight years. June was the one with the degree — the librarian. Grace was the helper, put on staff because they couldn't afford to pay another higher salary. June came up with the ideas — the monthly book club, a weekly reading series for children, for the three and four-year-old set. Grace was the one who conducted them, who returned the books to the shelves and swept the floor when the spring mud was tracked in, and made stern calls to borrowers who regularly neglected to bring the books back at all. None of that bothered her. She was paid to do it.

It was the talking, the constant talking — the way June never shut up from the moment she arrived in the morning until she left late in the day. It was the lack of dead air. Every moment had to be filled, and it was, with some of the most trivial garbage Grace had ever heard. She got the play-by-plays, the ongoing sagas. Nothing ever seemed to reach a climax or resolution. On and on it went, like everything else, for years, droning in her ears like the ceiling fan at the library — never realizing quite how irritating it was until she walked outside at lunchtime or at the end of the day, and suddenly, it was gone. That's when she heard it the most.

There was June and her mother. June and her husband. June and her kids. June and her thankless sister, Tammy. "Thankless," June said, "because she doesn't appreciate anything I do for her. Never has. And I should have seen it a long time ago when Tammy's first kid was born. I practically moved in to help her. Changed all the diapers. Washed all the laundry just so Tammy could sleep and soak in the tub and have her crying fits in peace. And what did I get? When I had my first kid, Tammy shows up with some pink bear and leaves in less than an hour! One hour! And of course, Tammy's kids are better than mine — which of course is nothing but a bunch of you-know-what. They might wear all the right clothes but at least my kids don't eat from the dog bowl or slap her in the face like I saw Tammy's son do once, just up and slapped her because he couldn't have a second Mr. Freeze before dinner.

"My husband is always at work. At work. Like our lives depend on him putting in seventy hours in a week. He doesn't even make that much money, and if he does, I sure as heck don't know where he's putting it. What's the point of working so much when you don't make any money? And what does he think I do all day?

"Tell me, Grace. How did we end up with husbands like this?"

Then there was June, and June — the month of June. It was *her* month — *her* lucky month.

For four weeks of the year, June's mood picked up. There was a bit of a bounce in her walk — expectancy, nervous anticipation. She walked around as though her life might change at any moment.

When nothing happened to June, which it never did, June always slipped into depression. She called in sick more often — almost every other week for the rest of the summer and into the fall, with greater frequency over the winter — doubling the workload for Grace. She was expected to cover for June, then help out a little more the day June returned — the day after the sick-day, because June still wasn't feeling well, but she made herself come in anyway.

She'd forget about her hair and her makeup. She'd wear the same old shoes with lifts that were worn away, and the same old skirts with hemlines that were never in style anymore. She was always tugging at them and pulling up her pantyhose, which were loose from too much wear, light beige and sickly looking on her legs. When they got runs, June threw them away in the metal wastebasket behind the front counter in the library, where they sat in the bottom like dead skin that had stayed on the bone far longer than it should have.

When Grace was in a generous mood, she could actually remember a time when June used to lay the books down on the counter with care. She could recall how they once sat in silence in different parts of the library on quiet days, reading. How June interrupted only occasionally to share something worth hearing, something she'd just read: the significance of Saturn in astrological charts; what the shape of our face can tell us; how birds fly in massive clusters and never collide.

Grace still remembered how things had started out — those first few months at the library. But they took up less space and were easily forgotten whenever she thought of how they ended — June throwing tape on ripped pages, not caring if one of her brown hairs got caught as she was sealing the wound, not caring that her kids' faces were filthy and their clothes seemed ill-fitting and grey — being held hostage to June's running monologue, which recapped every moment of the eight years in between — witnessing the flurry of activity that seemed to follow June through the front door every morning — chaos forming a distinct outline up one side of her disintegrating clothes, over her uncombed hair, and down the other side.

Grace had thoughts of leaving before, but there were very few jobs that paid as well in such a small town and she needed the money. The money. It was always about the money. Eventually, she hit upon the perfect excuse to steal time to herself every lunch hour, to put a halting hand out to any ideas June had about them spending it together, the way they once did.

"It's my only chance to read these days," she said one morning, and then repeated it every six months or so when June needed reminding that lunch hours were off-limits. Grace kept herself so busy in the library, straightening, dusting, sweeping — anything to make it look like there wasn't a second to read all day, except at lunchtime.

Grace would leave the library, get into her car with her sandwich and a book and drive around the corner, over to Henry Street, where she parked along the side of the road near the tennis courts. A baseball diamond and an acre or two of mowed grass took up the rest of the space between this part of Henry Street and John Street, on the other side.

In the winter, no one was around — or in early spring and late fall when the weather was still too cold. Grace came to think of it as her spot, and felt invaded and disappointed if she drove over and found some town trucks parked in her place, with ride-on lawn tractors and rakes and paint for the bleachers — everything to maintain the park during the summer. She would have to drive over to Edward Street and park near Grace Chapel, where the cemetery usually guaranteed some peace and quiet, unless they were cutting the grass on the same day. This only ever happened once that she could recall.

At some point, Grace stopped reading during lunch hours and started writing — random thoughts at first, pure play. She kept a large pad of lined paper under the passenger seat, a pocket-sized dictionary and thesaurus and two or three pens in the glove box. She began assembling bits, sketching with words, loosely at first, borrowing on June's melancholy, plagiarizing her melodramatic monologues, or plucking one good line from fifty she may have heard spoken that morning — one wayward line taken out of context, which would put Grace on an entirely different path. She'd write and write and

follow it where it seemed to want to go, astonishing herself
with the sudden appearance and usefulness of a pair of stinking
pantyhose sitting in the bottom of a metal wastebasket. To
whom did they belong? How did they get there? Where was
this wastebasket? And so on. Making it up along the way,
realizing she could.

Grace was taken from that moment on — irrevocably
taken by what was sitting there, waiting to come out.

As Steven and Grace drove along the Trent-Severn
Waterway, which links Lake Ontario to Georgian Bay and
passes through Lakefield, Grace was thinking that Margaret
Laurence's house wasn't that far away at all. Linked by way
of road and water.

Their usual drive would steer them through the village
of Frankford and along the back roads through the hamlet
of Glen Ross and back into Stirling where Grace would
mail her manuscript. As they made their way along the
water, the argument they'd had the night before hung
suspended in the steady movement of the car — echoed in
the wind coming from the doors that were no longer
sealed shut. The wear and tear and the changes in the
weather had shrunk the rubber trim and left them singing
along with an annoying rattle. It came and went and came
again whenever Steven hit a bump in the road or crossed
over railroad tracks.

Grace rode as the passenger — at the mercy of Steven's
good judgement — past familiar open fields and houses she
had come to know. She was an observer of who was
compulsive and neat and always on time with outdoor
decorations, and who was tardy and left tacky Christmas lawn
ornaments sitting out until March.

She saw their open pools all summer, whenever they
took a drive — saw them covered with their black sheets in
winter. She could tell who had snow blowers, and who
didn't, just by looking at the way the snow was piled along
the driveways. She felt sorry for the same family every time

she passed the same house, where rusted junk was parked in every conceivable space, where paint hung like flaking skin on the wooden siding, where someone still bothered to hang a basket of pansies from a hook outside.

Over her left shoulder, she could see Amanda — her small head bobbing with the bumps in the road and leaning too far over her tiny chest. Grace was afraid Amanda would end up with a sore neck, so she leaned back and gently pushed Amanda's head up. Amanda stirred and licked her lips. Ten minutes later her head fell forward again.

Grace eventually gave up trying to push Amanda's head back up and was distracted by the recollection of a red fox she had seen in the corner of a winter field — the same field she was passing now with a stretch of clover. The one that came before the *fall field*, which she named the *fall field* because of its forest of yellow and orange. Steven had stopped to take a picture of it last year, before the leaves were gone — a month or so before the first snowfall. Before the short weeks in between fall and winter when nothing is hidden and the forest stands undressed — its previously hidden holes and blemishes revealed — its inhabitants unable to scamper unseen. It stands in idle nakedness waiting for winter to cover it up, to lend some mystery once again.

As they passed by the fields, still striking in their summer greens, and through the village of Frankford, Grace was trying to remember what had happened with Dr. T. the night before, and why he had that strange look on his face when she showed up at his condo. She couldn't recall if anything happened, or if she had just fallen asleep, exhausted from another confrontation with Steven. He needed to blame someone. She needed to feel blameless.

She was also trying to figure out what she should do with the woman named Hannah who found her manuscript. Would she feel better for having made the call to her old love? Would she realize she wasn't missing anything in her life — that the search for parsley had been a lesson in futility?

They drove past the trail of houses on the outskirts of the small town and within a few kilometres they wound their way around a bend, past a string of transmission towers where something began to lift, where something always began to lift. Grace had never been able to figure it out. She used to think it had something to do with the bend itself, and the picturesque farms that suddenly appeared in the hills on the horizon.

"What is it about this turn?" she said. "I always feel a change — a real change. I feel it physically."

Steven shrugged. "A change in the polarity, I guess." He shifted in his seat and asked her if she had brought along anything to drink. She reached into the small cooler at her feet. It was filled with juice for the girls and a couple of cans of pop. She opened one for Steven and one for herself.

"Could it be the electricity?"

"Could be," he said. "The electromagnetic field."

Either that, Grace thought, or because the *transmission field* was where they always started to talk again, when they reached that point — the eighty-five kilometre mark. Which she knew it was because Steven always reset the odometer before their drives, always said, "another hundred kilometres" when they got home, when he shut the car off.

The eighty-five kilometre mark — the field with transmission towers — that's where he once told her she was a good writer, that she could transport him, that he didn't even think of her when he was reading what she wrote — he was immersed in the world she created.

It was also where he once asked her, "Did you decide to do it that day in Lakefield?" She knew what he was really asking. Is that where it had all started? She could see why he might have thought so. It was only a matter of months after their vacation at Stoney Lake when Grace came home from work on a Friday with her plan to cash in some bonds, to leave her job, to write her book.

On the day that Steven asked her about Lakefield, he wasn't accusing her. He had stretched a bit and sat up straighter. He even commented on how much he was beginning to enjoy their drives.

"Is that the day you decided, Grace?"

At the time, she had to think about it, had to think back to that afternoon on Regent Street. It had been almost two years. Finally, she answered him.

"No," she said, "not that day."

It wasn't a lie. And it wasn't the truth.

Chapter Nine

We meet twice in October. It is such a long month —
taking up almost five weeks on the calendar, and we
are feeling restless and out of sync with our lives.

It's the weather. It's boredom. It's the alignment of the stars.

We have our theories.

We meet on the first weekend and watch *sex, lies and
videotape*. Jenny brings it and no one can recall much about it,
except that Andie MacDowell was beautiful and she had
good sex for the first time in her life while cheating on her
husband with some bad boy who had an obsession with
videotaping women.

Jenny holds the videocassette in the air and tells us she
has all the bases covered with this one — the sex, for those
of us in this room who are having it. The lies, for those of us
who are having sex with people we shouldn't be. And the

videotape for Del, who should be having sex but is too busy making a documentary of her own.

Sex, I say, what's that? And what about Sally? What category does she fall into? She only thinks about having sex with a man who lives in a different time zone.

Don't worry, Grace assures me, there'll be another man for you, she believes this.

Grace sees my life in episodic segments — *the Johnny story, the Zeke episode, the Ben saga* — a constant and consistent source for the ambiguities of stationary love. Go-nowhere love, we call it. I move, she once said, with love's possibilities and inevitabilities chasing me and leading me at the same time. She said it as if I've achieved something everyone else hasn't — something admirable and pathetic at the same time.

It was meant to be a compliment.

She steals from my life, but still, it is Grace I turn to most often — for purely selfish reasons. She's the one who pays the closest attention. She remembers previous indignities and shortcomings as well as I do, and can recall incidents, and remind me of insights I forgot I had. She remembers my life as it if were her own — I find it tucked into her pages, disguised as someone else's — something I once said, something I did. I am preserved on paper — unrecognizably preserved — and everything I do is grist that goes to Grace's mill.

Late one night, under the lamplight in my bedroom, I found myself residing in an apartment building with a woman knocking at my door looking for fresh parsley. My name was Clara and I was busy pasting pieces of fabric into a scrapbook. The book was almost filled but I was empty and to top it all off, I didn't have any fresh parsley. The woman left me where she found me — at my kitchen table with a pair of scissors and a bottle of glue, wistfully fingering the small squares of cloth before me.

"Actually," I tell them, "there might be someone next week."

The midnight rambler, they ask. No, not the midnight rambler, I say. Someone who has a job. A job, they say. A landscape architect, I tell them. With a nice house in the country. A job and a house, they say.

But is he funny, they ask. They have to be smart and funny. And single, they say. Is he single and available?

Apparently, I say.

Forget the midnight rambler, they say.

I tell them I already have.

We watch the film and moan in our seats, mostly with envy over Andie's sexual awakening with the bad boy.

I think of Ben and then I scold myself.

I repeat — *I'm too old for bad boys, I'm too old for bad boys* — and then I sigh with the rest of them when Andie cries out with pleasure.

I didn't tell them that I preferred bad boys and that the someone else was someone I was willing to meet because Eliza wore me down with her unwavering persistence. "Mom, he's a hunk and he has a job!" "Mom, he has a big house, and a nice car, and he loves art!" "Mom, he's not a loser. Go out with him. Janey told him you're cool. She doesn't know any better."

My daughter chipped away at me with her not-so-subtle subtext. That — aside from her father — I'd never been with a man of substance, someone who could live up to her high standards, which she said weren't so high at all. Mine were just too low, flat on the ground as a matter of fact, stomped on really, practically non-existent, she said.

The next time Janey came over to our house I found myself sizing him up, taking in his daughter's dark brown eyes and her black hair and her heart-shaped face. Eliza said Janey was the spitting image of her father, and not her bitchy, stuck-up mother, who was living with some twenty-something computer junkie she'd been having cyber-sex with over the Internet, who just moved up from Montana so he could fuck her in person.

I was shocked, not so much by Eliza's directness and lack of embarrassment to even bring the subject up, but by her observation and conclusion — the way cynicism and unromantic reality had already made their ugly way into her young life. She was probably right. Janey's bitchy mother and her young lover were likely all heat and flame under the covers. That made it worse. To suddenly know nothing could make it past my daughter. Nothing in the lives of those she hardly knows, even less in my own life.

She is only seventeen and skinny as a rail — her body burdening her with growing breasts and menstruation and the pain and the mess and the inherent dangers that come with it — its lurking complexities still incomprehensible but hanging, nonetheless, above her head, out of reach.

It seemed to arrive all at once, even though it was really over the course of a few years. Her periods. Her burgeoning knowledge. Her pity for me. I had, she informed me, made too many bad choices. What was wrong with me, anyway? Didn't I like decent guys?

How could I say anything but yes — yes, I'll go out with him.

The first night I get together with Jonah, he tells me it wasn't really our daughters' idea to fix us up — it was his. He says it with a sureness that makes me feel chosen, hand-picked with as much care and enthusiasm as the impeccable antiques he has filling the rooms in his custom-built house — a house with a view on a cliff in the country — a home he designed himself. He tells me he made up his mind when he saw me making my way through the farmers' market once with Eliza. He recognized her and assumed I was her mother.

"It was the way you handled the zucchini," he jokes. "I knew then that I wanted you, that I had to have you."

Smart *and* funny, I think to myself, making a note to tell my film friends. I can already hear Grace's appreciation for the great line about zucchini.

He gives me the tour and shows me his many works of art — paintings and sculptures, which he talks about in a soulful, thoughtful way — the way Johnny Marks used to talk about the faces of the old men and old women he carved in the fence posts.

"I'm a collector," Jonah says, "of beautiful things."

We walk from room to room, viewing and stroking the smooth marble surfaces of a woman's shoulder and a man's thigh, and the rounded ass of a donkey kneeling before the gods, an empty Moses basket strapped to its back and a tattered teddy bear lying inside.

"Kind of tears you in two, doesn't it?" he asks. "Makes me think of sacrifice, or blind obedience. I've never been sure which."

"Something given up," I say.

"Then prayed for," he adds. "Isn't that always the way?"

I find out that his impressive house was never the matrimonial home. That he built it and furnished it and adorned it himself. That his ex preferred large bungalows with contemporary touches and he was more the nostalgic type, a lover of all things old. I think of Ben's shack and the ratty furniture and I decide I've liked bad boys for long enough.

I find him physically attractive, but I am just as aroused by his natural talent for making his surroundings so harmonious. And his shirts are clean and wrinkle-free and I can't see any signs of clumpy laundry detergent.

We talk about land and art and the particular challenges of raising teenage daughters. He tells me Janey lives with him most of the time and stays in town with her mother only occasionally, ever since the young boy moved in. That's what Jonah calls him, "the young boy from Montana." It softens the underlying emotion, as it's clear by the way he rolls his eyes that he doesn't approve of his ex-wife's sexual escapades with someone half her age, even though they are divorced, and according to Janey, not on speaking terms at all.

What can I say? I can hardly snicker and sneer, and I'm not about to explain the allure a younger man can have. I've fallen for it myself. I decide I'm not going to tell him that. Or that Hal used to roll his eyes the same way about me. It's what ex's do.

Thankfully, Jonah drops the subject and I am off the hook and don't have to pretend to be something I'm not, hiding behind a hypocritical mask — righteousness, and all that. I am relieved when we return to the subject of teenage daughters, this being our most obvious common ground.

"I try not to clip Janey's wings," he says, "but tell me. Is it possible for her to sit and neck with someone on that couch for an entire day without it leading to something else?"

"Not forever," I tell him.

"I hardly remember what it was like at that age," he says. "Sex, I mean."

"They tend to fall in love," I say.

"Now that you mention it, she does have that glazed over look in her eyes," he says. "And I've noticed she's been banging into more walls lately. I thought her feet had just grown and she hadn't realized it."

"In your teens and twenties, it's always about love," I tell him.

"I see," he says, crossing his legs, resting his chin on one hand, tilting his head, leaning in casual amusement over the direction our conversation has taken. I am grateful for the chance to talk about sex and love, having already exhausted everything I can say about oils and marble, and so I go on to tell him that when a young girl or young woman sleeps with a guy, she usually tells herself that he loves her — the *I love him, he loves me* thing — how it all changes in your thirties and becomes less about him, more about yourself. What I want. How often I want it.

I am aware of my own arrogance, speaking for all women everywhere, as though we are one big glob of female — this is what it looks like, this is how it thinks. "At least, that's what it was like for me," I add, "and some other women I know," just to narrow it down, chop the glob in half, set the other 50 percent free to claim it's about something else.

"And in your forties?" he asks, sitting upright, meeting my eyes, sending the rest of my dwindling cohorts scattering, heads down, bailing on me. He's cut to the chase; I paved the way, leaving my immediate future hanging before me, ripping the generalizations right out of me. Leaving me on my own, frantically searching for my personal opinion. If it isn't just about love, and it isn't just about personal satisfaction, what is it about?

Before I can even think of speaking, I think about shutting up, about not saying anything, which is what I would prefer at this point. For once Sadie McCann is choosing not to speak. Choosing? Or accepting? Accepting the failure of spoken language.

"In your forties, it's about communicating," I finally say, "about what you no longer have to say, or can say," as if I'm not entirely sure of what it is I'm saying, that I just couldn't think of anything else.

He smiles, either to reassure me, or because it sounds just as unclear to him, maybe even ridiculous — a real stretch even for someone as socially generous as he appears to be. He offers me another drink and doesn't seem to be in any hurry to end the evening. I decide whatever I said must have made some sense to him.

And the more I think about it — while I am left alone in his living room, left to fidget with my hands and wait in silence in the intimate space he created long before I ever came along — the more it makes sense to me. This need to communicate, skin to skin.

What can be said?

What needs saying?

Before the evening ends, Jonah kisses me. We stand near the wall of windows overlooking the valley below his house. He has shut the lights off behind us, to erase our reflections, so we can see the miniature lights from the farms below and the distant cluster of sparkling beads that map out the town. There is passion in his kiss and I respond with a desire that has been building for hours, fuelled by the oily nudes in framed canvases and the etched genitalia in the black and white marble, shelved and winking at me from various corners of the room. I am expecting it to go somewhere, but Jonah pulls back and cups my face in his hands and tells me, "There'll be plenty of time for sex."

It feels more like a deliberate interruption than a respectable period of waiting. "Sure," I say. "It can wait."

Grace would say he was behaving like a gentleman.

He's smart and funny, and he has manners.

Alex would say he's just relishing the anticipation while it lasts.

Which won't be for long, I think, as I leave. We have already made another date. My house. In three days. My kids will be at Hal's for the night.

I can wait, I can wait, I can wait.

When I get home, I discover Eliza has been waiting up for me. She opens the back door before I can reach the handle.

"So?" she says, before I even cross the threshold. "Isn't he a hunk?"

I step inside and in the light I can see the hopefulness and weariness on her face.

"He's very attractive."

She follows me through the kitchen and all the way up the stairs to my room, follows me in the darkness as I turn the lights off in every room I pass through.

"Are you going to see him again?" she asks from behind me.

"Wednesday," I say, and I admit I am glad that I can say it, that another date has already been set.

"Wednesday," she repeats, counting the number of days off in her head. I can hear the surprise in her voice as she says it and I tell myself, she forgets what I'm like, that I can be charming and captivating, even to a man like Jonah.

"Have you been waiting up for me?" I ask when we reach the top of the stairs and I have a chance to see the distance and disapproval in her eyes and I realize I'm no longer the mystery I once was for her. That the little girl gleam in her eyes will probably never greet me again.

"No," she says. "I had homework."

I no longer cook the right food, or use the right words. I don't wear the right makeup. She hates the way I leave the clothes in the washer for too long, or that I forget about them completely. She finds them scrunched up and wet, still sticking to the sides the next morning. She yells and accuses me of ruining them on purpose, says that I'm not paying her the respect she deserves, I've abandoned her, insulted her. My explanations of absent-mindedness or just plain busyness are scoffed at, unacceptable. I'm expecting too much tolerance and forgiveness from her.

"So it went well?" she asks, sitting on my bed.

"I think so," I say.

"You don't know?"

"I think it did."

"Well, how can you not know? It either did or it didn't."

"It seemed to go well," I say.

"Seemed? As in, not definitely."

"As in, I'm not a mind reader. From my perspective, it was a good night."

She gets up and stands by my dresser while I change — my answer too ambiguous for her to figure out, although I can see that she is trying. What exactly did that mean? Weren't Jonah's actions and reactions clear enough? What is wrong with me that I can't say for sure, without uncertainty, that the evening went well? What is wrong with me, she's trying to figure out with her tight mouth and her watchful eyes — what have I possibly done wrong to come home with nothing to say except, "It seemed to go well."

I have become a burden every bit as itchy and as painful to her as her swelling breasts. A daily reminder of what the future may hold for her if she doesn't get it right, doesn't memorize me and take stock of my faults and make a mental note to become someone else entirely.

What is wrong with me that I can't just say the evening went well, without feeling the need to add my own perspective? As if even a simple statement like "it went well" needs justification and ownership — a disclaimer that it is only my opinion. Not necessarily shared by anyone else.

I go to bed with the same question on my mind, wondering if it was there before or if Eliza planted the seed of doubt with her insistence that the night had to have gone one way or another, that I was being deliberately vague.

It *seemed* to go well.

Why wasn't that good enough, even for myself?

Somewhere between Sunday evening and Wednesday afternoon I decide I won't live with him. I'll still keep my own house and divide my time between the two. Our kids will become the best of friends. Eliza will have a sister, and once Adam gets over his crush on Janey, he'll have two younger sisters to look out for, to study and use as reference points as he tries to fathom the peculiar habits of the female species.

"You're obsessing again," Jenny spits at me when we meet on the street.

I decide we'll spend all of the holidays together, probably at his house — it's bigger than my house and it's in the country where holidays like Christmas and Thanksgiving should be spent. I'll cook. Jonah will mix the drinks and nibble the back of my neck while the kids go skiing or snowboarding down the hill behind his house. Music will play softly in the background. Snow will fall gently on the evergreens outside the kitchen window. We'll fall hard into a fit of lust on the kitchen floor while the turkey's spread legs lie waiting for my mother's famous oyster stuffing, and I'll believe in miracles all over again.

My Storyteller's Jacket will be complete with patches of blue Oxford cloth filling in the remaining empty spaces, rightfully claiming a prominent place. I'll hang it up in the back of my closet, next to other garments I no longer have a use for but can't bear to throw away — a memoir of my own making, in a coded language only I can understand.

"You can take him to parties," Del says over the phone, and it's true. I wouldn't have to stand in a corner and whisper the details of my latest affair, which, of course, demanded silence and discretion, for there was somebody else on the scene — wasn't there always somebody else on the scene?

I can take him to parties, and I can take him home, where my mother and Aunt Viv will fuss over him, and my Aunt Ruth will blush in his presence, and Gran will just come right out and say he's the best thing that's ever happened to me. What the hell took me so long? My father

will sit with him outside in the shed and drink beer and talk
about the land before them.

Hal will have to stop saying that I only attract losers.

Janey reported to Eliza that Jonah thought we got
along well. Eliza reported to Janey that I thought things
seemed to go well. They decided their efforts were
successful and I slipped in and out of visions of Jonah for
the next three days — watching myself make elaborate
meals in his kitchen, stretching the lust of early sex into
years of gratification. Letting myself give in to the rush, to
the chance that this time I just might let myself be taken. I
just might.

I'm getting dressed upstairs. Eliza is sifting through my
jewellery box, pulling out every pair of earrings, every bracelet
I own. "Why do you have to wear such big earrings?" she asks.
"What's with all the silver and turquoise, anyway?" "Don't you
have anything gold, anything classic?"

I watch her finger rings and bracelets she once begged me
to wear and remember her bony girl arms lined with bangles
of every colour — her small body wrapped in what she used
to call my gypsy clothes, then my cool clothes, until she grew
into calling them anything but clothes — drapery or funky
table linen.

"Isn't it time you went to your father's?" I finally ask.
Jonah is scheduled to arrive in less than an hour and I need
the time to regain my composure, to dress myself without my
daughter's disdain for my particular style, which is, she has no
problem saying, odd and unattractive and out-of-date. I need
time alone to purge her judgement and my own, to stave off
the feelings of impending doom. I sense that everything
good about that first night with Jonah could evaporate the
minute he arrives, because of this hour. This hour when I
need to silence my mind, to let in the flutter of birds and the
sound of disentanglement swaying on the wire above my
head, swaying in the screaming heat of an August afternoon.

Everyone has their place of return.

I try working my way back. Eliza clutters my path. I sit on my bed and remember how much easier it was when she was a young child — when my dates were once called dental appointments and doctor's appointments and nights out with some friends. Hidden, underground romances. Kept that way to protect my kids — in the days when the measure of my worth as a woman wasn't tied up in what I wore. When I wasn't the easy target I am now, and have been, ever since I bravely made the move from perceived asexual, nurturing mother to self-proclaimed woman with desires — who also happens to be a mother.

"I can dress myself, Eliza. I've been doing it for years."

She throws a pair of bamboo hoops across the room. "I'm only trying to help," she snaps before she leaves in a huff, knocking the clothes I've chosen to wear right off their hangers, off the door to my room where I had hung them only moments ago.

I don't bother chasing her. I yell instead. Yell to the heavy footsteps and the drawer slams and the whispered "fucking bitches."

"Don't forget your overnight bag!" I say. "I love you!"

"I just want to get dressed by myself!"

"Some day you'll understand!"

She walks out of the house without acknowledging a thing I've said, lets the screen door slam against my unwanted explanation, leaves me with the struggle of it — conjuring up the birds, the flutter, the smell of the sun-bleached earth at my feet as I walk Johnny Marks to his truck — remaining still, while the rest of me is already running after Eliza, swooping down on her with my repenting mother-arms while she defiantly looks the other way.

So much for getting dressed in peace.

Nothing about the night goes as I think it should. Eliza has stomped out of the house. I feel uncomfortable in my own clothes. Jonah shows up as someone else. Someone intense and jumpy, in a hurry to get past the first few minutes of the night, pecking me with a perfunctory kiss, walking past me into my kitchen, setting a brown bag down on the counter.

"Nice house," he says without looking around. "Do you
have a corkscrew?"

He opens a bottle of wine and pours two generous
glasses, takes his down in four or five gulps. I sip away and
watch him proceed to get drunk — first on red wine, then
on some single-malt Scotch I splurged to buy. He becomes
less jumpy and more talkative than I've seen him before, less
tentative about personal matters, less interested in his
surroundings, forceful really, bulldozing his way into the
details of my previous encounters.

Am I to judge this as a drastic change in personality?

I only have one other night to go on. Yet something has
changed since then and I begin to wonder if he's had his
own fantasies about me in the last few days, and if this has
made him uncomfortable, if I make him uncomfortable.

Was it something I said?

Did I greet him with too much enthusiasm?

We sit on the couch in my living room and I try to focus
on the few objects of art I have in my home, pointing to
some marble sculptures given to me by an old lover. But
Jonah is more interested in talking about my sexual history
and the histories of other women he's known — vividly
recalling their personal quirks for me. Speaking of them
fondly in the past tense, the way a person talks about their
children — grown up and gone — their annoying antics
distant enough to make them humorous.

I am surprised by how many women there've been. It
seems Janey's father hasn't been the poor lonely dad his
daughter thinks he is.

"I try to keep her sheltered from my relationships. You
know how it is. Why make them live through it, too?"

I wonder what he means by "live through it." He makes
a date sound like an ordeal. Perhaps, some of them were for
him. I could say the same for myself. I wrestle with the tone
he used when he said it and have another sip of Scotch and
decide that what he said could just as easily be interpreted as
an act of devotion to his daughter, a selfless gesture meant to
hide his bumpy journey to companionship.

And so I let myself be persuaded by his unflinching confidence, by his unfailing commitment to Janey, persuaded enough to smile and even call him thoughtful.

He is smart *and* funny, I remind myself.

And good looking, I can hear Grace saying.

And responsible, I hear Storm adding.

And he likes good Scotch, I hear Jenny yelling to me from the front porch of her house further down my street.

I decide all his talk about sex is just a prelude to the real thing. He rubs my feet and begins to kiss me in between all the questions and the answers, chugging Scotch and running upstairs to the bathroom in half-hour intervals. I forgive his overindulgence and his boldness, his lack of poetic comment, his teetering politeness, and blame it on too much drink and nervousness, brush over it with my overzealous desire to have him remain the possibility I thought he was.

He seems particularly interested in discussing the conditions of unions, the miscalculation that often precipitates quick departures, the nature of love's selfish impositions, and lust's copulative jig with self-abandonment. I can hardly keep up with him and think I've had too much Scotch for this kind of talk. Couldn't we just have sex?

"Everyone has an agenda in mind," he says. "You can't tell me otherwise," he argues even though I haven't disagreed. I haven't said anything, one way or another. I am only listening — listening to this person who insists that nothing in love or lust is unorchestrated, only forsaken when nothing else works.

"What about going with the flow?" I venture.

"Rivers flow. People don't," he says. "People will swim against the current if they think it'll get them what they want."

He goes upstairs to pee again. I can feel the Scotch swimming in my head and my libido is almost ready to go to sleep for the night, but what a waste that would be, I think to myself. So I light all the candles in my living room and open another bottle of wine and when Jonah comes downstairs, I suggest he spend the night. I tell him he's too drunk to drive and he grins and nods and holds back his urge to laugh at our silliness, our formality. As if it hadn't already been decided hours ago, about the time he walked through my front door. Probably before — the other night when I was told he had stood across the street watching me check the firmness of a large zucchini, relying on my sense of touch to tell if it was good or bad.

"I love the symbolism," Grace had said.

We make out on the couch after an unhurried, painfully slow ritual of undressing — something he chooses, something he guides. He comes in less than five minutes. I have barely started.

It happens, I tell him.

He passes out after that — his energy fizzled and spent. I go to sleep unsatisfied and wake up an hour later beside another version of this man of vision, of beautiful things — his angry mouth closed and screwed up in worry. His forehead the fleshy replica of a miniature washboard. Short, sustaining breaths banging weakly against the thin skin of his whimpering nostrils.

I take the package of cigarettes he has brought with him and go outside to sit on my front porch. I see myself silhouetted against the white funnel of a street light — from his point of view — the way he would see me if he sat up and opened the curtain and found me there, on the other side of self-abandonment, drained by lust's premature ejaculation.

I sit and I listen to what remains of the night. To the sound of the odd car turning a corner on some other street, comparing its distant, lethargic motion to the dangerously close and repetitive whipping whirl of a common night hawk diving for insects, impaling the sultry air with speed and skill.

The smell of myself keeps rising up every time I shift in my seat or put a foot up on a chair, exposing the aftermath of a failed union, the smell of contact edging me on with hope, with the surviving promise of something better the next time around. I fight to hang on to this even though I keep asking myself, Why do I feel so shitty? Why do I feel so shitty? Is it worth it?

Is any of it worth it?

After a while, I go back inside and spend the rest of the night upstairs. I fall into bed exhausted by the tightness in my muscles, by my refusal to let any of the answers come.

Sleep, Sadie. Sleep. Quit thinking. Quit talking to yourself. Just go to sleep.

In the morning, Jonah apologizes and invites me for dinner on Saturday. He will cook for me, he says. Do I like linguine and clam sauce? Please, he says. He wants to see me again. One more time, he says, just one more time.

I set aside last night's ambivalence and accept his invitation and close the door behind him with hope rising as the rest of the week goes by.

He's trying to make it up to you, Grace says.

At least he's not just going to disappear, like some people we know, Delaney adds.

And, fuck, he cooks, Jenny points out. He cooks.

There are wildflowers on the table, expensive sea foam-coloured linens, and antique crystal. Jazz plays loudly from every corner of every room. Do I like jazz? Would I prefer folk? Do I want salt and pepper on the table? Am I hungry?

The manic intimacy of the other night is being forfeited. We are starting over. The darkness and openness of our previous conversation, the disappointing sexual performance, the consoling and the scratching for forgiveness are no longer part of our short-lived history.

We are starting over.

He serves dinner and we talk about the professional dilemmas a landscape architect faces on a daily basis. The personal anguish he tells me he feels over ripping up the natural beauty of a wild tract of land to install an acre or two of the finest turf grass money can buy and a few conservatively placed rock gardens, usually with enough room for a couple of shrubs and an evergreen. I listen attentively and try to imagine what it must look like at his house in the winter and where he puts his Christmas tree, wondering if I'll still be around to find out.

"You must get a lot more satisfaction out of your work," he says, "teaching people how to read."

I help clear the table after dinner and we leave the dishes piled on the counter in the kitchen, Jonah insisting we leave them. Isn't it compulsive the way we're always in a rush to put things back in order?

"Order's never been a problem for me," I say.

"You mean you can live with the messes."

"I am a mess," I say, "if you call living by the rules order."

He changes the music, puts on Patsy Cline, and I feel the evening taking a turn in my favour.

"So you're a rebel?" he asks when he sits down beside me.

"No. But I like rebels," I say.

"So, what are you doing with me?" he asks and I have to wonder myself, with his orderly life and his respectable career and those perfectly ironed Oxford cloth shirts. I could say, You're a rebel in your own right. But it isn't true and it would be foolish to say he is. As if being a rebel is everything, anyway.

"I've never met a man who can make clam sauce like you can," I tell him, hoping he'll appreciate my comic side stepping. And he laughs, and he strokes the side of my face, and he pushes back a strand of hair and says, "Maybe you should stop looking for rebels and become one yourself."

"Then what happened?" Jenny asks.

We meet again during the last weekend of October.

Everyone is anxious to hear the story of Jonah, to get an update.

I am less than anxious to tell it, to go past the part where we fell to the Persian rug and made love for hours.

I talk about the movie Grace has brought — *Rachel, Rachel*, with Joanne Woodward. Naturally, it was Grace who brought it. She rented it the first time, too. It was the only

Margaret Laurence book ever made into a feature film, *A Jest of God.* I liked the book's title better. Isn't it better, I ask, as I ramble on. *A Jest of God.* And wasn't it shitty the way the virginal Rachel loses it to a guy who pretends to be something he isn't? I remember that part. I hated that part. You just don't know with some guys, do you?

Maybe you shouldn't go to Kauai, Sally.

Maybe Josh isn't who you think he is.

"Quit avoiding," Jenny snaps. "Tell us about Jonah."

"You mean the two-time guy," I say as I sip a beer and pull a patch of Oxford cloth out of my sewing box and try not to prick my finger as I thread the needle.

"Don't tell me he's dating someone else at the same time?" Grace asks.

"That would be the obvious," I say, "and there's nothing obvious about Jonah."

Silence.

I tell them about the linguine and clam sauce and the ripped buttons on the Oxford cloth shirt and how he didn't look like Johnny Marks, but he reminded me of him — the way he loved art and the way he challenged me, telling me to stop looking for rebels, to become one.

"That's something Johnny would have said."

I tell them that I was surprised later that evening, that in a horny rush to get down to business on the antique Persian rug below us, Jonah ripped the buttons right off his Oxford shirt — a true act of rebellion for someone like him, I thought, and I praised him for it. Not aloud, but in my own suspecting mind, to put to rest any resounding questions about why I was with him in the first place.

I tell them how sunrise woke us and found us still lying on the Persian rug and that I planted a kiss on Jonah's cheek, and excused myself, my bladder painfully reminding me of what I hadn't taken the time to do in the last twelve hours, when I was too busy making love.

When I returned to the living room, Jonah was gone, I say. I could hear him in the kitchen tackling the dinner dishes. His puddle of clothes had disappeared from the floor beside the couch. I put my own on and followed the sound of clinking glass and scraping plates.

"Good morning," he said as I walked in. He was trying to get the hardened clam sauce out of a pasta bowl. "Why don't you take a shower while I clean this mess up. Then I'll make you breakfast. An omelette okay?"

"Perfect," I said.

"I have an appointment at eleven," he said. "Sorry about the rush."

"An appointment on Sunday?" I asked.

"Some clients make life difficult," he said, and he continued clearing and scraping the dishes, shutting me out with the noise of it, with the task of cleaning up last night's disregard for orderliness.

I had my shower, I tell them. I came out and said nothing. I sat down at the table. The sea foam green napkins had been replaced by terracotta-coloured napkins. Jonah had put some classical music on. He was still wearing the same jeans and the same Oxford shirt, a few buttons were still hanging by dangling threads. He served the omelette, which was slightly burned on the bottom, and poured us both some coffee.

"Why don't you come over for dinner tonight, after your appointment?" I said to him.

"Can't," he said. "I'm taking Janey out."

"Maybe next weekend," I said, and I concentrated on the omelette and the coffee and tried not to pay attention to the way he stopped eating and pushed his plate away and sighed one of those here-we-go sighs.

"Sadie," he said, "there won't be a next time."

I swallowed and chewed and said as calmly as I could, "I thought we had fun."

"We did," he said, "and now it's done."

"Done?" Jenny says.

"That's what I said. Done. I'm sorry," he said.

"Did I do something wrong?"

"Nothing," he said.

"Then why end it now?" I asked him.

"Now. Later. What's the difference?" he said.

"He said that?" Delaney asks.

"What's the hurry?" I asked him.

"And what did he say?" Storm asks.

"He said he doesn't sleep with women more than twice," I say, and I can't describe how matter-of-factly he said it, so I leave that part out and keep to myself how he said it, as if I should have known this already, as if I should have said to him, Oh, okay — right. Shit, I wasn't thinking. Sorry about that, sweetheart. Instead, I asked him what the fuck he meant by that.

"What the fuck did he mean by that?" Sally asks.

"It means I have this rule," he said. "After I get a woman into my bed the second time, I don't bother anymore."

"You don't bother anymore?"

"I don't want any more."

"What kind of fucking rule is that?" I said.

"It's my rule," he answered.

"I don't get it," Alex says.

"He said he's a rebel in his own right, just not the kind I wanted him to be."

"He said that?" Delaney asks again.

"I never said it would go beyond this," he said.

"You never told me you had an agenda," I said.

"And you didn't!" he snapped back.

"I didn't deliberately set out to fuck your mind," I said.

"I'll leave that one alone," he said, and then he stood up and took his plate into the kitchen, left me sitting there wondering where the hell I was.

I tell them I went into the living room to pick up the rest of my things, found them scattered in the path of the morning's buttery rays that skipped along the Persian carpet and ran up the white walls — illuminating the paintings and the sculptures I had been so impressed with that first night. They were even more beautiful in the warm glow of creamy light, but now I could hear their conspiratorial whispers, revealing them as hand-picked props, part of the set design. Manufactured illusion.

I made my way down the hall into Jonah's bedroom and into his closet where I had noticed the row of Oxford shirts the night before. I chose the shirt closest to the open door, the one he'd reach for first. I removed a pair of compact scissors from my purse and cut a hole the size of my fist in one of the pockets — the left pocket — the heart pocket, so he'd hear my cries of foul play.

"You can't ever write about this," I tell Grace.

"I won't," she says, but I already have my doubts.

"If nothing else, I had expected him to be real," I say.

I don't bother telling them about the few minutes I spent at the front door of Jonah's house before I left. How I stood there listening to him tell me it didn't have anything to do with me — that I was a wonderful woman in every way. It was just a rule, something he didn't want to go into — I wouldn't understand, or maybe I would if I thought about it. He would like it if we could still be friends.

"Right," I said. "Uh-huh." And, "I don't think so." Monosyllabic answers to get me out the door so I could think, so I could take it in. He repeated his offer of friendship again, reminding me of the growing attachment between our daughters. From where I was standing, I could see the marble donkey sitting innocently on an end table, the sculpture Jonah said made him think of sacrifice, or blind obedience. Had he rehearsed that line? Or was it a slip, unrelated to the task at hand?

We start the film and watch the virginal Rachel fall willingly into the arms of a man who is pretending to be something he's not — or was it that he just hadn't told her everything?

Was he supposed to?

We watch, still feeling restless and out of sync with our lives as October comes to a close.

I decide on a blanket stitch — to put the whole thing to rest — and choose a place on my back, under my left shoulder blade, where I can still feel the wound, where it will be out of sight from my own eyes. Something remembered but not looked at often.

Jenny gets up several times for a refill and I am suddenly aware of the parallel stories that run through the film and her own life. The virgin. The man. The mother. The continuing threat of losing herself. *Jenny, Jenny.*

These Jests of God.

"I'm a collector of beautiful things," he had said.

I stitch his powder blue shirt onto my jacket and remind myself that art sometimes collides with life and then works its way back into art. Had I become part of his medium, just as he had become part of mine? That sounded like bullshit, even to me. But it gave it colour and shape and elevated it to tangible purpose. I had a place to put it. Besides, I tell myself, there's usually a grain of truth floating around in every load of crap. Fecal knowledge. Not necessarily worth knowing. Odorous and repulsive, even if it discharged from our own bodily life.

The shit we have to deal with, as Jenny would say. She drinks too much tonight. She passes out on my couch. I cover her with a blanket and leave her there. When everyone has gone home I go to bed and am awakened some time later to the sound of Jenny vomiting in my bathroom.

I clean her up and drag her into Eliza's empty bed.

"Are you okay?" I ask her when she moans and turns onto her side. "Go to sleep," I say as I lean over to brush the hair off her sticky face.

She giggles and motions for me to leave and mumbles things I barely understand. Something about caulking and bad toilet seats. Something else I can't make out at all.

I finally hear it.

As I stand in the doorway about to leave, after I've tucked her in and turned out the light, when she turns onto her back and takes her hands away from her mouth, I hear it in her boozy, weak, and delirious voice.

"I'm going to Hawaii," she says. "And I'm not coming back."

Jenny
LAKE PEOPLE

Chapter Ten

On a sunny Saturday in August, all Jenny could think about were the fish that must have spent their final moments gasping for breath in the bottom of her father's fishing boat. They'd left some of their shiny scales behind, floating in a shallow puddle near the middle, where a little lake water trickled in through an undetectable crevice. She put her feet up on the side of the boat to avoid them.

To look at her from afar, most people would think she was being dramatic, the way she was sprawled out, adorned with huge dark sunglasses and a straw hat with an exceptionally large brim — Queen of Catchacoma Lake, a woman of money being escorted to her summer home.

Summer home, my ass; the very thought almost made her laugh out loud.

Jenny was headed to The Cottage, a modest log shack

with cheap orange and green plastic lanterns strung across its narrow porch and a boathouse that sagged slightly to the right. If she looked dramatic, people would only say she was a little too much like her mother. That she'd inherited Georgia's flair for the exaggerated, riding in the boat as if she owned the lake. People on Catchacoma were used to Georgia's antics. They assumed Jenny would follow in her footsteps.

From the boat, Jenny waved to some of the lake people who have known her family for years — waved like the Queen of England — as her father rode the shoreline for a stretch before heading out to the middle of the lake. She tried to keep her balance when some waves suddenly appeared behind a larger, faster, more luxurious boat, which sped past them.

She tried to remain poised when the choppy water whacked the bottom of her father's small boat in steady hard-hitting rhythm. So hard she thought her tailbone was going to split in two right there on the aluminum seat, which didn't bend and didn't give, and hit her back with its steely coldness and nearly knocked her over.

When Jenny was halfway across the lake, a large cloud passed in front of the sun. It changed her train of thought — and transported her to woods where she could feel herself walking barefoot on a carpet of wet pine needles.

She should have been concerned — should have been watching out for the one needle that might be pointed upwards, its sharp prick threatening a sudden end to her blissful solitude. She should have been concerned, but she wasn't. She felt secure in the woods, assured that nature would not bring her harm. It was the same feeling she got when she heard the loons crying out from their lonely spots on the lake, and when she rode across the open water with her eyes closed.

She felt it in her spine.

The cloud passed, the light changed and put her back in the sunny present, in the middle of what was actually happening, at the edge of the next moment. She watched it come towards her. She forgot she was the one moving closer and closer to her immediate future. It was standing still waiting for her.

From her distant spot in the middle of the lake, Jenny noticed how small The Cottage looked. Smaller than it should. She tried to think back to the summer before, and the one before that. Surely, she had just forgotten this particular view. It must have crossed her mind before — the smallness of the place that loomed large even when she wasn't there — out there — on Catchacoma Lake, with the rest of her crew. One distant, uninterested husband, an aging, agreeable father, and two young daughters who still saw the place as bigger than it really was.

This was new, this attaching descriptions to everyone. Distant. Uninterested. Aging. Agreeable. She was no longer satisfied with saying — thinking — husband, father, daughters. Everything and everyone suddenly needed further explaining.

As they got closer, The Cottage still looked smaller than it should to Jenny until she realized the yellowy figure on the porch was her mother, wearing yellow shorts and a yellow top, sitting on the white and yellow lounge chair with a gin and tonic in her hands.

Even from a distance — even with the tired, steady hum of the Evinrude behind her — Jenny could hear the ice cubes clinking in the glass every time Georgia took a sip. The sound was that loud and that close.

On the evening of Day One at The Cottage, Jenny tucked her daughters, Rebecca and Katherine, into bed, in what used to be her room. The wooden particleboard on the floor was covered with a light dusting of sand carried in by the girls from the beach. "Bloody stuff gets in everywhere," her own mother used to complain when Jenny was young and tracked it in with regularity.

Jenny shoved most of it out of the way with the side of her shoe, pushed it under the beds Katherine and Rebecca were sleeping in.

The afternoon of Day One at The Cottage went as predicted. The girls swam. Jenny's father made dinner while her mother supervised from the lounger. Robert drank a few beers then passed out on the hammock near the water.

Once, when Jenny handed Georgia a freshlymade gin and tonic, she turned her arm just enough so her mother could get a good look at the bruises she'd been hiding earlier under a white gauze blouse. If Georgia saw them she didn't say anything.

Jenny kissed the girls goodnight then turned out the light on the small table between the two beds. In the darkness, she stood in front of the screened window overlooking the lake. With a child's eye, she saw the glow of the orange and green lanterns riding the surface of the black water. She stood there watching for a while, then whispered another round of goodnights to her daughters before she pulled herself away from the window. There was something about the lake and the way the trees swayed with indecision — *yes, no, yes, no* — something that stayed with her for most of the night.

On Day Two at The Cottage, Jenny asked her mother to show her how to make her famous peanut brittle.

"You mean to tell me, in all the years I've been making this bloody stuff, you never paid attention?"

"I had better things to do."

"And now you don't?"

"Now I want to know how you do it. The girls love it."

Georgia spent the next hour with Jenny, mixing ingredients with local gossip about Catchacoma Lake folk. "Word has it, Freda and Don's daughter, Edna, got herself pregnant. Imagine naming your kid Edna," Georgia ranted on. "Kind of suits her though, doesn't it? Looks just like her mother, too. Let's face it, that Freda has a face uglier than a warthog's ass."

It wasn't meant to be malicious, just colourful. "Why do people always have to be so damn boring when they talk," Georgia used to ask Jenny. "So polite and nice and sickeningly boring. Bore, bore, bore." Georgia considered it one of the great sins in life, to be a bore.

"You have to admit, though, that Freda's perfectly suited to that lard-ass husband of hers," Georgia continued with an air of superiority — not because she had it over Freda in the beauty department, but because she could talk that way and get away with it. She could criticize and joke and make it seem reasonable — right — challenging Jenny to say it any other way, making her the hypocritical one if she did. She couldn't dare say they weren't ugly people. Georgia had her there.

But why couldn't Georgia say she empathized with Freda, whose daughter Edna was young and unmarried and pregnant — in a real fix. Hadn't Georgia learned anything along the way?

Jenny wanted to ask her mother what made her so damn unsympathetic, but when she opened her mouth, something else came out. "Talk about the waste of a male gene," Jenny said, referring to Freda's husband, Don, and his lard-ass. It made her mother laugh approvingly, and it might have made Jenny feel good, like she'd won some kind of prize, if it hadn't felt so much like defeat.

One summer, Jenny asked the trees if she should sleep with her new boyfriend, Robert. They swayed in endless circles and kept reversing direction. She sat watching from the end of the dock until she was certain they'd given her a "yes." Then she stopped looking at them altogether, kept her eyes peeled on the boats riding the surface of the lake.

Jenny met Robert at a barn dance at her cousin Rachel's. She had just turned 19 and was home for the summer after another year at university in Montreal. Robert played bass guitar for a band that was made up of four self-taught musicians who drank too much and didn't work enough, and sounded best when you'd had a few yourself.

Rachel was dating the drummer, Pete. Jenny wasn't dating anyone. She hadn't had many dates in real life, only in her dream life, which she considered just as good at the time. There, she could end up in the arms of any man she chose — the handsomely disheveled editor of the school paper, the very sweet, very married English professor, or the reclusive Frenchman who lived in the apartment across the hall.

In the midst of their lovemaking, Jenny never saw their faces. She only saw bare backs and hair-covered legs and the curve of their buttocks. One was as interchangeable as the others in bed. Sometimes, she'd feel herself blushing when she met up with one of her dream lovers in real life. God, wasn't it great last night, she wanted to say.

Jenny's imagined trysts left her feeling intimate with men who barely remembered her name. Was she the only one who lived like that? It was too embarrassing to ask other girls, so she never bothered. Besides, they were all busy sharing the details of actual encounters. Why court humiliation? It was bad enough Georgia was always asking, "Are you still a virgin, darling?"

By the time Jenny met Robert, she was ready to try out her imaginary lovemaking techniques on the real thing. It became a goal she'd do anything to reach. Sex. Now. With him. Jenny calculated the quickest, most direct route to her destination of fornication was Robert's ego. Feed it. Get it used to the tiny tidbits she handed out, then when it was busy feasting on its own importance, let it think it has the power to seduce you.

Jenny was sure of herself. After all, she'd taught herself how to be right-handed before she was 10. No one else in the family was ever a lefty, Georgia had said many times. Her father once said he thought someone on his mother's side, a cousin or second cousin, might have been left-handed. No one in the immediate family was, Georgia repeated.

It took three years and many nights of tying her left hand behind her back and staying up to all hours practicing how to write with her right hand and brush her hair and open packages of gum. The process was so gradual her parents never even noticed until one day, years later, they were having lunch at a fancy restaurant for Jenny's thirteenth

birthday and she ate Poulet au Poire Crème with a solid
silver fork in her right hand.

When Jenny finally ended up in bed with Robert, it was
her left hand that explored his body. All her calculation and
concentrated efforts in altering the hand nature had given
her were lost in Robert's lusty appetite for another tidbit of
gratification. Any sense of self was swallowed up and freely
given to the thrusting and the hair-covered legs, and the
smooth buttocks. Every ounce of blood in her body went
rushing to the place where victory was about to come. And
it did. It was wet and sweet, even in its bloodied sting. Then
it left the room, along with Jenny's self-assurance that she
could control anyone or anything ever again.

On Day Three at The Cottage, Jenny and Georgia took the
boat across another section of the lake to Helen's Grocery.
Georgia had run out of tonic and limes. Jenny was on a
mission for the girls to get salt and vinegar chips.

Jenny sat at the rear of the boat, steering. Georgia was
in the front with her back to Jenny. She had tied a shocking
pink scarf around her hair to keep it from blowing on the
ride over. She turned her head from side to side, waving to
other lake people — some she'd known for over twenty-five
years, with whom she had shared births and barbecues,
deaths and drinks. She looked much older to Jenny. Her lips
were darkened with a deep red that only enhanced the lines
around her mouth and didn't go with the pink scarf at all.
Her eyes, hidden behind sunglasses too large for her face,
still squinted in the light as she spotted another summer
friend. Jenny could not remember what colour they were.
Blue-grey? Blue-green?

Georgia once told Jenny she made a mistake having a
child. Not that Jenny was a disappointment — just
something she really shouldn't have bothered doing in her
life. Georgia always believed she was destined to be a poet.
As a young woman, she had grand plans to travel to Europe
and learn her craft. A bold dream for someone who came

from the small hamlet of Minto — population twenty-six, if
you include the Reid's eleventh child who died before his
sixth birthday after being hit by a car. The way everyone
talked so much about him, he was still part of their lives, even
though his tiny, bent, and busted body lay beneath a tall
willow behind his house.

In my darkest hours
I think not of what I have
I obsess about my nails
What else matters
In the darkest hours
When what I have isn't what I am.

Jenny found the poem at The Cottage when she was 12, in
the back of the utensil drawer between a collection of flour-
dusted, butter-stained recipe cards. At the time, instead of
empathizing with her mother, Jenny could only think of her
father. What if he found it? How would he feel?

Russell Ridgeway was a hard-working man, an air
inspector for the government. A simple, genuine sort of
man, whose life changed when he met a petite redhead with
a penchant for drama. Georgia married Russell because
everyone thought she should. Russell married Georgia
because everyone thought he shouldn't.

Jenny contemplated throwing the poem out but couldn't
bring herself to. Her father never did the dishes anyway, and
he never reached in behind the utensil tray to find recipes.
He'd never find it, she thought, so she carefully placed it
back in the drawer between some recipes for carrot muffins
and honey-garlic chicken breasts.

Jenny and Georgia spent an hour at Helen's, which was
easy to do with Helen filling their ears about this person and
that person. She poured them both a shot of rye from a
bottle she kept below the cash. They drank from Styrofoam
coffee cups and added a splash of Coke so other lake people
who came into the store wouldn't notice.

Jenny played along with their self-deception every
time she went to Helen's. Only once did she ever point
out that people might be suspicious because their pretend

cups of hot coffee weren't steaming. They only fizzled with carbonated bubbles.

"No one pays that much attention," Georgia said, annoyed that Jenny even brought it up.

"Where'd you get those?" Helen asked, spying the bruises on Jenny's arm. They were more of a muted green by then, on their way to fading from existence. "You climbing the birches now, too?" she asked, snickering, turning away from Jenny's arm, winking at Georgia who was well known for perching herself on trees after a few drinks.

Georgia and Helen started laughing, recalling one white birch that was particularly difficult for Georgia to climb down at the Mayer's annual barbecue last year. The bark was still slippery from a morning sprinkle. Helen wasn't really interested in where Jenny's bruises came from. She had already moved on, never giving Jenny a chance to answer the question.

Jenny left the two women and their tree stories and their cold, fizzing coffees, and walked through Helen's store, filling a shopping basket with salt and vinegar chips and limes and tonic, and one of those romance novels you can read in a day — the kind you can half-read and leave behind at The Cottage and it doesn't matter. You already know how it's going to turn out.

After that first summer with Robert — the summer she lost her virginity — the next year of university was a blur. Jenny lived for the weekends when she could go home and sleep with Robert, who was playing with regularity by then at Shrine Clubs and Lions Clubs and the odd bar in the area.

Robert never went to Montreal, though he'd heard there were good strip clubs there. Jenny often dreamt of riding a Kalesh up the Mountain in the winter with Robert's arm wrapped around her. She pictured Robert as romantic and caring, and apologetic for not phoning, appalled that Jenny would even think the rumours about his one-night stands were true.

The truth was, Robert never apologized for anything, especially for what he did when Jenny wasn't around. He didn't need a ball and chain, he said. He needed a good time and freedom. If she loved him, she'd trust him. Didn't she know she was the only one he really cared about? No, it wasn't just the beer talking. I love yah, baby. C'mon let's stop all the bullshit. Let's fool around. C'mon, My. That's what he called her — My. *My* baby, *my* woman, *my* girl.

Jenny liked being *his*. It came at a price — but what didn't, she told herself every time he changed his plans at the last minute and forgot to call her. Like an underdressed woman waiting for a bus on a chilly winter's night, Jenny watched the clock and made herself think only of the warmth she'd feel once she stepped inside its narrow body. Content and safe, she'd ride past the rest of the world unaware of any previous discomfort. Then Robert would whirl by the next day, splashing frigid lies all over her thin coat, barely slowing down long enough to notice she didn't buy a word.

Being *his* meant being adaptable, she told herself.

If Robert taught Jenny adaptability, she taught him good grammar. After making love on weekends, Robert would take out his acoustic guitar and share his works in progress with her. He'd have songs written on folded pieces of lined paper stained with coffee or alcohol of one sort or another. She'd correct his grammatical errors and his spelling mistakes.

"That's why we're a good team, My," he always said. And in the aftermath of their lovemaking, sharing cigarettes and commas, tenderness found its way into the moment. Jenny knew Robert didn't share his songs with anyone else. He never even played them in public. Despite his apparent arrogance and beer-induced cockiness, Robert wasn't really sure of much in life, much less himself. Jenny knew that. It's what made him forgiveable.

On Day Four at The Cottage it rained. Katherine and Rebecca watched the only station the small black and white television had to offer. "Bonanza" reruns. "I Love Lucy." "Carol Burnett."

Jenny made poached eggs for breakfast. Georgia and Robert played euchre. Russell finished a complicated jigsaw puzzle.

Later that morning, Jenny lay down upstairs with her romance novel. Not in the guest's room where she slept with Robert, but in the girls' room — her old room where the window was open and she could hear the rain falling on the lake. Where the smell of the towering pines drifted in on the cool wet air and stroked her face with a reminder of how things used to be. She read for just a few minutes then abandoned the longings of a fictional woman in a fictional life. She watched the raindrops disappear into the grey tones of the lake and the woods. Even the green needles on the pines seemed subdued and barely stood out from the rest of the colourless scene.

For a while, the slate was wiped clean.

In the afternoon, Georgia decided to paint the girls' nails and do their hair in French braids. Russell and Robert stood before the map of Catchacoma Lake, which hung on the wall under a large, stuffed bass, and planned their early evening fishing trip. Jenny baked a strawberry-rhubarb pie then drew a hot bath.

She left the light off, preferring the softness of the grey day on the other side of the window to the harshness of the two sixty-watt bulbs above the sink. Before the tub was filled, she undressed and stood before the mirror and kept turning until her eyes caught the bruises on her back.

It was the first time Robert ever hit her. She didn't know what to do with it. Forgive him? Forget it? He had grabbed her arm, squeezed it hard, then he punched her several times in the back when she turned away. She heard his fist before it ever landed above her kidneys.

It had started off like any other argument, the usual verbal tug of war. But then he grabbed her, and hit her, and hit her again. He said he was sorry — a minute later, an hour later, that night, the next morning. He seemed scared.

He was drunk, he said. Drunk and frustrated. He said he didn't want to go to The Cottage again. It was too late, she said. Her parents were expecting them. The girls were looking forward to it. Besides, they couldn't afford to go anywhere else. It was either The Cottage or no vacation at all.

He didn't want to go, he said, again and again and again.

The argument took place a few nights before they left for The Cottage, when Jenny was racing around the house doing laundry and packing, after working all day, baking cakes and pies for a private school in Belleville. Robert's real estate career had its ups and downs. Half of his head was in it. The rest was picking away at the strings on his guitar. They had just bought a house on the nicest street in Stirling, where the maples laid a red carpet along the sidewalk in the fall. Jenny had to help out. That's how she did it — baking cakes and pies for local restaurants and catering companies and the school children of a few well-off parents.

Robert had gone out for a few drinks with some other agents. Jenny knew he was in a bad mood as soon as he walked in the door. Robert wasn't hard to read, just hard to live with. He was hot-tempered and unpredictable, but he was never a bore. At one point during the argument, Jenny almost said, "Okay, we won't go." But as she gave in on most disagreements, she didn't want to that time. It happened like that every now and then. Something surfaced. She knew it was going to be a bad fight. They'd had them before whenever she mustered the strength to stand her ground, which wasn't often. She didn't have the energy for it most of the time.

Had he really gone that far, she thought to herself when it was over. It seemed like someone else's nightmare. A friend, maybe. She would tell her to leave. She would say, it's only the beginning. She would say, leave now — it'll only get worse.

It wasn't until Jenny climbed into bed that night after the argument that she felt the full force of his blows — when she slid between the sheets, when Robert climbed in beside her as if nothing had happened, he had a right to be there. It wasn't until then that all her friendly advice and gentle warnings for an imaginary friend rose up as panic inside herself — when she finally admitted that, yes, it had happened to her.

If she had let it go, it wouldn't have happened. If she hadn't looked him in the eye and told him to go fuck himself — if she hadn't turned her back towards him.

Jenny lowered herself into a tub of hot water in The Cottage bathroom — so hot the water made her skin itch. She could feel it turning red and wished it would peel off a layer or two. Peel off the bruises. And the other invisible marks he had left all over her body — from the invisible touches, the invisible caresses that once upon a time were clearly there — telltale signs of the love that used to exist between them.

She wanted them all to be gone and done with.

When Jenny finished university, she came home immediately. She told her parents she wasn't sure what she wanted to do. She decided to take a year to think things over and took a job at Annie's Country Inn as a waitress, where she also helped out with cakes and pies.

One night Robert showed up at her parents' house in his old white Volkswagen Beetle. He was drunk. It was almost midnight. Jenny argued with her father briefly about being adult enough to make her own decisions while Georgia slept through the entire discussion. Jenny left with Robert and they drove out of town along some dirt roads, drinking lemon gin.

Robert pulled over when they reached the top of a steep hill on Boundary Road, where daylight provided a clear view of the quilted farmland below and the thin ribbon of road that split it down the middle. At night it disappeared and laid as a seamless black blanket that ushered the eye upwards in search of whatever light still flickered and twinkled above, to keep the darkness from completely taking over.

When Robert turned the engine off, the world narrowed. The road and the trees and the thick grass seemed to push Jenny towards the midnight sky, which felt reachable to her if she stretched her arm out the window far enough. It was perfectly silent out there on Boundary Road, except for the chorus of crickets and the sound of lemon gin making its way down Robert's throat.

"Pete knocked Rachel up." Robert passed the bottle to Jenny, jarring her out of her own thoughts. "I wasn't supposed to say anything, but what the hell. You'll find out anyway."

"But Rachel never — "

"She just found out today."

"I can't believe it."

"What can't you believe? How do you think these things happen?" Robert put his hand on Jenny's thigh and squeezed it tightly.

"What are they going to do?" Jenny asked, before she took another swig of gin — a long swig, not the short almost-nothing swigs Robert always teased her about taking.

"Pete's going to marry her." He took the bottle from her hands and sucked on the end and looked at her while he did it.

"He is? You mean he asked her already?"

"What did you think he'd do? You think he'd just say 'fuck you' and go lay some groupie hanging out at the bar?" He took another swig then passed the bottle back to Jenny.

"What would you do?" she asked, then immediately wished she hadn't. She wanted to round up the words that had so easily slipped past her, exposing her need for reassurance that what she was experiencing with Robert was real and wouldn't end up as some vague memory he'd recall, years later, as he drove along Boundary Road.

Robert took the bottle from Jenny's hands and swallowed before he spoke. "I'd never leave you. You know that." He put the cap back on the bottle, threw it on the floor near the gas pedal, and began unbuttoning her blouse. It seemed a fitting prelude to sex — this unexpected declaration that left no need for further conversation.

As they made love in the warmth of the cramped quarters of the car, Jenny let herself hear it over and over again. She worked hard to retain the pacing of his words, to remember the particular note he ended on, where he had placed the emphasis — *I'd never leave you* or *You know that* — until she wasn't sure how he had said it, what it had sounded like exactly. And so it became something else — lyrics to the music of the crickets, accompanied by the cries of satisfied lovers, muddled and mixed up with everything else. In the morning it would be lost entirely, when her own voice would take over once again and remind her that her period was already a few days late.

Day Five at The Cottage. Jenny woke up early and was eager to take a morning walk. The sun was a soft, golden yellow, stretching sleepy arms across the sky, touching clouds as they gently blew by, stringing the unknown of a new day behind them. Jenny loved sunrise. She was like her father that way. Georgia preferred sundown and slept late every day. Russell was an up-at-the-crack-of-dawn person.

Jenny found her father standing at the end of the dock sipping on a cup of coffee, standing before the lake that had been his place of solace for most of his married life. It didn't ask anything of him. It didn't have need for conversation and gossip and reassurance and constant understanding and rearranging, or moments of ugly truth, and years of self-deception and mutual deception and willingness to swallow it all, knowing he could have just walked away and left the whole damn mess behind.

Russell always got up early and went fishing. When he came back, Georgia had usually had a good breakfast waiting for him, and a kiss and a smile. He detected love in that smile, or at the very least, some sort of affection. It made his heart strong for the long day of antics and God-knows-what ahead. Maybe that was it. Maybe he was still there because she needed him and he knew it, even if she never told him and went out of her way to try to prove otherwise.

Jenny could still remember the first time her mother ever perched herself on a tree in public. She was only fifteen. They were at a hootenanny near Macky's Landing and all the lake people were there. Something had changed between that summer and the previous one. Georgia had begun acting younger and seemed liberated by the freedom of her rediscovered youthfulness. She started wearing lots of jewellery, and she began shopping in used clothing stores for "something different." She wanted to be different, she said.

Georgia danced at the hootenanny. So did everyone else. Georgia drank and sang loudly. So did everyone else. The night pushed on with the adults mingling and carrying on as adults do, and children of all ages were running around out of control, getting away with things they normally couldn't.

Jenny was sitting with Donna and Carole Dunning on a grassy hill beside the dance floor watching all the boys when everyone suddenly started pointing to a large birch tree nearby. There, sitting near the top of the tree, was her mother, with one leg resting on a large white limb, the other dangling in mid-air. Georgia was waving at her audience, holding up her drink, toasting her own victory, being the one who could stand out.

Russell laughed with the rest of the crowd. What else could he do? Scold her? Ground her for the rest of the summer? Yell? Fight? She'd only remind him of how much she gave up to give him a good home and the child he wanted so badly. Jenny laughed, too, but only after Donna and Carole told her she was lucky to have a crazy mother who wasn't boring, always telling her what to do. Jenny watched her mother with a confusing mixture of shame and pride.

That night, after the hootenanny, when Jenny was getting ready for bed, she went downstairs to use the bathroom, but the door was locked. Her father was in the kitchen making a cup of tea for Georgia. "Your mother's in there," Russell said.

Ten minutes passed and her mother was still in the bathroom. Jenny went to the door and listened. She couldn't hear anything — no running water or flushing toilet. She knocked on the door. Nothing. She knocked again. Nothing. She banged on the door, loudly, and shouted for her mother to answer her. Nothing.

"Something's happened to her," Jenny yelled to her father.

Russell came to the door and hit it hard several times. "Georgia, unlock the door now!" he demanded, then waited

with unease and impatience for something to happen. He
kept his eyes on the floor, at the line of light across the
bottom of the bathroom door, to avoid eye contact with his
daughter who also stood staring at the floor.

"Georgia," he said again, with urgency and resignation
and weariness.

"I'm coming, I'm coming," she finally mumbled. There
was a fumbling and the sound of the lock being released.
Russell hesitated for a second or two, then opened the door
as Jenny stood behind him. Georgia was still sitting on the
toilet with her pants around her ankles and her head on her
knees. She was sleeping. She had awakened long enough to
unlock the bathroom door and then had drifted off again.

Russell took one look at her and shook his head. "Jesus
Christ, Georgia," he said just before he walked away. Jenny
heard the screen door on the porch slam behind him. Georgia
didn't hear a thing.

For a fraction of a second, Jenny thought about leaving
her there, but she would have to use the bathroom herself
soon. She stood in the doorway looking at her mother with
disgust, which quickly turned into empathy when she
remembered the words of the poem she had found a few
years before. Is this where Georgia had ended up? Sleeping
on toilets in someone else's clothes?

Jenny nudged her mother awake and managed to get her
up off the toilet. She dragged her drunk and heavy body
upstairs and threw her into bed, onto the old, lumpy
mattress. Georgia was in a haze. She reached for Jenny and
asked her to lie down, to keep her company. The two of
them lay in silence in the dark room under a blanket of
disappointment. Georgia stroked her daughter's hair, twisted
it around her fingers, played with it as though she were a rag
doll — a child's beloved rag doll.

After a while, Georgia started whispering. At first Jenny
couldn't make out what she was saying. She asked her
mother to repeat it. "It was a good party, wasn't it, Jen?" She
said it louder that time, trying in vain to separate her words,
still coming out tied together, slurred and not sounding the

least bit sorry. Jenny wanted to slap her. She wanted to
knock the fuzzy, red-eyed look right off her face. Georgia's
eyes were only halfway open, roaming freely, without focus,
around the room. Jenny wanted to slap it away, and might
have, if she didn't see that her mother was crying — not
openly, with a lot of sniffling and gasping. Her eyes were her
only betrayal — her tears quietly reflected in the dim light
coming in from the hallway.

It was cool that night. The smell of the sand and the
lake seemed embedded in the blankets on the bed and were
just as strong smelling as Georgia's perfume and gin-soaked
breath. Jenny pulled the blankets up to her mother's neck,
tucked them in behind her, and watched the antics of the
evening slowly disappear from her puffy, wet face as Georgia
fell into a deep and undisturbed sleep.

Russell stayed outside for some time. The summers weren't
so hard for him. It was the rest of the year when he wasn't at
The Cottage and there was no place to get away from it all.
He had to rely on the pictures of the lake he had hanging in
his workshop back home to get him through. Jenny just had to
close her eyes and she was there. The Cottage was always
there. Only once or twice did she ever need it to be there and
it wasn't. She closed her eyes and — nothing.

She still remembered it well. The taste of despair came
in the form of rum and Coke as she sat waiting for Robert's
first set to end. It wasn't sitting well. She knew it wasn't good
for the baby. She needed it for herself.

At what point do you know despair has parked itself at
your doorstep? Jenny tried to remember the exact moment.
How long had it been? A couple of weeks? A month? Despair's
the only thing that stops a ticking clock. Life gets suspended
and hangs there in front of you until you're exhausted from
looking at it. That month seemed like a lifetime as her life
flashed before her — life with Georgia and Russell — her time
with Robert — then back to Georgia and Russell.

The taste of the rum and the Coke stayed with her until
later that night, when she stood beside Robert outside the
back door of the bar in the cool October rain, when every

line Jenny had memorized on Robert's face began losing its definition. The half-circles around his mouth and the deep ridge that cut into his forehead when he was concentrating — working out a new song. It all slipped away and became unclear and unfamiliar to her.

"Why haven't you called me?"

"Been busy."

"Haven't you thought about things?"

"What do you want me to do?"

"Can't you be there for me?"

"Can't you just take care of it?"

"Why are you doing this?"

"I'm not doing anything. It happened. It was an accident."

"I thought you cared."

"I do."

"And this is how you show it?"

"You're too young to have a kid, My. So am I."

"I'm 21, Robert, not 16."

"The timing is bad."

"Can't you just be there?"

"For what? What are you going to do? Have it? Abort it?"

"I don't know."

"What do you mean, you don't know?"

"Don't you give a shit about me?"

"C'mon, My, I've gotta get back in. I've got another set."

"Why are you doing this?"

"I'm not ready to settle down! Can't you understand that?"

"Did I say I wanted to get married? Did I say that?"

"What do you want from me?!"

"You said you'd never leave me."

When she said it, Robert's face changed. The frustration and the anger softened and something about the moment made Jenny think of the night they had spent on Boundary Road. She remembered how it started raining just as they were about to leave, after they made love and finished the lemon gin. Robert had stepped outside the car to urinate before they drove home. The car lights illuminated his back. There was a steady swishing sound from the windshield wiper and a fleeting knowledge that she would always remember the moment. Something about his back to her, and the rain, and the way Robert stood looking at the long, narrow road ahead of them, the way he stood alone, the way she felt — with him, but alone.

"Look, I can't do this," Robert finally said that night outside the bar. Then he opened the door and went back inside, left her standing there, left it up to her to decide what would come next.

Jenny was already treading water, trying to keep her head afloat. She made plans on the way to her car. She decided she would tell her mother, that she would need Georgia to get through it. Just before she pulled out of the parking lot, she heard the band start up. The music boomed from behind the thick walls of the bar and became clearer when a group of under-age teenage girls opened the door and made their way inside. That's when she heard it. That's when she recognized it. The song she had helped Robert with only weeks before. He'd forgotten to tell her he had finally found the courage to use his own material on stage.

On Day Six at The Cottage, Jenny and Robert took the girls fishing before breakfast. Out on the lake, Jenny realized that she hadn't spoken to Robert much since they arrived. He tried to make love to her in the middle of the night but she rejected him. He didn't try to persuade her. Jenny knew he wouldn't. Not there.

In the boat, Jenny pretended to read her romance novel. Really, she was watching Robert place squirming worms on fishhooks. Their guts smeared his fingers. He dipped his hands in the cool lake water and wiped them on his jeans, then threw the lines out and handed the rods to the girls. Their little hands eagerly grasped the handles.

If she left Robert, where would she go? What would happen to Katherine and Rebecca? Would they hate her? Would they be poor and have to live in some dingy apartment in a building that should be condemned?

If she could just start the next paragraph in a new life, she thought. It was so easy in those damn books. The paragraph before, the damsel's in distress. Next paragraph, she's in the arms of a handsome man on her way to the airport to fly off to the castle he owns. Oh, didn't he tell her? He's rich — the next best thing to the king of a tiny country nobody's ever heard of, where it's warm all year and the green fields in the hillside are sprinkled with beautiful villas and storybook farms.

Robert didn't make enough to afford two places and Jenny only made so much with her baked goods and they had just bought their house. She had waited a long time for the house. She didn't want to give it up. But he had hit her.

Rebecca had noticed. Katherine hadn't. Jenny was afraid Rebecca had heard the argument, but she accepted Jenny's lie about trying to catch a heavy glass bowl as it was falling out of the cupboard. It was the strained look on her face — an adult's concerned look on the face of an eight-year-old. That hurt Jenny more than Robert ever could.

He did hit her. He didn't just grab her arm. He hit her back. Punched her. More than once. Three, maybe four times. It bugged her that she couldn't remember exactly how many times. It was something she thought she should know.

When Rebecca was born, Robert beamed with pride and love and was nearly bursting from it all. Jenny had never seen him like that before. It lasted most of the first year, then things returned to normal.

When Katherine came along two years later, Jenny sensed some disappointment — another girl, and Jenny's last child the doctor had said. The birth was difficult. Yet, it was Katherine who managed to steal her father's heart. She was playful and stubborn and moody, just like him, not pensive and sensitive like Rebecca. Rebecca was like her grandfather — far too sentimental for her tender age. She looked out at the lake the same way Russell did.

If Jenny left Robert, Rebecca would have to give up her room and the rainbow Jenny painted on one wall, as well as her small closet with its tiny cubby holes, where she neatly displayed her shoes and hid her Easter eggs so Katherine couldn't find them. She would have to give up everything. Goddamn bastard, Jenny thought.

That's how the fishing trip went — without incident. After an hour or so, they headed back with the chosen ones flailing around in the bottom of the boat. By the time they reached The Cottage all but one had stopped moving. Robert said it wouldn't be long before it stopped, too.

He headed inside with the girls, hungry for the pancakes and sausages Georgia promised to make. Jenny told them to go ahead. She had to take the beach towels off the clothesline. She was barely aware of what she said. She only knew she had to stop the *thud, thud, thud* from the suffocating fish left behind in the boat.

It became the topic of the conversation later, over lunch — the mystery of the missing fish.

"Little sucker must have flung himself right over the side," Robert said.

Jenny tried hard to swallow a mouthful of bass, then excused herself to go lie down. Her act of liberation didn't make her feel as good as she thought it would. The *thud, thud, thud* stayed with her most of the day, fading in and out over a game of horseshoes and during a walk down the road with the girls after lunch. Her breathing was short and difficult. She told herself it was just the heat.

By four o'clock, Jenny decided to join Georgia on the porch for a gin and tonic. The girls went to Helen's with Robert and Russell for an ice cream. By that time, Georgia had already had several drinks. Jenny heard the ice cubes at eleven in the morning while Robert was cleaning the fish.

Funny, the things that make you look at your watch, Jenny thought. It would be important if Jenny was being called to the witness stand to provide an alibi for her mother, or Robert, if they were suspects in a crime — say a murder. She'd be able to tell the prosecutor exactly what time they were at The Cottage because she had looked at her watch when she heard her mother's ice cubes while she was on her way outside to hand Robert a sharper knife to clean the fish.

None of it would do any good, of course, if Jenny was the one they killed.

Jenny fetched her mother and herself another gin and tonic. Georgia had already set foot in that familiar territory Jenny referred to as the "swollen tongue phase." Words sometimes inherited an extra syllable. Letters were occasionally dropped. It was one of Georgia's more irritating phases to Jenny, unless she'd had a few herself — an ounce of tolerance never hurt.

The "swollen tongue phase" would only last for two more drinks, then Georgia would enter the "cooking impaired phase," when everything gets overcooked because she doesn't want to stop drinking long enough to sit down and eat. "Just keep them on low," she'd yell to Russell who was patiently babysitting steaks or ribs or chicken breasts, basting and turning and moving them around to the few spots where the charcoal wasn't burning so hot.

If Jenny was ever going to talk to her mother about Robert, she knew she'd better do it in the "swollen tongue phase." The "cooking impaired phase" was usually short-lived and short-tempered before the final "life's wonderful phase" kicked in, when everything and everyone is beautiful and wonderful. That's the phase when Georgia miraculously gives in to the affectionate side she's been closely guarding all day and openly displays her warmth with slurred compliments, strong embraces, and soft kisses goodnight. Wet nothings, Jenny used to call them when she was young. Georgia didn't have the energy left at that point to pucker her lips and give her daughter a real kiss goodnight.

Of course, the "life's wonderful phase" was always in jeopardy of ending suddenly whenever Georgia went to the bathroom.

"Robert hit me."

Jenny didn't know any other way to enter the conversation. It came blurting out — the whole story. Jenny had hoped to be detached about it. Reserved and detached with the voice of an unaffected narrator telling the story of some stranger's life. Nothing at stake. Nothing close to the bone. Instead, she felt like a schoolgirl telling the teacher about the school bully who just pounded her. She wiped her tears on the back of her hands, and when they were soaked, she pulled her T-shirt out of her denim cutoffs and used that.

Georgia thought about offering Jenny her napkin but realized it was already wet from the condensation dripping from her glass. She hated the way the summer heat made her glasses sweat. She particularly hated it at the time because she should have been able to offer some comfort to her distraught daughter and that napkin was too wet to do any good.

As Jenny sat there sobbing, Georgia's mind wandered back to how she used to feel about summer, when she was younger, when she wasn't sitting on The Cottage porch, drinking all the time. How spring always made her feel light with the promise of something exciting hanging around the corner. How she'd nearly go out of her mind waiting for the summer holiday to begin. She'd be able to go swimming with her friends at the quarry down the road and ride motorcycles that belonged to older boys. Anything could happen.

"Maybe next summer you should go someplace else," Georgia suggested to Jenny. "Life can become too routine. Just because you always want to come here doesn't mean your husband does. Your father's the one who wanted this place, you know, not me. You think I liked the idea of coming to the same place every summer? I spend the rest of the year in the same place, doing the same thing. You'd think I'd be able to go someplace different in the summertime — but no. Your father wanted to buy this cottage and I've spent every bloody summer for the past twenty-five years sitting here on this goddamn porch looking at the same goddamn lake, talking to the same goddamn people."

Georgia got up to head inside for a refill. She left the weight and the burden permanently carved into the seat of the fraying lounge chair behind her.

It was on The Cottage porch that Jenny had told Georgia she was pregnant with Robert's baby — that he thought she should have an abortion. She was 21 and felt like a child who had done something bad. She wept openly and hated herself for it. She knew how much her mother hated emotional encounters.

Georgia circled it, picked it up, made it all about her own life and told Jenny it was just as well Robert was running away from her, that Jenny shouldn't marry the first man she slept with anyway. Georgia did. Look where it got her. "Trust me, darling," she had said, "you marry the first man you sleep with and you'll spend the rest of your life wondering what you missed out on."

"I thought he loved me," Jenny cried that day.

"Most of us do," Georgia said as the afternoon wind picked up, pushing the lake against the shoreline, rippling waves of absolute failure towards The Cottage, rustling through the leaves of the trees around them. The tall skinny pines swayed and creaked as though they might snap at any moment, like cheap wooden toothpicks. A loon called out from somewhere further down the lake.

Georgia took over after that. She made the appointment with the doctor. When he asked if there was any possibility Jenny could carry the baby then give it up for adoption, it was Georgia who said no.

She lied to Russell about Jenny needing some sort of gynecological procedure — "woman's stuff." She sat by Jenny's side all day in a hospital in Kingston and only ever left the room twice to put money in the parking meter across the street.

Georgia's hands were shaky most of that day. She kept looking at her watch and at the clock on the wall in the hospital room.

"They said you can be discharged at six, maybe a little sooner if the bleeding stops."

She was anxious to leave, to get home to pour herself a drink. It was already long past the hour she usually started. She kept drinking coffee, which only made it worse. She kept reapplying lipstick, kept getting up to look out the window at the street below, kept sitting back down in the chair beside Jenny's bed.

Jenny went in and out of sleep. She would open her eyes to find Georgia beside her reading a magazine, flipping through the pages so fast it was obvious she didn't even have the patience to look at the pictures. Sometimes, Jenny would open her eyes and Georgia would be standing near one of the other beds. There were three patients in the same room. There was Barb, a university student who was alone, who smiled every time she woke up as if she were at a sleepover — a girls' party — happy to find her friends still with her in the morning. And there was Lynn, a young mother of two, whose husband stayed with her behind a drawn curtain.

Only first names were used. No one wanted to share anything more. They'd never see each other again, hopefully.

It rained on the way home. Georgia drove in silence on the dark, slick roads, and only ever spoke once. "You always liked the sound of the rain on the rooftop. Close your eyes, darling. Let the rain put you to sleep."

Jenny couldn't remember ever saying anything about liking the sound of rain on rooftops.

When they got home, Jenny went right upstairs to her room. Georgia poured herself a drink before she even took her coat off, said she was chilled to the bone, that a good stiff drink would do the trick. Later, she came upstairs and sat on the edge of Jenny's bed while Jenny pretended to be asleep. "It's over now," Georgia whispered. She gave Jenny a weak kiss on her forehead then staggered out of the room and down the hall.

On The Cottage porch, Jenny swallowed a mouthful of gin and tonic and watched a grey spec come into view from across the lake. It almost disappeared — the sun's reflection on the water bounced off its metal sides, drowning it in the harsh afternoon light. Jenny strained to keep it in sight — the tiny spec that was carrying a million moments of her life as its cargo. It should look bigger, she thought.

Georgia spotted the boat off in the distance, too. She knew the bobbing blur was Russell. She could tell by the way he zigzagged around and came at the choppy waves from a slight angle, to lessen the impact of a bumpy ride. Georgia had always been irritated by the way Russell did that. Whenever she was at the helm, she drove straight through the waves no matter how big, damn the consequences.

"There have been times in my life when your father's made me so angry, I've wanted to haul off and whack him." Georgia gritted her teeth as she said it. "The man just knows what buttons to push, and damn, if he doesn't go ahead and do it even when he knows he shouldn't — when he knows what it'll lead to."

The night of the argument, Jenny didn't hug Robert when he finally came home. She didn't kiss him or ask him how his day was. She kept running past him with her list of things to pack, asking him where the sleeping bags were, where he put his bathing suit — she couldn't find it. She was tired. She'd had a long day. She had to pack everything herself. She didn't care what kind of day he'd had. He'd come home late. He'd been drinking.

She could still see him standing in the doorway, taking his tie off, throwing his keys on the kitchen counter, grabbing a beer from the fridge. He didn't look happy. He looked tired. Drained. He went into the living room, played his guitar, played nothing in particular. Some parts were recognizable. The rest seemed like random plucking, off key and without rhythm.

She could have stopped for a moment and asked him how his day went. She could have taken five minutes to put her arms around him and say hello. She could have, if she'd thought about it.

Who was that woman, darting around like some half-dead fly, buzzing and banging between two panes of dirty glass that hadn't been open since last fall?

That's how Jenny saw herself, on The Cottage porch, after a few gin and tonics and the distance of a week between the two events. A fly stuck between two panes of dirty glass, creating havoc with its own frustration.

"So maybe it was my fault?" she said to her mother.

Georgia got up out of her chair again and let out a long sigh, which bothered her a great deal. Sighing was for middle-aged women who couldn't cope and couldn't think of anything to say, who resented being put in a position where they were forced to say something. For they no longer had the boldness of youthful bluntness on their side, and they hadn't yet discovered the freedom of being an old woman, of no longer caring what they said because anything they said would have some grain of truth to it.

"You just have to get on with it," Georgia said with another sigh. Then she took their glasses inside for a refill.

When Jenny was 7 or 8 — she couldn't remember exactly how old she was — she fell on the slippery dock one afternoon after a storm had passed. A splinter cut through her knee. She ran into The Cottage crying. Georgia pulled the splinter out and soaked Jenny's knee in peroxide. Jenny couldn't remember Georgia wiping her tears or telling her everything would be alright. She could only remember sitting on the counter by the sink, her body still jerking from the aftermath of tears and her mother working in silence, cleaning and bandaging the wound. When Georgia was finished, all she said was, "there, good as new."

Jenny didn't object to another drink or to the others that followed. The gin was starting to drown the heaviness in her chest, helping her breathing return to normal. She could even smell the pine trees again, and the gas from the Evinrude as Russell's boat approached the dock.

Day Seven. Something about the lake soothed Jenny's hung-over body. She had tried aspirin at three in the morning, hoping she'd wake up feeling better. Two hours later, she was still tossing and turning in agony. She went downstairs and tried a glass of milk then brought it right back up in the kitchen sink, just missing some plastic glasses that didn't get washed the night before, which still smelled of gin and limes. The sky was getting lighter — the way it does just before the sun makes its way into the day. Jenny had stood in the darkness of The Cottage looking out at the lake. It seemed to promise relief.

She quietly changed into a pair of shorts and T-shirt and headed for the boat, moving quickly. She didn't want her father to wake up and ask to come along. She wanted to be alone where she was going, wherever that was. She pushed off from the dock and placed the oars in their notches, preferring to paddle into the arms of Catchacoma, past the sleepy cottages and the huge granite boulders, past the occasional patches of undeveloped land and other familiar landmarks.

Jenny paddled for at least a quarter of a mile down the lake then anchored the boat several feet from the shoreline. She was thinking about a hundred different things until she finally slipped into the lake. That's when she decided she wanted everything off. It was heavy and clinging and suffocating.

She removed her T-shirt and bra, then peeled off her shorts and underwear with one hand, while she hung onto the side of the boat with her other hand. The water felt good on her vagina and buttocks. Her breasts floated free of their binding support. The cool, still water lightened her limbs and allowed her graceful movement without much effort on her part. She stroked the water with the gentle eagerness of a new lover, then spread her legs like the wings of a butterfly and thrust forward — farther away from the boat and the Evinrude and everything else that reminded her of everyone else.

Only last night's dream stayed with her. Jenny was in the kitchen at The Cottage baking cakes for private school students. Georgia was sitting on the counter near the sink. There were hills of flour all over the kitchen floor. Jenny could hardly move. She was frustrated because she couldn't remember how much flour she was supposed to put in the cakes. When Georgia opened the utensil drawer to get the recipe, Jenny saw fish in the slots of the plastic holder instead of knives and forks. Some of them were still moving.

Georgia took out a card and closed the drawer. Jenny didn't want the card, but Georgia insisted. Jenny reluctantly took it from her mother's hand, which was small and childlike, not at all like the hand of an adult woman. Georgia jumped off the counter and began putting handfuls of flour into the mixing bowl. Jenny looked at the card. It was blank, except for a dot halfway down from the top, like a period — the end of a sentence about nothing.

As she turned onto her back and moved her hands and feet just enough to stay afloat, Jenny could still see the card vividly. The lake no longer felt cool. She was warm and comfortable and thinking that if you stay in something long enough, it will lose its elements of discomfort. You'll get used to it.

If she could just stay there, she thought. If she could just make the swim last forever, and remember to keep the layers off — to remain naked.

She could stop talking like Georgia. She could leave Robert and be on her own and read more books and meet with friends for a coffee without worrying about the time, and take a night course and volunteer more at the Literacy Centre. She liked teaching people how to read. She liked making a difference — something that lasts and doesn't leave crumbs behind.

A muskrat watched her from its spot near the shore. She returned its intense stare until it dunked its head below the surface, reappeared further down the lake, disappeared again, reappeared once more, each time gaining a few feet, moving closer and closer to her.

The muskrat reminded her of Robert's disappearance and reappearance, how he made his way back, appearing suddenly on the street a few months after the abortion. She was walking along, not paying attention to anything going on around her, walking towards the drugstore when all of a sudden he was there, standing across the street behind his Volkswagen, staring at her.

She stopped walking when she saw him and stood staring back. She was going to say something and motion for him to cross the street, but he walked away. He walked further down the street, stopped once to look back at her, then he disappeared down an alley between some stores, then disappeared altogether and headed west to Edmonton where his uncle ran a real estate business. He reappeared two years later with his hair cut and his face plastered on dozens of *For Sale* signs on the freshly mowed lawns in town, with a renewed interest in the woman he always thought of as *his*.

It wasn't so hard for Jenny to start over with Robert, to set aside what happened before. It wasn't as deep a wound, as tragic, as near as it had once seemed before he walked back into her life and asked her to marry him, to be his forever.

It wasn't so hard. Georgia had given her the tools. She had taught Jenny many times over that what can be true and certain and felt with all her heart one minute can just as easily be seen as magnification, emotional impairment, and over-reaction the next minute. It can be cleaned up, realigned, and relabelled — stored away, forgiven, and forgotten. It rarely had any lasting effect and was almost never felt with the same intensity again, even if it did keep coming up — kept reappearing in a lesser form in times of weakness and inebriation. Usually, it reappeared as something else.

Georgia didn't welcome Robert back with open arms, but soon enough she was playing euchre with him, drinking and keeping up with him, planting wet nothings on his cheeks before she said goodnight. Everything else — what happened before — fell away, landed in the same place she put her drunken tirades and her embarrassing bathroom naps.

Jenny swam until she was too tired to swim any longer, until she was out of breath. She made her way back to the boat. She knew Robert would be waiting for her. She pulled her body out of the water and put her wet clothes on again.

Robert told her he wanted to pack up and get on the road early, that he wanted to leave right after breakfast. She remembered him saying it the night before, just before she passed out. At least she thought that's what he said. He usually did. The night before the day they leave, he always makes sure she knows they've reached the end of their vacation at Catchacoma Lake.

Georgia said goodbye to Jenny at The Cottage. She said she wasn't feel well and didn't think the boat ride to Macky's Landing would do her any good. Jenny noticed how red her mother's eyes were. Her blue-grey eyes. Probably last night's gin.

Georgia put her sunglasses on to hide what Jenny could see — to hide the private tears a mother sheds for her daughter. That's what Jenny told herself — that Georgia wept silently for her, that she was only pretending not to as she stood at the end of the dock, waving, blowing kisses to the girls, yelling at Russell to stop at Helen's on the way back. Grab a few limes. Don't forget.

She got smaller and smaller as Jenny and the rest of her crew zigzagged back across the lake — smaller and more like the mother Jenny always wanted her to be. Cleaned up. Realigned. And relabelled.

It was one of Jenny's last summer vacations at The Cottage with Robert. He only came back to Catchacoma Lake once or twice after that. Jenny went every summer, without fail, with Rebecca and Katherine, and left Robert at home, with his guitar and his own ideas about a good time. That went on for about eight years.

She never told Georgia about the near misses — the times she thought Robert was going to hit her again. How he yelled just an inch from her face, spitting on her eyelashes — the way he pushed her across the kitchen floor until she was backed against the cupboards, the round brass knob of the utensil drawer pushing into her spine. She never told her mother any of it. Not even after a few gin and tonics on The Cottage porch in the mid-afternoon sun and lots of colourful talk about the lake people. Georgia never asked, either.

When Jenny finally told her parents she wanted to leave Robert, they offered to lend her money so she could keep her house, pay Robert off, and rewrite the mortgage. She accepted.

It was Georgia who handed her the cheque. Jenny took it, held it in her left hand — held it tightly all the way to the bank.

It is a decent house — yellow brick with pale pink and slate blue gingerbread trim. Jenny still hasn't taken down the bamboo blinds from her front porch. They flap in the November wind and hide the canvas folding chairs and the small tables behind them, which she has also forgotten to put away.

Chapter Eleven

"Jenny's not coming tonight," I say when they ask. "She has the flu."

I stand at my front door and look out the window down the street. I can see her car in the driveway, but only one light is on in the house — the bathroom light, upstairs. I make a mental note to go over tomorrow and help get her porch ready for winter. Her beloved porch, her second home.

Jenny starts sitting outside in this other room, her outdoor porch room, as early as April, as soon as the snow melts and the air warms up, turns from freezing cold to just plain chilly. When the frost disappears and the earth starts to give under her feet, cushioning her eager steps while she inspects her gardens and looks for displaced bulbous gifts, transplanted by the neighbourhood's industrious squirrels.

She wears a heavy sweater and a spring coat while she

rakes the flower beds and picks up last year's decaying blooms, stuffs them into whatever box she can find, then returns to her seat on the porch where she sips from a coffee mug. Hours later, and only when she is chilled to the bone, will she go inside.

The fall isn't any different. She wears an extra sweater or two, or a winter coat, and stays outside as long as she can — raking, sipping, delaying the inevitable.

It seems the whole town rakes at the same time, plants at the same time, goes to bed and wakes up at the same time. They make the short walk to the same stores on Mill Street and Front Street, which look just as old inside as they do outside — preserved, and with all the charm of a carefully constructed movie set. They move in and out of the screen, picking up their parcels from Del at the Sears Catalogue Store, eating breakfast at the same cosy hole-in-the-wall, ordering flowers at Sally's for this birthday and that funeral, waving hello to the town cop who knows most people by their first name.

All over Stirling, they've fixed up their porches with folk art and hanging baskets and furniture that isn't made of plastic. They sit out there and watch each other come and go — sit and see themselves up one street and down the other in the tiny space, in the façade that greets the rest of the town and makes an impression and leaves any chance for a deeper look parked out there, near the front door, where entry is made welcome to a select few.

It is different on Sundays at 136 Anne Street. I can see Georgia arriving with Russell, carrying an aloe plant for Jenny's kitchen window sill, or a crocheted tea cosy, just like the one she bought for herself at a church bazaar, or a wooden knife holder, just like the one Russell made for her.

Jenny says Georgia seems confused about whose house it is. She's plugged night-lights into all of the bedrooms, despite Jenny's protest. She even had Russell build shoe shelves in Jenny's closet, the way he did for her own closet.

On Sunday afternoons in the summer, I can hear Georgia singing, after she has sipped for hours, belting it out from her seat on the front porch, "do your boobs hang low, do they wobble to and fro," until Jenny's latest boyfriend either joins in or leaves, drives off in his car, embarrassed by Georgia's constant poking to sing along, to explain what's the matter with him, do songs about boobs offend him? How can they? We all know what you're after with my daughter.

The last one she chased away was the good-looking hippie who makes silver jewellery in the back of the hardware store. Georgia offered to French braid his hair, told him his ponytail was boring, boring, boring.

My own mother never meets my lovers. They come up in conversations, mentioned in passing. Nothing much is ever said about them. A name, an occupation if they have one, current marital status. I tell her about them so she will know I am not like her. I don't tell her the details so she'll think we're not that far apart.

I like to think the day will come when she'll ask me for specifics. How many have there been? What were they like? How long did it take me to realize I was allowed to enjoy it, too?

I think that day will probably never come, or if it does, it will come just before she dies, on her deathbed — a sudden interest in the life that has gone on around her, all around her, while she kept to herself, kept her urges neatly arranged in the bottom of her sewing box, in a corner, on spools she never fingered, never dared to unravel, to use.

What was it like for you, all those men, all those years, she will ask. Her hair will be spread across the pillow. It will be white and brittle. Her eyes will be afraid, her mouth curled downward, dry and cracking and thirsty for the details.

Did size ever matter to you? How many sizes have you come across? Did you ever do it upside down?

Why do you look so surprised, she will say. Do you think I've lived a lifetime without thinking about these things? Do you think I've not paid attention to what the rest of the world has been doing, to what you've been doing? Tell me though, how many of them have you loved? Then she will tire and drift off to sleep and never wake up to hear what I have to say for myself.

For now, I say I'm seeing someone. Are you still seeing him, she will ask later on. No, I'm seeing someone else now, I will say. This word *seeing* floats back and forth between us, open to interpretation and palatable, as we try to stay connected while we separate, if such a thing is ever possible.

"Are you still seeing Ben these days?"

"As far as I know," I say, without getting into it.

"What's he doing now?" she asks, then waits for my answer.

I hold out for as long as I can, thinking, and when I speak I say it in a way that signals the end of our conversation. "Fishing," I say quickly, with finality, with *I have to hang up now* riding on the tail end of a few more words. "Ben's still fishing," I say, with laughter just around the corner, with a pathetic joke coming at me from somewhere straight ahead, with my mother's stillness weighing heavily on my chest just before I say goodbye.

"If Jenny's not coming, can I use this mug?" Delaney asks.

She makes a cup of tea and settles into a chair with a large coffee mug Eliza gave me a hundred years ago — what seems like a hundred years ago — with a red heart on it, and the words *We love you, Mom* scribbled in black. It is Jenny's mug on film nights. If she comes over and finds out that it's dirty, she washes it. She refuses to grab another mug, or God-forbid, a real wineglass.

I've never caught her drinking at work, although she is hardly ever without a mug in her hand at the Literacy Centre. Once, I couldn't help myself. When she left the room to collect the mail, I wandered over to her desk and checked the contents. It was black and smelled like coffee and didn't taste like anything else was in it.

She never drinks during the day, except on weekends — something I noticed long ago, one spring afternoon, while Jenny was busy churning peat moss into the soil in her flower beds. I saw the white liquid that almost filled her coffee mug, could smell it as I sat on the top step, as I leaned over to one side near the edge of the porch. There was a dead mosquito floating along the surface.

Often, when my phone rings late in the day on a Saturday or Sunday afternoon, it is Jenny calling to tell me about something she's decided on — no more letting Georgia chase away her boyfriends, no more letting Robert miss his support payments. Her voice is louder than usual. She swears more. She spills her guts while she slurs her words, gets her thoughts jumbled, falters, then quickly catches her own incoherence, repeats herself slowly to maintain control over her unreliable voice, apologizes for blowing off steam, apologizes again before hanging up. Vowing one more time to make some changes.

When I see her the next day, she is quiet and slightly shaky, eager to mention the gist of the telephone conversation, lessening the urgency without admitting what we both know — that she has already let the idea go and is already accepting how unlikely it is that anything will change.

I say nothing about these phone calls, about any of it. How can I when my own indulgences and excesses have led me to the same place — backtracking — shaking in the aftermath of my own conviction, unable to live within its power and its fury for more than a few hours. It flares, it fizzles. I am hopeless.

Hopeless and horny and hopeless.

Ben called last night from a phone booth at the Becker's store and in thirty seconds he gave me the play-by-play of what's been happening. He's been stuck, he says. For months. Stuck with the girlfriend who won't leave. He doesn't want to hurt her. He doesn't have the stomach. He doesn't have the energy. Could he please come and see me? He needs me. He wants me. Please?

I am hopeless.

"You're horny," Grace says.

"Horny and hopeless," I repeat.

"Better than being horny and hopeful," Sally says.

Did you tell him you might go to Kauai, we ask. Yes, she says, yes — and he wants her to come. But it's a stupid idea and it'll only ruin everything and then she won't have him at all and so what's the point, and he's married and she has the store and it's a stupid fucking idea and so she doesn't know, and what if he isn't what she thinks he is? Then she'll be stuck there with the sun and the lava slopes and the palm trees and the mountains and the emerald fields of taro and nothing else.

"If you don't go, you'll never have anything else," I say.

"If she goes, she'll pay a price," Grace says.

Storm stirs in her seat and lets out a sigh. We've all begun to sigh a lot. We used to smoke cigarettes and exhaled our frustration and dilemmas with each drag. Now, we hardly ever smoke and spend a good part of the night pushing pockets of air up from our diaphragms to release what we cannot contain.

"Sometimes you have to pay a price to have that in your life," Storm says.

"But he's married," Grace says. "What about that?"

"But he may not be happy," Alex says.

"You keep saying that," Grace says sharply. "Every time the subject comes up, you say that."

"Because it's true," Alex answers her.

"Then get out," Grace snaps back.

Silence.

I sip on a beer and wonder if Ben has been thinking about me as much as I've been thinking about him. Wonder why I never believe he is, when I should know that if I'm thinking about him — chances are he's thinking about me.

"Proof," I say. "We all want proof." And they look at me like I have two heads until they hear what I've said.

"Why do we always choose avoidance of guilt over what could be the direct route to our own happiness?" Delaney asks.

"Because we're supposed to," Grace says.

"Because the world tells us we should," Alex adds.

"Because films like *The Bridges of Madison County* make it impossible not to," I say.

"I hated that fucking film," Sally says.

"Meryl Streep should have gone with her lover, Robert Redford," I say.

"It wasn't Robert Redford, it was Clint Eastwood," Delaney corrects me.

"She should have stayed with her husband," Grace says.

"What for?" Alex says.

"Because it was the right thing to do," Grace says.

"And is it right to live life falsely?" Alex asks.

"She was just bored," Grace argues.

"She found the man she should be with," Alex says.

"If something like that ever happened to me, I hope I would have the courage to go for it," Delaney adds.

Grace lets out a sigh. "Who says she didn't feel that passionate towards her husband once upon a time?"

"C'mon, Grace, give your head a fucking shake," Sally cuts in. "That husband of hers had about as much passion in him as Clint had in one finger. His fucking baby finger. She should have gotten out of that fucking truck and gone with Clint, and you know it. Jesus Christ, for once just take a chance and say what's really on your goddamn mind instead of spouting all that self-righteous shit that comes out of your mouth."

"What do you know about it, anyway? You haven't been married. You haven't even had a long-term relationship."

"I haven't had one because I haven't wanted one."

"Well, not having one won't keep you from feeling the loss, will it?"

"What the hell do you think I'm going to Kauai for, Grace? To see the goddamn volcanoes?"

Silence.

I tell them I think not going is worse.

I tell them that the night Ben and I got stuck, I was considering love. Love and all that goes with — what can rise up out of conjugal affection.

I tell them that in my state of prolonged attachment to Ben, I could feel my ex-husband, Hal, inside of me once again. Not the Early Hal, who wore his hair down to his shoulders and made bonfires at two in the morning so we could hear our future crackling brightly before us. Not the Later Hal, who didn't bother at all, the vitality sucked right out of him, out of both of us. We had used each other up. In the cottage, in Ben's bed, still stuck, it was the Middle Hal I felt, the slender, tapering form between my legs as he performed dutifully for himself in the final years of our marriage. I had already begun to disappear from beneath the heaviness of his life. We were only making messes, something to be cleaned up with the back and forth friction of a Maytag and a cup of laundry detergent thrown in with the sheets.

We've been apart longer than we were together, yet Hal shows more interest in my life now, a post-marital curiosity about the men I date, the friends I have, the highs and lows of my job. He pays more attention to me, makes frequent comments about my hair, how toned my arms are, have I started lifting weights?

I've gone from being his everything, to his nothing, to his ex. The possessive *his* still applies and he seems happy to have it that way, to still have me in his life. He comes to my birthday parties. I've been to his house for dinner.

I tell them that in the cottage, in Ben's bed, I had enough time to close my eyes and return to them all. Hal and Zeke and Jonah and so on, and so on. It was that long and that short — my life flashing before me in the artificial brilliance of a Technicolor dream, only my eyes weren't closed and my head wasn't on the pillow. It was propped up by my elbow and my arm while I watched Ben breathe and the curtains blow in the breeze from the lake, as I listened to the sound of my own creation gently lapping along the shoreline.

The night Ben and I got stuck while making love, I had already decided to move on. I sat alone on the dock on the kinder side of midnight, retracing our unintentional steps. They lacked the usual pretense and concentrated energy of a serious courtship but landed us in a heap of shared history anyway, in spite of our belief it was only ever meant to be a fling, something to while away the dead time, forgetting that time itself forged bonds. I hadn't been with a man for a while when I met Ben. He was escaping commitment. Over a year later, we had become something.

On the other side of midnight, I could already see it falling apart, losing my patience with all the talk about indecisiveness and personal journeys, belittling his small ideas because they weren't big enough, lucrative enough, enough to make any goddamn difference at all — chastising him for his too-small steps because I wouldn't be able to stand the pace. He was going nowhere, and he was dragging me along with him. We would learn not to make love.

On the dock, I was already resenting him for making me think I was better than that, that I shouldn't settle, shouldn't make the same mistake twice, that I should learn not to praise his rebellion. It was poison to praise it — what makes him his own person — then expect it to go away because I couldn't stand the thought of being encumbered by it. I decided I was two-faced and didn't know how to live with the courage of my convictions, let alone his, which would never be enough to sustain me.

I was prepared to let it go when he walked back down the narrow path from the cottage carrying two cold beers and hopes for my own metamorphosis in his hands. Could he show me the way? Him — with his detergent-smudged Levi's shirt and the smell of fishing all over his jeans, embracing impulse in the middle of the night, assuring me there wasn't anything more important to do under the infinity of a stellar sky.

I tell them that under the infinity of a stellar sky, I started thinking of Johnny Marks and the bumps and grooves of the old men and the old women he carved in the fence posts — the ones he said already knew what we would know someday.

I tell them that on that dock that night, I was already hearing their whispered wisdom, and it was telling me it's only ever too late once, and then it is gone.

They leave under a starlit November sky, with Alex carrying the film we didn't watch — *The Whales of August*, with Bette Davis and Lillian Gish, two elderly sisters trying to decide if they should give up their ancestral home.

I stand at my front door and wave goodbye and watch as they get into their cars and drive away, taking the chill of the night with them. I look down the street at the yellow brick house with the pale pink and slate blue gingerbread trim — looking for signs of life in a house that is completely dark, except for the one room, upstairs — recalling what Storm once said about the attachment of place. How long after someone has gone, you can still feel their pulse in the bricks and the mortar and the clapboard by which you've known them.

I stand there and watch until they are gone and then I stand there a little longer, wondering what time Ben will show up, and whether it's too late for us to become something more.

Storm

MISSING PICTURES

Chapter Twelve

Sometimes, when she's in the bathroom or standing at the kitchen sink, Storm leans as far as she can into the left side of the window to see the red brick building, her face touching the glass until it comes into view. She looks out on impulse, or because someone has just gone down the road. She has a good ear.

She can hear the memory-seekers coming, can hear them driving alone or with their middle-aged sons and daughters at the wheel — after-dinner and after-church forays, a little look back. They speed past the Rogers horse farm, easing off the gas as they reach the top of the knoll, then nothing. They sit there in front of the old red brick schoolhouse, the engine idling, saying the place has hardly changed at all, until they take their foot off the brake and drive away, kicking gravel, disappearing with a slow fade out.

Drying off after a hot bath or rinsing plates after dinner, Storm will feel a sudden need to look out the window at the small red brick building in the distance. Half-hidden behind two maples that used to knock on the tin roof whenever the wind picked up and blew across the fields from the north, or the west, or the northwest. A quarter of the compass bashing against their weathered skin. The two of them *tap, tap, tapping* like old friends, making sure she was safe inside before the elements arrived in full force. How still they used to stand after the wind died down. Calm, quiet legs of the gods, stripped naked during the winter months until the warmer winds blew in spring and dressed them in the colours of the season. Greenest-green against the blue summer sky, laying scalloped jewels at her feet in fall — ornamental offerings of continuity, come what may.

Storm cleans the Minto School every month. She walks down the road with her plastic bucket filled with cleaners and dust rags — even in the winter when the wind whips across the open fields she has to pass to get there. It seemed silly to drive such a short distance, to miss the slight shifts in perspective by arriving too quickly, to waste the gas driving less than a quarter of a mile.

Will told her to take the car even though she's been walking to the vacant schoolhouse for some time now, keeping up with the dust and the mice, until they find another tenant. Will and Storm own the converted schoolhouse. They've both lived there, at different times in their lives, before they ever decided on a life together. It is like all the other one-room schoolhouses that dot the back roads of rural Ontario, of rural anywhere.

Storm reminded Will that when she lived in Kingston, she used to walk for miles, block after city block, in all sorts of weather. To get to work, to shop, to visit a few pain-in-the-ass clients who insisted she couldn't write a good commercial without *seeing* what it was she was writing about. They didn't trust her imagination, couldn't understand how she put the missing pictures on the radio in thirty-second clips, didn't know she could pull rabbits out of hats and help them sell a store full of sofa-beds without making the five-block walk to see the ugly things for herself.

She couldn't tell them it would be harder to lie if she saw the truth. If she saw the inferior quality, and couldn't help but notice they had only one sofa-bed priced at $299, even though they wanted her to say the walls were *bursting with hundreds of brand name sofa-beds* in every style and colour imaginable, *priced as low as $299!*

"It wasn't a lie," she told Will. "They had one at that price. It was in the back of the store, the last one you'd ever see, and only if you were looking for it."

She knew he was only mildly interested in what she was saying. That he could do without hearing it altogether. That he listened only because she brought it up out of the blue, as if it was still important, as if the time she had spent living in Kingston, away from the back roads of Stirling, had actually taken place. Will rolled his eyes, gestured understanding, and let that part of their conversation end.

On her way to the schoolhouse, Storm regretted making room again for her days working in radio, regretted even thinking about the exaggerated inflections and the tiresome background music and the same old-same old lines. She was surprised it was all still there, a stopwatch ticking in her mind, counting off the proper order of things: tell them what you're going to tell them — tell them — tell them what you told them. Three steps to a structurally sound commercial.

As if she thought about these things deliberately. As if it mattered if she did. It was years ago, another life — history.

She could say all that, and make her way down the road to Minto School, S.S. No. 19, circa 1872. Even still, she got an uneasy feeling, as if she was betraying someone. All because she remembered something she used to do. All because it had nothing to do with who she had become.

Storm wrote radio commercials for ten years, after working her way up from secretary-receptionist in just twelve months. She went from typing lists of lost pets and school bus cancellations to writing ad copy without much trouble at all. She was a natural.

She did what came naturally for the next decade of her life. She lived with Paul, a salesman at the radio station for just as long — minus a month and three days.

Storm learned early on the easiest way to write a radio commercial was to cast herself in the starring role, close her eyes, see it as she would want to see it if she was the one who was buying a new dress or having her Tarot cards read. What would be the motivating factor? What would make her act? What would she be thinking, feeling, seeing?

Gotta look good. Feel fat. Gotta find the perfect dress.

She would play with this, roll it around in her own mind. After several years, even that wasn't fun. She eventually found a shortcut. She wrote first to amuse herself, then substituted and rewrote with nice words, left all the bad words cut and pasted to the underside of her desk, but only after she'd had her way, her fun.

Hey, all you've gotta do is get your fat ass down to Penny's Ladies' Wear, buy black, and hey, lucky you, there's a sale on too! Reward for covering that fat ass in high fashion. Hey, never mind that we didn't solve the problem of your fat ass. Stay tuned. In a moment, you'll hear about Keep It Up Fitness, *where there's no sweat in making a difference in your life!* Magical machines *take it off in no time! It's so easy! And* it works! *Soon, you'll be shopping for new clothes, in the dress size you've been dreaming of! And hey,* Keep It Up Fitness *even has* fifty percent off *coupons for* Penny's Ladies' Wear — more incentive for *losing that disgusting fat ass now! What could be* better?! *What could be* easier! *What could make you* happier! Healthier! Sexier!

Storm could make herself overweight. She could make herself uncertain about her future. She could make herself lonely, depressed, in need of a divorce lawyer. Broke and shopping for a car. Young and stupid and ready to drop a fortune on a glamorous wedding your friends and family know you can't afford. A man, worried and anxious about not having enough life insurance. Single and looking for fun. Married and looking for the perfect anniversary gift. Typing words she used the week before, and the month before that, and the year before that, for women's clothing stores and health food stores and the Sixth Annual Psychic Fair. What difference did it make if they all sounded the same?

She passed through her days listening, over and over again, to what she had become. A cast of thousands whose rushed scripts were filed away in the metal cabinets next to her desk. Whose presence was always being requested on copy information sheets with instructions like, "just do what you did before, but differently," written in the illegible scribbling of another frantic sales rep who had promised the client the moon and gave Storm one hour to deliver it.

Twelve hours later, it was blaring over the station monitors, jammed in between station breaks and weather breaks and the overstocked "oops-we-screwed-up-so-you-save" sale at the ugly furniture store. It followed her into the bathroom at work and into a neighbourhood bar after work, where Storm and Paul made the transition from colleagues to couple — never very successfully. It followed her into the car on the way back to their condo, and was there again first thing the next morning when the radio alarm clock pulled her from a deep sleep, with opening lines and sell lines and closing lines that she worked, and reworked, until there was no possible way to work them again.

Christmas and New Year's and Easter and graduation and summer holidays and back to school and Thanksgiving. Spring tune-ups. Fall tune-ups. Spring cleaning. Fall decorating. Home shows and car shows. Strawberry season and apple season. Father's Day and Mother's Day. Boss's Day and Secretary's Day. Boating season and hockey season and gardening season and snow-blowing season. New arrivals, birthdays, funerals. Weddings and anniversaries. Divorces and therapy.

Storm used to dread Christmas most of all. She could hardly stand to write one more commercial about the perfect store with the perfect gifts for everyone on your list, could barely stomach writing another Christmas greeting, sending best wishes from them and theirs to you and yours. She knew everything would be on sale at sixty percent off in just a matter of days, had already written Boxing Day commercials a week or two before Christmas, urging you to spend, spend more, buy more, get more for your money, *save* on all Christmas decorations, and paper and bows and tape.

January would bring on the weight-loss clinics with their New Year's specials for losing all that Christmas fat. Easter was for selling spring dresses, pushing rent-a-car companies to make that special trip home to visit the family, sending flowers across town or across the country, visiting nurseries for spring bulbs and grass seed.

Graduation was for computers and jewellery. Summer holidays for boats and trailers and golf clubs and bus trips to Niagara Falls. Back to school was for more computers and cars and new clothes. Thanksgiving was like Easter all over again, for sending flowers across town or across the country, for pushing rent-a-car companies to make that special trip home to visit the family.

And then it was time for Christmas before she knew it, with *only three months to shop*, dropping hints in October to *book that cruise now and save* hundreds of dollars. Take her to the Caribbean for Christmas! Take advantage of *early bird specials!* Yes, it's coming sooner than you think. *Act now! Don't delay!* Think *Christmas* and start shopping *today!*

For ten years, Storm lived out of sync with the rest of the world, separate and apart from everyone who was counting off the days left to shop, slushing around the snowy streets, running here and there. Rushing home to deck the halls and mail Christmas cards, while Storm wrote about Boxing Day sales and New Year's resolutions to quit smoking and lose weight and take that dream vacation to Las Vegas in the spring. While the snow fell and Santa stood on a street corner collecting money for the Salvation Army and Storm could never figure out what day it was.

There was no escaping it, even at home. Paul was always chasing her down, asking her what she thought about this client and that concept. She retreated to the bathroom when she got sick of listening to him ride the airwaves, checking out other stations, stealing ideas.

He used to talk about being in the "steal" business. The "iron and steal" business, he called it. His mother, a woman who had had seven children, whose husband left her high and dry, cleaned houses and ironed other people's clothes to feed her family, while Paul went around stealing boxes of Kraft Dinner and cans of peas from local grocers to help out.

"She used to iron. I used to steal," he'd say every time, as if he were sharing it for the first time. Wearing his stolen youth like a badge of courage, while he listened for ten seconds to this station, thirty seconds to that one. Listening to commercials and weather breaks, to news sponsors and station promos. Looking for a way to put a spin on it, to steal it, what did she think?

There wasn't any place to go but the bathroom. She'd close the door, muffling the streak of noise coming from the living room, certain she'd have a few moments alone. And she did, for a while. He never barged in, at first. That came later on, years later, something new to make up for what was falling away, when politeness and space were freely given at the office and left there at the end of the day.

Once, during Christmas dinner, Paul asked Storm to think spring and help him come up with some kind of promotion for sales.

"Just forget snow, forget Christmas. Think sunshine and grass and what can you come up with?"

Think, Storm, think. Come up with something. Whip it up. Be creative. Use your imagination. Picture spring. Flowers. Mud. Spring jackets.

Don't look outside! Don't look at those huge snowflakes. *Don't look!* Forget and focus. So she thought spring. Mud. Flowers. Spring. Mud. Flowers. Spring and storms and love on a cold, wet balcony.

She thought about one night the spring before, when they carried their lovemaking under a blanket out onto their eighth-floor balcony, which had solid steel sides. Unless someone was standing on another balcony a few floors up and over to the right, they couldn't be seen, Paul said, and who would be outside on a night like that anyway, with a heavy spring rain coming down in straight sheets, moving over the building steadily with big, fat drops, the cool water washing them, keeping them fresh, energizing them, lending them endurance as they put their basic need for each other on display to the world.

There was always a chance they might be seen.

It was Paul's idea. That's how it started. Public displays of their most intimate moments. Before they ever lived together, flirtations were part of their workdays. Paul would brush up against Storm at the coffee machine, lean over her at her desk, leave his cologne on the back of her neck.

She met him in the bars after work, was always thrilled to see him waiting for her while he wooed everyone around him, telling jokes. She watched waitresses put a hand on his elbow whenever they passed by, touching him, saying something to him, always saying something to him, never speaking to her, dismissing her with their side glances.

Storm didn't care. She knew she was the one going home with him, who would take his jacket and his tie off, and unbutton his shirt, and lay beside him until morning. She could hardly wait to steal his attention, was nearly crazy when he did his double takes when he saw her coming through the front door of the bar, when he followed her to the bathroom in the basement and waited until she came back out, then snuck her into a dark corner near the telephones, told her they had to go home right away — no, forget it. It was too late. Now, he said. Now.

One Easter weekend Paul made the obligatory visit to Storm's parents' apartment in Stirling, to eat turkey and make small talk. She could see his dislike for the whole situation. She knew it was going to be that way. He didn't usually go home with her. He didn't like small towns, or family functions. He hadn't bothered with his own family, his brothers and his sisters, not since his mother had died.

Storm took Paul out for a drive that afternoon while the turkey was still roasting, while her parents fussed in the kitchen, arguing. She drove Paul past the farm where she grew up. Partly to delay leaving what was still so familiar, partly to delay returning to her parents, she made their way back into town along back roads.

They were driving past a clump of trees that lined the road and hid a shallow dip in the ground on the other side of a split-rail fence, when Paul said, "Pull over here. I want to make love to you right now. I'll go out of my mind if I don't." He was rubbing her vagina, rubbing his fingers hard over the seam in her jeans. His other hand was down her top, pinching her breasts. His mouth was wet all over her ear as he bit it and sucked it. He was breathing heavily, moaning, begging and demanding. She was practically coming as she drove the right side tires into the ditch.

They leapt through the tall grass, laid down behind some trees, made love with their clothes half-off while the odd car passed by. Storm could feel the eyes of the passers-by looking to see, to see where they were, what was going on. Paul said there was no way they could be seen. Did she want to stay and make love all night, move out onto the road, under the stars, see how long they could make it last before someone came along? Would she make love to him forever? Would she stay with him forever?

She was going to ask him what he meant. She never knew for sure. But he was making her scream other things. Whenever there was an empty hole in their conversation Paul always filled it with his mouth and his fingers and his penis, whatever worked at the time. Whatever made her needs switch from emotional to physical, until she cried out *it's enough, it's enough.*

On the way back to Stirling, he didn't talk about their forever future. He was only amazed at how many stations he could pick up out in the middle of nowhere. He flipped around the dial all the way into town. Their crotches were still moist, smelling, competing with the stale scent of their immediate past, the dust from the road leaving a trail of powdered grass growing in the ditches along the way.

Years later, she was on the balcony of their condo riding him as a storm approached from the west. She could hear the thunder rolling in. It was still off in the distance, with a flash of lightning too far away to be concerned about just then. Yet, it was there, flashing in the periphery of their relationship, a reminder of what had always been. What would always be.

Storm knew how life with Paul was going to unfold, just as she knew the morning light would eventually greet her the next day. She could count on that. She would be regurgitating the same, same old words. She would meet Paul after work for a drink. They'd go home for dinner, talk about commercials and clients and clients and commercials — anything but where they were going. There wasn't anything to say about that that she hadn't already tried to say.

She knew he did and didn't want her. That his eye and his mind wandered, that he had convinced himself he needed her, so he was hanging on. Asking her to write commercials after hours. Asking her to make love to him, to make his dinner, to trim his hair — fulfill his basic needs, keep giving him reasons not to walk, not to desert, never expecting the end to come at all.

She told Paul it was time for her to leave. He laughed. She told him again. He didn't laugh that time. She told him once more. He didn't understand. He loved her. He thought she loved him. She did. She does. She can't anymore. He didn't listen. He cleaned the table and didn't talk and kept to himself. She knew he was looking for a way to sell her. Sell her, keep her booked. Keep her there.

Later he took her, pulled her clothes off, had her near the tree. Like always, he made her forget what she had said, for a few moments, for as long as he stayed on top and behind and below and in her. For as long as he could keep it up, every day, every chance, taking her, trying to inhabit every inch of her, but he couldn't get past the crevices, couldn't penetrate what had already let him go.

He worked hard, came at her from every angle, saved his best lines for last, held her hostage to his pitch. She thought he was beginning to enjoy himself. He always loved the chase, the odds, the bullshit it took to make them buy the illusive, the intangible — airwaves. He thought he had engaged her, made her part of the creative melding. That he had her using her skills at masquerading and spinning, and had her writing non-truths and embellishments, diminishing what previously surfaced to save them both, lessen the blows, the impact. He thought he had almost closed the deal. He walked tall around the apartment and the office, confident and cocky, while he sniffed without stop, uncontrollably and unconsciously. It was all she could hear.

She told him she was leaving, but he didn't listen. He thought she was bored or wanted a baby or a house in the suburbs. He thought she was forgetting all the good things they had going for them. She told him she was leaving. He said she wins. He would be whatever she wanted him to be, if she could just tell him what the fuck that was. Describe it, he said. Write it down. Spell it out for him.

She wrote, *goodbye* on a piece of copy paper and left it taped to the fridge. Eventually, he sent her a large cheque for her share of what they owned — the ugly furniture, the condo, the new car they had just bought — a cheque large enough for her to survive on, without him. His note, accompanying the cheque, said he didn't understand what went wrong, didn't understand her sudden urge to flee, but he finally understood why her mother named her Storm and it wasn't just because she was born during a particularly bad one.

She figured he had probably forgotten that her first name was Jean-Anne, that Storm was really her middle name, more of a nickname-middle-name, even though it was on her birth certificate. She didn't respond to Paul's note. She cashed the cheque to live off the money, to buy herself some time. She was sure Paul had probably never noticed the way a storm moves in, the way the wind is fierce, then slows, then stops altogether. The way the sound falls off and coats the air with stillness. The way the birds fly frantically about, then disappear, and the way the trees whisper *here it comes, here it comes*. It must seem sudden, she thought, when you're not paying attention. Paul was the kind of man who never noticed the rain until it began to fall — and even then, he was always surprised to see it, as if it had come out of nowhere.

He hadn't noticed that his interest in her had perished, had become five minutes of attention in a crowded bar after work, asking her what she wanted to drink, talking about a client he sold advertising to, a client she wrote for. He believed he was conversing, was keeping her content in between the other conversations with clients and colleagues and the waitresses who kept touching him. Where did she want to go for dinner? When did she buy that dress? What did she think of the way the commercials for the ugly furniture store turned out? Did she think a two-voicer would be better — a conversation between a man and a woman, fighting over which sofa to buy. You know, make it funny. Could she make it funny? Be funny, he said. Humour sells. Or make it sexy. Sex sells. How about funny and sexy? Could she do that?

Storm moved back to Rawdon Township, back to familiar territory, where the rolling farmland was home to some of the oldest rocks on earth — limestone and black chert and granite. Where fossil rocks could be found in its low valleys, and thick layers of sedimentary rock, and glaciallycarved ridges and rivers wound reminders of its geological history throughout that part of Hastings County.

She couldn't think of anywhere else to go but home. She rented the furnished schoolhouse from Will over the phone, sight unseen, not knowing what it would be like inside, only remembering the maples and how they glowed orange and yellow in the fall against the red brick building. She had passed them hundreds of times in her youth, by school bus and by car. On the way into town, whenever she left and returned to the farm around the corner where she grew up. They were always part of the journey, were still there when she lived in Kingston, where the streets are lined with thousands of trees just as magnificent.

Storm moved into the schoolhouse with two large suitcases of clothes. Sometimes, in the middle of the night during those first few weeks alone at the schoolhouse, Storm would wake up to the sound of nothingness. She had forgotten how quiet it was in the country. How quiet and dark. Sometimes, she would get up and look out the window into the blackness, unless the moon was full and illuminated the land before her with its yellow-white light. Sometimes, she would just lie in bed and listen to nothing, and let the spring air cross the room and brush her cheek. Let her lungs take it all in — all the midnight country air she could swallow at one time. Let it run to the top of her skull and fill her head with certainty. She really did leave. She really did save herself. The noise was really gone. Turned off. Unplugged. Like the radio on the shelf in the kitchen, locked on the same mute station. The monotonous repetition of suggestion silenced by her own hand. The cord wrapped neatly behind the back, its lifeline strangled by a single Glad twist-tie.

In the schoolhouse, Storm was awakened by the morning light, by the sound of crows flying overhead. She had stopped using a clock radio to wake up, had stopped caring what the weather would be like, didn't know what was happening in the rest of the world — couldn't take it in.

When it was cold, she put a sweater on. When she was hungry, she ate. She spent hours reading the books that lined the shelves in the living room. Will told her some of them were his, some were left by other tenants, some were there when he bought the place years before. *Gemmology; Astronomy; The Zodiac; The Book of Runes; The Great Artists of Yesterday; The Best Jobs for Tomorrow; Persuasion; A Jest of God; Surfacing; Fear of Flying; Passages; A Guide to Growing Herbs; Raising Chickens: The Complete Handbook.*

She walked into the feed store in town and bought half a dozen chicks. She tried to remember the last time she passed through those doors and smelled the oats and grain and barley. The last time she saw the sons of the men she used to see sitting in the front on wooden chairs, smoking cigarettes and pipes, talking shop, and the weather, and the moisture. There was too much moisture, too much mud to get to the fields and sow the seeds. The sons watched her with curiosity, wondering what the hell she was doing buying chicks, going into the back of the store with Will where he grabbed a few bags of feed and pointed out the laying mash she'd eventually need for healthy eggs.

Storm took the young chicks home and made them beds of clean straw in the chicken coop behind the schoolhouse, watched them nestle under the heat lamps. She fed them, gave them water, looked forward to the day when she would hold their warm eggs in her hands, when she could nourish her body with their small white gifts. She was envious of their obvious purpose, of their simple requirements.

When she needed a walk, she went into the fields behind the schoolhouse, or down the road and around the corner, past the farm where she grew up. She could still see the fieldstone foundation of the barn partially hidden by thousands of overgrown thistles, and remembered how she used to ride the roads on the school bus twice a day, every day, passing a landscape she's never quite forgotten. The route, the houses, the barns, the type of cattle and horses that grazed in the fields, the cars and trucks that were parked in the driveways. How the bus dipped below ridges of cut earth and split-rail fences, and rode above deep, grassy ditches passing the small heads of spring-born calves that looked up as it went by — how she always expected it to be the same. And it was, until the afternoon the bus turned the corner and slowed, and everyone pointed and shouted *Oh, my god*, and was just as shocked to see it levelled and charred, still smoldering in the later afternoon. A mere memory of what they had passed that morning when it had stood looking brown instead of black, yellowed and lightened by the early light.

The barn was caved in, gone, leaving Storm with nothing to say. At least she didn't remember saying anything. Maybe she gasped. She must have gasped, but she couldn't recall the sound. She only remembered sucking in the stale dusty air of the bus, inhaling thoughts of burned horses and baby cows. *Change* getting stuck in her throat — the finality of it lodged in her windpipe as she made her way off the bus towards the smoking barn, away from the voices of others.

Will said he remembered the fire. Old wiring, wasn't it? He remembered it because his father was a volunteer fireman back then and he got called out that afternoon and left Will to run the feed store. Will was only 18, just out of high school.

Storm remembered seeing him at the store whenever she went in with her father, remembered how skinny he was then, with his tall, gangly legs and messy hair. They never spoke to each other. He had filled out nicely by the time she saw him again, by the time she arrived at Minto School with her two suitcases of clothes and a decade of noise still swimming around in her head. She liked the fact he didn't talk a lot, didn't take up all the space, the way Paul did with his constant bantering, pitching, and manipulating. Will was quiet.

"Did you love him?" Will asked, shortly after they started seeing each other.

"Yes, I think so."

"You mean you don't know?"

"I mean it's gone now, whatever it was. Does love go away?"

Will sat there silent for a moment.

"I would like to think it doesn't," he said, the way he would always say it — answering her, but not giving her the answer she thought she needed. He never knew what she was really asking. Neither did she.

A year later, Storm was travelling the same road she had stopped with Paul to make love on. It was Christmas Day, after dinner with her parents. She was beside Will in his truck, heading home, passing the same clump of trees she'd had sex behind, which had grown taller and thicker. At the time, she still lived in the schoolhouse by herself. Will was living in the farmhouse down the road. As they drove past the familiar spot, Storm told Will a bit more about her life in Kingston. He listened attentively, then said, "You belong here." The roads were covered with snow. They travelled without talking for a while. When Will eventually spoke again, he told Storm that everything that had happened before that day no longer mattered, that they were starting a new life together. She embraced what he said. It seemed to make sense to her then.

When Brian was born, it seemed as though time had just begun. Everything from before just fell away to the operating room floor and was swept up with the bloodied green towels, thrown out along with her placenta. While he lay sleeping in the glass crib at the foot of her bed, Storm looked out over the small city of Belleville and could see the twinkling lights and the distant stream of car lights, and could only think of how far away she felt from it all.

Late in the night, only hours after Brian was born, Storm strained to hear Will walking up and down the hall with their son. He had taken him out of the room to give her a chance to sleep. She even stopped breathing so she could hear their footsteps, a cry — anything. But she could only hear the dinging of the elevator's arrival and the hushed voices of the nurses working overnight. She couldn't hear the shift she felt in her life. She couldn't hear anything remarkable or relevant — nothing that signified a crossing over, a closing off.

Storm wrapped the cord on the radio the same way every time a tenant left the schoolhouse and she went over to clean, left it silenced on whatever station it was last broadcasting — golden oldies, easy listening from Rochester, classic rock from Toronto. That's how she heard Will and Brian driving into town to the feed store, heard the weight of Will's truck on the road and the clanging of metal on metal as the shovel in the back bounced with every bump and pothole they hit. There was nothing else to listen to.

Storm unplugged the radio last winter when Adrienne Moore left, left it tuned to the classical music station Adrienne always listened to, put it on the shelf next to the canisters of flour and sugar she emptied out, dusted it along with everything else.

No one else had moved in since then, yet Storm kept up with the cleaning anyway, and when she got inside, the first thing she did was look for her cigarettes. She found them tucked into the corner of one of the kitchen cupboards, next to an old bottle of cognac with less than a third left. She sat them both down on the table — for later — for when the job was done. She had her routine and a cigarette and cognac were part of it.

She had come to the schoolhouse for the mindless tasks of removing dust from the tabletops and cleaning the toilet bowl. Put the cleaner in, scrub, flush, and you get results. Storm was happy with the simplicity of it, eager to remove the dirt and the dust, certain that if she cleaned the place long enough and hard enough, she'd remove the residue that had permeated everything around her, which Adrienne left behind, which Storm still hadn't been able to shake.

Once, when the schoolhouse had been vacant for over a year, Storm and Will ran ads in the Toronto papers. People from the city had rented it before. A potter. A reclusive gemmologist. It was worth a shot.

Adrienne Moore was the only one who responded to the ads, a history teacher at a high school in Scarborough who wanted to rent the schoolhouse for an undecided period of time, perhaps only a few months, she had said over the phone. She was on a sabbatical but wasn't sure how long she'd be staying. She wanted to move in as quickly as she could. Will and Storm decided a few months' rent was better than no rent at all and accepted Adrienne's request for an open-ended arrangement.

Storm guessed Adrienne was at least ten years older than her, that Adrienne had to be around 50, although it was hard to tell for sure, she was in such good shape — as it turned out Adrienne was actually 58. Storm thought if she didn't dress so conservatively, if she didn't carry herself with such reserve, with such concern for appearances so common to her generation, she'd easily shave a dozen or more years off.

Adrienne moved in that July, with her suitcases, a box of books, and several bottles of cognac, which she said she needed as much as the books and the clothes, maybe more. She asked about a radio, didn't care about the television, or that she could only get two channels on a clear night. She didn't seem to mind that she shouldn't flush every time she went to the bathroom, and that the well might run dry in the summer if she used too much water.

Adrienne was happy with the way the place looked, and that the phone was a private line, and not a party line — which she said she remembered her grandmother having in the countryside outside Toronto, near Ajax, years ago, when it was still considered the countryside. She particularly liked the monarch butterflies glued to the bathroom wall, perched on painted flowers — found out that Storm had collected them from the road, already dead, and put them in an eternal garden on the pale yellow walls, gave them pink and purple flowers to suck nectar from. Storm told her she didn't see the point of leaving them rotting in the rain on the road, or having their wings ripped by the tires of passing cars, explaining why she didn't just leave them there, why she interrupted nature, even if she shouldn't have, she couldn't bear to know they were outside being crushed under a pair of Michelins.

Yes, yes, Adrienne nodded, her fingertip touching the back of the larger monarch, barely touching it, if she touched it at all. She would see them from the tub — watch their static flight through the flowers and escape all other thoughts she might bring with her racing mind in a hot bath. She'd find distraction in their familiar patterns, which she thought she knew but had never had the chance to see, not really. Not while they were flitting around in the midday sun, moving, always moving through their fragile lives — flicking an image her way, letting her believe she's seen them, she knows them.

That's why she had come to Minto School, wasn't it? To stop. To live in unfamiliar surroundings, with Will's hand-me-down furniture. His mother's cousin's cherry-coloured sofa, his grandmother's dining room table, his father's mother's sister's bedroom suite, his yard sale lamps. With banged up pots and pans and someone else's first set of china, Storm couldn't remember whose, only that two of the plates had chips. She used to keep them on the bottom of the stack and never used them unless she had to.

What else had brought Adrienne Moore to the schoolhouse? What ever brought anyone here, Storm thought, other than the need to stop for a while.

Storm started with the bathroom. She crouched down and leaned over the bathtub. Her legs cracked. She worried that it meant something. That it had always meant something, those cracking legs she's had for as long as she could remember. She never told her doctor, or she might have and he mumbled something that wasn't worrisome, or else she'd remember. He never made a move to check it out, didn't send her for tests of any kind, and he would have if he thought there was something to it. But he didn't.

"You worry too much." Will had just said that to her that morning.

"You're obsessive. Borderline paranoid." Paul had told her years ago. She didn't remember why, only that he said it as he was leaving the room, heading into the kitchen, and that he wasn't looking at her when he made his observation.

Storm ran enough water to moisten the scouring cleanser, then began scrubbing a bathtub that wasn't even dirty, that only had a small spot of dust near the drain, barely visible. But, she was there anyway. Might as well fill the time. Make it sparkle. Keep it spotless, the way she always did. Hunched over. Breasts flattened against the cold side of the tub. Backside high in the air, the way Paul always liked to find her, unable to resist the angle, the way she made it so easy for him to slip in and take her away from the porcelain and the powder, stop her in the middle of the job. Stop her. Claim her. Have her. Then leave.

"Paul the tireless," she called him when she eventually told Adrienne about her life before.

Adrienne was curious, to say the least. She hadn't known Storm very long when she found out about Paul, only a few weeks, and could only go by what she saw. She knew Storm by the farmhouse she lived in down the road, and the antiques that filled it. The way it was always clean, except for the Tonka toys rolling across the kitchen floor that belonged to the young boy who stood between his mother's legs, hiding, peeking out. And the nice husband, Will, who ran the feed store in town, who made his wife tea and stood behind her chair and massaged her neck the one time Adrienne visited and he was there.

Up until then, she only saw Storm when she made her trips to the dump every Thursday morning, taking Adrienne's garbage with her in the back of the truck, with little Brian beside her eating peanut butter sandwiches cut in quarters — his mother wiping his mouth, kissing the top of his head, and ruffling his hair.

She couldn't picture Storm hunched over, taking it from behind on a bathroom floor — not the way Storm described it, as if it went on all the time. Never waning as the years went by. Never letting up. Not even at the end, when everything else between Storm and Paul was winding down.

"He liked that position, did he?" Adrienne asked only after she remembered it didn't matter what she said there at the schoolhouse, that the whole thing was temporary. She could inquire, could take things even further if she wanted to. She wasn't staying.

"He liked every position," Storm answered.

"He didn't ever really go behind, did he?" Adrienne was aware of the inhibition in her own voice. It gave her away, revealed her as the unworldly person she saw herself as. Unworldly and limited in her own curiosities. Still, she had gone further off course than she ever expected she would, than she would have even thought she could if you'd asked her fifteen years ago.

"Oh, no. No, not that," Storm replied with equal inhibition in her voice, then went on to tell Adrienne about that one time, early on, when Paul almost entered her there. He was going to, but she turned around, and was angry that he'd ever think she'd want to, angry that he'd want to hurt her. It would definitely hurt. She'd already heard that from other women who said they'd never do it again.

"But you know," she said to Adrienne, who agreed it would probably hurt a great deal, she didn't know herself, "I doubt I'd be so angry if the same thing happened today, if Will ever tried, or if I was still with Paul and he tried again. I don't think I'd take it the same way, or see it as the insult I saw it as then."

It almost made Adrienne tell. That personal revelation of Storm's made her want to. The words sat waiting their turn at the end of her tongue, which she bit, and bit again. She didn't know Storm well enough to tell, didn't know her and wouldn't ever know her well. She wouldn't be there long enough for that. On the other hand, she knew they could tell each other anything and it wouldn't be hanging over their heads years later when they had an argument. It wouldn't become a dirty secret they could dangle in each other's face when things no longer worked well between them. There was no threat of permanence, of inhabiting the same place for long, and Storm had already gone first. She had already shared some things she said she never told anyone before.

It all seemed too fast though, her relationship with Storm — her acquaintanceship, which carried with it all of the expectations and intimacies of an older, more slowly developed friendship. And besides, Adrienne wasn't used to talking about it. She changed the subject with as little disruption as she could, making the shift from sex on bathroom floors to the history of Rawdon Township with a single line.

"Thank God for the freedom to enjoy good sex these days without getting pregnant every time out, the way women used to," she said. Before Storm could reply, Adrienne went on. "Did you know there was something called a maternity home over on the eighth concession back in the fifties?"

"No, I didn't," Storm said, unsure of where their conversation had gone, afraid that all the frank talk about

Paul's libido had been too much for Adrienne. She didn't know why she even brought it up. She shouldn't have, but Adrienne had asked, had kept it going.

"I read about it in the book I got from the library." Adrienne was still talking about the maternity home. She glanced at the burgundy-coloured book on the table in the dining area. "Apparently, the nearest hospital charged more money for maternity care if the patient lived outside the city, so some woman opened her home up out here for them."

"Now that you mention it..." Storm said and left it dangling. She was going to say she remembered hearing something about the maternity home, but wasn't sure she had, but must have if it only closed a decade or so before she was born. Why hadn't she heard? She knew about the general store and the blacksmith's shop. The buildings were still standing at the four corners down the road — someone's house, someone's garage. But a maternity home?

"Over three hundred babies were delivered over a ten year period in this poor woman's house," Adrienne said.

"Three hundred!" Storm repeated.

"She was a nurse. A bloody saint, I'd say. Imagine all the sleepless nights she must have had, as well as her husband and her own children. How could anyone ever sleep with so many babies passing through under one roof!"

Adrienne laughed, shook her head, mumbled "imagine," "my, God," "so many babies" and other incomplete thoughts.

"Do you have any children?" Storm asked.

"No," Adrienne answered, with nothing more. Then she offered Storm another glass of cognac. She didn't want to be rude — cutting Storm off with a "no" she knew was flat and uninviting. Storm was the only person she knew in Stirling, who had been good enough to let her move in just days after they had talked on the phone. Who would let her leave whenever she wanted to. Who took her garbage away and checked in on her periodically, with excuses about checking the well, checking the window frames to see if they needed repainting, checking everything and anything and nothing at all. Staying for tea, or standing outside, talking, skimming the surface in the sunshine. The weather. The news. The best antique shops.

Adrienne poured more cognac and let Storm linger on a Saturday afternoon, as she seemed to want to. She picked up the pace, skipped over the space she'd put between them by her unwillingness to talk personally, and continued circling the subject of women's lives in Rawdon Township. What it must have been like having babies in maternity homes and back rooms before that, and log shanties before that, with only a robe or a quilt or oiled paper covering the door, keeping out the wind, the rain, and the cold winter snow. Keeping the conversation rooted in a past neither one of them could call their own.

That summer, the rains stayed clear of Rawdon Township and brought steady days of sun and heat. Storm began to have a more than usual interest in the uneventful happenings at the schoolhouse. Adrienne came and went, mostly stayed put and kept to herself, kept close to home. Storm could see her outside, digging around in the small, neglected gardens, or sitting on the green and white lawn chair, reading the history book she talked about so often. Adrienne said she liked to know who walked the ground before her. Storm could see her fetching her mail from the box across the road. She seemed to get a lot of mail for someone who didn't seem tied to any other human being, none that she talked about anyway.

Storm ran into Adrienne every now and then in Stirling, at the grocery store or outside the library. They stopped and talked briefly. Adrienne always crouched down to greet Brian, stood back up to tell Storm about the pesky chipmunks that were eating all of her birdseed — what she came into town to buy, where she had to go next. It was as if they were old friends with not much to say — sharing insignificant annoyances and itineraries on the street, promising to see each other soon. Storm knew that would only happen if she made a point of dropping in on her, which she would. She couldn't seem to stay away for more than a week or two at a time.

It was different when they met up at the schoolhouse. "You look tired," Storm could say, without the undercurrent of something resembling embarrassment over running into each other in town, away from the secluded confines of the schoolhouse, out of context. "You look a little pale, is everything alright?" she could ask Adrienne without it sounding out of place. Adrienne would always answer, "I'm fine, I'm fine, not much sleep last night, that's all." But she seemed to appreciate Storm's concern. It seemed to nudge them closer each time Storm inquired.

"Slow down going by," Storm would tell Will on their way in and out of town. "Just checking, keeping an eye out, you remember you once did the same yourself." She'd take in as much as she could in the few seconds it took to pass by, looked straight ahead quickly if Adrienne suddenly appeared from the side of the house, carrying out water for the gardens. Storm wasn't that eager to be seen. She retreated the same way whenever Will walked into the kitchen just as she was stretching to see the schoolhouse out the window, leaning into the glass to see nothing she hadn't already seen a million times before.

She was ashamed of her own nosiness, yet she kept looking. She wasn't sure why, wasn't sure about this need, this compulsion of hers, this living in a constant state of waiting, waiting for something to happen.

"What do you do out here all day?" Adrienne had asked Storm when she first moved into the schoolhouse. She only ever asked once. It seemed that in a very short time, Adrienne found the answer herself, in her own busyness, in the seemingly trite and mundane chores of looking after a homestead. When she had asked, Storm made it sound like it couldn't be enough, not enough to fill a life, not important enough, especially to those who've never lived in the country, who walk around thinking life only happens in the fast pace of cities, big or small.

She was content now to spend her days feeding her family. Feeding cows and chickens, and taking walks with Brian on the farm looking for groundhogs and blue jays, painting pictures in primary colours, taping them to the fridge, running the house, cleaning the house, showing her son how the light filters through the lace curtain on the front door window. How it casts flowers made up of tiny pink squares on the staircase when they come downstairs in the morning.

She had chosen a new life. She cannot complain. She was happy, most of the time. She was no longer frantic, most of the time. Her life no longer whirled by. She had slowed time down, as much as anyone can. Once, she almost made it stand still.

When the bathtub was clean, Storm turned to the toilet. She raised the lid. She flushed and saw the familiar scummy ring about the bowl, left there by the hard, stagnant well water that hadn't moved since the last time she came by.

When the water finished flushing, before it had a chance to rise up again, she sprinkled the bowl with a generous amount of cleanser — more than she needed — afraid one day it would eat its way through the aging pipes that carried her wastefulness out back, away from the schoolhouse, to the corner of the lot where a sumac grows and spreads on a moist bed.

She sat on the floor opposite the toilet, waited for the cleanser to loosen the mustard-yellow ring, and remembered using the toilet in the schoolhouse for the first time. How she closed the bathroom door, not quite all the way. How she was able to relax knowing no one would burst in looking for a Q-Tip or after-shave, closing her up, embarrassing her, leaving her unable to continue, the way Paul used to. Barging in on her to find something, or to relieve himself while she sat soaking in a lavender bath, leaving his smell behind, apologizing for the interruption, making light of it, saying they must really love each other — selling her on the idea.

That's what happens when two people live together and there's only one bathroom. Lighten up. Relax. It's only me. Will never barged in on her. He called the upstairs bathroom "her" bathroom and he built a smaller one with a toilet and a sink off the kitchen before she moved in, before they were married, so there'd be two bathrooms and she'd always have her privacy. Even when she lived in the schoolhouse and Will started coming around and spending the night, he never interrupted her, not even in the winter. He put his coat on and walked outside, came back in and washed his hands in the kitchen sink, dried them on the tea towel and never said a word about any of it, ever.

Adrienne said that never would have happened back in the days of outhouses, or backhouses, as they were once called. Women always had some distance between themselves and their mates when they went to visit "Mrs. Jones," and could pretty much count on not being interrupted when they sat several feet away from the main house, on a seat that was bitterly cold in the winter, using old Eaton's catalogues as toilet paper, reminding themselves to grab an armful of wood on the way in.

"It was expected," Adrienne said. "That's why the woodshed was always built halfway between the privy and the house."

It was a small price to pay for privacy, Storm thought. Carrying a load of wood under your arms on the way back in. She would have gladly obliged. "A woman needs privacy," she said to Adrienne. "Don't you agree?"

Adrienne didn't answer right away. She lit a cigarette and exhaled the first drag for such a long time, she was blowing out her own breath after the smoke had already cleared and was making its way across the room, dissipating, settling onto whatever furniture lay in its path.

"I've had privacy all my life," she finally said, turning away as she said it, choosing to look instead at the maples outside. They were swaying in a light breeze, their vibrant colour beginning to fade, turning a lighter green, a yellow-green, that early September kind of green, thinned by summer's drought and the onset of cold nights.

Adrienne could have left it at that, could have left her words hanging in the wistful air, but Storm knew now. She knew that Adrienne's statement was not made with bragging pride or gratefulness, that privacy had been granted to her, not by choice, but by consequence. She also knew Storm wouldn't pursue it, that she would leave it swirling around in the cigarette smoke, letting it land and disappear. It was Adrienne who didn't want to let it lie still any longer, silent behind her rib cage — the heaviness that had followed her from Scarborough, east on the 401. Then north on this highway and down that back road until she had arrived at Minto School, where she had to learn all over again how to make do with what was given.

Storm scrubbed the toilet, rinsed the brush in the sink under hot water, then cleaned the sink, then the mirror above the sink. Tub. Toilet. Sink. Mirror. Working her way from the floor up. It was then that she realized she forgot to pray when she heard Will and Brian going down the road before. Forgot to stop, put everything down, close her eyes and beg. *Please God, please, please, please, bring them back safely. Please God, please.*

She set her Windex down. She stood next to the butterflies on the wall. She cupped her hands and closed her eyes. She repeated it twice, to make up for the lapse of time, whispered the same words the same way, as if changing them might break the spell that always brought her family home to her.

When she was finished she gathered up the cleaners and turned off the bathroom light and left the room, remembering Adrienne's words the one time Adrienne caught Storm standing still, head lowered, eyes closed, near the front door. When Storm thought Adrienne was busy in the kitchen pouring drinks just as Will and Brian were going into town, passing the schoolhouse, honking the horn three times, the way Will did.

"What are you doing?" Adrienne asked.

"Praying," Storm said, feeling awkward about being caught in her small act of paranoia. "I always pray that they make it back safely. I know it seems silly, but I can't help it."

Adrienne stood there looking exasperated and irritated and sorry for her all at the same time. "Don't you know?" she said, making more of a statement than asking a question, with impatience stringing the words together a second time. "Don't you know?"

"Know what?" Storm asked sharply. She was just as irritated and exasperated that Adrienne wouldn't just leave it alone, wouldn't pretend she never saw her in her moment of private pleading. "I don't know what you're asking me," she added. Don't screw it up for me, she wanted to say. Don't make me feel like an idiot for praying for my kid's life.

Adrienne hesitated the way a mother hesitates to explain the truth about Santa Claus and the tooth fairy and the seemingly friendly strangers lurking about the streets. She considered letting the next moment carry it away altogether, and she would have if she could have, but she had already made too much of it.

"Don't you know," she repeated, this time with a voice that was powerless and frighteningly certain. "Don't you know, it has nothing to do with you. Nothing at all."

Adrienne said the doctor called every night from Toronto to tell her how Sam had made out that day, and to read what Sam had written to her. Personal notes with references only a lover of many years would understand. Which, God willing, would pass unnoticed by a doctor, who for unspoken reasons, was willing to act as the messenger — the remaining link between them — who dropped the notes in the hospital's outgoing mail so she would have them. So she would have something.

He didn't say it like that, but Adrienne said that's what the doctor was really saying. She knew by his tone and by the way his words dropped off after that. He knew who she was. Sam would have told him to ensure his silence, so nothing was ever said about her to Sam's wife or to any of his children — this mystery woman who waited by the phone every night, the closest she could get to being there.

He must have found a way in, must have found a way to make the doctor feel alright about what he was doing. Sam was good at that, making the uncomfortable more comfortable, the wrong seem right, at least right enough to keep it from seeming unbearably wrong, the kind of wrong you can't normally live with.

The notes came in envelopes, stamped and paid for by the hospital, and were written in Sam's shaky handwriting — something new to Adrienne. She wasn't so familiar with his handwriting. She only ever saw it on cards for her birthday. *Still. Forever yours, Sam.* The way he always signed them.

Adrienne told Storm she couldn't picture Sam's hands shaking. They were always so steady, always on her somehow. Around her shoulder, on her leg, cupping her face as they made love in the afternoon sun, which warmed his back and the carpet below them. It entered through a wall of windows and bathed them in the clear light of day. As they saw it, it was right. Right for them.

She couldn't picture Sam writing the notes. She couldn't picture him lying in a hospital bed, a tube keeping the airway open, steeling his voice, his body withering away from cancer. Holding a pen and a pad of lined paper. No matter how hard she tried, she could only see him getting out of her car, stopping midway, with his legs hanging out the door, leaning back to kiss her again, saying he'd see her next week. Closing the door. Walking over to his car which was parked in a lot three blocks from the insurance office where he worked — the parking lot where they often met late in the day to go out for coffee, or a drink, or take more time and head to Adrienne's apartment. She couldn't picture anything else.

Storm cleared the top of the bookcase in the main room — the living room, if you had to call it something. There was nothing to separate it from the dining area and only a small island of cupboards told you the kitchen was over there.

In the main room — the living room — she cleared away a collection of pinecones and rocks, set them down on the seat of a nearby chair, took away an odd assortment of candles, some burned away, others with blackened wicks barely started. She dusted the top of the bookcase and scratched away at some pin-sized drops of wax she must have missed the last time. She hadn't been very thorough and was aware of the distraction. She hardly felt like she was there at all in some ways — going through the motions one minute — savouring it in another, taking a ridiculous amount of time to sit down and dust between the crevices of at least a dozen pinecones in various shapes and sizes.

"They're good for starting fires," she had told Adrienne when she showed her how to use the wood stove and how to keep a good fire going. How to let it die out before she went to bed, to keep the oil furnace turned down low during the day, let the wood Will cut heat the schoolhouse and fill it with the smell of burning hickory. She sometimes saw Adrienne in the fields out back, collecting pinecones, filling the old apple basket Storm gave her, bending down in her red cloth coat, carting her goods back home.

Adrienne didn't mind the work — making a wall of logs behind the wood stove, hauling it in from the pile Will dumped near the back door, and covering the windows with plastic sheets for extra insulation during the winter months. Stapling them from the inside, the way Storm told her to — starting at the top, stretching them out as she went along for a smooth surface that didn't obstruct her view too much.

There wasn't much else to do some days, Storm told her, but look out the windows at the snow gathering in the corners, covering the naked branches of the maples and drifting across the driveway — keeping you inside, without so much as a wish to be anywhere but inside. Blanketed by a white sheet of guaranteed privacy, left to sit there and occasionally drift off to sleep in one of Will's hand-me-down chairs.

"I've had privacy all my life," was all Adrienne had said that day they talked about bathrooms and outhouses, but it was enough. Enough to sink her head to her chest and pull her knees up to her aching stomach. To wrap her body around the years of moments that only existed in her mind and in her gut. The blanks she had filled in out of necessity.

Sam never barged in on her in the bathroom, the way Storm said Paul did. Sam and Adrienne never shared a bathroom. The only time he used her bathroom was after they made love, to shower himself off, and when there wasn't time for that, he just washed himself with one of her floral washcloths, left it hanging soaking wet over the side of the tub behind the shower curtain. Left his sperm in a spent condom in the bottom of the garbage pail, which Adrienne had to rinse out.

He would urinate, but Adrienne didn't recall a single time he sat down and left his lingering smell. Never. Wasn't it silly that they were talking about it at all. The private bodily functions of the men they'd loved? The bodies they would never touch again.

Any recall seemed better than the rock hard truth and its unyielding coldness. Its sharp edges pointedly reminding them that those men were gone forever from their physical lives. If that's what surfaced — those revealing bathroom tales — it was better than not having anything.

Sam couldn't go at all anymore, the doctor said. He was having problems with that, too. Martha, his wife, ran through the halls, chasing nurses, begging for suppositories — something — anything that helped to relieve him and gave him back some dignity. Martha, not Adrienne, who helped him get to the bathroom and waited for something to happen.

"This is probably all too much for you," Adrienne said.

"No, it isn't. It's okay," Storm answered before she had a chance to think, to let the truth rise up, form the words, speak them. She stayed and listened for hours and found out all about Sam and Adrienne and the affair they'd been having for thirteen years. She walked home later feeling his impending death behind her. She turned around and heard his shallow breath whispering in her ear while her own breath pushed forward in a white cloud before her in the chilly November air.

She could picture him, was sure of what she saw. She tried to let it go as she made her way home in what little light was left of the day. Will and Brian would be wondering where she was, she thought, what was taking her so long. She knew Will would already have the chicken in the oven and he would warm her hands when she got in. That he would smell cognac on her breath, and cigarette smoke in her hair, that he would leave all questions until later, after Brian was in bed.

He would say it's too bad, too bad Adrienne was alone. He would give her that. He would leave it at that. Paul would have said Adrienne couldn't expect anything else. That it comes with the territory when you screw around with someone else's husband. You don't exactly have the right to hold his hand when he's dying.

Everything was about action and consequences with Paul. With Will, everything was about destiny. Paul thought he had landed Storm because he sold her on his charm and good looks and dazzling personality. Will thought he ended up with Storm because circumstances and fate had brought them together. The timing was right.

There was truth in both versions. That's the part that always confused her. If Paul could have her because he set out to — if Will could have her because she showed up, which was really her choice because of Paul's actions, not his choice, or was it? If it wasn't Paul's, and it wasn't hers, but became hers — she made a choice and left and ended up with Will — what part was controllable action? What part destiny?

Sometimes, after she's had a long day with Brian's endless how-comes and whys, and Will has kept her in conversation about the feed store and the things that need doing around the farm, Storm excuses herself and grabs a magazine to make it look like she might be a while. Then she heads for the small room upstairs at the end of the hall. The only room with a locked door, the one room that can give her a little time away.

Storm sits in the bathroom and reads, or doesn't read. She lingers, lingers in the instant distance, in the chance to hear her own mind's questions and quandaries and banal observations. The toilet seat is cold. The rain is heavy. Did fate land her there? The effortless narrative that repeats everything she ever thinks, which starts to fade when she flushes and leaves the bathroom and heads back downstairs where sound effects and conversation take up most of the room again.

That night, after Adrienne told her all about Sam, Storm walked home with a number of bathrooms floating through her head. When she reached the end of her driveway, she turned to see the schoolhouse once more. She could see the smoke rising from the chimney and the yellow of the lights from inside, which were softened by the plastic covered windows, hazy and filtered. Adrienne was alone again, left with nothing but the company of her private thoughts and possibly regret for telling Storm everything, what seemed like everything.

She was probably waiting for the phone to ring, Storm thought. She might fix herself something to eat, or run a hot bath, or drink cognac all night long. Light candles. Sit in the dim light listening to that classical music station she liked so much. Reminisce about nights not so lonely, in the arms of Sam who managed to get away, who made a great effort to be with Adrienne, who risked everything to be with her.

Adrienne said she was used to being alone. She was used to living off a few moments of pleasure — stretching it out — using it to fill the rest of time. She could make it last longer if she had to.

The naked trees that lined the road between where Adrienne was and where Storm stood were hardly moving in the slight wind. Minto School sat aglow in the eerily quiet early hours of a late-autumn evening. Storm watched for a moment until the smell of roast chicken and the sound of familiar voices beckoned her to come in from the cold. She took one last look at it — schoolhouse at dusk — then stepped inside, away from everything that had followed her home.

Storm dusted the tables in the living room. She used lemon polish because she liked the smell, because she never used anything else. The amber liquid left a lemon-scented memory of other homes. Only one had offered privacy, and only for a short time, before Will started coming around, before she married him and moved into the farmhouse he was renovating down the road. That's how it seemed to go. He started coming around. She married him, moved in with him, bore his child.

Sometimes, it felt like she never lived in the schoolhouse. Sometimes, it felt like she never left.

Before that she lived in Paul's condo, for nearly ten years. Before that she lived in a basement apartment on Albert Street in Kingston, where her aging landlady walked heavily above her head, nosed around, and hummed songs Storm hadn't heard in years. It was all she could afford. She went to Kingston to make her own way, to find her way and get away. It seemed far away then, at 19, even though it was only an hour by car.

Storm kept quiet on weekends and in the evenings after work when she came home from her secretarial job at an investment firm. She kept the volume on the television turned down, didn't laugh too loud on the phone. She made love to boyfriends in the dark without making a sound. Jumped up and down when she landed a job at the radio station. Played music loudly when she packed her clothes and moved out. Made love to Paul with vigour in the middle of the kitchen floor before she left, screamed her head off when she came.

Before the dark and dingy basement apartment in Kingston, she lived in Rawdon Township, in a farmhouse with a stovepipe that ran through her bedroom, making it the warmest room in the house. Where older brothers lurked in corners behind half-closed doors, leaping out at her when she least expected it, to scare her and entertain themselves, to keep her on her toes. She could hardly stand to stay in the room with the door shut in the winter, it was so warm. The heat crackled in the pipe that poked up through the floor and ran above the doorway into the wall. She left her door ajar and could never tell if someone was standing on the other side. She could hear everyone passing by on the way to the bathroom, could hear them flushing, washing, bathing.

Storm squirted lemon polish on the tables, rubbed, made it last, went over and over the same spot several times. She wasn't ready to leave yet. She always had trouble leaving the schoolhouse. Whenever she was finished cleaning, she walked around and inspected her work, checked and double-checked to make sure she shut the taps off fully and all the lights were turned off — delaying her departure. She stood in the corners, saying goodbye all over again to each room, to every angle of the small and peaceful space — forcing herself not to listen as it begged her to stay, to put her feet up and stay for just a bit longer.

She vacuumed the living room, along the tops of the baseboard, in between the coils of the braided rug and underneath the cushions and along the back of the cherry-coloured sofa — every place she could think of. Storm always called it a couch until Adrienne came to stay and called it a sofa. Sofa sounded better.

Adrienne kept the place pretty clean, cleaner than most of the tenants who passed through. She rearranged the furniture slightly, which Storm rearranged after Adrienne left. She preferred the sofa facing the doorway and the front windows. Adrienne preferred the chairs facing the doorway and the front windows and reversed the order of things, placed the sofa so it looked towards the dining area, its back to the door.

Storm told her the new arrangement felt strange. Adrienne said she would move everything again when she left, she was only there a while longer. She had to return eventually, to her job, her apartment, her real life.

"I came to extract myself," she said simply and left it at that. She always left it like that, with no where else to go, no way to pursue it, no point really. Her words were brief and exact.

She had come to wait out Sam's death. It was unbearable for her to be in the same city, a few blocks away, unable to see him. Unbearable. Unfair. Cruel to them both. Impossible on her part, she wouldn't survive it.

Sam knew where she was. Adrienne described the schoolhouse in detail over the phone one night. The doctor put him on. He said Sam wanted to talk to her. She filled him in on the history of the place, talked without response, then finally got a breathy "terrific" from him. A note had come the day before. *Am trying to talk a little each day. Doctors say it's better if I talk a little. Hurts more if I don't talk. God, I miss your face.*

Storm said she didn't mind the rearrangement of the furniture. Really, she thought the change was good. Adrienne should feel free to do whatever she wanted to with the place for the time that she was there. Really, in the whole scheme of things, it didn't matter all that much.

Adrienne collected pinecones and rocks, and placed them next to the ones Storm had collected. It was hard to tell which ones Storm had picked and which ones Adrienne had brought back. Eventually, Storm forgot about the tiny markings that once identified the cones she had gathered from the woods. She couldn't remember which of the long, skinny ones had reminded her of a limp penis — Paul's limp penis. For some reason, only his penis. Had Adrienne been thinking the same thing? She had also collected some long, skinny ones, had held them in her hand and felt their undeniable shape.

Adrienne went to flea markets and picked up blue bottles and lined them along the window-ledge in the kitchen. She picked up a new quilt for the bed — an antique quilt with blue and red stars and circles and half-moons against a creamy background. She made snowflakes out of paper and left them taped to the windows in the dining area, where they still made their way down from the sky against the glass. Storm never bothered peeling them off. She left them up all year, on purpose, relishing the foolishness of it, the rebellion, even if it was only about a few paper snowflakes on an old window-pane. Why couldn't they stay up all year?

When she lived in Paul's condo, Storm used to hang a plastic green Christmas wreath with fake plastic red berries on the front door on the first of every December, twisting the wire around a hook several times so no one could steal it without a lot of work. She'd hang the same grapevine wreath with the same bunch of Indian corn on the same hook on the first of every October. She left the door bare in the spring and summer.

She used the same artificial Christmas tree every year — hauled it out from the locker on the first floor, used the same red and gold satin balls and multi-coloured lights, played the same Carpenters' Christmas songs while she decorated the tree, drank rum and eggnog, and longed for a Christmas that didn't smell of plastic. She shrugged and made the best of it and got all sentimental hanging a porcelain ball with *First Christmas Together* painted on it. Even that last Christmas together, when she knew it would be their last Christmas together, she felt her heart move to the right of her chest at the very thought of it being the last time she would place their special ball on the tree. She knew she'd leave it behind in the locker, along with the plastic wreath. Paul would find it one day and throw it away. Cheap plastic reminders. All for the sake of tradition, to maintain the proper order of things, make them feel they were sharing a life together.

In her basement apartment, Storm always unpacked the same twenty-inch artificial tree she used to have in her bedroom as a girl and placed it on top of the television, screwed in the flicker light so they'd blink on and off, on and off. She placed cotton balls underneath the tree to make a blanket of snow and wrapped old jewellery boxes in Christmas paper with small bows for presents under her mini-tree — for her pretend Christmases. They weren't real ones. Not the way she wanted them to be. The way they would be when she married Will and had Brian and they walked back into the woods to cut their own tree, dragged it back to the house, and strung popcorn and cranberries and white lights around its prickly arms.

The first Christmas she spent in the schoolhouse by herself, Will took Storm out into the woods and chopped down a small Scotch pine. He carried it back on his shoulder and set it up inside for her. It was the kind of tree she used to write about, like the Scotch pines and blue spruce available in the parking lots of the A & P and Loblaws and in all the nurseries, where you could find Christmas trees and door swags and cedar garlands. Everything to bring an old-fashioned Christmas into your home. *Decorate early! Shop now! Get ready for Christmas so you can enjoy the holidays! Hurry! Just thirty-one shopping days left!*

Every year now, Will and Storm and Brian went out to cut their own tree. Every year, Will strung multi-coloured lights along the front of the house and all the way up to the top of the evergreen in the corner of the front yard. It sometimes reminded Storm of the plastic tree with the same red and green and yellow and blue lights she had had with Paul. Not always, just some nights when she caught a glimpse of their reflection in the snow and remembered the way they used to bounce off the white walls in the apartment, where she sat in the dark and waited for Paul to come home from another client Christmas party.

In the kitchen, Storm took a damp cloth and wiped the dust off the cupboards and the counter. She opened the drawer, checked for mouse shit, ran her fingers over ladles and salad servers and slotted spoons she used to use. She told herself they were stupid things to be sentimental about. She remembered Adrienne washing them, stacking them in the dish-rack, the way she missed rinsing some of the soap that ran down the handles, settled into the bottom of the utensil holder, and left a grey, slippery scum that Storm found after Adrienne went back to Toronto.

She only saw Adrienne washing dishes once, that one night she asked Storm to stay for dinner. That night the phone didn't ring and Adrienne paced back and forth the length of the schoolhouse, through the living room towards the front door, turning around, walking back to the dining area — the front of the class where the chalkboard once was, the teacher pacing up and down the aisles between the desks, the *clump, clump, clump* of her shoes while the children were scribbling, concentrating, pretending to be doing something worthwhile. Storm useless, wordless, waiting for

Adrienne to sit down.

Storm told Adrienne she went to Minto School for the first two years of her education, until 1968 when it was closed, along with all the other one-room schools. Adrienne said she remembered reading something about that, about the closing of the little schools. What was it like then, she asked. Did Storm remember? Where were the desks placed? How many students were there? Who was the teacher? Storm hardly remembered anything about it. Miss Ketcheson, she said. The seats were hard and there were paper snowflakes on the windows in the winter, tulips in the spring, red and yellow paper leaves in the fall. She liked the smell of the glue and wanted to play with the fat pieces of chalk. She couldn't remember ever speaking in class. She remembered raising her hand, so she must have, but she couldn't recall what her voice sounded like.

"Something must have happened," Adrienne said, still pacing.

Storm searched for something to say to ease the burden, to give Adrienne a reason not to think the worst, even though Storm was thinking the worst, was almost sure it had to be the worst. Still, she didn't want to say, didn't want to be the first to bring up the possibility that the end was no longer nearing, it was there, suddenly, as suddenly as anything ever is when you expected it to come later — or not at all.

"Maybe Martha took him home again. Maybe he's doing better and they let him go." Storm put a smile in her voice. She could do that. She could smile and be bubbly. She could fake it.

She could read a radio commercial over the phone to a client with enthusiasm and proper inflection, pretending his annual spring dress sale was the most important, best thing that was happening in the world. She could smile as she said *The biggest sale ever! Save like never before! Beautiful dresses in every size!* She could sound interested while she menstruated and popped Tylenol and gave a pushy, interrupting sales rep the finger as he slipped her some last-minute information on a bar napkin — sales points for a new pet store that was sponsoring the five o'clock news, starting that day.

Besides, Storm thought, she wasn't stretching too much. It was possible. It had happened before. Sam had gone home before, in September, for almost two months. Adrienne didn't hear a word. There weren't any letters. No nightly calls from his doctor, except when Sam first left the hospital and the doctor called and told her about it.

One morning during that time Sam was home, Adrienne said she actually forgot. Forgot for just a while. She woke up without thinking, only saw sunshine as it spread across the quilt on her bed. She felt a quickening, as if there was something to look forward to. She showered and ate breakfast and went outside to collect some fall leaves. She brought them inside, pressed them between waxed paper the way her grandmother had taught her, and placed them in between the pages of the history of Rawdon Township, in front of a picture of Minto School. She forgot about it for a while, then paid dearly for it when it came back, and hated herself for forgetting in the first place.

"He's too sick to be at home anymore," Adrienne said, setting aside her urge to lash out, to throw it in Storm's face, and smack her with it. What good would it do? Storm was only trying to help her, the only one there.

"His regular doctor probably just didn't make it in today. Maybe he has a cold and Sam wouldn't tell anyone else to call you. He wouldn't take that chance."

Adrienne stood in front of the paper snowflakes looking out into the black night. She couldn't see it really. The light from the candles and the one lamp that was on in the living room were distorted in scale but clearly there, on the bubbled window-pane, on the wrinkly surface of the transparent plastic sheet. Storm's face was there, too — a long way off, round and shaped differently, expressionless, or rather, her expression didn't make it as far as the window. It lost its definition somewhere between the sofa and the other end of the room.

She could make tea, Adrienne thought. She could pour some cognac. She could make Storm go home. She could run a bath. She could try to read. She could walk outside under the moon and let the crunch of the snow take her someplace else. Let the cold air slap her back to getting past this part of her life, making it history. She could deal with history, with what was.

"What can I do for you?" Storm finally asked, as much for herself as for Adrienne, knowing, even as she asked, knowing the only thing that would help wasn't possible. Adrienne couldn't be there. She couldn't see him. She couldn't know where he was, what he saw out the window, what he smelled. She couldn't hear the nurses outside in the hall, or the dinging of the elevator every time someone came and went. She couldn't see the tube of mush that fed his decaying body, the way he'd grown used to the feedings every fours hours. The way he still smiled at his own reflection in the mirror every morning when he woke up, saw a ghost there in the middle of the night, realized it was his own face barely illuminated by the small bedside lamp.

Storm could picture him.

She could picture Sam turning on the larger lamp, taking the darkness away, reassuring himself, seeing his grey hair in the mirror, and his ears, one bigger than the other — still one bigger than the other, one cropped slightly on the top. It was the forceps, his mother had told him. She told him when he was a boy. A boy who was embarrassed by his ears, feeling deformed, wanting to keep his hair long so it covered them. They looked identical at the bottom.

Adrienne mentioned Sam's ears once. Storm never forgot. His ears. The hospital. The tubes of mush. It was enough for Storm to work with. And the white teddy bear with a red heart and a card that lied, that said it was from the girls at the office. Storm could picture it on the window-ledge, how its white hair formed a halo in the sunshine, the way it dulled in front of a dark sky when it rained. How it smiled at him — its eyes never looking away, always asking him *why, why, why*.

He was sitting up. Yes, Storm thought. He was sitting up, looking out over the city. Nothing was moving, except a plane jetting above the skyscrapers, a bit of smoke rising from distant factories. He winked at the bear, but really he's winking at you, Adrienne. He reaches over, brushes its soft cheek with his finger. Really, he's touching you, Adrienne. He picks you up, holds you, wants to be with you again — wants to meet you in the parking lot, to slip away to your apartment, to hold you forever.

Can't you feel him?

He holds you, holds the colour of your face, radiating life's heat against the plaster walls. The walls are plaster. Cold, shiny plaster. A light, pleasant colour, almost a non-colour, but he no longer notices. The room is quiet. He's the only one there, in his private room, with his bed near the window, and a table on one side where he keeps his notepad and pens, and a closet where his coat and a pair of slacks and a shirt hang ready for him. His shoes tucked into one corner, a dufflebag with underwear and socks beside them.

Martha takes his dirty underwear and socks home every night. She washes them, brings them back the next morning, and puts them in the dufflebag — leaves at least a dozen clean pairs in the bag. She sits down beside him, tells him about her day, makes the smallest detail seem interesting, stretches life in all directions, doesn't mention she spent the better part of the night staring at the living room ceiling. She helps him go to the bathroom, shaves his face while he sits up in bed, cuts his hair, hates to shake it off the towel into the garbage can — the living, greying hair — puts a few strands in her pocket when he isn't looking, takes them home.

Storm stopped there.

For God's sake, she thought. His hair. In his wife's pocket.

She told Adrienne she needed to use the bathroom. She left her alone standing by the dining room window, straightening the curled edges of the paper snowflakes behind the plastic sheet, rubbing the spots where the tape was, rubbing them, warming them, to keep them sticking against the freezing glass.

Storm sat on the toilet and barely peed. She forced it. Anything to make a trickle. She knew Adrienne could hear and would wonder about it if nothing came. A little did, then stopped. Storm sat there — so long her feet fell asleep and she had trouble getting to the sink to wash her hands. She stood there shaking one foot at a time until the prickly feel went away. Until the urge to tell Adrienne went away.

Yes, she could do it. She could tell Adrienne all about Sam's world, what his world had become, what Storm could only guess his world had become because she didn't really have a clue. But what good would it do? What possible good could come from knowing your lover's wife was carrying her dying husband's hair around in her pocket? Besides, Adrienne would know. So would Storm. She would always know it had come from her own world. That she had gone inside and given voice to the images and lent them to Sam and to Adrienne. That Storm would never see them the same way again.

Barn in afternoon light. Storm stood in the middle of the barn floor, where grass had found its way through old concrete, where the stone foundation surrounded her and a few windows were still intact. Everything else — the walls, the roof, the stalls — was gone. She stood near the spot at the front of the barn where her father had kept a radio hanging on a large nail, on a beam above her head. She told Will she used to listen to it constantly, when she was cleaning the barn and helping her father milk the cows.

She told him her father used to get stale chips from the Hostess distributor in the city and bring them home for food for the few pigs they had. She told him she stood over a white plastic barrel, opening bags of Doritos and Hickory Sticks, dumping the contents, eating some, dumping some, eating some, dumping the rest while she listened to dedications and Top-Forty Countdowns — to country music and classic rock. That she used to listen late at night to non-stop news and talk-radio, and W-NNNNN-BC in New York City, while she waited for a calf to be born, or because she had nothing better to do, never imagining she'd end up further down the dial one day. A messenger for meaningless messages — stale, meaningless slop. A pig's supper.

Will listened patiently and told her he used to listen to the same stations, then he asked her to marry him. He made love to her on the barn floor the same way he talked. Certain and paced. *He will be my private foundation*, she thought, as she lay there on the cool concrete with Will inside of her, on top of her, sheltering her from the elements that lay waiting, unpredictably, in the air above and beyond them.

It is only now that Storm can look at that picture and see the significance of the wall-less, roof-less structure around her.

Storm finished cleaning the kitchen, gave the radio a quick swipe with the dust cloth, left it until last, as usual. She knew no one was there. That Paul was probably out selling, pushing the owner of the ugly furniture store to buy more, more, more. That no one real answered the phone anymore. That computers played voice-tracked breaks and time-checks in between cuts of pre-assembled music and digitally recorded commercials, while announcers were out getting their hair cut or shopping for groceries or drinking in some bar in the middle of the afternoon listening to themselves — to the magic of being there, and not being there.

She sat down at the dining room table, poured herself a cognac, and lit a cigarette. She heard Will hit the horn three times quickly as he drove by, was thankful for the safe return of her husband and son, said so three times, as always. *Thank God, thank God, thank God.* She pulled out a brochure on fall leaves with pictures and descriptions. She pulled out the history book Adrienne left behind, pulled out the waxed paper and opened it, and laid the leaves on the table.

The last time Storm cleaned the house she found the book on one of the shelves in the living room, saw the maple leaves behind the white waxy sheet. She figured Adrienne had collected them from the trees out front. Storm didn't expect to find the other leaves behind them and wasn't sure what some of them were. A brochure had come in the mail, since then, advertising a resort with a view of the fall colours. Storm brought it along, to look up the unfamiliar leaves and found White Ash and Shagbark Hickory and Speckled Alder in Adrienne's collection. She decided she'd look for them on her way home, now that she knew their names. She wondered if Adrienne knew what they were and if that's why she picked them in the first place. They were pale and unspectacular next to the orange and yellow glow of the maple leaves.

When she was finished her drink and her cigarette, Storm walked into the kitchen to rinse her glass, walked through the spot she always imagined was the place where Adrienne fell apart. She didn't see her so much as she felt her, felt Adrienne sitting on the floor, leaning against the cupboards below the sink, her knees bent, her face buried in her hands, her shoulders heaving — fighting it, letting it go.

"Sam died last night." Adrienne had said it plainly, with a degree of control. "I'll be leaving tomorrow."

The doctor had called to tell her. He told her Sam had asked him to, a long time ago, when there wasn't any hope left. Adrienne said the doctor seemed relieved that it was his last call to her. The mistress. It had to be uncomfortable for him. It wasn't easy for anyone, that kind of arrangement.

"You have to like wanting," Adrienne once told Storm. "To settle for a man like Sam — a married man with too much history with his wife ever to leave her. Wanting becomes your real companion. I could always understand the history bit. How could I ever say I didn't? I rant and rave when they tear down old buildings. I'm a history teacher, for God's sake."

Storm shook her off. She rinsed her glass then felt it again, like she had before, felt something smearing on the floor beneath her feet. She told herself, maybe this time she really did spill something — some cognac or some water. She hoped for something wet as she bent down to check, as she ran her hand over where it should be.

Adrienne wrote one letter, about three months after she left the schoolhouse — at Storm's request. She said she was

back teaching and that she went to see Sam often, that she
felt okay about it. She could always say she was looking for
an old friend if Martha showed up. She could roam around
the graveyard for a while to make it believable. She had it
all figured out.

On her way home from the schoolhouse, Storm made a
point of looking for White Ash and Speckled Alder, and
spotted some Shagbark Hickory right away. A car passed by
her and an elderly couple waved. She heard them slowing
down behind her, then stopping, going over old ground,
unaware of the continuum of history, knowing nothing at all
about the slow extraction of Adrienne Moore, how she
looked up just as Storm walked into the kitchen and stepped
into her private moment. They only saw a familiar road and
a woman carrying a bucket, holding the hammered gold
leaves of Shagbark Hickory and the thin, leafy fingers of
dark red sumac.

When she got home, Storm shoved the leaves in
between some withering maples on her front-door wreath —
a grapevine wreath that's weathered and lightened over the
years. She admired it briefly, fussed, and made a slight
change. Then she went inside and forgot about it
completely, until the next time she saw it and remembered
where it came from.

Chapter Thirteen

It is early December when we meet again for film night. The naked tree season, as Grace calls it. Those few weeks between the time the fall leaves disappear from the trees and winter begins, when nothing is hidden and the forest stands undressed and exposed — its secret life unable to move about unseen. It stands in idle nakedness waiting for the first snow to fall, to lend some mystery once again. Grace has described the naked tree season before, in a passage from *In Search of Parsley*, which still hasn't been picked up by a publisher and keeps her up at night wondering if she really has anything worthwhile to say — if she said it well, or if she failed, somehow, to say anything at all.

Storm says in the naked tree season you see things more clearly, when the world isn't coloured with distracting summer greens or the vibrant beauty of autumn, when you can't help but see the truth in its monochromatic starkness. There is nothing disguising it — nothing covering up the truth about a woman sitting alone in a schoolhouse, completely and utterly alone. You can't help but see it for what it is.

"Do we have to be so goddamn gloomy?" Jenny yells from the kitchen. She is drinking heavily tonight and even I find it difficult to be around her.

"What's with her anyway?" Sally whispers.

"But Adrienne chose to love Sam," Alex says.

"Not this bloody love stuff again." Jenny walks back into the room with my mother-mug full of white wine, spilling some on the floor when she sits down, making no effort to clean it up.

"Is love a choice?" Delaney asks.

I asked Ben the same thing the other night. Is love a choice?

We've gone from secretly meeting at his cottage — where the girlfriend is no longer allowed to live but shows up frequently unannounced — to meeting at my house when my kids are at their father's and I am home alone. Home and alone and awake late at night when Ben shows up at my door. He said he was easing her out, he wasn't good at this heartbreak stuff. Wouldn't a clear break be better, I suggested. No, he said, and I wasn't sure if it had more to do with them or us. Did having her in the picture keep things moving slowly between us? What would happen if we were suddenly free to love each other without the complication?

Do I have a choice, I asked him.

About what, he asked me.

About loving you, I said.

He seemed perplexed and didn't bother answering me. He told me I think too much, I think too far ahead. Can't I just let it go? Can't I just be with him?

Can't I?

It didn't help that he was rubbing my feet in bed and telling me how beautiful my arches were, and my toes, and my ankles, and my legs, and every other inch of me. I was eyeing my Storyteller's Jacket, which hung like another part of me on a dressmaker's form in the corner of my room, with a piece of Ben's black Levi's shirt still sitting in the left-hand pocket. It remains unstitched — our story incomplete. My unwillingness to be finished with him keeps me from finding its place among all the rest, to give it its fitting end, as I have given it to those who've come before.

"It's the sex," Jenny says. "You just don't want to give up sex with the midnight cowboy."

"The midnight rambler," I correct her.

"Isn't it always the sex?" Jenny adds. "That's what fucks everything up. That's what'll get you into trouble, Sally."

"It's not just the sex," Alex snaps. "That's so insulting to them both."

"Then what is it?" Grace asks. "If it isn't the sex, what is it then?"

"God, your mind is closed these days, isn't it?"

"What the hell is that supposed to mean?"

"You just don't get it, do you?"

"Maybe she doesn't get any," Jenny quips.

"Fuck you, Jen."

"Christ, you people are serious tonight," Jenny says, gulping, spilling, gulping some more.

Silence, a shifting in seats. Stereo sighs from the corner where Storm and Delaney exchange concerned glances.

I put the movie on in a hurry — *The Trip to Bountiful*, with Geraldine Page — and try to run through it quickly in my mind, what I remember of it. An elderly woman goes home to her parents' house in Bountiful, Texas. It's a pilgrimage, a last trip home. Will it make things worse tonight, or settle us down? I can't remember what buttons are pushed, and I am afraid to push the one that says *Play*.

I'm afraid not to.

Grace is sulking, Alex is near tears, and Jenny is looking for a fight.

Storm and Delaney stick to their corner, out of the line of fire.

Sally is unusually quiet.

I feel a sudden urge to retreat to my bathroom, where strangely enough everything is working well for a change. The toilet seat is still screwed tightly to the base, my faucet no longer leaks, and the caulking job I did months ago is still holding fast to the side of my tub, sparkling white and smooth, with no imminent signs of mould.

"Ben," I said when he was here. "Are you real?"

"Am I what?"

"Are you real?"

"Real what?"

"Real."

(*Pause*)

"Yes."

Halfway through the movie, Jenny passes out, then wakes up. "Isn't it over yet?" she slurs. "Christ. What's the big deal about going home?"

She passes out again and we leave her there to sleep off what I've just discovered is two bottles of wine down her gullet in less than three hours, never mind what she had before she came. She sleeps and she stirs and she keeps mumbling, "It's on the porch, it's on the porch." We find it funny, and then not funny, and then not so funny at all.

"She's killing herself," Sally says.

It is the only thing Sally says all night.

No one knows but me. No one knows about the walk Sally and I went for last weekend, how we wound our way through the streets of Stirling and found ourselves standing in front of the house she grew up in.

"It's going to snow soon," she said. The wind was blowing strong, blowing her hair in front of her face and into her mouth as she spoke. "I can feel it, you know. Usually, weeks before it starts."

She pulled at the hair that was sticking to her lips and I could see they were purple and quivering slightly and I knew she was talking about her parents and the snowstorm on the day they were killed. She held the top of her coat closed with one hand and tried to keep her hair back with the other. There was a button missing and her neck was wide open. She'd forgotten her gloves and her hands were red and freezing. I gave her one of mine and kept my bare hand in my pocket. She did the same. It was too cold to stay there, too important to leave.

"They've never felt dead to me," Sally said.

A shutter on one of the windows was loose and banging in the wind. The place looked rundown. Even I noticed how neglected it was.

"They never felt alive to me, either."

There was movement in the living room window, someone pulling back a curtain and then letting it close again. It was dark inside and we couldn't see who it was. A child? A woman?

"They never went anywhere."

We could see a quick flash of flesh — a brief glimpse of a hand. And then it was gone and the picture remained the same. The neglected house. The lack of life around it.

"I think I have to go," Sally said. "Don't you think I should go?"

There was Sally, her hair getting caught in her mouth, the banging shutter.

The sound of birds fluttering in the back of my head.

The distant glimmer of the dumping ground on Johnny Marks's sister's farm.

I could see it as I followed him along the narrow cattle path. We were heading for the pond in the back twenty acres of the property; a small forest of evergreens and pine and the odd white birch — just three or four more fields of tall tickle grass and uncut hay away. I could see the reflection of the sun bouncing off an old milk bottle or the windshield of some old car, a shimmering light from somewhere off to the right. I didn't mention it or suggest we go there. I didn't want the distraction or the delay. I only wanted to carry on down my own inevitable path.

I knew what would be there. I'd seen dumping grounds before — on the farm where I grew up, and on the farms of childhood friends, holding the garbage and decaying junk of previous generations, most of them started decades before the advent of community garbage disposal sites. There would be a pile of disintegrating tin cans and dirty glass bottles — most of them cracked. Irons worked to death and discarded. Probably a radio or two with the back ripped off, half the guts missing, yanked by someone who thought the parts might be useful one day. Licence plates all bent to hell, a rusted-out car, or an old tractor, or both. Maybe a pram, with torn, discoloured material and missing wheels, scrunched up like an accordion, its baby-carrying days long gone and forgotten by most, except the one who pushed it along pebbly country roads.

The pile would stand in statuesque stillness in a corner of a field too rocky to plow, too thistle-ridden, too steep and too small to use as pasture. It would appear suddenly. They always appeared suddenly, unnatural and out of place, a sculpture of still life heaped onto the land of continuous movement, of seed, growth, and harvest.

"It's not as far as it looks," Johnny said, turning around to make sure I was still behind him, still enthused about going to the pond even though I had already mentioned I was late, that Hal was expecting me home hours ago.

"That's okay," I answered, although I wasn't sure if we didn't get there soon, I wouldn't turn back. Johnny had already shown me the faces of the old men and the old women he carved in the fence posts along the road and in the field behind his sister's house. I had already stayed for two beers and a ham sandwich, had already spent the better part of the early afternoon on the front porch with him, talking, and shifting in our seats, opening our legs wider then we should have from our opposite positions on the cool cement floor — helping ourselves to indiscreet looks at the unrevealing crotches of our jeans. It was the idea of it. Relax, I told myself. It was allowed here, with him.

I followed Johnny down the cattle path because I couldn't imagine the day going any other way — just leaving, bidding each other farewell and I'll see you around. I wiped the first signs of perspiration from my forehead with the back of my hand. It had turned out to be a muggy day. The temperature had climbed considerably since the morning when I told Hal I was going out on a delivery.

"I suppose you're already in hot water." Johnny grabbed a blade of grass as he walked and began chewing on one end.

"I'll probably be grounded for the rest of the week," I joked.

He turned around and walked backwards, to face me. "You don't seem too concerned."

I could see the reflection of light from the dumping grounds just beyond his head. "I am. But I'm not," I said.

He turned around again to watch where he was going, then turned his head once more to look at me. "Good," was all he said and he kept walking.

When we reached the end of the field, we joined up with a laneway wide enough for a tractor to drive through, where the grass was only a few inches tall. Johnny said he was trying to keep on top of it, that his sister told him not to bother with the hay fields. They had hired a farmer down the road to cut them.

Although he loved the country, Johnny wasn't adept at farming. It was all he could do to remember how the gears worked on the tractor and to cut the grass in the laneway without taking a chunk out of the fence that lines it.

"What can I say? I'm not exactly Farmer Brown." He tripped as he said it, catching his shoe on a rock.

The laneway only went so far, down to the opening of the last field of workable land, and we were soon traipsing through another field of tall tickle grass. That's what my mother always called it, because of its green, fuzzy, caterpillar-like flower at the end. She used to pick it on her walks through the fields behind our house, bringing a few strands home to tickle us. Sometimes, she brought back pretty stones, or fossil rocks, or small pieces of smooth driftwood — something to show for her time away. Usually, it was tickle grass.

I followed her once. I hid behind the wide trunks of trees along the fence-line and behind clumps of spreading lilacs and watched her as she made her way through each field in one of her house dresses — her apron still tied around her waist. She often forgot to take it off.

It seemed she never planned her walks. She always left in haste. I never knew if it was because of her own sudden need to flee, or because my father would show up unexpectedly, taking a break from plowing or cutting, giving her the opportunity. Or if they had planned it all along — that morning — and just didn't bother telling any of us, to lessen the risk of intrusion, of someone pleading to go along. Whichever way it was, she often left the house with her apron on, dashing off before anything could stop her.

She looked younger out there, without a pot in her hand or one of my younger sisters or brothers in her arms. She looked like she might keep walking forever, like she might leave her mother-shell behind and run naked the rest of the way, or start spinning around on the hilltop in the field just before the dumping ground — spinning until she made herself dizzy and fell, but she didn't.

I followed her from far behind — half a field — not letting my eyes wander for even a second, for she was unpredictable. She would stop suddenly at the edge of the next field, or in the middle of it, where the tall grass stretched on beyond her. She would stand rigid in its flowing waves with one hand above her eyes against the sun, helping her to see what was ahead of her and to the side of her. More of the same.

Sometimes, she'd stand for what seemed like ten minutes and I'd get cramps in my legs or in my shoulders from holding the same position, tempted to call out to her, to reveal myself and bring relief to my own aching muscles. To get rid of the loneliness that seemed to surround her as much as the tickle grass. I was frightened by the way she stood there, by what unknown thoughts were racing through her mind, making her abandon her steady pace, stopping her from moving. I was used to seeing her always moving.

Once, she turned around and I barely had time to dive into the grass to escape notice. If she saw something suspicious moving quickly, she made no attempt to discover it. I lay still against the dry ground — my skin itchy and red from the impact of my landing, from scraping up against the reedy stems of the grass. I waited, knowing I might lose sight of her altogether, possibly wanting to — for I couldn't erase the image of her turning around, of knowing something was behind her, of feeling watched in her privacy.

It was the first time I realized I could inflict pain on her, if I wanted. I was 13 at the time. My mother was 35.

When I came out of my hiding spot in the grass, I continued in the direction I thought she went in — down the path that led the cattle to a trench in one of the fields in the back of our farm. But I didn't see her. I stood in a field of uncut hay, hoping she wouldn't see me from some other spot on some other hilltop. She was nowhere in sight and I felt as though she had disappeared from the face of the earth.

I began to head back when I heard a sound coming from the direction of the dumping ground. I made my way carefully, keeping low to the ground, and found her there, smoking a cigarette and rooting through some of the garbage, wiping the dirt off a milk bottle with her apron, setting it aside.

I never knew my mother smoked and I wondered if she'd stolen the cigarette out of my father's pack, or if she had her own stashed away somewhere in her dresser drawer. She looked elegant, the way she held it between her fingers, the long drags she took, and the way she blew the smoke in the air, with her head tilted upwards. As if she belonged on a stool in a bar with silk nylons and high-heeled shoes and nails painted red. Not sifting through the disintegrating artifacts of my father's family, flicking her ashes on top of their garbage.

I watched her from behind a thicket of cedars, watched while she sat on a boulder and finished her cigarette. She spoke twice, in a lowered voice. "I remember those," she said. She was looking at the heap in front of her. She didn't make any attempt to pick up whatever she was looking at. There were bottles and cans and soiled plastic dolls and strange mechanical kitchen utensils I couldn't figure out. She sat there for the longest time. She took her shoes off and rubbed her feet. She stood up and stretched, her arms reaching for the peacock sky above her. Then she sat down and lit another cigarette.

"Shit," she said, as she exhaled. "Shit. Shit. Shit."

Johnny and I never made it to the pond. We wound our way through the openings of two different fields and up a hill where we could see the pile in the corner below us. The wind had picked up, but it was too warm to do any good. We were both perspiring.

"Shall we keep going?" Johnny asked me.

"No," I said. "I'd rather sit here for a while." I wasn't interested in seeing the pond anymore. I didn't care about it. I'd seen ponds before, skated on them in the winter, fished out of them in the summer. I didn't care. I didn't care that I wasn't going to make it the rest of the way, or that I was late beyond late, and that my husband might be worried or mad.

"Can we make love here?" Johnny asked before we had a chance to sit down.

"Now?"

"Am I being too blunt about it?"

"Yes. And no."

"Yes, we can make love. And no, I'm not being too blunt?"

"Yes, you're being blunt. And no, it's not too much. I guess it's not too much."

He stood there still chewing on the same piece of grass he'd picked earlier, waiting for my answer. I was buying time with my hands on my hips and worry on my face, looking out at the fields below us, which led to more fields and more fields beyond them. There wasn't any sign of a road, or a break in the landscape, although I could see the shiny silver roof of a barn and the rounded dome of a silo close by.

"If it's a dilemma, let's skip it," he said. "It doesn't have to happen."

"Not here," I said.

"You're right. It's not the prettiest place."

I could see a small piece of glass, what remained of the windshield of an old car, and the way the sun was hitting it, throwing it back at the open air.

"We can go back to the house," Johnny was saying, only he sounded far away. "Whatever makes you comfortable."

I could see my mother sitting on a boulder near the pile. I could smell her cigarette as my young hand pulled out a cracked milk bottle full of old butts. I could feel how long she'd been going there, what she left behind every time she walked away. It reached through me, wanting a place to be put down, recorded and made important.

There was nothing around.

I stood in the absence of paper and canvas, on the barest spot of a bed made mostly of thistles, reaching for the nearest form I could find.

I reached for it again, and again, and again, until I heard it adequately rendered in my own unrecognizable voice.

"Ben?"

"Yes."

"Shall I love you?"

"You don't need my permission."

"How about your blessing?"

"Alright. God help you if you love someone like me."

(*Pause*)

"God help me if you don't."

"It's not just about love and sex," Sally said as we stood outside her parents' house.

"I know."

"I keep feeling like there's something I need to hear. You know what I mean?"

"I think so."

"Like there's something I need to know and I'll only find it there. Does that make any sense to you?"

"Yes."

"Am I being silly?"

"To want to find out?"

"To believe it's there in the first place?"

By the time Geraldine Page makes it back to Bountiful, Texas, Jenny is vomiting in my bathroom once again. I hear her and make my way upstairs and find her on the floor lying in her own sickness.

"Is that blood in there?" Delaney asks from behind me.

"Yes," I say. "She's vomiting blood."

"I'm calling Georgia," she says and she leaves and I can hear her in my bedroom, on the phone, waking Georgia out of a boozy sleep to come and fix what she cannot see.

"You're her mother," I hear Delaney saying. And I can see her all over again: Delaney with her head out the window of my car, with a video camera in her hand, taping the perfect set of clouds moving gracefully across the perfect sky. Sally, in front of her parents' house with her hair in her mouth and all of her hopes pinned on a place far, far away. Myself still obsessed with rendering another version of what I saw that day when I followed my mother to the dumping ground on our farm.

Delaney

WHEN WOMEN LOSE THEIR MOTHERS

Chapter Fourteen

Until the article appeared in the *Stirling News Argus*, no one had any idea Delaney was capable of doing something extraordinary. They were surprised. So was she. Surprised, but not surprised.

She looked at her face in the black and white picture below the headline and still saw what she used to be. Even back then, when she stood in that grassy field behind the barn, the wind's whispered predictions told her *something* was going to happen to her one day. She remembers everything about it. The monochromatic hills in the distance. The chill that ran up her back. The swell of her belly and its frightening call for strength she didn't think she had. It floats through her veins, like all the rest. Edited bits of time.

She thinks that way. In chunks. Scenes. Words. Dialogues and monologues and the way the light looks at sundown as it

turns orange and rides the wires along the highway to
someplace else. She can recall the gestures and the tone of
voice and exactly what was said, and not said. It's all the space
in between scenes she doesn't know what to do with, except
to see it with tomorrow's reminiscent eye.

Local Producer Makes It To Big Time! the headline read, with
a poorly written story below. Front-page news, placed
beneath an even larger picture of the Stirling Tykes hockey
team — the tiny child faces beaming with pride over
winning the latest tournament. *Tykes Victorious Once Again!*

Except for a handful of friends and the few women she
had interviewed, most people in town didn't even know
Delaney had produced a documentary. She didn't talk about
it. Her husband, Drew, was the one who leaked it to the
press, to Donald McIntyre, who played hockey with Drew
every Thursday night. For the following week, it was the
talk of the town — how the girl at the Sears Catalogue Store
was really a producer and had just sold her documentary to a
national cable network.

"You've been leading a double life," old Bart Cooney said
when he came in to order a nightgown for his wife's
birthday, guessing at her size, which he'd forgotten or never
knew. Delaney offered her own body to his aging eyes, for
comparison, and didn't mind the extra minute he took to
look at her breasts. What harm did it do?

Suddenly, people she hardly ever saw came into the
store to pick up a new catalogue. Where they in yet? An
excuse for a glimpse at oddity. What did they expect to find?

She still wears her hair the same way — long, and in
need of a good cut. She still passes the same crooked picture
of Christ on the wall in the hallway that connects the Sears
Catalogue Store to the rest of the old Stirling Hotel, where
Delaney lives with her husband, three teenage boys, Drew's
mother, Opal, and the few roomers upstairs.

She still gets dressed every morning in a bathroom that's
dark and dingy, with a tap that never shuts up and never
stops dripping reminders of what needs to be done in the
old place. A tube of Scarlet Ice lipstick sits on the metal

shelf below a mirror that's turned brown in the corners and stares back at her with a hazy fog that never clears. Maybe, that's the point, she thinks. Dim the light and it'll all go away and fade into deception, or some place called survival.

It's barely bright enough in the bathroom to see the patchy rust marks painted by hidden, leaky pipes that moan and groan and shriek from behind the walls — let alone the true colour of her Scarlet Ice lipstick. Not orange-red, or burgundy-red, or too bright and cheap looking. Just red. Iced, and muted slightly. The kind of red that doesn't bleed all over a television screen.

Regular customers lingered when they came in to pick up parcels wrapped in dull grey paper, their secret contents known only to Delaney, who reads the description on the computer-printed labels. Honestly, what did everyone think they'd see? *Say, that was some news I read about you in the paper.*

She still lives down the hall, still sits on the same brown plaid couch with rips that run alongside fat gold stripes and swallows you up in two decades of dinners spilled by one kid or another who refused to sit at the table. Shepherd's pie, macaroni and cheese, vanilla ice cream. She still cooks in a kitchen that seems out of place the way it's set up at one end of the living room, with enough counter space to hold a mixing bowl, a carton of eggs, and a well-used Fanny Farmer cookbook with greasy fingerprints all over it.

She still passes the same back door that leads to the small yard behind the hotel, where she hung three different types of birdfeeders on a single maple and transplanted clumps of wild black-eyed Susans in front of the crumbling fieldstone foundation of a nearby building. Their faded, petal-less heads quivering in the winter wind.

She passes the back door to get to her cramped bedroom, where she sleeps on the same huge waterbed she's never gotten used to and watches a new state-of-the-art television that sits on top of the same dresser she's always had. A frosted glass candy dish she ordered years ago from Avon sits on top of that, filled with safety pins and tarnished pennies and earrings that no longer have a mate. Faces, framed in oak and brass and floral fabric, stare back in disbelief from either side of the television set. *This time in my life won't end, they say.* In the most prominent picture, Jesse, the woman Delaney calls mother, stands in front of an antique hall tree in the baby-blue rayon dress she wore to Delaney's wedding. A fake white corsage, improperly pinned, leans forward in mid-air. She smiles shyly for the camera before stepping out of sight.

A small silver frame sits at the back, behind the larger frames, and holds the only lasting image of Delaney's real mother, Claire. She is almost ten years younger than Delaney is now and is leaning against a willow tree, posing, pretending to be at ease with being photographed, with being there at all. She is impatient with the process, anxious to leap out of the black and white background and someone's self-serving need to document her.

After nearly twenty years, Delaney still feels the same way about the place she lives in — at home and not at home with the transient ghosts of the hotel who roam around the rooms looking for something to do. Drew's mother lives upstairs in a bedroom with a private bath and claims all rights to the parlour, the nicest room in the whole joint with its well-cared-for antiques and fancy, custom-made wall of curtains.

The parlour is off limits to Delaney's three children, who also have bedrooms upstairs, along the back of the hotel, and to the roomers who live down a separate hallway along the front, whose doors are always open, their televisions spewing out constant chatter. Wet, hacking coughs from tired, smoked-out bodies rise above the steady hum of game shows and the fastest, most effective relief for constipation.

Delaney noticed but didn't say anything when Charlie Sawyer stumbled in with a bottle half drunk and sticking out of a coat too thin for the weather. He gave Delaney a glance of indifference and made his awkward way up the stairs to a room at the end of the hall, where guests were once pampered with crisp white cotton sheets, fresh flowers, and homemade full-course meals. As they washed up for dinner, music would drift up the wide wooden staircase — a call for gaiety from the prancing fingers of a ragtime player piano in the dining room downstairs. Delaney heard Charlie close his door so he could enjoy the rest of his bottle in private, without the wanting eyes of other permanent guests intruding on the few ounces of comfort he had left. He was oblivious to the excitement going on downstairs. The constant ring of the bell on the back of the store door was only a minor irritation to him as the curious continued to saunter in to take a look at this woman who was someone other than she appeared to be.

And so it went, for several days, then everything quieted down again at the Sears Catalogue Store on Mill Street in Stirling.

A few weeks earlier, after she closed the store at noon on Saturday, Delaney went out to the small cemetery beside Bethel United Church in Rawdon Township and stood in front of Jesse's grave. The ground was frozen and didn't give at all under her feet. The trees were winter-bare and lifeless and, except for the streaks of noise from speeding traffic on the highway where the cemetery sits, it was dead silent.

Spring will bring the sound of tractors plowing up fields, she thought, and cows crying out their readiness to be milked as they lug their bulging udders all the way to the barn. Booming drums and wailing guitars will scream from open windows in the summer, thrown Jesse's way like stones kicked up from the shoulder of the road. There might even be a wedding or two in the church next door, where ushers and grooms will stand outside in the back, near her stone, smoking one last cigarette before the ceremony, swearing and joking about how marriage kills good sex. But at this time, on the day that Delaney stands by Jesse's grave, it is still dead silent.

She noticed a bouquet of dirty pink plastic flowers lying half-buried in the snow close by. She wasn't sure if it belonged to Jesse, if one of her sons had placed it there, or if it had blown over from some other grave. She put them in front of Jesse's name, packing the snow around them to keep them still and straight. Jesse should have flowers, she thought, and when she stood back up, Delaney's eye caught sight of the barn and the house and the drive shed.

That's the thing that struck her. That Jesse spent the last forty years of her life living on a farm only a glance to the left of her grave. A single field was all that separated her life from her death. In the smallest amount of time, Delaney could lift her eyes from the slab of granite that speaks Jesse's name in muted etchings and see her life summed up in three rundown buildings. A barn, a house, a drive shed.

Jesse Reid. Mother of. Wife of. Friend of. *In God's keeping* carved in stone. She lived there, she's buried here.

It was easy to simplify things, standing there for a few brief moments before Delaney returned to her car. Too easy, she thought. And that's what she was left with. That, and *what next-what next-what next?*

It was over. All the late nights and early mornings viewing and reviewing and stealing pockets of time here and there to get it done. All the sacrifice and self-discipline and self-doubt and complete surrender, the reasons for talking to Neil, taking trips to Montreal, the excuse for spending so much time alone in Room 15. It was all over now.

When Delaney met Neil Grayman for the first time the year before, she told him in verbal point form that she grew up as a foster child. That she'd spent the first two years of her life with a single mother who couldn't cope and the next ten years with families who thought they could. She told him she remembered certain rooms and certain smells, the occasional display of hesitant affection that would come her way, the dishes she was expected to do, the kids she was expected to instantly like, the affinity she had with bouncing rubber balls.

She told him because she didn't think she would ever see him again and if he was going to help her in the few short hours they had together, he might as well know who he was dealing with. Otherwise, what was the point? She couldn't pretend she was something she wasn't, and she wasn't some film grad who had connections and know-how and a nice budget courtesy of Telefilm Canada. She read about those people in the *Toronto Star* arts section every weekend. That's where she read about him, Neil Grayman, veteran documentary producer.

She's the mother of three boys, she told him. Her eldest was turning 20 in another year. Yes, yes, she knows she doesn't look that old, because she's not. She's only 35. She got pregnant at 15, married at 16, and the baby came four months later. You know how these things happen, don't you? In the crapshoot of life, she got pregnant the first time out. Can we move on?

And she did. To the point of her visit — her documentary — and how she lost the only woman she ever thought of as her mother two years ago, the wife of a dairy farmer who took her in when she was 12. How on a slow day in the Sears store she was cleaning the mirror on an antique hall tree when the words *When Women Lose Their Mothers* came into her mind. Just like that.

She didn't see it as a book or an article in *Chatelaine* — she's not good with words anyway. She saw it as a documentary, which she at least had some possibility of making because she's good with a video camera. You have to be with three kids and birthdays and first steps and last days of school. She just didn't know where to start. Could he give her a few pointers? She brought her notebook.

Yes, she lied when she called him out of the blue and said she had a tape she wanted him to look at. Yes, she did make it sound like she already had something finished. Would he have bothered with her if she hadn't? Would he forgive her? Could he help? Can she use his bathroom?

Yes, he said, to everything.

On her way home from Montreal that first time she met Neil, Delaney watched a continual pan to the west as the train left its dark tunnel and crept out into the late afternoon light — past the backs of crowded row houses downtown, where laundry flapped in the smoggy breeze and children played in the safety of a familiar street. It picked up speed past business towers and church steeples and Mount Royal, a compressed cityscape that buzzed with life on the other side of the thick silencing glass. It glided past one field after another — the longest part of the journey — past patchy snow and black split-rail fences, interrupted occasionally by short stops in the least attractive parts of one town or another. Cornwall. Brockville. Kingston. Train platforms and people popped up in the middle of her thoughts. The insecure embraces of departing lovers. The strained greetings between aging parents and adult children who've made another obligatory but disappointing visit — the regret, the unreasonable expectation. They accompanied her home for a while then faded into unimportance as she drifted back into the remaining light. The light that remains even when the sun has gone down — dark and illuminating at the same time, the way it glows and makes the snow in the fields look blue and unreal.

When she boarded the train, Delaney placed her purse and coat and the scuffed up navy leather schoolbag she found at a yard sale last year on the seat beside her. She didn't want to risk unwelcome company, the drain of making small talk. She wanted time to think about her meeting with Neil, about what she had done that day.

She was pleased with herself. She ordered one of those tiny bottles of rye and mixed it with ginger ale. She was on a train, having a drink, after spending the day with a talented documentary filmmaker, in a city with signs she couldn't read.

She had taken two cabs, with drivers who barely spoke English or French, and spent a half-hour reading *The New Yorker* in the train station. She had never read it before.

She had seen a copy of it earlier on the table at Neil's, beside a stack of video tapes, in a living room full of African artifacts and a menorah Neil told her he had brought back from Israel. He liked to travel, he said. Large shells that begged her ears to listen to the ocean's tales sat on a shelf near the window, lined with dusty plants in need of a drink. Delaney looked around for some hint of a woman's touch. Was he married? Divorced? There were no signs of children. No obvious clues to define him. His phone never stopped ringing. He'd call back, he said. He was busy. No, he hadn't looked at it yet. Yes, later today or tomorrow, for sure. One call took longer than a few minutes, longer than all the rest. Delaney could hear Neil yelling at the person on the other end. Something about being delayed because his editor got the flu; he'd get the fucking thing done as fast as he could; don't think for a minute he's not sick of working on the goddamn thing at this point and is really pissed off because he had to postpone his trip to Mexico. She listened as she stood near the window looking out at the mountain in the distance and the park across the street.

Neil had given her instructions on how to get to his place, his home, where he worked. She was going to grab a cab from the train station, she said, and didn't know the city at all. She'd never been there before. Where did he live? He told her what route to have the cab driver take, to make sure she didn't end up getting the scenic tour at five times the cost. "They'll take you up the goddamn mountain and all the way to Dorval if you let them," he warned her. But she made it, using the map she had drawn on a piece of old stationery from the hotel back in Stirling — when it was a hotel. The Stirling Hotel, which used to be the Sterling Hotel, with an *e* for the sterling service it promised, after it was Stirling House, with *i*. Either way, she was far from the bricks and mortar that contained her life.

Standing in Neil's home, she pulled off the dead, dried out leaves from the plants on the window-ledge. If a woman lived there, wouldn't the plants be watered?

"I'm a compulsive pruner," she said when Neil walked back into the room. He held out his hands to take the leaves. Delaney released the crumbling brown bits. Several landed on the floor.

"Do you go around pruning everybody's plants?"

"Just my own. And now yours."

She followed him into the kitchen where he put the dead leaves in the garbage. He started to make coffee and spilled milk all over the counter as he reached for yet another ringing telephone. She told him to sit down at the table and let her do it, that he was a real klutz, and was he always this much in demand?

"I have to tell you, Delaney. This whole thing is a bit strange."

"What is?"

"You showing up like this. It's like you just landed here, out of nowhere. You call me up out of the blue. The next thing I know, you're telling me the story of your life, you're pruning my plants and you're cleaning my counter."

"I'm sorry."

"You can't learn how to made a good documentary in one afternoon."

"I know."

"It's taken me years. You might have the desire and even a natural talent for it, but it takes more than that."

"I don't have more than that."

What did he think? That she had all the time in the world to do this? That she could go back to school and learn? That she had the money to do anything about it? Hadn't he heard a word she'd said?

When she told Drew she was going to Montreal to talk to a documentary filmmaker, he frowned and asked her if it was really necessary, to spend money they didn't have. His carpentry business had been slow for a while. Couldn't she just talk to him over the phone? Delaney told Drew she had to make the trip and that was that. It could be her Christmas present for the next ten years. She didn't care. Drew didn't argue. They'd been married long enough to know when there was room for argument and when there wasn't. Their signals, which would be dismissed as nervous twitches and flat tones by outsiders, were unmistakable and final and had wound their way into the marriage years ago, like patterns of conversation and lovemaking, with a life of their own.

"You're going to have to come back here again, probably

a few times, so I can view your footage." Neil stayed in his seat, as instructed, while Delaney finished making the coffee.

"That's not a problem."

"I can lend you a few good books about filmmaking. You can send me your questions before you interview anyone. Do you have a fax? Or you can call."

"I'll call."

"You're going to have to find a way to tie the whole thing together. You are going to script it. How are you going to edit? Where are you going to edit? What about music? These are all things you have to think about."

"I know."

When she was leaving, Neil stood at the top of the stairs to his walkup, waiting with her for the cab she insisted on calling despite his offer to driver her to the station.

"I'll do everything I can to help you," he said just before the cab arrived. Then he kissed her goodbye on both cheeks. "That's the way we kiss in Quebec," he said. Then he kissed her on the mouth, quickly, "the way you do in Ontario," he joked.

Drew was waiting for her on the platform at the Belleville station. She could see the car in the parking lot and their youngest son, Joel, who turned 13 that week, sitting in the front seat. She was only twenty minutes away from home, a short drive up the highway back to Stirling and the old hotel. She walked behind the other passengers, down the aisle and off the train, with *The New Yorker* and books on filmmaking in her schoolbag and the taste of rye in her mouth.

Delaney set up shop upstairs in Room 15, down the hallway from the rooms her children slept in. She placed a reconditioned VCR on top of Jesse's old dresser and a used television on a table below the window. She placed the books Neil lent her beside it. *A Quest for Vision; The Documentary; From Here to There: Getting It On Film.*

The dresser was given to Delaney after Jesse died, when Orville decided to leave the farm and move into town. She got the old hall tree, too, which once stood at the bottom of the staircase in the farmhouse. Where Jesse always kept the latest Sears catalogue in the small compartment under the seat. Where her sons hid forbidden things, like cigarettes and stolen Jell-O crystals from the kitchen cupboard, in the pockets of Orville's good tweed jacket, which hung on the hall tree with a layer of dust because he never wore it.

Jesse and Delaney used to steal the boys' stolen Jell-O crystals and go for a walk down the road, and talk.

Delaney got the hall tree and the dresser — things Jesse's three sons didn't want — as well as most of Jesse's personal belongings. Perfume bottles, and the doilies they sat on, the silver brush and comb set, Jesse's few bits of jewellery and clothes Delaney said she'd take to the Salvation Army, which still hang in the closet in Room 15. Lots of polyester and rayon in size sixteen with the pants hemmed to fit Jesse's short legs.

There's a picture tucked into one side of the dresser mirror of Jesse standing in the very same room, taken years ago. She was about 16, a young woman who had just left her family in Marmora and moved to Stirling to work in the shoe factory — before she married Orville Reid and moved to the farm. It was the only time she had had to herself and she spent it in Room 15 of the Stirling Hotel.

For a couple of years, Jesse slept and dreamed and woke up there. Her window overlooked the small yard at the back of the hotel where four long lines of linen dried outside on wash days. She ate downstairs in the dining room. She ate good meals, cooked by Drew's mother, Opal. Sometimes, she helped with the dishes. She didn't have to. She was paying room and board. She didn't have to do anything.

Jesse used to spend a lot of time upstairs in her room, ironing. She ironed everything, even her bras. She was obsessed with the way her clothes looked. They had to be perfectly straight, without so much as a hint of a wrinkle.

A woman. A girl. A country road. Red hands. Green hands. A
light summer rain keeps them cool as they walk. They can
smell the dirt on the road and the moist wood smell of the
bark on the trees and the cedar split-rail fences that embrace
them with two endless arms.

Jesse says she's afraid. One minute she's laughing
hysterically at the noodles she spilled all over the kitchen.
The next minute, she's bawling because Orville never takes
her out to dinner.

"It has to be the menopause," she says.

"Maybe you're just tired," Delaney offers. Before she
moved to the farm, she didn't know what menopause was.
Hadn't even heard the word.

"No, it's the menopause," Jesse says with certainty.

"How do you know?"

"My own mother got it early, too. Nearly drove us all
nuts. Nearly sent my father packing." Jesse picks up a stick
and wags it in the air with a strawberry Jell-O stained
hand. "As long as you go on cooking and cleaning for
them, they'll put up with anything, I suppose. Don't you
think, Del?"

Delaney could still picture Jesse in her kitchen, cooking
roast beef dinners every morning. Watching soaps in the
afternoon. Washing overalls with manure on them. Three
boys to feed, to fight with, to plead with. A large old house
to clean. A car she couldn't drive. A job she didn't get paid
for. A husband who never took her out to dinner.

Television was her refuge, her rage. People got dressed
up and ate in restaurants. They drank champagne and
toasted their love. They didn't have endless loads of laundry.
They didn't milk the cows when their husbands got drunk
and were hung over. They had a career and a driver's license
and passionate sex.

Menopause? Delaney remembered Jesse's red face, hot

one minute, cool the next. She remembered her uninhibited laugh. The unexpected, uncontrollable tears.

She could still hear Jesse's wild laugh — in the middle of the day when she bent down to reach for a dull grey parcel in the bottom bin, when she was walking across town to deliver catalogues, when she sat in Room 15. She could still smell Jesse's White Shoulders perfume. Bisquick biscuits baking in the oven. The freshly printed pages of a new Sears catalogue.

Links in the chain.

Eventually, Delaney decided to bring the picture of Claire upstairs. She sat the silver frame on the dresser just behind and to the left of Jesse's picture. From there, Claire stared back at her daughter from alongside a willow tree — stared past her really, the way she always did whenever Delaney sat opposite her in the plastic covered red benches of a restaurant in Toronto, the smell of splattered grease competing with Claire's department store perfume.

"I brought you something, Del." Claire reached into her purse and pulled out a handful of cereal box prizes she'd been saving up since their last visit. Sugar and cereal dust still clung to the cellophane-wrapped prizes.

Delaney tried to picture her mother at a kitchen table in the morning sunlight, eating a bowl of Cheerios or Shredded Wheat, but she couldn't. She had a vague memory of her mother standing at a counter in a flannel nightgown, pouring some cereal into a bowl. A red plastic bowl, which she handed to Delaney. She must been under the age of 2, because after she turned 2 she never lived with Claire again.

"What kind of cereal do you eat?" Delaney asked.

The slight smile Claire was wearing before fell into her scratched porcelain coffee cup. Some of the skin on her cheeks dropped to her chin and the perfectly plucked half-circles, which arched over her chocolate eyes, melted into two straight and heavy lines.

Claire lit a cigarette and ordered another coffee from a passing waitress then made as much small talk with the woman when she returned as she could, to buy herself time to regain her composure. The coffee was great. Could she have more sugar? She really shouldn't. It all sits here, you know how it is. But she'll have some anyway.

That's all it took for Claire to change scenes, to change the subject, to come back stronger than ever.

"Ask me what I did last week," she said. She leaned forward over the table with a big desperate grin on her face and took Del's hands in hers. Dramatic gesture. They both went back to acting like mother and daughter.

"What did you do last week?"

"Guess."

"I don't know."

"I auditioned for a part in a play and I got it!"

"You did?!" Delaney put as much enthusiasm as she could into her response even though she was still thinking about the fact she hadn't had breakfast with her mother in six years.

"It's a small part. I'm only on for about fifteen minutes, but I've got a few good lines." Claire let go of Delaney's hands and leaned back, one arm folded around her waist, the other holding her cigarette again.

"What play?" Delaney asked, hoping her interest in Claire's struggle for the stage would get her something.

"It's called *The Day Ends*. It's a love story." Claire waved her cigarette in the air. "Some actor who's been in theatre forever wrote it."

"Can I see it, Mom?"

"It's really not worth seeing, Del. It's hardly a part at all."

"But I really want to see — "

" — Maybe next time, Del."

Claire's eyes followed the traffic outside the restaurant. She sighed and Delaney couldn't tell if it was boredom or disappointment. Disappointment that Delaney had spoiled her only bit of good news with a request for further contact.

"How about some rice pudding?" Claire asked. "They make great rice pudding here, with raisins and whipped cream and cinnamon on top."

"I'm not hungry." Delaney wanted to ask her when she had tried the rice pudding there? Who was she with? What day was it? Did she eat there all the time?

Claire snuffed out her cigarette, rubbing its amber nose in the glass ashtray over and over again. "Aren't you happy for me, Del? Tell me you are."

"I am, Mom. I'm really happy."

"It's not much, I know, but it's something. Please just be happy for me and leave it at that, for now."

That was the last time she saw Claire. Delaney was 8. Claire was 27. The picture of Claire against the willow tree was taken the year before outside the house Claire was boarding at on Springdale Boulevard in Toronto. Delaney never went there. Claire always met her at one restaurant or another and they sometimes went shopping downtown at Eaton's, or rode the streetcar and bus out to Kew Beach in the summer where Delaney collected stones. Coke and Canada Dry and brown beer bottle glass softened by the sand and the waves of Lake Ontario and rounded into brown and green and clear stones — human debris made beautiful by the soothing forces of nature. Occasionally, Delaney found cobalt blue ones or red ones. She never tired of searching for them, walking along the water's edge with her back hunched over for hours, risking a cut from the odd sharp one that wasn't ready to be snatched from its sandy bed. She never got so used to them that they lost their mystery and their magic. They were rare. Even at the tender age of 7, Delaney knew she would probably never find glass stones like that anywhere else. That's how old she was the last time she went to the beach with her mother — 7. Last time at The Flamingo restaurant — 8.

At the end of the day, she did what she always did. She gave most of the glass stones to Claire, who put them in her canvas bag and promised to add them to the rest of her collection on the windowsill at home.

Perfume bottles on doilies on the dresser. Raindrops on the leaves. Ironing board set up in the corner. Neil told Delaney to make a list of images to shoot and use in the documentary, to make it more intimate — images other women would relate to, images that meant something to her. *An empty bed with the covers pulled back. Housecoat hanging on a door. Glass stones on a windowsill.* She would drop them into the final cut.

The women she had lined up to interview promised old photos. She commissioned one of the women — a fabric artist named Beth — to create a piece on the theme of mother-loss and would tape her working on it at various stages.

She would take another woman named Pam out to the property of what used to be a country estate where she grew up with a difficult mother. The tree-lined driveway led to the foundation of what was once a grand home, burned to the ground in a fire several years ago. She planned to have Pam sit on the front steps of the foundation and read a short story she had written about her mother's wedding dress.

She would have Sally make the symbolic bouquet she'd been unable to work on before and place it on her mother's grave.

Neil approved of Delaney's list and her plans and told her she was a very visual person. She talked to him on the phone, in between customers who constantly interrupted her train of thought with their pickups of bed linens and kitchen gadgets and lingerie with stiff lace that scratches and makes you red in embarrassing places just before you leap into bed with your lover. She mailed him a list of questions for her interviews.

Neil said she was a natural and gave her one final piece of advice before her first interview. "Stay open to letting the interview go its own way." It was the final bullet-point in a check-list he'd been giving her for weeks. Stay open. Use natural light whenever possible. Check the sound. Check the white balance. She wouldn't want to go through everything twice. "Something always gets lost the second time around," Neil had said. "Truth dissipates. Turns into half-truths. Embellished versions of vague memories too distant to recall in detail." Make sure they're not wearing red, or polka dots, or large stripes. Don't forget the tape. Take extra tape.

Delaney stood by a roll-top desk, where black and white photos of a woman and her daughter were carefully placed. The daughter, Beth, now a grown woman and successful fabric artist, was fixing her hair in the bathroom upstairs. A handmade rag doll was sitting on the desk, its limp neck buckled under its heavy head, which hung down over a picture of itself and a young girl and the mother who made her. They were all in her hands now, Delaney thought, her inexperienced and inadequate hands. She almost walked out the door.

Weeks later, when Neil viewed the footage from the interview, he said her shots of the doll's face and the pictures it was looking at were haunting. Haunting was good, he said. The lighting by the window was perfect. The sound, excellent. Did she want to go out for lunch?

He took her to a restaurant on Saint-Laurent where a magazine store occupied the other half of a small green building. She didn't see a name anywhere and the restaurant had windows that opened up onto the street, which only let in car fumes and cigarette smoke and the aftermath of too much perfume.

Delaney had bought another copy of *The New Yorker* at the magazine store to read on the train on the way home. She wanted to see what plays were on. She still had her last copy at home in the top drawer of the dresser in Room 15. She had read it cover to cover, re-reading the descriptions of the plays several times. She wanted to know what kinds of stories were making it to the stage, what situations an actress might find herself in.

Claire used to say you had to become the part, or, if you were lucky, you would walk into a part that was already you. She said that on her good days she was animated, in love with the script that allowed her to be someone other than who she was. On a bad day, she didn't want to talk about it.

Neil and Delaney sat in a corner of the restaurant near the front windows. He seemed to enjoy having her around, giving her advice, teaching her the language of film. Did she ever think of moving to a place like Montreal? For the workshops and the film festivals and the bars where writers, producers, and directors hang out? After lunch they went for a walk on the mountain. It was late spring. The last time she had seen Neil it was still wintertime. The next time, it would be early fall. Editing time. Neil said they'd have to work at night in the post-production studio he always used. All night. Overnight. It's cheaper, he told her. It's when filmmakers with low budgets edit, like he did years ago, when he made films for different reasons than he does now.

Where would she sleep during the day? How would she get around? Where would she get the money for a hotel? For meals? For the editing time?

Neil said she could stay with him, and so finally she asked, "What about your wife, or your girlfriend?"

"She's not around much."

"Your wife? Or your girlfriend?"

"We live together. I've never been married."

"Is she in the film business?"

"She's a photographer. She travels a lot, taking pictures for travel brochures."

A couple of grey squirrels raced in front of them, across the paved path up the mountain, into the woods on the other side and up a tree.

"She wouldn't mind if you stayed. We have a guest room."

Delaney couldn't picture it, unless the girlfriend was out of town. She couldn't picture sleeping in a room down the hall or across from theirs if *she* was there, waking up in the middle of the night to use the bathroom and running into Neil or his girlfriend who might be going to the kitchen for a glass of water. If it was her, she'd struggle for something to say, not wanting to talk to her at all, then dart off back to bed. If it was Neil, she'd want to drink wine, sit in the living room in the candlelight, and talk about imagery and memory and the nearly impossible and wonderful process of putting them on film or videotape.

She didn't want to know about his girlfriend, or the friends he's known all his life, or the summer cottage in the Eastern Townships. She wouldn't be able to lie there in the fashionable pale blue and white striped sheets she imagined were on the guest bed. Not without him beside her, his head on the pillow facing her, talking to her in the voice she had come to know and looked forward to hearing while she stood waiting for his call behind the counter in the Sears store. Waiting in what used to be the confectionery store and office of the Stirling Hotel.

Years before, Delaney had found a couple of antique filing cabinets in the back room. She hauled them out, cleaned them up, and put them along one wall of the catalogue store. The empty compartments offered nothing surprising. No hints of secret lives, no remarkable words scribbled in another century that might be timely and confirming, a fateful find. She didn't find anything inside, just a little historical dust and a registry from a year that didn't stand out from any other year, except that the journeys of few souls were recorded on its thick, yellowing paper. Someone named Mavis Hendenson from Cornwall, Ontario, checked in on December 20, 1898.

When quiet periods came along, Delaney stood in the front window and looked across the street at the same view that always greeted her. The upholstery store, a hair salon, and the old fire hall, stripped of its tower and bell and converted into someone's home with a barber shop downstairs, the street level. Spring rains, fall leaves, and dirty, slushy snow were all that ever changed the view.

The covered bridge and Rawdon Creek, the Mill Pond and the IGA grocery store, the pizza joint and the doctor's office at the corner — all sat outside her view. But she saw them in her imagination. Until the phone rang and took her to a place she couldn't describe but had been before — on a beach picking glass stones, on a country road eating Jell-O crystals off her hand.

Delaney decided she'd have to try and save a little extra for a hotel. It wouldn't cost too much. She'd only be there for a few

days, if she prepared well and marked her tapes and made most
of the editing decisions before she went back to Montreal.
Drew would make her pay, though. He was already making
her pay, in small ways, for her trips to Montreal and the huge
phone bills and the new digital video camera she took out a
loan for. It wasn't so much what he said or didn't say. It was
how he left the room after she told him what the long distance
charges added up to and how he rolled over to shut her out
when she said she needed to make another trip to Montreal.

"Mail him the tape."

"I'm not mailing it. I want to sit down and talk to Neil
and make sure I'm doing things right."

"Turn the television on. Copy what they do. What do
you have to keep going back to Montreal for?"

"Because he wants to help me and I need help. Don't you
understand that?"

"I understand it costs a hundred bucks every time you
get on that goddamn train. That's what I understand."

On the mountain, Delaney declined Neil's invitation for
the guest room, saying she'd be fine in a hotel, as though she
did it all the time. In truth, other than living in the old
Stirling Hotel, Delaney had never spent a night in one.
Never spent a night alone. She went from Claire's desperate-
to-love-but-incapable hands, to a blur of hands in foster
homes, to Jesse's Jell-O-stained hands, to Drew's groping-
but-in-the-long-run-responsible hands.

She thought about that all the way home on the train
that day. After her walk on the mountain with Neil. After
their lunch at the nameless restaurant. His patient viewing of
her tapes. She thought about how she would pack two
suitcases, one with her taped interviews and her edit decision
list. Another with enough clothes to last a week, in case she
had to stay a little longer. A travel iron — the one she saw in
the Sears catalogue. And a couple of bottles of wine.

She would stay downtown and drink wine in the
morning when she returned to the hotel after a night of
editing. She would have the front desk call and wake her up
at three in the afternoon and wander down St. Catherine

Street to Eaton's, and eat in restaurants that still looked the
way they did twenty-five years ago, like The Flamingo in
Toronto. She'd take long baths. She'd make a documentary.
She'd check in and stay a while before continuing on her
journey, like Mavis Hendenson from Cornwall did in
Stirling in 1898. It was something to look forward to.

Delaney finished her interviews in early July and sat and
viewed them for hours at a time in Room 15 of the Stirling
Hotel, a stuffy room with only one window and a small
inserted screen that provided about eight inches of relief. She
had to wait until the evening to work, had to wait until the sun
set in the back of the hotel before she could start, until it knelt
behind another building on another street, taking its
unbearable heat with it. She liked to watch the way the light
changed on the dresser in the corner and on the pictures of
Jesse and Claire. Yellow to orange to pink and red. This shift in
angles and colour seemed to make it alright — forgivable that
she found herself completely wrapped up in the task at hand,
able to shut out the looks of neglect and astonishment that
came her way from every member of her family. From Drew
and the boys. From Drew's mother, who seemed unclear about
what it was Delaney was doing in that room every night.
    Delaney was a little astonished herself, for different
reasons. Astonished at how simultaneously difficult and easy
it was to walk away after dinner and leave Drew and her sons
to their own devices, to getting their own dessert, to wading
their way through the daily pool of disagreements and rivalry
without her side-line refereeing. They weren't young children
anymore. They didn't need her the way they used to. Still,
they didn't like the distraction of the documentary. It meant
she wasn't waiting in the wings for a sign they needed her
help — dishing out even portions of apple pie, sewing the
underarms of their favourite T-shirts. After dinner, she'd take
care of the dishes, enlisting their help once in a while for the
benefit of future wives, then announce her departure and not
see them again until the morning.

It was a burden she carried. A burden of change, of not being there at the drop of a hat, as she had always been. A necessary burden. A depleting one. Another one to add to a growing pile she'd been gathering, like the dust under beds in rooms she could barely find the time to clean. The difficulty and the ease. If she felt the pull of domestic guilt over not being there, she also felt the pull of freedom from its suffocating clutches whenever she ascended the wide staircase to Room 15. She wanted someone else to keep up with the cooking and the cleaning and the conversations with customers about nothing, about the weather and the relentless heat, which, of course, was like no other summer they could remember.

Drew's intolerance fluctuated and was more noticeable on the nights he didn't play baseball or coach baseball, when he stood in the doorway and watched a few seconds of an interview and hated how inaccessible it was to him. He couldn't be part of it, had nothing to say about it — something new in their marriage.

They had set up house together when Delaney was just 16 and Drew was 18. They had three children, paid bills, celebrated Christmas the same way every year, made love with familiarity and weathered storms they never knew were coming. They got past bouts of anger at one another for stealing each other's youth, past Drew's steady date with booze before he left a job he hated and started his own business. They got past the depression Delaney experienced after her third child was born, when she stood in front of a mirror and cried at the sight of the incision and the flab around her middle, with no purpose but to remind her of what she'd never be again — hip-bones-sticking-out skinny, young and full of energy. She was only 21.

Delaney didn't mind that Drew didn't hang around Room 15 and make suggestions, or ask her who the woman on the screen was and what her story was. There was a need for space and he found it in the baseball fields and she was finding it in Room 15 — and if she could be there and on the bleachers at the baseball diamond at the same time, everything would be perfect. She was thankful when he closed the door behind him. She wanted to be left alone to deal with the burden of dead women's lives, which she carried around the hotel all day, every day, to the laundry room, to the kitchen sink, to places where she couldn't help but hear their pleas to tell their stories.

Upstairs, pages of notes sat in her lap with underlined headings. The Beginning, The Middle, The End. It's a storytelling medium, Neil had said. "Tell a story with their words, their pictures, your images."

A stack of photographs lay on a bed, which she had moved into the room weeks before. A couple dozen tapes, carefully labelled, lined a shelf Drew reluctantly hung for her. Master tapes in DV format, work tapes in VHS format, the way Neil told her to do it.

The Beginning, The Middle, The End. She wrote it on a piece of paper and taped it to the dresser mirror, above the VCR, above Claire in her silver frame, beside Jesse. She had no idea where to begin. She didn't know what order to place the images and the interviews and the photographs. Freeze frames from the private newsreels of a fabric artist, a florist, a woman of money, and their dead mothers.

From the dresser, Claire and Jesse watched her. The evening sky's extended arms of light brush-stroked their faces in deep yellows and pinks and resurrected the faces in the sky Delaney used to see from her bedroom window at the farm. The faces of a thousand souls who once rode school buses and streetcars, who lived in cities and small towns and on farms, who had jobs and families, hobbies and dreams, first dates and last rites. Who appeared before the sun set, then pulled apart in myriad colour, slowly drowning in a black and magenta sea.

Delaney used to look for Claire's face in the thin grey strips of cloud, not knowing if she'd recognize it or not. It all depended, she thought, on whether Claire would have died shortly after the last time she saw her, or if she had died five,

six, ten years later. Would she know her if she saw her? Even
five years could make a big difference in a person's face if life
threw its worst at you. Claire might have started drinking to
drown the guilt Delaney imagined she felt for abandoning her,
or to convince herself the bit parts she was getting in this play
and that play would lead somewhere someday. The alcohol
would have destroyed Claire's beautiful skin, loosening and
wrinkling it. Regret lining her forehead, her cheeks.

Jesse had said Delaney was wasting her time looking for
Claire up there. She wasn't dead. Delaney would know,
somehow, someone would have found a way to let her know.
No, no, no. Claire wasn't dead, silly girl. She was probably
in the arms of some handsome leading man who had
whisked her off to his cosy den after closing every night for
champagne and seafood and red roses on a table set with
solid silver. Or she had met a handsome businessman. They
were always handsome. She had met him at The Flamingo,
on a cold and windy night. He offered to pay for her dinner
when Claire realized she left her purse on the bus on the
way over to the restaurant.

Claire wouldn't ever know her longest running role was
that of the muse in the life of a menopausal farmer's wife —
a part she had landed without even trying.

When the incandescent light from the street took over,
when the colours in Room 15 had faded to shadows, Delaney
surrendered to the bits of life that laid waiting on the
videotapes, to the faces in the crimped and curled photographs
on the bed beside her. She turned on the only lamp in the
room and went to work, piecing together the stories of a few
dead women.

On Sunday, October 14, Delaney checked into Room 537
of the Holiday Inn on Sherbrooke Street in Montreal. A
rainy day. She had promised Drew she'd skip the skyline
view and stay closer to the ground, in case a fire should
break out and she had to escape by the staircase. He said
he'd call every afternoon at three to wake her up, that she

didn't need room service. She opened the curtains to a view of office buildings with mirrored windows that hid phone calls, meetings, pensive moments spent looking across the way at her room — and memories of other meetings and family vacations in other parts of the world. The room smelled of fresh bars of soap. The air was stale and confined, like the air inside the box of a new toy — plastic and man-made, without any signs of life. Water marks and shaving cream and misdirected hairspray were wiped from the bathroom vanity. The heads of sleeping lovers and business travellers were beaten out of the pillows. Fingered brochures and information sheets were replaced with fresh ones and carefully arranged on the table near the window.

The room had been vacuumed, dusted, and disinfected by women who saw the same messes and cleaned the same bathrooms and made the same beds over and over. The rooms were small, uniform compartments, like the drawers in the Matchbox car collections Delaney's sons used to play with. Room 537 was her home for the next few days.

Delaney hung her blouses in the closet, set her new travel iron on top of the table, and lined the bathroom with her makeup and shampoo and Scarlet Ice lipstick. She put three bottles of red wine in the bottom drawer of the one dresser. Placed Jesse and Claire on the top. Put her lingerie in the second drawer — lingerie she didn't really need and didn't bother showing Drew. It came in the last shipment before she left. Bras and a travel iron in a dull grey Sears parcel with her name on it.

She called Neil shortly after she checked in. A woman answered. Then Neil's voice, welcoming her. He talked quickly, in a slightly higher pitch than usual. Was it nervousness? Excitement? She was there — all his. He had to know she cared for him. How could he not? Neil was helping her pass through — through what she didn't know, couldn't articulate. Movement of some kind. She had been feeling it ever since the day she was cleaning the mirror on the back of the hall tree in the Sears store and the words *When Women Lose Their Mothers* came to mind.

Strange, she hadn't realized it until then, hadn't known
that's when the movement started. She could have sworn it
had always been there — at Kew Beach, at The Flamingo,
on that grassy hill behind the barn at Jesse's farm where the
wind whispered predictions of this very moment. It took her
that long to get there.

Who would have thought *there* would be a Holiday
Inn in downtown Montreal with suitcases full of clothes
and videotapes and too many women swimming around in
her head?

She could remember sitting on the window-ledge in Jesse's
room, the window open, the smell of cow manure blowing
in. She could see the barn where Orville milked forty head
of cows and the large trough of water when he drowned the
barnyard cats' kittens in a grain sack.

"Why doesn't he get them fixed?" She turned towards Jesse
who was lying on her side on the beige chenille bedspread.

"He won't spend the money."

"But it's so cruel."

"He says they don't feel a thing."

"And you believe it?"

"I have to."

Dead kittens. Milking cows. Roast beef dinners at noon.
Jesse Reid's home. A back shed full of flannel shirts and mud-
covered rubber boots. A party line that rang two long and
one short. Lime green sheers on the dining room windows.

Delaney met Jesse the summer she was living with Anne
and Paul Canning and their children in Scarborough,
another foster family who rated a six according to her
personal scale. Six meant the food wasn't bad, she had a
room of her own, and they didn't pry too much, didn't ask
her about the last family or the one before that, like some of
them did. Actually, they didn't ask her anything about
herself. They lost points for chewing their food too loudly
and for insisting she join in the family discussions about
everything, from what kind of dog to get, to where they'd

spend their summer vacation. They voted to spend a week at the farm of Anne's cousin, Jesse.

Delaney fell in love with Jesse the minute she met her. She was standing in the middle of the kitchen with flour on her face waving a wooden spoon in the air, screaming at her three sons to wipe the cow shit off their clothes before they stepped into the house. "Oh, why didn't the good Lord send me a beautiful daughter like you?" Jesse said. Then she winked at Delaney who winked back at the short woman with the ingredients for apple pie all over her apron.

Jesse sneaked out early one morning with Delaney, with a box of cherry-flavoured Jell-O crystals in her pocket. They went for a walk down the road, the dew still clinging to the tall roadside grass in see-through beads of water. On this first walk, Delaney and Jesse were joined by the ghost of Claire, by her estranged relationship with her parents, by her brief and obsessive affair with Delaney's father, whose last name became his daughter's first, and by her waning visits with Delaney that ended one day outside a restaurant in Toronto, without warning, without drama.

"You mean to tell me, she just never showed up again?"

"Never."

"Did you call her?"

"She left town."

"Couldn't they track her down? Those social workers. Don't they know how to do that?"

"They couldn't find her."

"I don't understand. I'd have given my right arm for a daughter." Jesse opened the box of Jell-O crystals and poured some into Delaney's hand. "I buy three boxes of this stuff every week and it's a miracle if one of them ends up in a bowl in the fridge." She poured a small mountain of crystals into her own hand and the two of them walked on, licking and talking.

"All those times I lay in that hospital holding another baby boy, bawling my eyes out," Jesse said, shaking her head. "Orville thought I was just happy to have another baby. Another farmhand to help out around here." She turned to Delaney. "He didn't see my disappointment. Men never see things like that, you know. You have to spell it out for them and even then they don't see it. Not the way you want them to."

Unseen animals scurried in the grass as Delaney and Jesse made their way around the corner past the Southfork Ranch strawberry farm where Jesse worked every year, picking berries on her knees — to get out of the house, to make some money of her own. They passed the strawberry farm enough times that week for Delaney to imagine the blue sign with its strawberry-coloured letters before they even turned the corner. They sneaked their walks in here and there, when Anne was taking a nap or wanted to read in silence, while Orville and Paul and the other children helped with the hay.

Jesse and Delaney wound their way back and forth — yesterday and today — until they found themselves at the end of the week suggesting to Anne that Delaney move to the farm. There were hushed discussions in the parlour, in the kitchen in the middle of the night, from behind the closed door to Jesse and Orville's room, down the hall from the room Delaney slept in.

Anne and Paul were having conversations about it, too — detached, theoretical conversations. Jesse was fighting tooth and nail for her, dredging up every single time she could remember that Orville had let her down, failed her in some way, and threw it at him until he finally said okay to his last chance for redemption. He didn't say a word to Delaney except good morning and goodnight. Jesse's sons, Kyle, Chris, and Ken, one younger and two older than her, were concerned about which room she would get. It didn't matter to her. It didn't hurt. She only saw them as clothed bits of flesh — extensions of Jesse she could put up with if she had to.

Three weeks later, after several visits with her social worker, Delaney went back to the farm with all the clothes she owned, a few glass stones, and a picture of Claire. She was given Kyle's room, who was moved into Chris's room —

the largest room in the house at the opposite end of the hallway. Jesse helped her unpack and took pleasure in pointing out all the things she had done to make the room just right for a girl. How she ordered pink and white bedding from Sears and washed up the quilt her own mother had made her for her thirteenth birthday, which had been stashed away in a box in the attic.

She found Claire's picture and looked at it several times. "You have her nose and her eyes," she said. "She looks frightened. She looks like an actress."

One day, Jesse came into Delaney's room with a small silver frame. She opened the back and removed the photograph from inside, then handed the frame to Delaney. "You should have a proper frame for that picture of your mother," she said. Jesse watched as Delaney put Claire inside the frame and sat her on the dresser.

"Thank you," Delaney said.

"It'll keep her in a safe place," Jesse told her. She was still holding the picture she had removed from the frame.

"Can I see that?" Delaney asked.

"This silly thing?"

Delaney nodded.

"It's just some old picture of me," Jesse said dismissively. But something in the picture caught her attention and wouldn't let her look away so quickly. "I was only a few years older than you are now," Jesse said. "Room 15. In the old Stirling Hotel. That's where I lived when I worked in the shoe factory, before I married Orville and moved out here."

Delaney didn't know then what a woman searches for in an old picture of herself. For what survived the journey to the present, for the casualties that didn't make it. The parts of herself she mourns when she looks into her own youthful eyes and realizes she no longer lives behind them.

"That was a long time ago," was all Jesse said when she lifted her head. She handed the picture to Delaney, then went to work putting the freshly washed sheers back up, humming old love songs in the face of the day's harshest light.

By the time Delaney rode the elevator downstairs to the lobby of the Holiday Inn, Neil was already parked out front, waiting for her. She could see him on the other side of the huge glass doors. He was looking in another direction and didn't notice her coming towards him.

She hadn't slept well the night before and spent the better part of the day going over her notes, trying to visualize the scenes she had pasted together in her mind. Would it work? Had she thought things out well? Made the right decisions? Self-doubt had followed her into the bath after lunch, where she soaked and fretted for a good half-hour. She tried deep-breathing. She tried visualizing the sunsets in Room 15. She dried herself off and took a moment to think of something else — what lingerie to wear? The black bra and underpants? Or the beige ones with white lace?

She rode in Neil's car in beige and white lace underneath a pair of jeans and a white blouse and the black leather jacket Drew had given her last Christmas, which she had ordered and placed in his hands. She told him the least he could do was wrap it, which he did, in some leftover blue shiny paper his mother used on all of her gifts. No bow. No card. It sat under the tree, without surprise and far too much tape.

In the car, Neil talked about *Duddy Kravitz* and The Main, and St. Viateur bagels, while Delaney watched hundreds of unfamiliar faces walking streets she'd never remember. A succession of tiny shops and bars and restaurants whizzed by and promised to look different the next time she passed them. Tomorrow. The next day. The day after that.

At the studio, she met Jean-Claude, the editor Neil worked with. He made cappuccino for everyone and wasted no time getting down to work. It was just as well. Delaney was forced to focus, forced to block out the closeness of Neil's leg as he sat beside her. She focused on all the dials and switches and computerized equipment; she smelled the new wood from the custom-made cabinets that surrounded the room and held more monitors and more computers and more dials. This was where they would pass through the lives of a number of dead women and their daughters. Photographs would be scanned. Interviews would be cut, then cut again to include or get rid of a gesture, a blink of an eye, a word that seemed out of place and unnecessary.

The framed pictures of Jesse and Claire were in Delaney's schoolbag. She brought them along for luck after berating herself for her juvenile superstitions, after spending an hour deciding which bra to wear. There was no need to bring them out. They would find their way into these other stories — stories that were also their own. The story of daughters and mothers, and what happens when they go missing.

It was a morbid subject. Drew had said so. So had some of the friends of the women she interviewed, who hadn't yet lost their mothers. They thought it was morbid, too, a real downer.

Neil didn't say that. He said it was a good subject. A universal issue every woman eventually deals with. It would probably sell well. Then he caught himself and realized none of that mattered to Delaney.

Neil thought it all had to do with Jesse. He didn't know about Claire and the brush with her life that was about to take place in a high-tech studio on The Main. He might miss her altogether. The glass stones. The clouds in the sky. A half-drunk cup of coffee. Delaney had buried Claire deeply, in images that were simply meant to move the story along.

Drew called the next afternoon at three, as he said he would. Delaney was already awake, lying in bed listening to the rain on the windows. When she had wakened earlier, she was startled and didn't know where she was — a familiar feeling that had greeted her as the light of a new day nudged her awake. Before she went to live with Jesse on the farm, she often woke up not knowing where she was. How could she? She had lived in one house with a bed along one wall one minute, and before she knew it, she was sleeping in another house in another bed that jutted out into the middle of the room, with nothing to put her back against, no safe corner to retreat to. Drew said everything was okay. The boys were already asking when she'd be home. He'd call again tomorrow.

When Neil drove her back to the hotel at 5:30 that morning, she thanked him several times for sitting with her through the editing process. She wasn't paying him to be there. He had volunteered to stay up all night, every night, until the job was done. He used to do it all the time. He missed it. He had told her that before. Perhaps he forgot. Perhaps he was still figuring it out — that he missed being what he used to be — and was talking out loud, to himself, circling what was really bothering him, dancing around it, getting used to the idea that it was there in the first place.

Neil parked the car near the hotel entrance and walked her to her room. It wasn't safe, he said, for her to be walking through the hotel at that hour. She thanked him again.

"Is it ridiculous to invite someone to stay for a drink this early in the morning?" Delaney asked.

Neil hesitated, but only for second. "In this case, no. But I should get home."

"I only meant a drink." She hated saying it, but made herself say it anyway, for the sake of their working relationship, for the sake of her own ego. It was the end of their workday. That's all — a drink after work.

"I know," he reassured her, but he didn't. He didn't know. His eyes told her he didn't. Was that disappointment she saw? "Rain-check?" he asked. Did he want to stay? Is that what she was seeing?

"Sure," she answered, "rain-check."

No, wait a minute, she wanted to say. Wait, I didn't mean one drink, I meant several. I meant a bottle or two and a few hours together. You know what together means, don't you?

"I'd love to stay and talk all day, I really would." He was still standing there, near the door, with his hands in his pockets. "I could probably talk to you forever," he said, "but this morning just isn't good."

She had a glass of wine after Neil left and watched the rain darken the concrete on the office buildings and the street below. She could still smell his after-shave, or cologne, or whatever it was, competing with the bars of soap in the bathroom and the smell of clean from the busy hands that had passed through the room hours before — after she had left for the editing studio. If life were a play, she thought, Neil would have stayed. He would have found his way around the beige and white lace lingerie, which housed what no other man had ever touched. Drew had been her only lover. Was she looking for a new lead? Neil had said forever. *He could probably stay and talk to her* forever. *Forever* had never been within Delaney's grasp.

Was it forever she wanted? Or just a moment? A single moment when she would lose control and finally know what it was that made Claire fall so intensely in love, made her so incapable of coping — with life, with the child her great love left planted in her belly. A leading man who came into her life and mesmerized her and fed her loving lines for weeks and weeks, using words he spoke on stage — so every night she was reminded of what he said the night before, when she was opposite him in their own private play. She loved him with all her heart, Claire had said. She was having his child. He disappeared. He didn't want to know. He was gone. Another play. Another city.

"Maybe she's landed a part in a play and she's met up with him again, and they're still in love," Jesse used to say, standing at the kitchen sink, washing the yellow beans they had picked in the garden. Used to say, as she mopped the mud from the spring rain off the floors, as she filled Halloween bags with suckers and chewy taffy candies and small bags of potato chips. Settings changed. Scenarios changed. Jesse played one reconciliation card after another, but she never changed the final scene.

"You just never know how these things are going to turn out, Del. He could have come back from wherever he's been all these years and met up with her again. He could have realized what he gave up. You. Claire. She's a looker, that girl. No man's likely to forget loving a woman as beautiful as she is."

"It's too late, Jess. There's no way that would ever happen."

"You don't know that."

"Nothing like that happens in the real world."

"Remarkable things happen in the real world, Del."

"Or nothing happens."

"Alright. Sometimes, nothing happens," Jesse gave in. "But sometimes, something remarkable happens." She looked like she believed it.

It was silly to compare. Neil was different, a leading man with his feet on the ground. He wasn't going anywhere. He had a life before she came along and it would still be there after she was gone, when she packed her suitcases and went home with the rest of the women she had dragged along on her journey. Life would go on. Delaney knew that. She knew all of that. It was just harder to take now.

She finished her wine and decided to head out for a while. There was a restaurant on St. Catherine Street she wanted to go to with her notes. She had to focus on the task at hand. The night before, they had loaded the interviews into the system and scanned the photographs and worked on the first few minutes of the documentary. She was working without a script. She wanted to let the women she interviewed tell the story. She had spent weeks in Room 15 listening to them in bits and pieces — a sentence from Sally, a paragraph from the others — until their voices became one in her mind.

Delaney showered and got dressed and walked on floors that didn't creak with every step, like the plank boards in the hotel back home. The pipes didn't rattle when she turned the water on. The pressure from the taps was strong and steady, not trickling because one of the roomers was running a bath. She couldn't smell Charlie Sawyer's whiskey breath, or the plastic wrap around the new Sears catalogues. She knew she was somewhere other than where she had always been, and Claire was following her. Delaney could smell her. In the perfume she dabbed on the sides of her neck. In the lipstick she put on then patted with a Kleenex. In the elevator that carried her to the lobby. The smell of Claire was everywhere. In the rain that hit the pavement, with its smell of wet concrete, of city streets. In the smell of new leather at Eaton's, where Claire used to shop in Toronto for purses and gloves. In Dunn's Delicatessen on St. Catherine Street, in the cigar a man was smoking in a booth next to hers.

I know I haven't seen you for a while, darling. I've been so busy and I wasn't feeling well for a while there. Is everything okay with the Keetings? Are they treating you alright? Damn, that cigar smoke reminds me of my daddy. That son of a bitch. Best thing I ever did was to keep you away from him, and her. The only thing they were good at raising were dogs. Goddamn bulldogs. Christ, I always hated those things, with their big, floppy lips and those frightening teeth sticking out. You ever see the teeth on one of them? I'm rambling, aren't I, darling? I'm sorry. I ramble when I'm nervous. God, you're beautiful, Del. That's the worst part. Seeing him every time I look at you, reminding me I'm not good enough to you. You deserve better, baby. I hope you know I only want what's good for you. You'll remember that, won't you? It's not so bad this way, is it? Damn, there ought to be some law about smoking those god- awful things in a restaurant.

Delaney ordered dinner and went over her notes. That night they would make real progress, Jean-Claude had said. She was well organized and had mapped it out like a screenplay, or a theatrical play, in three acts. *The Beginning, The Middle, The End.* It wouldn't take too long, he told her. A few more nights and it would be in the can and she'd be finished with it.

INTERIOR — HOUSE Beth, the fabric artist, sits with the rag doll in her lap. **CLOSE-UP** of Beth's hands stroking the doll, lifting the doll's arms, twisting the doll's hair. **Voice-over**: Beth talking about the time her mother told her she was dying. **Cut to: PICTURES** of Beth and her mother taken a few years before. **Cut to: CLOSE-UP** of the rag doll as Beth cups her hands around its waist and holds it like a child. **Cut to:** Beth in the chair, saying she still can't believe her mother's gone. That she can still smell her perfume and the way it got absorbed into the pieces of fabric she carried around the house, from room to room, whenever she was working on one of her dolls. **Cut to: CLOSE-UP** of a picture of Beth as a young child sitting on a chair holding the same doll.

Fade to: INTERIOR — FLOWER SHOP Sally sits in the front window of the flower shop as the traffic moves along the street behind her. She twirls a single yellow rose in her hands and talks about the car accident that killed her mother fifteen years ago — the suddenness of the loss, the drive to the cemetery in a limousine, sitting in the back seat wondering why everything else hadn't stopped. People were still driving and shopping and standing in the street, talking, as if nothing had happened. **Cut to:** Clouds in the sky, as seen through the back window of a moving car, looking up.

Cut to: EXTERIOR — COUNTRYSIDE Pam is driving her car down a country road talking about the house she grew up in. How it burned to the ground two years after her mother died in a nursing home at the age of 65, from Alzheimer's and years of alcohol abuse. **Cut to: PICTURES** of a stately home and Pam as a teenager, sitting on the front step. **Cut to:** Pam getting out of the car and standing before a charred foundation, talking about how much her life is still tied up in a house that no longer stands. How its ashes were carried by the wind to places she'll never find. **Cut to: CLOSE-UP** of tall grass blowing in a field.

When Jesse first got sick, Delaney was 14, almost 15. She knew Jesse had breast cancer and that they had taken her left breast off. That's what Jesse told her when Delaney saw her after the operation. Jesse was lying in a hospital bed. "They had to take it off." She said it quietly — a hushed secret.

Jesse was pale, with dry lips and helplessness swimming around her reddened eyes. Delaney looked at the wall of windows next to her bed. It was lined with flowers in need of water, dried out from the gusty fall winds on the other side of the glass.

She wanted to ask Jesse where they put it — her breast. Did they throw it out with the garbage, with uneaten plates of grey chicken and tasteless cold potatoes? Or did they burn it? She wanted to ask her if it hurt. Did she feel lopsided? Depressed? Like someone else? Could she come home now? Could she forget about this? Could she just sit up and put some makeup on and come home and make dinner and sit on the edge of her bed at the end of the day and listen to her as she goes over the details of some silly argument she had with some girl at school and tell her she handled it well?

"You must have spilled something," Delaney said, and she brushed a small red spot on Jesse's nightgown — her white one, with the blue violets on it. Jesse grabbed her hand, hard enough to make it hurt. She didn't speak, but her grip on Delaney's wrist screamed with anger at the breast she no longer had.

It wasn't until the ride home in the dark in the back of Orville's rusting Ford Fairlane that Delaney realized it was Jesse's blood she had wiped, that it had seeped through. She let herself cry as she curled up in the arms of the blackness around her, thankful for its dark return every time the bright lights on oncoming traffic passed by.

The next day, Delaney took over the cooking and the cleaning and shopped for groceries. Kyle drove her into town and waited in the car, listening to the radio and smoking cigarettes.

When Jesse came home, Orville left the farm chores to the boys and drove her to chemotherapy appointments in Kingston, over an hour away. If they lived in Toronto, Delaney thought, a handful of hospitals would be only minutes away. It was a thought that wrapped a cape of isolation around her shoulders. Corner stores and huge shopping malls and city blocks were a thing of her past. She realized she had one then, and that it was something she couldn't get back.

She hadn't thought about it that way before. She was too busy being impressed by how many stars she could see at night in the country, where kids swam in roadside quarries instead of fenced-off neighbourhood pools with too much chlorine and over-eager lifeguards, and where farmers drowned kittens and walked cows named Annabelle and Clementine down the road to the butcher. In the country, they always came back in a hundred carefully wrapped pieces. Brown paper bits with blood stains and black scribbles that went into a large freezer in the back porch.

At night, Orville puttered around the barn, taking longer than usual to feed the cows. He talked less and smoked more, the burning orange glow filling space, preventing unwelcome conversation about lost breasts and the cost of a good prosthesis.

Jesse's appointments were always during the day, when Delaney was at school. When she came home, Jesse would be in bed, sleeping. She never knew how sick the chemotherapy made her until one of Jesse's appointments fell during the Christmas holidays. When Orville brought her home, Jesse stepped inside the house and grabbed onto every piece of furniture, every wall and every railing she could and scurried upstairs to the bathroom. She didn't make it that one time Delaney saw her. She vomited all over the runner on the floor in the hallway. She sobbed as Orville cleaned her up, then limp with fatigue and humiliation, she let him put her to bed.

After that, Orville went straight to the barn. His life had been reduced to a series of chores that he carried out without complaint or any sign of it being too much. Milk cows. Drive to chemotherapy. Clean vomit. Put Jesse to bed. Feed the cows. Milk the cows. Shovel shit. Say goodnight to the kids.

Delaney sought solace in a boy named Drew, who had finished high school and was working at the IGA grocery store, stocking shelves. His father had died the year before — he knew all about sickness and death. He drove his father's old car, which squeaked when it rocked when they finally did it.

By spring, everything had changed. Jesse's chemotherapy was finished and she began feeling better, and eventually strong enough to take over the household chores once again. She seemed to find pleasure in every task. She stood outside in the warm sunshine, singing and cleaning windows, her prosthesis jiggling with the rest of her body as she scrubbed the winter's dull dirt away, revelling in her own emerging reflection with the willow tree behind her, and the fields in the distance — plowed and ready for another season of bountiful crops.

She didn't know the fall harvest would include news of a baby.

Delaney had thrown up after breakfast five times in one week. "Are you sick, Honey?" Jesse asked the first and second time. The third and fourth time, she didn't say anything. The fifth time, she met her upstairs in the bathroom and told her they had to talk. Delaney ran out of the house.

Everything looked brown and beige from where she stood on the grassy hill behind the barn. The other hills in the distance, the fields that stretched beyond her, separated by dark fence-lines and the piles of white-grey field stones that supported them.

The October winds were making waves out of the long grass, which made Delaney queasy and angry that her stiff body couldn't be carried off, couldn't be swept away by the waves, back to Kew Beach, back to Claire, back to before everything else that happened. Drew had offered marriage. An abortion had offered freedom. A deceiving form of freedom, she concluded. She couldn't. What if the child had Claire's eyes? Or her cheekbones or her slender arms?

Her own life suddenly seemed just as desperate as Claire's — what she knew of it. The crowded bedrooms, the morose silence that descended when harsh words subsided. How Claire left school and friends behind to stroke the keys of a Smith-Corona, to help pay for groceries and a mortgage on a house that wasn't hers. How she was left behind by a man who accompanied her with imaginary appearances in a bar that smelled of wasted lives. Claire said she didn't think she'd ever get away from him, that she'd ever forget him.

The wind crawled up Delaney's back. The sky darkened. Something fluttered from down there. She would be alright, she told herself. A crow cried from the top of a dead tree.

Geese flew overhead. The wind wiped her face. She would find her way.

Delaney married Drew a month later, on her sixteenth birthday, and moved into the Stirling Hotel after the wedding, taking the memory of the grassy hill behind the barn and the wind's words with her. Jesse came by every week and called every day. She sat in the Sears store with Delaney, one nursing baby after another, and ordered new dresses for church, which she had to fight with Orville to drive her to every Sunday. Grace Chapel, in town. Near the water tower. She could sing there. Delaney went once or twice a year, just to hear her. Jesse sang with two other women and stood in the middle. Everyone said she had a lovely voice.

The sun was already up when Delaney and Neil left the studio the next morning. Neil came up to her room for wine, to celebrate the progress they had made.

"To mothers," he said, holding up a glass that had been wrapped in white paper in the bathroom.

"To mothers," Delaney joined in, tapping her glass against Neil's. She opened the curtains to let the morning light in — not all the way, just enough to cast a warm glow and let something of the outside world into the room, to remind herself she was drinking wine at seven in the morning while the rest of the world was eating Shreddies and rushing off to work. She liked living in opposite time. Being where she shouldn't. Doing what others weren't.

"Is this what you used to do?" she asked Neil. "Drink wine after all-night sessions in the studio?"

He was sitting in a chair near the table, his legs stretched out with his feet on the bed. They would leave their mark, she thought. The corners of his heels would leave an impression in the quilted abstract on the bedspread until the clean hands showed up later and ripped them away into a heap on the floor.

"Wine. Beer. Whatever was around," Neil was saying when she tuned back into the conversation. He drank his glass in a few gulps. Delaney filled it again, and her own.

Neil was fairly quiet. In the studio, he hadn't said much, either, offering his opinion when he thought it was crucial, but otherwise he sat back and watched as Claire and Jesse flickered unwittingly before him in between sound bites and photographs and chunks of time in other lives unknown.

Pam's mother sat on white wicker on the screened porch on Saturday afternoons and listened to opera on the radio and drank tea with lemon slices and a shot of vodka. Beth's mother made rag dolls out of her dead husband's shirts. Sally's mother traveled the world with *National Geographic* every weekend on an overstuffed paisley sofa.

They made their pilgrimage with their stories packed in handsome leather suitcases, or worn, splitting vinyl bags, and they perched themselves on others' shoulders — heavy and burdensome and familiar and comforting. This one married late in life. That one had six children. Another one never knew her mother, who died when she was born. Surface details. Gaping holes everywhere. Incomplete submissions from inside pilgrims' luggage, left behind to be recorded by those who may not get it right.

Neil said he didn't have much to say. Jean-Claude's a good editor, and she knew what she wanted. He was only there for reassurance. Reassurance and the pleasure of her company, he told her.

"I couldn't have done any of this without you." The wine loosened sentiments that had been building since her first trip to Montreal, and stood with her in the front window of the Sears Catalogue Store as she watched the seasons change. It followed her into Room 15 where she pieced together the stories of a few faces in the sky, and put her to sleep when Drew rolled over in frustration with the amount of money she was spending, leaving her back cold and exposed to the empty space between them.

"Someone helped me once." Neil shrugged. "It was my turn."

"Still, you didn't have to. Not this much." Delaney took a sip of wine to hide behind the door she had just opened. What did she want him to say?

Neil grinned. "You pruned my plants. I owed you."

The sun bathed his face in golden tones of generosity and kindness, which could only come from the difficult times he must have made it through, whatever they were. The great levellers that bring us back down to where the rest of humanity lives, after we've soared, however briefly, on the wings of the extraordinary — producing the documentary of the hour, the book of the month. Something that makes us think we're different from everyone else.

Could it be he's just a kind person? What was she looking for anyway? Why couldn't he help her, then go his separate way and never see her again? What would be so wrong with that? What made it so painful to live with that?

"You should get some sleep," he said, putting his glass down on the table. He stood up and stretched. She was sitting on the bed, forcing a smile. He let his arms fall back to his sides, then pulled out his car keys and played with them.

Delaney stood up and walked him to the door.

"How about dinner later, before work?" he asked. "You must be tired of eating alone."

She put the chain on the door after he left, then washed their glasses out in the bathroom sink and set them upside down to dry on a clean hand towel. She must have said yes to dinner. She didn't remember. She remembered him standing at the door, the jingle of his keys, his mouth on hers. She must have said yes because when she walked through the lobby at five that afternoon, Neil was sitting in his car outside waiting for her.

INTERIOR — ARTIST'S STUDIO Beth works at her desk, piecing together a collage of fabric, and talks about the last year of her mother's life. How she visited her mother every week, to wash her floors and vacuum. How her mother kept saying, "Why don't you sit down and talk to me," but Beth always said, "Too much needs to be done. I'll sit down later," and then she never did.

Cut to: EXTERIOR — GARDEN Sally stands outside a neglected garden in the back of the house she grew up in and talks about all the time her mother spent planting perfectly straight rows of impatiens, which only died in the fall. Then she had to do it all over again in the spring, and this went of for years and wasn't it a waste of time? She was angry that her mother didn't come inside the house and suggest Sally come out and help her, and now it occurs to Sally that she could have walked out the door and offered to help just as easily. Then they would have been together, instead of one outside and one inside with a freshly washed window between them. **Cut to: PICTURE** of Sally as a young child in the window that overlooks the garden. **Cut to: PICTURE** of Sally's mother wearing a straw hat, leaning against the garden shed, holding a hoe.

Fade to: EXTERIOR — CHARRED FOUNDATION Pam is sitting on the front steps of the burned down house she grew up in. She reads a passage from a short story she wrote about her mother's wedding dress. How her mother wanted Pam to wear it on her wedding day and how it fit just right. How she got married and had children and did all the things her mother did, and lived her mother's life, until her mother didn't remember who she was. Then Pam found the courage to become herself. **Cut to: PICTURES** of Pam and her mother in the same wedding dress. **Voice-over:** Pam talks about one of the last conversations she had with her mother, who asked Pam if she still had the wedding dress. Pam knew at that moment her mother would die soon, there was a certain look in her eye — that moments like that just appear out of nowhere and tell you what you need to know. **Cut to:** leaves on the trees blowing in the wind. **Cut to:** a weathered barn door flapping in the wind.

Orange hands. Purple hands. Delaney and Jesse went for a walk down the road, for old time's sake — just a few months before they realized Jesse was dying. Claire was with them, as always. Jesse had her living with a gentle, older man in a suburb of Toronto, who took her to the theatre on weekends and to Florida for the winter. A quiet life, with a little dabbling in acting every now and then, and lots of time walking the beach in Orlando, remembering, knowing it was probably best to leave it alone.

"She would know it wouldn't do much good to show up now," Jesse said, pouring a little orange and grape Jell-O crystals in their hands. She looked thin, and even though Delaney saw her often, she only now noticed the appearance of a collarbone. Jesse walked slower and breathed heavier. They turned for home after a short distance. The wind had picked up. Orville and Drew and the boys had gone for a swim at the quarry down the highway. They left a note. Jesse and Delaney had tea.

Sometime in the late afternoon, they began to hear a loud banging noise from outside. They looked out the kitchen window. The barn doors hadn't been locked and were threatening to break off the hinges as they flapped in the wind.

The phone rang. "Get the phone, will you, Del?" Jesse asked. When Delaney turned around, Jesse was already outside. Delaney stood in the kitchen talking on the phone to Kyle, watching Jesse as she crossed the driveway and headed for the barn. She saw Jesse's slacks and blouse blowing against her shrinking body. Her hip bones and shoulder blades seemed more prominent, sticking out from behind her polyester blends.

From where she stood, Delaney saw one of the barn doors swing open and catch Jesse in the face. It knocked her back a foot or two. Her lip was already swelling by the time Delaney ran out to her and brought her back inside. Jesse's eye was covered in blood from a cut above the brow. Delaney grabbed some ice and a wet cloth and tried to wash away the petrified, vulnerable look that stared back at her. Death had whacked them in the face, and in that moment, they both knew Jesse Reid was living on borrowed time.

She wanted to die at home. Delaney brought groceries and
kept up the housework. Orville stayed in the barn or sat in
front of the television.

"Can't you even wash the fucking dishes," Delaney yelled
at him one day. "You don't cook. You don't clean the crumbs
off the counter. You can't even fill a sink with soap and water!"

She was tired of running two households. Drew and her
boys were complaining that she wasn't around enough.
Jesse's fading light told her to be around more. She moved in
temporarily and grew tired of cooking and cleaning up for
Orville and making every single decision about what to eat,
what dress Jesse should wear for the funeral, what type of
coffin to buy.

The small breaks Jesse's sons and their wives could give
weren't enough and they returned to their work and their
homes and their own families, relieved they had someplace
else to go. They didn't have to look into Jesse's dying eyes day
after day after day, and the dirty dishes piling up in the sink
that took precious time away from their last weeks together.

Orville Reid stood in the kitchen the day Delaney yelled
at him, his shoulders drooped and surrendering, waiting for
death to lift the veil of ineptness that surrounded him. "Jesse
always did the dishes," he said, with sorrow and regret
quietly wrapped around every word. Then he went upstairs
and lay down beside his wife.

Delaney never complained again. She made his meals
and cleaned up the table and washed his dirty overalls and
held him after she held Jesse's hand, when the last note of
singing hung in the air above her lifeless body.

After they took her away, Delaney stood in the doorway
of Jesse's bedroom recording every detail with her mind's eye.
The empty bed scene is how she came to think of it. A slow pan
around the room past the bed — the white percale sheets
and white duvet pulled back in a messy clump, the imprint of
Jesse's head on the pillow on the right side of the bed. The
impression of her own elbow on the other pillow, supporting

her head as she lay beside the woman she called mother just before she died, stroking her with cool water and hours of wordless affection. The late afternoon sun shone through the sheers on the window and spread a yellow screen across one corner of the bed onto the hardwood floor. The doctor had opened the curtains after he pronounced Jesse dead — to let the light in, to let death out.

Delaney recorded the barely used perfume bottles that lined Jesse's dresser, their putrid, dark perfume fermenting from Christmases and birthdays past. There were a few pairs of Orville's thick, grey socks, which needed mending, sitting on one side of Jesse's pink velvet jewellery box, its broken ballerina frozen in movement — her tiny, stick-like image reflected in the bevelled wall of mirrors behind her. A silver comb and brush were angled just so, with several strands of hair still clinging to the vinyl bristles. A note in Jesse's writing to *clean out drawers* was tucked into the side of the large dresser mirror. A pale green housecoat hung on the closet door — the arms folded up twice to keep them from getting in the way of making Orville's favourite blueberry pancakes.

Delaney recorded the cracks in the ceiling and the clock on the night table that insisted on moving ahead. A washcloth was still floating in the water in the basin on the floor. Everything was still buzzing with life in the dead silence of the room.

She recorded it again and again and again, so she'd remember what the room looked like with Jesse's fingerprints all over it, and to know a life had been lived.

At dinner that night, Neil talked to Delaney about her next project, whatever that might be. He said she didn't need him anymore. She could fly on her own with the next one. He hoped there'd be a next one. He didn't like the thoughts of her going home and not ever doing this again. It would be a waste, he said. She really was a natural.

Delaney told him she was just happy to have found a place to put everything. Some of it, anyway. Neil didn't know what she was talking about. He didn't ask and she didn't explain. Let's stay in touch, he said. He'd hate to not know what she was doing with her life. He didn't say anything about the kiss earlier that day. Neither did she.

They went to the studio after dinner and finished the documentary with Jean-Claude. They cut shots of Sally putting a special wreath on her mother's grave, and Beth hanging the fabric art with two women embracing amidst symbolic rites of passage, and Pam standing nearby as a crew bulldozed the foundation of the house she grew up in, while she talked about her plans for a log cabin, too small and rustic to ever have met with her mother's approval.

At the end, Delaney insisted on a montage of images despite Jean-Claude's advice for a quick and clean exit. *An ironing board set up, waiting. Glass stones on a window-ledge. An empty bed with white covers pulled back. Perfume bottles on a dresser. A cup of coffee, with lipstick on the rim. Footprints in the gravel of a rain-soaked country road*, which disappeared behind the closing credits.

A year before Jesse died — before anyone even knew she was sick again — Delaney saw her sitting in a truck with a man named Ron, a widower who went to her church and drove her into town and back every week. Delaney was delivering catalogues early on a Sunday morning when she saw them together. They were parked along Edward Street, not far from Grace Chapel. It was too early for church. They were sitting in the truck, drinking coffee in Styrofoam cups. Jesse was laughing. So was Ron.

She looked content, Delaney thought. She no longer had to fight with Orville to take her to church every Sunday. She had someone she could talk to about the hymns she sang. Jesse told Delaney that Ron took her out for coffee every week, before or after church. Delaney assumed that meant in a restaurant. She didn't know their friendship had demanded the privacy of Ron's truck on a quiet street with a couple of take-out coffees.

Delaney watched her from behind a bush further down the street. Jesse looked like she might never get out of the truck or let it take her back home. She looked like she might go with him, this man, Ron, if she were someone else who could do it and live with it. Delaney even thought, for just a second, that the day might come when she wouldn't ever see Jesse again. But Sundays always brought her back to the farm, and she stayed there until she went across the field to lie forever in the small plot Orville secured for them years before, when the church next door wanted more land for a larger parking lot and bought a chunk of the field from him.

Delaney left the cemetery a few weeks ago, after the story came out in the Stirling newspaper. Neil had mentioned the documentary to a friend of a friend who was the executive in charge of programming for a national cable network and it was airing that night. She headed back to the Stirling Hotel to watch it with her family.

Drew sat with his arm around Delaney to watch *When Women Lose Their Mothers* on television. The boys were sprawled out on the floor. They couldn't believe that she had done it, now that is was on television, with commercial breaks, like everything else.

At one point, an image of passing clouds filled the screen, shot from the back seat of a car, looking up — the way it looked from a child's point of view. An eight-year-old child who climbed into the back seat of a taxi outside The Flamingo restaurant and said goodbye to her mother, the way she always did. With a peck on the cheek, and an embrace that lasted long enough to take in the smell of Claire's neck and carry it all the way back to whatever house she was living in at the time, staring up at the sky along the way.

That's how the day ended. Delaney watched the passing clouds on the screen with all the yearning and clarity she could stand.

Cut to:

EXTERIOR — BRICK HOUSE — NIGHT

Chapter Fifteen

It is a Friday night in early January. The snow has been falling for days, coating the trees and the rest of our immediate world with a thick blanket of white, lending mystery once again and changing our perspective. A neighbour walks his dog past my house. He can see in. I have forgotten to close the curtains, as usual. This man with the dog doesn't know the women who are seated next to me and near me. He can't make out our faces — faces he's likely seen before somewhere on the streets of Stirling. All heads are turned in one direction, transfixed, and out of sight. If he looks closely, he might notice that one head is missing. He'd also notice the absence of bottles of beer and glasses of wine. We are drinking herbal tea and ice water and behaving ourselves tonight. We are doing it for Jenny, who sits in a corner of my sofa, shaking slightly, sipping tea from my mother-mug.

She will not stay long. She has only come to watch
Delaney's documentary and then she will go home, where
she sleeps a lot lately and tries to limit her visits with
Georgia, who comes by and doesn't argue about staying for
such a short time. She can't drink anymore at 136 Anne
Street, and an hour is about all she can handle. "Herbal tea
tastes like goddamn dish soap," she told Jenny, "except that
banana cinnamon one. It's the only one you'll get me to
drink, if I have to drink that bloody stuff with you."

This man with the dog probably can't see that it is Sally
who is on the screen now, sitting at her worktable in the
back room of her store, sharing the significance of a roadside
bouquet she has chosen to make for her mother's grave.
Tiger lilies and Queen Anne's lace and wild black-eyed
Susans — roadside flowers that reappear every year in the
same spot where her parents were killed.

"At least she had the guts to go," Jenny says.

On the screen, Sally trims the stems on some Queen
Anne's lace. *It used to bother me that these flowers grew there*, she
says. *It used to bug the shit out of me that something so beautiful would
come out of the ground at that exact spot. But it doesn't anymore. Now, I
think, something beautiful should rise up from there.* She lifts her head
and looks directly into the camera and asks, *Don't you think so?*

"I hope she'll be okay," Grace says.

Everyone agrees and shares their concerns.

I can only remember that cold and windy day when we
stood outside her parents' house, when Sally felt the snow
coming and she told me she'd be alright, no matter which
way it went. That, even if things didn't work out with Josh
in Kauai, she'd be fine with being stuck with nothing but the
sun and the lava slopes and the indigo and turquoise waters
off the rugged Na Pali Coast.

"At least I'll have something to talk about when we're a
bunch of old broads sitting around on your front porch,
sharing stories," she said. "I can't think of anything worse than
not having anything to say when you're old and wrinkled to
shit and your tits are hanging down to your knees. Can you?"

No, I can't, I say.

But what will I say? After Sally has told her story about Kauai and what happened with Josh. When I am old and struggling to keep my own stories straight in my aging and unreliable mind. When I start telling the same stories, over and over again, and my friends are forced to listen for the hundredth time about the night Ben and I got stuck while making love. How it was a night like all the others I'd seen at Oak Lake, with the same dark sky that greeted me every time Ben called and I drove out in the middle of the night to see him — on the wheels of one long-ago moment.

They'll sit patiently and listen and nod in recognition as I tell them once more about the day I met Johnny Marks, the day he brought his grandmother's chair in for refinishing, when I walked him back to his car. How there had been the birds and their flutter as they picked up and flew away above our heads in a single, sudden move of force and unanimous decision. The smell of the parched earth below my feet. A feeling the canvas had been wiped clean and was waiting for me, only I mistook it for the sound of serendipity, buried all the rest beneath an unexpected love and the accidental explosion of my own deafening sexuality.

Will they remain respectfully silent when I tell them how I simply failed to hear anything else? Will they nod in recognition, having done the same things themselves?

"Ben?"

"Yes."

"Do you ever get the feeling you missed the point of a particular moment?"

"Is a moment ever about just one thing?"

"Probably not."

"I miss the point of most moments, Sadie." He pauses. "Don't worry, Sadie, it'll be there in the morning."

"What will?"

"What you thought you missed."

Quit talking.
   Quit thinking.
   Go to sleep, Sadie.
   Sleep will take care of this.
   Go to sleep.

The man with the dog who walks by my house doesn't see that I am sitting in my Storyteller's Jacket. That the black patch from Ben's shirt is still in my pocket, waiting for conclusion, as I try not to bring it to one too soon, as I try to get used to the loss of footing, to the sensation of being stuck with myself for good.

The man with the dog who walks by my house doesn't see that Alex and Grace are sitting close together tonight and not arguing, or that tears well up in Delaney's eyes when a shot of passing clouds fills the screen. He doesn't see Storm handing her a Kleenex, or Jenny putting an arm around her.

He only recognizes the scene — a group of women settled into the same spots in the same house, with the same flickering blue light illuminating the room with a series of moving images. It hardly catches his eye.